To Amelia

I hope you
reading the book.

All the best

Andrew Cavarr

23/3/2017

G000112257

Andrew Covarr, a retired modern languages teacher, was born and raised in Johannesburg, South Africa but is currently resident in the United Kingdom. He is married to Claire and has one daughter, Rowena. He likes folk/country music, bird watching and going on family holidays to the Mediterranean.

Dedicated to my daughter Rowena and the students of Tonbridge Grammar School, past and present, whose encouragement and support enabled me to finish this book.

Andrew Covarr

GONE FOR A SOLDIER

AUSTIN MACAULEY
PUBLISHERS LTD.

A CIP catalogue record for this title is available from the British Library.

ISBN 9781785548383 (Paperback)
ISBN 9781785548390 (Hardback)
ISBN 9781785548406 (E-Book)

www.austinmacauley.com

First Published (2017)
Austin Macauley Publishers Ltd.
25 Canada Square
Canary Wharf
London
E14 5LQ

Thanks to my friend Richard Lomax for his help.

Part 1

Heading Out

Chapter 1

My name's Lincoln French and I'm getting on a bit now. Have been for a while. You know you're getting old 'cos things don't work so well anymore. It takes a while to climb out of bed in the mornings and there are a few unexplained aches and pains when the weather cools, but I can't complain. I've had decades more than I ever thought I'd have and there's not much wrong with me. Genetic modification and cellular renewal has ensured that I live a comfortable life, and although there was a time when humans had to die after only eighty years or so, that time has long passed. Living now for well over a century is commonplace and I have no doubt that the time will come when we won't have to die at all. Work on genetic modification is advancing all the time and who knows, I might still be around when that happens. Here's hoping.

Because of a lifetime of military service I am permitted to live on Earth, once again a beautiful planet that has undergone major repair, climatisation and regreening since the climate change disasters all those years ago. The planet has been climatically controlled now for centuries, and advances in genetics have made it possible to revive thousands of previously extinct species. I have a place on the island of Ithaca. It's scenic here, and peaceful, and a man can't ask for more at my time of life. This terrace runs the length of the house and there's nothing I like better than to sit out here in the evenings with a glass of wine or a beer, and look out at the sun setting over Kefalonia and the Ionian Sea. I never get tired of it and have given strict instructions that when I go they are to plant an olive tree out front and use my ashes to fertilise it. If it lasts, that tree and its descendants will stand looking out at the ocean for thousands of years and I'll be a part of it.

It could all have been so different. After leaving school I was immediately caught up in the war – volunteered in fact – and although I managed to get through physically and mentally unscathed, quite a few I served with spent months or even years trying to get over the trauma of it all. I still mentally shudder at experiences I went through and things I saw and did, but I have managed to put all the death and destruction down to something that had to be done at the time. It certainly resulted in a better future for the Union, the Protectorate and the Republic (or the Imperium, as it was known then), but I'm getting ahead of myself. I'm like that sometimes – start to reminisce and drift toward the edge. When that happens, just go along for a while. It won't be long before I'm back on track.

I look at my campaign medals lying on the table in front of me, including the Interplanatery Union Star of Honor, that I received a long time ago now for the small part I played in the war, and remember that I was young once, my life stretching out ahead of me like the endless plains around the town of Oasis where I was born and raised. It was so flat, they said, if you looked out towards the horizon you could see the future. I didn't know then just how eventful my future would turn out to be but I remember how, from a time when I was very young, I would stand and gaze out at the emptiness of it all. It was mainly farmland and water as Ironmarsh is an Agri-orbital and I would look up at the planet Proserpine, containing the capital of our solar system, Dakota, and imagine myself travelling there. I felt restless, like our town, even our orbital, was too small, too claustrophobic. I longed to go and see Dakota. I'd been to the virtual city and had travelled spellbound through the streets, gaping at the crowds, the buildings and the never ceasing movement but I never did get to Dakota itself as a kid because the orphanage in which I grew up had no cause to send me there. I spent my childhood either going to school or out working on the farms. I once tried summer camp but I found that boring. Little did I know, in a childhood spent in and around Oasis, that I would not only get to know Dakota well, but so much more. By the time I was twenty-two I had fought my way through great swathes of the galaxy and seen some things that still have the monsters scuttling towards me in the night.

I can't say that I had a particularly unhappy upbringing. I was found at the front door of the orphanage, a few days old, screeching (they tell me) in a basket with my name on a label. The ensuing search for my mother ended when they found her hanging from a beam in a seedy motel on the outskirts of town. I guess she must have had her problems because the judge handed down a verdict of suicide. Nobody bothered too much finding out who my father was and I've never been interested in looking for him. Some folks get hung up on this sort of thing but I reckoned that if he wasn't interested at the time he certainly wouldn't be later on. It was clear that he didn't want much to do with my mother or me so it was probably best I left well alone. I'm sure I'd only have been disappointed but I've hung onto that basket and the label.

I was taken in and remained at the orphanage until I left school. It wasn't always easy. I'd see parents and their kids together around town and try to figure what it was like living within a family, having your own room, spending time doing things together, and the love and closeness associated with it all. At times like that a wretched loneliness would cut through me like a rusty cheese wire, leaving me stranded and forlorn, and feeling completely alone, but I learnt to look after myself from way back and I made some good friends through those years. Also, I knew enough about family life to know that, quite often, these were the last places anyone wanted to be.

The orphanage was well run, unlike some I've heard of and while we weren't in any way molly-coddled, we weren't abused by the staff or bullied too much. They were a hard bunch in general and not really given to any sympathetic understanding of the problems of youth, but fair and straight with us for the most part. Those of us who made it grew up tough as titanium and from an early age I knew that I had to fight my corner or go under.

We were sent to the local schools and I received a good education. I wasn't what you'd call a scholar but I did my best, worked hard and came away with good grades in all the subjects I took. Turns out I was good at most sports and played rugby, basketball and baseball. I liked long distance running and I learned to box, even received a few prizes in the inter-school competitions which ensured that I wasn't given a hard time by the older kids. During my time at the school, I also developed a love of words and reading, thanks mainly to a particularly brilliant language teacher by the name of Sawyer. He gave me some good advice early on, too, when he found me snivelling about life not being fair. He held me by the shoulders and knelt down on one knee to look into my eyes. 'Lincoln, the only person who is going to look after you or make things happen is you. You listening?' I nodded, wiping my eyes with the back of my sleeve. 'Fair is a meaningless word, son. Remember that. It has no meaning in reality except as a place where you can find a rollercoaster ride. If something turns out to be fair, it's by chance. You understand?' I nodded again.

He looked at me, making sure that I was listening. 'Here's the thing, Lincoln. There's nobody in this galaxy who is going to shape your life except you, got it? Nobody. In your case you don't have any family, which makes what I'm saying even more important. You are going to be the maker of your own destiny. Get that into your head and life'll be what you make it. You got that?'

'I understand, sir,' I said.

'Wait here.' He disappeared into the toilet and came back with some tissue paper. 'Wipe your eyes, Lincoln.

Remember, too, there's nothing wrong with crying, as long as you're crying about something worthwhile.'

I stood there drying my eyes, starting to feel better.

'One more thing. Deal squarely with your fellow humans and you'll find life won't be that bad.'

He ran his classes like that too. We were encouraged to think for ourselves and to work independently. Sometimes those lessons got a bit out of hand but mainly they worked. Above all, I don't recall him ever punishing a kid for anything and it's a rare person who can say that. He always took you to one side and discussed what you had done wrong, encouraging you to take part in the discussion. At the start of every lesson he drilled the 'golden rule' into us: 'Treat others as you expect to be treated'. I've never forgotten the advice and have tried to make those my guiding principles ever since. They've stood me in good stead and, turns out, they're mainly true.

I graduated from high school without knowing what I wanted to do with my life, except that I needed to move on. Staying in Oasis was not an option even when the head man called me into his office a few days before I was due to leave. 'Come in, Lincoln, have a seat.' He was behind his desk, leaning back on his chair with his hands clasped behind his head. 'How you doin'?'

'I'm okay thanks, Mr Clinton.' I sat down in the chair on the other side of his desk.

He leant forward, resting his forearms on the desk. 'You thought about what you want to do with your life? You've got some good grades, especially in English,

Maths and Physics. The rest weren't bad either, including Art and Music.'

'Thanks, Mr Clinton. I was pleased with my grades but haven't yet decided what I want to do.'

'What about going on to college or university? You could do well. Your sporting skills would come in handy.'

'Yeah, I thought about that but truth to tell I don't feel like studying any more at the moment. I'd prefer to go and see a few places, even if it means doing some casual work for a while.'

He nodded and smiled at me. 'Tell you why I called you in. I'd like you to stay on here. You've been an excellent role model for the other kids and it'd please me no end to have you on the staff. I need good people and they're not that easy to find. You won't believe how many backsliders there are out there and we'd even help you with any further studies or courses you want to do.'

The offer took me by surprise and while I felt pleased with his appraisal of me, I couldn't see myself staying on – not immediately anyway. 'Uh, thanks Mr Clinton. It's a great offer and this is the only home I've ever known but I have to go. I want to travel, see some new places. Who knows, I may not like it out there and come running back but I figure I have to try at least.'

'Fair enough. Think about it though. Wherever you find yourself, don't forget us and, as long as I'm here, that offer stands. You intend travelling alone?'

'Yes, sir, although Cisco and I have arranged to meet in Dakota. He wants to join the military. After that, well I'm not sure. Guess I'd like to get to know Dakota before going any further.'

'Okay, good luck, Lincoln. I'm sure you'll do well wherever you end up.' He stood up and shook my hand. 'Take care. And I can tell you, Dakota's a great place.'

I thanked him again but knew I couldn't stay. A few days later I collected my possessions – there weren't many – and headed for the station. I had a fair amount of money in the bank, what with my adulthood allowance, which every citizen of the Interplanetary Union received on turning eighteen, and the money I'd saved from the farm work and so felt confident about being able to survive in Dakota while I figured out what I wanted to do. Mr Sawyer was at the station to see me off. He embraced me and then stood back, holding me by the shoulders. 'Good luck, Lincoln. And take care. There's trouble coming with all this bellicose talk from the Imperium. Bunch of lunatics, if you ask me. You ever back this way drop in and say hi. And don't forget to take a good book with you wherever you go.'

I patted my bag. 'Downloaded quite a few,' I said. 'And thank you for all the help during my time here.'

'No problem, Lincoln. It's been a privilege knowing you and working with you. Look after yourself out there.' He turned and walked away and I never saw him again. By the time I did eventually get back to Oasis he had died. But I went and stood at his grave for a while. I was in need of some quiet time round about then.

Chapter 2

There were a few moments on that station when I almost turned and followed Mr Sawyer back to town. I watched his receding back with something akin to fear and found myself hesitating about getting on that train. You must have felt the same at some time in your life – a sudden uncertainty about the step you're taking. I'd spent my life around Oasis and had mainly enjoyed it. I could think of no concrete reason why I wanted to leave, just the desire to see some other places, try something new.

Sawyer disappeared through the gate and the spell was broken. The uncertainty vanished and I picked up my bag and walked towards the platform and the train. The news headline caught my eye: 'Imperium insists Protectorate has the right to independence'. I always keep myself informed of what is going on and knew enough at the time to know that the rise of aggression within our neighbours, the Imperium, over the past few years had become more than a polite talking point.

The trouble was brewing in a sector of the galaxy known as the Protectorate, a group of eighteen solar systems that lay along the edge of the Union, separating us from the Imperium, a political entity very different from our own in that it was a one party, authoritarian system that brooked no dissent from within its population.

Changes of government occurred periodically, usually accompanied by violence and a wholesale culling of the previous administration but we had rubbed along over the centuries without any major incidents. Even though our two systems were diametrically opposed, both sectors tended to mind their own business and not interfere with the other. Up to now any minor incidents had been handled diplomatically via the Intergalactic Council but the latest change of power within the Imperium had resulted in a government which showed far greater aggression towards the Union. Corruption, greed and incompetence by successive regimes had impoverished the Imperium and their eyes now turned to the rich natural resources of the Protectorate. They were claiming that the Protectorate had traditionally been a part of the Imperium and that it had been 'forced' to become an ally of the Union; nonsense of course but it was becoming dangerous nonsense.

The Protectorate had its own government and a fully democratic political system, and had been firmly allied to the Union for fifteen hundred years, a situation unlikely to change in the foreseeable future given a recent referendum which had resulted in 97% of the population voting to retain the status quo. They looked to us for their protection, and they remained happy for the Union to have a military presence inside their territory. The Union in turn found the Protectorate to be an excellent source of minerals, metals and other valuable resources, and were pleased to have this friendly zone as a natural buffer between themselves and the Imperium.

The Imperium, of course, chose to ignore the vote or claim it was rigged. It was also unhappy about the continued advance of genetics and the spread of artificial intelligence through the Protectorate, fearing that the Imperium itself would become 'contaminated' and succumb to modernity. It was becoming clear that robots could do most things far better than humans and many of them (Artificial Intelligence Units as they were called) were already very human in their appearance. We humans, too, were benefitting from genetic modification and technological improvement, and I saw no problem with any of it. It meant longer and better lives for us and our descendants and, for the most part, a far superior mode of living. However, it clashed with the conservative outlook of the Imperium and their Supreme Leader was yelling about the 'sanctity of the human'. I wasn't sure what that was supposed to mean but he was becoming a real pain. If the Imperium wanted to remain wedded to the past that was fine by me, but they were threatening the peace and stability of our whole way of life, and the Zardogan system was close to the firing line. We had, in the distant past, been a part of the Protectorate but had, about nine hundred years previously, chosen to transfer to the Union. Nobody was sure anymore why that had happened but any trouble could affect us directly. As it was, the present leadership of the Imperium had mentioned Zardogan and how it too had been 'forced into the Union'.

The Interplanetary Union itself had not been at war for as long as anybody could remember. We had, over the millennia, striven for peace and had gone out of our way to live in harmony with our neighbours, including the Imperium. I knew from my history lessons that when we were a young species and confined to earth, we had constantly been at each other's throats but that was not the case now and the hostility of the Imperium was worrying to say the least. Any act of outright aggression against the

Protectorate would force the Union government to take retaliatory action, but it had been so long since anything like this had happened that anybody who counted was running around like a headless chicken. The small federal military forces – made up of army, marines and space-navy – were in no state to fight a major war or any war for that matter. Anybody joining the military, like my friend Cisco, could expect to undergo basic training and then spend their time on ceremonial duties or helping to police the frontier systems. The chances of being involved in any actual fighting were fairly remote but it seemed that this was about to change.

While I was thinking about all this the train started moving and I had my last view of Oasis for a while. As we rounded a bend coming out of the station the town came into view, nestling against higher ground and looking pristine in the light of the morning sun. I promised myself that I'd come back some day, that I wouldn't forget where I came from and I kept looking at Oasis until it disappeared from sight. The train rose to its floating height above the defined track and quickly gathered speed. Within minutes the display in front of me indicated we had reached maximum speed of 2000 kilometres an hour, making the journey to the spaceport about forty-five minutes.

The excitement began to build inside me with the realisation that I was actually on my way. Oasis was situated on Ironmarsh, an orbital that had been constructed and put in orbit around the planet Proserpine, which contained the system capital, Dakota. The Zardogan system contained a further five planets, all uninhabitable but which were used for scientific and commercial purposes, mainly mining and the extraction of minerals and elements. There were also numerous orbitals, all constructed for human habitation and most in their own orbits around our sun. Ironmarsh orbited Proserpine at a distance of 300,000 kilometres, a four hour journey by standard shuttle, which is how most people travelled. My seat was booked and I thought about how it would be, travelling off-surface for the first time. I had done some virtual travelling but this was going to be the real thing and I sat back and let my mind wander. In no time at all, I was out among the stars, at the start of the next stage of my life.

The train journey passed uneventfully and we were soon decelerating towards our destination, passing though residential areas and, as we got nearer, industrial units needed to supply the port. The spaceport came into view in the distance, giving the appearance of a compact city centre with skyscrapers clustered around. The train kept slowing until it finally came to a stop and I joined the other passengers and stepped out onto the platform. I knew that in the grand scheme of things this was a pretty small spaceport and that the technology wasn't quite as advanced as in some parts of the Union – we still walked off the train whereas the technology now existed to transfer seats and even whole pods straight onto a ship – but I was nevertheless awestruck. It was as if, on leaving Oasis, I had passed through a portal and emerged into some other world. The place seemed to me to be incredibly busy, with people and moving walkways everywhere. The whole concourse was enclosed and I didn't have much time to look around before being alerted to move onto Walkway three by my wristband. My journey had of course been logged beforehand and I followed the instructions until I entered the ship and took my seat. I felt a bit dazed but excited at the same time. It seemed I was a million kilometres from Oasis and about to start a great adventure. I had no idea just how great that adventure would be.

Having ordered coffee, I settled down and was starting to virtually explore the ship when a girl about my age sat down opposite me. She nodded and smiled and I guess I did the same. I can't really remember because my heart had started hammering inside my chest and I was finding it hard to breathe normally. She was, bar none, the most beautiful girl I had ever laid eyes on although she seemed completely unaware of the effect she was having on me.

Don't get me wrong. I'd been around girls all my life. The orphanage and the school were mixed and I'd had my fair share of entanglements. Getting past the warden and into the girls' dorm was a rite of passage and I lost my virginity in a hay barn to an older girl when I was 15. I frequented the few clubs that existed in Oasis and my last girlfriend and I had been together for about eight weeks before she decided she'd had enough of me. My pride took a bit of a knock but it ended pretty amicably. This was different, however, and had me reeling.

The girl was dressed casually in a pair of jeans and a red tee-shirt that seemed to fit her like a second skin. She had large green sparkling eyes, a dusting of freckles and a thick mane of tousled dark hair that hung down just past her shoulders. Both her wrists were wrapped in bangles and bracelets, she wore hoop earrings and all of her fingers and both thumbs contained some type of ring.

'Wow, I'm starving,' she said. 'You don't mind if I go ahead and order something?'

It took me a moment to realise that she had said something. 'Pardon?'

She smiled and what a smile that was. 'You okay with me sitting here eating something? I'm really hungry.'

'Uh...yeah...please,' I stammered, 'go ahead. I've already ordered a coffee. Just waiting for it to come.'

She placed her order and then sat back and looked out of the port hole. I tried to continue exploring but kept glancing at her and found it impossible to concentrate. I was tongue-tied and flustered and was rescued by the arrival of the coffee which the attendant placed on the table in front of me. He spoke to the girl. 'Your order will be arriving soon, miss.' There was very little expression or emotion in his speech and I realised that we were being served by an Artificial Intelligence Unit (AIU). They were becoming more human every day and I reckoned that within fifty years we wouldn't be able to tell the difference. (I was right. Nowadays it's virtually impossible to tell the difference and if it wasn't for the 'AIU' on their right hand I don't reckon you could. I'm involved in a campaign to remove the 'AIU' as it's discriminatory but I'm getting sidetracked again).

'Thank you.' She smiled again and my heart did a double somersault. 'I'm looking forward to it.'

The attendant moved on and I took the bull by the horns. 'Hi, my name's Lincoln.'

'Hello. Collette,' she said. 'You going far?'

'To Dakota,' I said, far too eagerly. I sounded like a kid out on his own for the first time and she caught it.

'Your first time to Dakota?' she asked. 'Where are you from?'

'Sounds that obvious huh?' I said. 'From a town called Oasis, here on the orbital. Born and raised. You?'

'Dakota. Like you, born and raised. Actually, I've just come from Oasis. I've been out to the festival with a few friends. They're staying over until tomorrow but I have to get back. From what I saw, it's not a bad place.'

I thought it best to be upfront. 'It's okay, I guess, although I can't really judge 'cos the truth is, I...I've never been anywhere else. Unless you count the farms and small towns round about.'

'Really? So this is your first time away from home, your first time off-surface?' She smiled – that smile again that set my heart hammering. 'You're going to find Dakota totally different from Oasis. Are you just going for a visit or something longer?'

'I mean to stay for a while, get to know the place. I've just finished school and thought I'd go and have a look around.'

'Sounds good. Have you got a place to stay?'

'No, not yet. Thought I'd find something when I got there. Someone told me the info centre at the spaceport could help.'

'I guess they could. That's probably the best place to start. And find some place in the centre near the spaceport. That's where all the action is. You'd be bored out in the suburbs.'

'Thanks, I'll do that. You live in the centre?' I took a sip of coffee.

'Not yet. I still live with my parents. We're to the north of the city. I've got one year of school to go and hoping to go to uni after that.'

'Yeah? What do you want to study?'

'Not totally sure yet but I'm veering towards architecture. What about you?'

'To tell the truth I haven't a clue at the moment. Right now my mind is focused on just getting to Dakota and finding a place to stay. After that, I guess I'll need to find some kind of casual work...in a bar maybe, something like that.'

Collette's food arrived and she started eating. 'Mmmm that's good. I can't believe how hungry I am. Help yourself to some fries.' She pushed a basket of fries towards the centre of the table. 'What about your folks? I guess they live in Oasis. You have any brothers or sisters?'

I took another sip of coffee and helped myself to a couple of fries. 'Not that I know of. I was brought up in an orphanage. Never had a family.'

Her drink was halfway to her unbelievably gorgeous mouth and she held it there and then put it down slowly. 'I'm so sorry,' she said. 'I didn't mean to pry. I just...'

'Hey, don't worry. I'm okay with it. It's just how I grew up.' I gave her a very brief outline of my life so far. 'What about you? Tell me about your family.'

She hesitated. 'Well...my life couldn't have been more different. There's my older brother, Gabriel. He's 24 now and busy with his post-grad at uni, where he works. I live at home with mom and dad. We...we're a really close family. Sometimes I think they're boring and set in their ways and we have our differences and arguments but we're really close.' She was looking at me and I saw the start of tears in her eyes. 'I can't imagine growing up without a family, my family...'

'Please don't feel sad on my account. You're extremely lucky to have a loving family around you. And it's obvious that you're all really close. As for me, well...I was lucky too. The orphanage I grew up in was a caring place and the boss actually offered me a job there a couple of days ago. Okay, I never had a family as such but on the plus side I have learnt to look after myself and all in all my upbringing wasn't that bad. Believe me, it could have been a whole lot worse. And anyway,' I said, desperately hoping to cheer her up, 'if my life had been any different I wouldn't be sitting here talking to you.' I smiled at her and reached out for another fry. 'May I?'

She took out a tissue, smiling back at me through her tears and causing me to almost stop breathing again. 'Please go ahead.' She sipped at her drink. 'I'm rather glad that you did end up sitting here talking to me,' she said, looking straight at me. My heart jumped like something demented. Did she really say that?

'Me too. I don't, uh, want to sound too corny but you're, well...er...um...do you have...er...are you seeing anyone?'

'I don't have a steady boyfriend, if that's what you mean.' She laughed. 'It must sound totally boring, but I've spent the last year immersed in my studies and haven't done much else. This trip to Oasis was an end-of-exam occasion with a group of friends. What about you? Do you have a girlfriend?'

'No. Not for a while. Like you, I was busy with exams and didn't really think about much else.'

We were interrupted by the announcement that we were about to lift off. The ship was completely automatic and had no need for any human crew, being piloted on a prepared flight plan by an AIU especially constructed for the purpose. However, society still insisted on a human pilot being present even though there hadn't been any mishaps with the AIUs for over a century. It was the human pilot who spoke to us. 'Good morning, ladies and gentlemen, and welcome on board the *Stardust*. The ship is a Mark three Helios of the latest design and is, as usual, piloted by an AIU. I am the human standby pilot. My name is Gerald Doubtfire and I will be on the flight deck for the duration of the flight. We will lift off for the journey to Dakota on Proserpine in about ten minutes. According to the flight plan the journey will take four hours twenty-two minutes and we will reach a top speed of 75,000 kilometres an hour. Please feel free to visit one of the viewing platforms during lift off or, alternatively, you will be able to view the lift off on any one of the vision units throughout the ship. Artificial gravity within the ship will be adjusted as appropriate during the flight but you should not be aware of any change at all. The crew of the *Stardust*, AIU and human, will be more than willing to assist you with any questions you may have and it just remains for me to wish you a pleasant flight and onward journey.'

'This is your first flight,' said Collette. 'You must go to a viewing area for the lift off. It's an experience you don't want to miss.'

'Great,' I said. 'I was hoping to do so but didn't want to sound too…you know… eager. You coming?'

Collette laughed. 'Sure. I can still remember how thrilled I was my first time off-surface. I was going on holiday with my family to visit Wild in the Environment System and I insisted on visiting the viewing platform during lift off.' We made our way to the nearest area and I found myself in a transparent pod with clear views on all sides as well as above and below. Being well travelled, Collette found the best spot and I looked out at the buildings and structures that surrounded the ship and to which we were still attached. As we stood there, however, they started moving away from the ship and disappearing below us. I couldn't decide whether we were moving upwards or everything around us was disappearing into the ground but it soon became apparent that we had moved vertically on a giant platform and were standing waiting to lift off above the surrounding structures. There was a definite hum from the ship now and before I knew it we were on our way, moving vertically and rotating to the left, with the surface moving away from us at a terrific speed. I looked down between my feet and saw the spaceport becoming very small within seconds. The whole area looked like a miniature of the original in no time and then we started moving forward and up, gaining speed all the time until the horizon became a definite curve and the sky started turning dark. I tried to find Oasis but failed to recognise it. There were a number of small towns dotted across the orbital and any one of them could have been my home town. I looked down and realised that we were leaving Ironmarsh's atmosphere and entering the vacuum of space. The artificial gravity worked because throughout the lift-off I hadn't experienced feeling any different. The space outside the ship became completely dark and we were outside the orbital's atmosphere and heading for Proserpine and Dakota. I kept looking at the orbital. It was my home and I hadn't been anywhere else. I found myself thinking fondly of my time there, of Oasis and the orphanage, the people I had grown up with and some of the more memorable experiences I had gone through. I thought about Mr Sawyer and Mr Clinton and, weirdly, I thought of my last girlfriend, Dolores, and wondered what she was up to. I told myself again that I'd go back someday and forced myself out of my reverie.

The view of space from the pod was unbelievable and I just stood and stared around me in silence. The number of visible stars was immense as our system lay in one of the galaxy's inner spiral arms. I turned towards Collette. 'You're right. I wouldn't have missed this for the world,' I said.

'I know. It's awesome. I've experienced it before – more than once – but I never get tired of it. I find it quite humbling to think we're a part of it, have even shaped some of it and yet we are really insignificant. When you think that there are countless billions of galaxies…' I nodded and thought about the progress we had made as a species. There was a time when we thought the universe revolved around us, that we were somehow different from the rest of life on earth but that changed thousands of years ago as the knowledge regarding evolution and genetics advanced. Even before we left earth with the discovery of hyper travel, it had become universally acknowledged that we were just one more species of ape, related to all other life on earth, who had happened to evolve along a certain path. That path, involving an enlarged brain and the ability to think and speak had brought us to this, enabling us to exploit and settle parts of the galaxy, to construct worlds and for me to be standing here on a ship travelling in space. Collette looked at me. 'You seem far away.'

'Yeah, just thinking…all this…and being on a ship for the first time. Would you like to go and have a wander…a look around?'

'I'd love to. Let's start at the top and work our way down.'

We had a good look around the ship and settled down in one of the numerous coffee bars dotted throughout the ship. We continued talking and ordered more snacks and drinks. The four hours passed in a flash. Collette had captivated me completely and I found myself dreading the end of the journey and the thought of her walking out of my life. It turned out she was having the same thoughts about me. I was plucking up the courage to ask her out, or at least arrange to see her again, but she got in first.

'Lincoln, I'd really like to see you again. I don't normally do this but I don't want to get off the ship without...I don't know...getting to know you better. It's just that I've really enjoyed being on the journey with you and...I'm probably gabbling a bit but...'

'No you're not. I was thinking exactly the same thing and was just about to ask you if you'd like to...you know...go out somewhere. I don't like the idea of never seeing you again.'

She looked at me. 'I'm really tied up for the next couple of days but why don't you come round to my place for lunch on Sevenday, or does that scare you to bits? Meeting my folks, I mean. I'd like you to meet them and Gabe's going to be home for the weekend. Am I being stupid? I think I'm starting to gabble again...'

I hadn't felt this good in anyone's company before but the thought of meeting her family and actually sitting down to lunch with them all did scare me to bits. My face must have been a picture because she suddenly looked quite concerned. 'Lincoln, please don't worry. They're the friendliest people in the galaxy and you'll be made to feel right at home. Say you'll come. I really like you, Lincoln, and want you to meet my family. They...'

'Okay, okay,' I laughed. 'If you're sure they won't mind I'd be happy to come to your place.' While we were talking the pilot again came over the intercom. 'Gerald Doubtfire again. We've entered Proserpine's atmosphere and are making our approach to the spaceport at Dakota. We will be touching down in twenty-five minutes. As with the lift-off, you should not notice any difference in gravitational pressure. If you wish to watch the landing, you can make your way to the viewing areas or make use of the virtual viewing units located throughout the ship. I would like to thank you for choosing Final Frontier Flights and hope you choose to fly with us again soon.' We made our way to a viewing platform and I watched in awe as we came in to land. We approached the landing platform far more slowly than we had left it and I was able to get a good look at Dakota. It was vast and lay on the coast, stretching inland through green hills with a wide river (the Cairo) running through it. I was fascinated by the ocean, never having seen anything like it on Ironmarsh. 'We're out there towards the north,' said Collette, pointing. 'And there, almost below us is the centre and the spaceport. That's where you want to be.'

I nodded, trying to imagine what it was going to be like, living in such a huge city. How was I ever going to get to know the place? We came down vertically, slowly rotating until we touched down gently on the launch pad, which then sunk into the port itself.

The spaceport at Dakota was all I imagined and more. It stretched in all directions for as far as the eye could see and it felt that there were more people in that spaceport than I'd seen in the whole of my life. I'd never seen anything like it, even though I knew that this was not among the largest ports in the Union. There must have been at least fifteen ship berths and thirty platforms with trains arriving and departing all the time. Endless numbers of people swirled around me in a never-ending stream and on the main concourse there were an infinite number of shops, cafes, restaurants and businesses, all incredibly busy. Escalators and lifts carried people up and down the two hundred or so floors of the place, while a spaghetti junction of moving walkways conveyed people to all parts of the port. I just stood, trying to take it all in until Collette grabbed my arm and pushed me further onto the concourse. 'Told you it would be different,' she laughed. She pointed over to the far side. 'The information centre is over there somewhere. I'm sure you'll find it. I'll give you a call and we'll arrange to meet on Sevenday so I can take you to my house.' Her expression changed and she became more serious. 'You still want to come don't you?'

'Of course,' I said. I looked around. 'That's if I ever find my way out of here.' I said it light-heartedly but I was genuinely nervous.

'I've no doubt you can look after yourself. I've got to run. Have fun getting to know this place.' She looked at me intently. 'I'm really pleased I met you, Lincoln.' She stepped close and gave me a kiss on the cheek. 'Speak to you soon.' And then she was gone, lost in that swirling, crowd of humanity and I was left standing on my own trying to remember which direction she had said the info office was in.

Chapter 3

I got lost of course. The signs pointing me to the information centre were clear enough but if you ended up on the wrong walkway, as I did, it wasn't long before you were a long way from where you wanted to be. I wasn't the only one. Hundreds of us seemed to be wandering around looking vacant, but the locals were helpful by and large and I eventually made it to the info centre, which itself seemed like a small city. Organising a place to stay took a couple of hours and I ended up renting a small apartment that had been specially commissioned by the city for newcomers like me – one bedroom with shower room and one other room that combined lounge, kitchen and dining room. I signed three months in advance with the option to extend the period if I so wished. I also managed to work out where I was going to meet Cisco. He had given me the name of a downtown bar and I was to meet him there the next evening.

I decided to walk to the apartment as I figured this would give me a chance to have a look at the city centre. After finding my way out of the station, I downloaded a city map on my wristband and set off. It was amazing. After a life spent in Oasis, the centre of Dakota seemed like something from a futuristic novel. It was vast, with grid-iron pedestrian walkways stretching to infinity and shining skyscrapers soaring into the sky. The crowds were even denser than in the station and all vehicular traffic travelled at least 100 metres above the ground. There was a subway system as well and all over the city were ranks of bicycles which were free if that was the way you wished to travel. I stood and gawped for a good few minutes and then headed for the apartment. I let myself in and experienced a feeling of real happiness with the realisation that this was my space, which I didn't have to share with anybody else unless I chose to. It was an unbelievable feeling of personal freedom which I had not experienced before and I stood there just taking it all in. Although the apartment was small, it seemed gigantic after a lifetime spent in bunkrooms. I walked around the place and out onto the balcony and let that happiness seep into me. After a while I took one last look around and set out to explore the city in earnest. I spent the day getting to know the area around the apartment, seeking decent restaurants and bars and just looking to see what else was on offer. It seemed that I had chosen well because the area contained everything that anybody could want.

I didn't feel like staying in that first evening and went to one of the pizzerias I'd seen during my exploratory travels. I found a table outside, ordered a beer and gave Collette a call. 'Hello, Lincoln?' Her voice worked its magic, reducing me to blubber and leaving me feeling helpless. I couldn't believe that I'd only met her that morning or that these feelings I had for her ran so deep. She'd been in the back roads of my memory all day but I now started to seriously miss her. I realised, with some surprise, that, more than anything, I wanted to see her again, imagining her sitting opposite me at the table and felt an overwhelming sense of longing. Two days to go until I saw her again and joined her family for lunch at her place. That rocked me back a bit, I can tell you, as I tried to imagine making small talk around a family table.

'Hi, Collette. Thought I'd check and see that you got home alright. Wanted to make sure you didn't get lost.'

She laughed. 'As if. What about you? How'd you get on? I was going to call but you've beaten me to it.'

'Fine. Just sitting down to have something to eat and enjoy a well-earned beer.'

'Great. Sounds like you have got yourself organised. Have you found somewhere to live?'

'I have. I managed to get a pretty decent apartment. The info people were really helpful. I'm off Euclid Square. Seems to be a good area, there's everything here.'

'Euclid Square? I know it. Well done. I'd like to see the apartment. Are you still coming Sevenday?'

'Definitely. I...I've been thinking about you today and, well, if I'm going to be straight with you, I can't wait to see you again.'

'Being straight with each other seems a good idea. I feel the same way. I'd love to see you again but I'm stuck until Sevenday. Shall we meet at the port? That'd be easiest I think.'

'Yeah, good idea. At least I know where that is. What time?'

'I'll meet you at the *Café Esperanza* on the main concourse at eleven. Also, it's my turn so I'll call you tomorrow. What are you going to be doing?'

'I'm going to see if I can find a bookshop I've heard about. They apparently stock old fashioned paper books. That'd be something to see. Also, I just want to check the place out some more. I aim to be a local as soon as possible. At the moment I stick out like a sore thumb, stopping to gawp every few seconds and checking my map.'

She laughed again and the sound of it set me quivering. 'I'm sure you'll be one of us in no time. Don't forget where you come from, though. I think it's important to have roots.'

'Don't worry. The old joke about not being able to get Oasis out of the boy applies. It'll always be home.'

'Good. I'll call you tomorrow. Look after yourself, Lincoln. I can't wait for Sevenday.' My heart leapt like a gazelle. Hearing her say that flooded me with all sorts of feelings – all of them good.

'Okay, Collette. Speak to you tomorrow.' I stared at the wristband for a while, wishing somehow she was still there as a feeling of well-being enveloped me, of something worthwhile, something rare and wonderful that needed to be nurtured, and safeguarded with every fibre of my being. I felt that, against all the odds, we had connected in a way that was really special. At that stage, sitting there in the warm evening air, I nevertheless told myself not to be stupid, not to jump the gun, anything could happen. I tried to convince myself that someone like

Collette would have dozens of guys interested in her, that she could take her pick, which might not include me. I might be just a fleeting interest but deep down I didn't think so. Underneath the confusion, I sensed that we had found something worth keeping, and that we shouldn't let it go. The chances of something like this happening, even once, between two people were vanishingly small.

I ordered a pizza and another bottle of beer and sat watching the world go by. Euclid Square was a cobbled area and filled with all sorts of shops, bars, cafes, restaurants, galleries and small businesses. Like the rest of the city, all vehicular traffic either travelled way over our heads or underground. The square itself was filled with people – families, groups of friends, couples and singles of all shapes, sizes and colours – scanning the various menus, checking out the shops and galleries, real and virtual, or just taking an evening stroll. I have never forgotten that first evening in Dakota and the serenity and quiet joy that I felt, thinking about Collette and looking at the peaceful, happy scene out across that square. It was quite dark by then and the lights around the square gave the place a magical look. I didn't know it, but our world was soon to be violently disrupted for a while and it would take a titanic struggle to get back to that peace again.

Chapter 4

I was up bright and early the next morning and went for a run. I have kept in shape all my life and a big part of that was regular running when I was younger. It is the most satisfying form of exercise I can think of and I liked it best just running on my own. I had entered a few organised runs and races but they did nothing for me. All that faffing around beforehand and endless waiting for the start of the thing. Going out early in the morning when very few people are about, running through empty streets, the sound of my feet pounding against the road surface, and taking in the sights and sounds of a place waking up was what I found most exhilarating. I decided that it would also be a good way to get to know my new neighbourhood. It seemed strange, as I set out, not to be running through the familiar streets of Oasis but that soon passed as I crossed Euclid Square. Some of the café owners were putting out tables and chairs and a few shops were in the process of opening. It was a beautiful morning, with a blue sky overhead and I had run quite a distance in no time. There were a few other runners around and I worked out a route as I ran, keeping to the streets around the square and getting to know the area. I memorised the street names and tried to remember where certain shops and other places of interest were. It was fun and I found it exciting that this was now the area that I would call home. After about an hour I returned to the apartment, showered and sat out on the balcony having breakfast, thinking about the day ahead. I was going to meet Cisco that evening and decided that it would be a good idea to try and find some kind of employment, preferably within walking distance from the apartment. I sent Collette a message: 'Hi Collette, have just got in from a run. Going to try and find a job. Missing you and hope you have a good day xx'.

I finished breakfast, washed up and set out towards Euclid Square. I figured this would be the best place to find casual work, hopefully in one of the bars. It would be a great way to meet people and I didn't mind trying my hand at that kind of work even though I'd never done it before. The first few places I tried took my details but weren't hiring at that time. However, I was pointed to the other side of the square where they'd heard there was a vacancy at the *Mockingbird*. I found the place and went inside. It was a great looking bar, very modern, beautifully decorated, spotlessly clean – the kind of place you'd want to go for a drink and where you'd want to spend an evening. I could imagine it being very popular. There was a man behind the bar concentrating on his e-paper. 'Friggin' nutcase,' he muttered just as he saw me. 'Sorry, pal, wasn't talking about you. It's this Supreme Leader fella. How can I help you?'

He was huge, with a massive chest and an equally massive stomach and arms to match. His curly black hair was cropped short and his dark eyes looked straight at me in an open, honest manner.

'Morning. I'm actually looking for work and I was told that there could be a vacancy here. Thought I'd try my luck.'

'Yeah? Well now, I may be able to help. It so happens that I have been let down by a scum-sucking sonofabitch who...never mind. You ever done this sort of thing before?'

'No, 'fraid not but I'm a fast learner and not scared of work.'

'Mmm...you look alright but I need to know whether you're trustworthy. Been let down too many times. Come on through. I need to have a talk with you before we get any further. Name's Jacob by the way and you call me Jake I'll kill you.' He extended his hand and gripped mine like a vice.

'Er, no problem. Jacob it is. I'm Lincoln.' I looked at him. 'You can call me what you like.'

He smiled. 'Sense of humour. I like it. Go through to the office. I'll get a couple of coffees.'

I went and sat down at Jacob's desk. Like the bar itself, the office was clean and well-furnished in a modern style. I figured Jacob to be someone who liked things done properly. He came in with two cups of coffee, sugar and cream on a tray which he placed carefully on the desk and then went round and sat in his chair. 'Help yourself.' He pointed to the tray. 'How come you're looking for work? You look like you should be studying or something.' He was looking at me pretty intently. I told him about my circumstances and how I wanted to see a bit of the galaxy before settling down, starting with Dakota.

'Interesting. You seem pretty straight to me. Anybody I can speak to who can vouch for you? I've been ripped off by two employees – one skimming off the top and the other drinking more than his fair share. That's not going to happen again.'

'Fair enough,' I said. 'Please feel free to call Mr Clinton. He's in charge of the orphanage and I'm sure he'll vouch for me.' I gave him the details. He asked me more personal questions and, over coffee, we had a general chat. I guessed he was sizing me up.

'Okay,' he said, 'here's how we'll work it. I'm gonna give this Clinton guy a call and then I'll let you know yes or no. I'll call you this afternoon. That okay with you?'

'Fine,' I said. 'I'll wait to hear from you.' I finished my coffee, shook hands and left. I was hoping that he would take me on as I liked him and thought I'd have no problem working for him. The bar was within walking distance of the apartment and I'd start to feel part of the local community. My wristband buzzed. 'Hello Lincoln. I'm missing you too. I hope you find something suitable. Have a good day, will call later xx'. I was once again overcome by a feeling of real happiness. I just let it ride me, standing there with the morning sun on my face, taking in my new surroundings. I felt great and was confident about getting the job. After all, old Clinton had offered me a job himself so felt sure he'd put in a good word for me.

I got on one of those bicycles and spent the rest of the morning exploring the area around the square, going considerably further than my run had taken me, memorising streets and visiting places of interest, including the bookshop I'd heard about. I spent a good time in there, trying to imagine a time when paper books were the norm and seeing, for the first time, what real shelves of books looked like. Mr Sawyer had often spoken about such a time and I reckoned that he wished he'd lived then. I didn't share that wish as I knew enough to know that when we were confined to Earth, things weren't exactly rosy and that the life of the average human in our time was infinitely better. Very few diseases were life threatening, thanks to major advances in medical science, genetic manipulation, modification and repair. This had also led to organ replacement being commonplace, with organs being grown in the lab, and we had learnt how to switch on the genes that enabled us to regrow severed limbs and spines. Pollution and the threat of climate disaster were a thing of the past and the vast resources of the galaxy meant that scarcity was virtually unknown, especially in the Union which, either by luck or judgement, was run pretty efficiently. I think the secret of our success was to be found in the tolerant nature of our society. Tolerance had become the watchword as we slowly, over thousands of years, realised that a totally tolerant society actually worked best. It allowed responsible freedom of thought and action on an unprecedented level and encouraged innovation throughout society. The idea of imposing your will or ideas upon others had no hold in our society at all, although it appeared that those threatening the Protectorate were intent on imposing their will on billions of unwilling citizens. It was a worry but I thought that the authorities would be able to sort it out before anything too serious happened. I was wrong. Even as I stood there soaking up the sun, events were skidding in a wrong direction. It wouldn't be long before my life and any future I had envisaged changed out of all recognition. On that warm sunny day I was standing in the path of a galactic firestorm.

I parked the bicycle back at Euclid Square and started walking towards the apartment when my wristband went off. 'Seems you're okay, Lincoln. Mr Clinton thinks the sun shines outa your ass.' Jacob laughed. 'Wish I had someone thought as highly of me. You still want the job you can have it. How's about you start Firstday? That suit you? I'll pay you weekly, Firstday to Firstday.'

'Thanks, Jacob. That sounds great. What time on Firstday?'

'Get round here about nine and we'll run through the details. 'Til then.'

I got back to the apartment and Collette called. 'Hi, Lincoln.'

'Collette, you okay?'

'Absolutely fine thanks. Been thinking about you today and wondering what you've been up to. I guess I could've messaged but I don't want to be too pushy.'

I laughed. 'You? Pushy? Who'da thought? I figured you for the shy, retiring type.'

'I am. I really am. I normally wouldn't say boo to a goose but somehow I found talking to you, I don't know, sort of easy and natural. I still can't believe that you're coming here on Sevenday to meet my family. I'm so looking forward to it, but you must believe me, Lincoln, when I tell you I don't normally invite boys...men around here after speaking to them for a while on a ship. I just never do that sort of thing. My family are as surprised as I am and I can see my dad is really curious about you. I've had to take some flak from Gabriel but know he is dying to see what all the fuss is about.'

I laughed. She sounded and looked so earnest, wanting me to believe her. And I did. 'I believe you,' I said. 'We just hit it off and I have to tell you that I feel...well I feel unbelievably happy sitting here talking to you. I don't mind admitting that I'm pretty nervous about meeting your family though. It's not something I do every day or have done very often. You sure they're okay about Sevenday?'

'Of course,' she said. 'They're looking forward to meeting you. And please don't be too nervous. I promise I'll look after you.'

I smiled. 'In that case I'll be fine. I see you've had your hair done. It looks great.'

'Thanks. Just had it cut and layered. What have you been up to today?'

I gave her a brief outline of the day and she told me that the *Mockingbird* was a well-known bar among all the young people she hung out with. They often came there as the atmosphere was good and the owner was friendly. 'It'll be a pleasure to serve you, ma'am,' I said. 'What'll it be?'

'Ooh, such a handsome barman,' she said. 'Make mine a large scotch on the rocks.' She laughed. 'Hardly. I can just about manage a small glass of wine. I usually have something non-alcoholic. I'm afraid I'm not the drinking type.'

'Me neither. Got roaring drunk once – actually it was with Cisco – but I didn't like the feeling of not being in control. I also felt pretty grim the next day and had no doubt made a complete idiot of myself. That was the first and last time although I enjoy a beer now and then.'

'You certainly don't look like the drinking type. Aren't you meeting Cisco this evening?'

'Yes. We go back all the way to elementary school. He asked me if I wanted a fight. We rolled around for a while and got a bit dusty before being separated. We've been friends ever since. He's one of the good guys. Wants to join the military but the problem is, it looks like he might be seeing more action than he thought if this aggression isn't sorted out.'

'I know. It's worrying but my parents seem to think it'll come to nothing and that the authorities will ensure that things don't get out of hand. I'm not so sure. From what I've seen of the imperial leadership they appear to be quite mad and capable of anything.'

'Yeah that's for sure. And the authorities aren't really in a position to do much at the moment. We can only hope some sense prevails.'

We continued talking for a while and finished the conversation by telling each other how much we were looking forward to seeing each other. 'Sevenday's going to be special,' she said. 'I just know it.'

'It is,' I said, 'and I'm looking forward to meeting your family. I just hope I don't make a complete fool of myself.'

'You won't. One thing that struck me right from the start was how you came across as being able to take care of yourself. I think you're one of those who could handle most situations. It's certainly one of the things I found attractive about you.'

I laughed, 'I'll take your word for it and I'll see you Sevenday.'

'Eleven thirty at the *Esperanza*. Give my regards to Cisco. I hope to meet him sometime. Bye, Lincoln. Look after yourself.'

Her face faded and again I found myself staring at the band wishing she were still there. I went and showered, got dressed, grabbed a bite to eat and headed downtown on the subway, which was a pleasant experience. The whole system was ultra-modern with fast, silent trains that worked really efficiently. Before I knew it I was at my destination and soon found the place, where Cisco was seated at the bar chatting away to the barman and two women. He saw me come in, 'Heeeey, Lincoln, my man. Come on over. You're a sight for sore eyes brother.' We hugged each other and he turned to the group. 'This is my best buddy Lincoln I been telling you 'bout. Lincoln, meet Hector, Cheryl and Amanda.'

'Nice to meet you,' I said.

'Your usual?' I nodded. 'Hector, two cold ones please and whatever Cheryl and Amanda are drinking. So, how are things going pal? You finding your way around the metropolis?' The drinks arrived and Cisco excused us. 'We gotta bit of catching up to do. Have a good evening you two. Hopefully we'll see you again sometime.'

'Bye, Cisco, Lincoln. Nice to meet you and thanks for the drinks.' Cisco led me to a table near the back of the bar.

'Nice people, Amanda and Cheryl,' said Cisco, waving his bottle in their direction. 'They're engaged to each other, gonna be married in a few months. I'm also getting to know Hector – it always pays to keep in with the barman. So, pal, you've made it to the big city. Salud.' We clinked bottles. 'It's great to see you again. The flight okay?'

'Cheers buddy. Great to see you too. Yeah, the flight was great. Can't believe I'm actually here, off the orbital.' I didn't mention Collette. 'What have you been doing with yourself over the last few weeks?' I said.

'Well, been settling in here really and going through interviews for the army. Gotta nice little apartment not far from here and been getting to know the city. Bit different to Oasis huh?'

'Just a bit. I've got a place three stops down the line near Euclid Square. Nice area, full of bars and restaurants, plenty of night life. Got me a job in one of the bars. Start Firstday.' I took a sip. 'You mentioned the army.'

'I'm in. Passed the medical four days ago and you see before you a future federal infantryman. They've brought the training forward. Gotta report for training day after tomorrow at oh ten hundred. Suh!' Cisco saluted with a flourish and lifted his bottle.

'So soon? Hey, well done. You'll make a great soldier. I can see you kicking ass out there on the frontier. Mind you, you might be doing more than that if this whole thing kicks off.'

'Yeah, wouldn't bother me at all. I've been following these imperial pricks. Bunch of fucking primitives who seem intent on taking us back to the earth-age. Have you heard them? Back to basics, some fucking drivel about society not being moral enough. All this shit about the Protectorate being historically a part of the Imperium. Also talking about how we need to stop the development of AI and "review our progress with genetics". Unbelievable.'

I smiled. 'I agree but I hope the authorities can sort it out. Anyhow, let's just enjoy ourselves this evening'

'Yeah. I'm gonna be up against it for the next eighteen weeks. I got twelve weeks intensive on-surface training and then six even more intensive off-surface. Sounds like hell but I'm looking forward to it.'

'Well, it's what you've wanted to do from way back and I'm really pleased for you. I haven't a clue what I want to do yet, except travel a bit, see some new places. Another?' He nodded. I went up to the bar and got two more beers.

'We're going on to a club in a while,' Amanda said. 'We've finally decided on a wedding date and we feel like celebrating. Would you two care to join us?'

'Congratulations. Sounds good. I'll speak to Cisco. I'm sure he'll be up for it.'

He was. We joined the two women and made our way to a club not far from where we had met. It was a great night out and Cheryl and Amanda were unbelievably happy. They had decided to get married in the spring of the following year and I wished them everything of the best for the future. 'I hope you two have a long and happy life together. Are you planning to stay in Dakota?'

'Definitely,' said Amanda. 'It's a great place, although I'd like to see some other parts of the galaxy. I'd love to get to see Earth someday. That'd be something, especially with all the repair work that's been done.'

'Yeah, me too,' said Cisco. 'The place where we evolved into humans, where we originated. Just imagine. Seems that a lot of extinct species are being revived as well. Apparently the planet is going to be declared a neutral zone, accessible to all sectors.'

'I've heard that the Intergalactic Council has agreed to limit the population of Earth to three billion, mainly civil servants, military, that kind of thing. That's a thought, Cisco, you'll be able to live there one day,' I said.

He laughed. 'Don't think I'll bother. Too far from home and from the little I've seen of Dakota, this seems a fine place to stay. Cheryl, you fancy giving the dance floor a go?' The two of them made their way to the dance area while I went and got some more drinks. Amanda and I stayed sitting, relaxing, chatting and I couldn't help thinking about Collette and how I would be seeing her again the next day.

We eventually left the club in the early hours and I said goodbye to Cisco. 'You take care, my friend. Don't try and be some kind of hero.' We hugged each other.

'Don't worry 'bout me pal. I'ma be just fine. Looking forward to it. I'll keep in touch, let you know how things pan out. Might even get to see you when I get some leave. You take care too. Good luck with the bar work, hope you have a great time here in Dakota. See you soon.' Then he was gone and I found myself sincerely hoping he would be alright. We'd been friends a long time and in a way he was a brother I'd never had.

Chapter 5

After going for a run the next morning, I got ready to meet Collette. I couldn't believe how excited I was and found myself dressed and ready to leave far too early. Euclid Square was only about twenty minutes' subway ride from the spaceport and I was at the station with a lot of time to spare. Calm down, I kept telling myself, everything is cool but I was as jumpy as a kitten on hot coals. After spending time wandering around the concourse getting myself more and more nervous, I eventually sat down at the *Café Esperanza* and found the whole thing with Collette overwhelming. I was still coming to terms about my feelings for her and just sitting there, felt a deep yearning to see her. I imagined her walking through the door but then I was suddenly filled with doubt. Would we still be the same with each other? Would that initial attraction still be there? What if she had had second thoughts and was just going through with this to be polite? Maybe I should call her. No, better not – I'd only sound like an idiot. What would I say anyway? Maybe I could make some excuse why lunch wasn't such a good idea after all…and there she was, walking towards me, smiling and looking like a million dollars. I stood up and the next thing I knew we were hugging and kissing each other, neither wanting to let go. After a while we sat down, still holding hands. 'I don't know what's happened Lincoln but I couldn't wait to see you. It's been...I've wanted to...I just couldn't wait to see you.'

I reached out and brushed a strand of hair from her face. 'I can't tell you how I've longed to see you. I just know that I'd rather be with you than anywhere else.'

'Me too. My friends thought I was acting differently. I kept drifting off, thinking about you. One of them even asked me whether I'd met someone special.'

'I think we should keep this between the two of us for now. I don't want to be having long conversations with your family about our feelings for each other,' I said.

'Agreed.' She laughed. 'Let them think we're just good friends, although I doubt we'll be able to fool them for long. Especially Gabe. He knows me too well. Shall we go?'

Collette lived about thirty kilometres to the north of the city in an area known as Ferndale. We took the suburban tram, the only vehicle to travel at ground level, very modern and floating smoothly along, passing through some beautiful parts of Dakota. Ferndale itself was an area of verdant hills, beautiful tree lined avenues and large, stately homes. The closer we got the more nervous I felt. I hadn't quite realised how different our upbringings had been and I was reminded just how little we really knew each other. This was an extremely wealthy part of the city, of the whole system. The houses all lay well back from the road, with winding driveways, carefully manicured gardens, perfect sweeping lawns and spreading trees. A definite feeling of opulence hung in the air and I briefly wondered what Collette's family was going to make of me. If the storybooks were anything to go by, we'd be at loggerheads, with her father totally against us being together, and then things would settle down – or not as the case may be. Or it wouldn't be anything like that and we'd get along fine. I usually got along with people so I hoped for the best. Nothing around Oasis could begin to match this. We had been chatting but I was now silent, taking in the whole scene. Collette smiled at me and held my hand in both of hers.

'Seems a nice place,' I said, as we stepped off the tram. 'Your house near here?'

'Five minutes' walk, that-a-way,' she said pointing to our right. She put her arms around me and stood there looking up at me. 'I don't want you to be nervous or feel awkward in any way. You okay?' I couldn't believe the feeling of happiness that surged through me. I pulled her closer and kissed her.

I looked back at her, into those beautiful sparkling eyes. 'I'm fine, just a bit overwhelmed I guess. Didn't realise just how well off your family was. I mean…these houses…this area…I've never seen anything like it, certainly not around Oasis. What did you say your dad does?'

'I didn't but he is a civil engineer. He has his own business and also advises the system government, and sometimes the regional government, on all matters to do with urban planning, engineering projects, stuff like that. I…I guess I've never really thought about it, having grown up here, but I suppose we are well off.' She looked up at me again, slightly worried. 'It doesn't make any difference to the way you feel does it?'

'Of course not. I was just interested, 's'all. And let's face it, for a boy from an orphanage on Ironmarsh, this place is impressive.' I laughed. 'I wouldn't even mind living here myself. I can see me sitting out on one of those verandas sipping a cocktail. With you, of course. What about your mother?'

Collette grabbed my hand and laughed. 'She is a high school principal. Not my school, I'm glad to say. Her school is near the centre. We're here,' she said, and pointed to an imposing gateway and paved driveway that wound between two rows of beautiful mature Beech trees to an even more imposing house. Here goes, I thought. Just don't screw up. We walked up the driveway to the front door which was opened by a grey-haired man in formal dress. 'Thank you, Cameron.' She turned to me. 'Cameron, this is my friend Lincoln, Lincoln French. Lincoln, this is Cameron, who has been with us since before I was born. Lincoln is from the orbital.'

We shook hands. 'Very pleased to meet you, Mr French. Your name has come up in conversation quite often over the past couple of days. I trust you have found life in Dakota to your liking.'

'Nice to meet you, Cameron. I've been here in Dakota for only a few days but so far so good. And please could you call me Lincoln. I feel a bit awkward being called Mr French.'

'Of course. As you wish.' He turned to Collette. 'Collette, your parents, Gabriel and Rachel are in the conservatory and are eager to meet your, er, friend.' He winked at me.

'That's enough, thank you, Cameron,' laughed Collette. I followed her through beautifully decorated and furnished rooms towards the conservatory which I imagined was at the rear. 'Nothing much gets past Cameron but then maybe I have spoken about you rather a lot.' We reached the conservatory, itself a large elegantly furnished area where I finally met Collette's family. They were sitting in comfortable chairs talking and stood up as we came into the room. 'Hi, everybody. Meet my friend Lincoln. Lincoln, my mom and dad. This is my brother Gabriel and his girlfriend Rachel.' Collette went up to them and hugged each one in turn.

A tall woman, slim and elegantly dressed in a summer dress came towards me. She had dark hair and a friendly, smiling face not unlike Collette's. She extended her hand towards me. 'Hello, Lincoln. My name's Georgia and I'm Collette's mother. Welcome to our home. We have heard quite a lot about you – all of it good, I might add. This is Collette's dad, Stanford.'

I shook hands with them all. 'Mrs Grenville, Mr Grenville, Gabriel, Rachel. Pleased to meet you.'

'Hi, Lincoln,' said her dad. 'Come and join us. What can I get you to drink? There's just about anything you'd care for. Collette, what about you?'

'A cold bottle of beer would be good,' I said.

'Just a fruit juice for me please, Dad,' said Collette.

'How are you finding life in Dakota, Lincoln?' said Gabriel. 'Are you settling in okay?'

Her dad handed me a beer. 'Yes, really well thank you,' I said. 'I've got a place to stay in a lively area and have even managed to find some casual work which I start tomorrow. It's all a bit different from my home town of Oasis on the orbital but I would like to stay for a while and get to know Dakota. From the little I've seen it seems to be a great place. And I've been very fortunate in meeting Collette and all of you.'

'Yes, Collette has told us how you two met on the ship and how you both get on so well,' said her mother. She laughed. 'It's very brave of you to come to lunch but you are more than welcome. We're having a barbecue. I hope you like that sort of thing.'

That 'sort of thing' was out of this world. Collette had been right. They were the friendliest people in the galaxy and I couldn't have been made to feel more welcome. They weren't fooled by the 'just friends' charade either. Collette stuck pretty close to me and it turned out to be one of the best days of my life. The family were very interested in my upbringing and the life I had led in Oasis, and I found myself telling them about my childhood in the orphanage. We also talked at length about the threatened conflict and the problems it would bring if it happened. I was made to feel very welcome, as if somehow they wished to compensate for the fact that I had no family. I got on particularly well with Gabriel, highly intelligent and very amusing, whom Collette obviously adored. That family was exactly how I imagined a functional family to be, and I couldn't believe how fortunate I had been in meeting Collette. Given the trillions of humans that inhabited the galaxy, the chances of it happening was so small as to be almost impossible. I realised that if I messed things up with Collette, I could regret it for the rest of my life. Even after the short time I had known her, I instinctively felt that I would not want to live my life without her. I sat there in the sun, in that beautiful garden amid those friendly people and felt a deep contentment. Whatever happened, I had to hang on to this.

'I don't want you to go, Lincoln,' said Collette later as we took a walk around the grounds. 'I want you to stay here forever.'

I smiled. 'Not sure what your folks would say about that but I don't want to leave you either. This has been a brilliant day and I'm so impressed with your family. I can't believe how welcome they have made me feel here.' I stood gazing back at the house. 'Sometimes, back in Oasis, I would wonder what it was like being part of a family. This is how I imagined it should be.' We walked back towards the house and joined the others. I felt I ought to be going as the last thing I wanted to do was outstay my welcome. No matter how nice the people are there comes a moment, especially on a first visit, when it's time to go.

'I hope you've had a good day Lincoln and that it wasn't too stressful,' said Georgia, smiling. 'It's been lovely meeting you and I've no doubt we shall be seeing more of you.'

'It's been a wonderful day, thank you, and I hope to see you all again soon,' I said.

'It's been good to meet you, Lincoln,' said Gabriel, shaking my hand. 'I'll be in touch. Maybe we can go out for a beer sometime.'

'I'd like that,' I said. 'Thanks again, Mr Grenville, Mrs Grenville. 'Bye, Rachel. Nice meeting you.' I headed for the tram, accompanied by Collette. We walked down that road holding hands, enjoying the warm evening air and the silence, and waited at the stop for the city tram. Dakota had a fantastic public transport system that enabled you to get anywhere at any time. 'When am I going to see you again?' I said.

'I'm out with a few girlfriends tomorrow evening but I want to see you as soon as possible. You'll have to let me know what your work schedule is like. Call me tomorrow and we'll arrange something. Soon.'

'I'll do that,' I said. 'I'll know about my schedule tomorrow morning. You take care. And thanks again for a really great day. I loved every minute of it.' We kissed each other and all too soon the tram arrived. 'I'll call you tomorrow,' I said.

Collette smiled. 'Take care, Lincoln. I can't wait to see you again.'

I arrived back at my apartment and turned on the news. Out in the Protectorate, an enormous force of imperial troops had captured the Halcyon system and were advancing on Lindfield and Jerendasien. Union military and naval bases had been overrun and the personnel either killed, injured or being held prisoner. The Supreme Leader was saying that his demands were being ignored by the Union government and that he had had no option but to act as he had. He was ranting on about the Protectorate being finally put on the path to righteousness. He solemnly declared that their 'beloved' Protectorate had, after centuries of 'slavery' by the forces of modernism, now been liberated and would soon be fully incorporated into the Imperium. He added that all Union personnel would be repatriated but that military bases and other Union property now belonged to the Imperium. A great number of civilians had been killed or injured and these were to be 'regretted' but for the future of the Protectorate as a part of the Imperium it was a price worth paying. I sat there stunned, unable to comprehend properly what was happening. I couldn't believe it. Did these people think that the Union was just going to sit back and agree to all this? Mind you, right then I wasn't sure myself what we were going to do. The thought of the Union going to war was shocking in the extreme and I still naively thought the two governments would get round the table and sort it out. I didn't realise that my life was about to change forever.

Chapter 6

When I arrived at the *Mockingbird* the following morning the federal government had issued a formal warning to the Imperium to evacuate the Protectorate, release the prisoners or the Union would have no alternative but to retaliate.

'Yeah, like that's going to get them out of there,' said Jacob, fuming in front of the holovision. 'The federal government needs to stop pussyfooting around and go kick some ass. Friggin' nutcases, attacking the Protectorate. I mean, what next?'

'Morning, Jacob,' I said. 'Seems like these people mean business.'

'Yeah, but this needs to be nipped in the bud before any more damage occurs. President Joyce is due to make a statement in about half an hour. Let's hope she knows what she's doing. Nothing like this has happened for centuries.' He shook his head and turned to me. 'You wanna coffee? We'll run through your schedule and I'll give you some rudimentary training. I'd like you to be behind the bar, serving drinks and coffee, if that's okay. I'll do the till and keep an eye on the rest of the place.'

President Joyce addressed the Union and, looking tired, solemnly informed us that the Protectorate had been attacked without provocation and that she regarded this as an attack upon the Union itself. Billions of our citizens were now under threat. She waffled a bit and I guessed that she was in a state of shock, but I was also impressed by the basic steeliness of her address. She left everyone in no doubt whatsoever that, as long as she was president, this act of war was not going to be allowed to succeed. She told us that all requests that the enemy forces evacuate the Protectorate had been ignored and that we were now at war with the Imperium and their allies. She was quite truthful about the fact that at the moment the Union's armed forces were not up to the task of waging war but that this situation was going to be rectified with the utmost urgency. She finished off by looking straight at the camera. 'The Protectorate has, for well over a thousand years now, been closely allied to the Union and looks to us for its protection. And who is to say that the Union itself is free from threat of attack? The Interplanetary Union which, for thousands of years has stood as a shining beacon in the galaxy and our whole way of life, based upon tolerance, democracy, human rights and the rule of law, are now under threat.

'I am determined that this unprovoked attack will not succeed but for that to happen we are all going to have to work together. Our armed forces, although well trained and equipped, are very thinly spread. I want those forces to be reinforced and to become the military we need as soon as possible and so I am calling upon you, any able bodied citizen between standard age 18 to 35, to volunteer to join our fighting forces and to become engaged in this struggle to safeguard the Union. I would like you to report to your nearest military recruitment office so that the build-up of our forces can start immediately. All industry and commercial activity is going to be put on a war footing with immediate effect. Only by working together, standing shoulder to shoulder, will we prevail and I mean to prevail. However hard the road, however long it takes. Thank you.'

Jacob and I looked at each other. '18 to 35 standard. That counts me out,' said Jacob. 'What about you?'

'Well, I'm nineteen but never thought of myself as a military type. I…I don't know what to think. I know for sure that I agree with most of what the Union stands for and regard the Protectorate as part of us really…but to go and fight…in the military…I just don't know.'

'You've only just started here,' laughed Jacob. 'All I need now is for you to go and join the army. Let's get on with your training in the meantime. Who knows, that speech may have brought the Imperium to their senses, although I doubt it.'

There weren't many customers that morning so I was able to get some good training from Jacob. I had guessed right in that Jacob was something of a perfectionist and wanted things to be done correctly. He ran a very successful café-bar and he meant to keep it that way. That suited me as I also prefer to work in a successful, efficient environment. Even at that early age I had learnt that if everybody does their bit properly, things works better and it's easier for all concerned.

However, while I got to know how to make various types of coffee and mix different drinks, the news got steadily worse. Satellite images from the Halcyon system showed that a huge force had captured the capital city and a number of orbitals, with imperial officials stating that the Halcyon system, weary of the decadence of the Union, had elected to become independent and invited other nearby systems to join them. We all knew this was a lie. This was being done by force, against the will of the people. The news from Halcyon suddenly cut off and we realised that the enemy must be in control of all transmissions from that area.

'Where the hell did that force come from,' shouted Jacob, 'and how come the authorities never knew about it?'

I just shook my head. Being able to capture an entire system would have required a large force and, like Jacob, I found it hard to believe that the authorities hadn't seen what was coming. The Union government must have been in a deep sleep or in denial. My thoughts turned to Cisco. He was busy undergoing basic training but no doubt would soon be in the thick of things. I wondered again about volunteering but decided to wait a while and see how things panned out. I didn't want to join the military only to be told that the whole thing had been sorted out. Collette called. 'Lincoln, have you heard the news? You're not joining the military are you? I won't let you. You can't...'

'Whoa, slow down. Yes, I've heard the news and no, I haven't joined anything. I'm probably being over optimistic but I'm still hoping that common sense prevails. In the meantime, I'm learning to be a barman.'

'Good. Keep on being a barman. I know we have to build up our forces but...'

'Collette, I don't know what to think at the moment. Joining the military was not something I had considered but if I'm going to be straight with you, I can't rule out joining altogether, given the present circumstances. Did you watch the president's address? I was pretty impressed even though she seemed to be in a state of shock.'

'Oh, Lincoln, I'm so worried. Both you and Gabriel fall within the president's age range for volunteers, and Gabriel has said pretty much the same as you. He also won't rule out joining up if he feels it's the right thing to do.'

'It's a new situation for all of us. For the most part we're just going to have to play it by ear. And please don't start worrying on my account yet. As I said, common sense may prevail and I'm as confused as anyone. One thing I am sure about though is that I can't wait to see you again.'

'Me neither. Listen, I'm out with some friends this evening but will see you tomorrow I promise.'

'I'll hold you to that,' I said.

'Bye, Lincoln. I hope your new job turns out okay. Can't wait to see you.'

'You too. See you later.'

I had a three hour break in the afternoon and was back at the bar at five when it started getting busy. It was a really popular place and I was kept busy serving drinks, making coffee and clearing tables until the end of my shift. It was demanding physical work but I liked it and found talking to the clients easy and pleasant. Jacob had a great way with the customers and I could see why the place was popular. He was at home with everyone, no matter what their age and went out of his way to make them feel welcome, whether they were regulars or first timers. The atmosphere in the place was very relaxed and the service first class, although the news from the Protectorate dominated the conversation. As far as I could gather most people were shocked and getting angrier by the minute. I know I was.

Chapter 7

The next day brought more bad news. All government property in the areas that had been overrun had been seized by the enemy forces and ships of the federal navy attacked as they tried to return to their bases. The personnel who had been taken prisoner had not been released and the Imperium was sounding more confident and aggressive, demanding that the federal government withdraw entirely from the Protectorate or 'face the consequences'. Most systems were still in federal hands but the forces stationed there were small and not in any condition to withstand a major attack. Citizens of the Protectorate were appealing directly to the president over the television, asking for help and begging not to be abandoned to the enemy. It seemed that the trouble was spreading and that the Imperium had more forces at its disposal than anybody had realised.

It was the sight of those people appealing to the president that made my mind up for me. What was to prevent the Zardogan system from falling into imperial hands? I couldn't imagine living under that kind of draconian authority and so made my way to the nearest military recruiting office in Dakota. I got there early and was immediately ushered into an office, where a smart looking woman in uniform stood up to welcome me. 'Pleased to meet you, Mr French, and thank you for coming in. I am Staff Sergeant Brindford and I understand that you wish to join up as a result of the present crisis. Please have a seat.'

'Thank you,' I said. My thoughts turned to Cisco. 'I would like to join the army, the infantry, if possible.'

She smiled. 'A good choice and at this stage we are able to grant your request. You will be required to undergo a medical and a basic literacy test. There are various forms to complete and, should you still wish to go ahead, you will be required to complete a verbal affirmation, after which you will be a provisional member of the army. Any questions?'

I spent two and a half hours at the office completing various forms, attending an interview and undergoing a medical test and a very basic literacy test. At the end of it I found myself sitting opposite a fierce looking individual. He was carved from hard rock, with close cropped hair and an impeccably ironed uniform shirt. His name badge said 'Staff Sergeant Ellard' and when he spoke I could not help but listen.

'Mr French. You have been provisionally accepted into the army. You are required to report to the infantry base at Black Tree Canyon on Fiveday at oh eight hundred where you will present yourself at reception. I have sent you details of where it is and how to get there. Once there you will undergo eighteen weeks basic training – twelve on-surface and the remainder off-surface. At the end of the eighteen weeks, and provided you have successfully completed the training programme, you will become a fully-fledged infantryman.' He sat looking at me.

'Er, I…er…thank you Mr…er…Sergeant Ellard.'

'Any questions?'

'Er, no, not really,' I said, my mind whirling with the enormity of the step I had taken. I thought of Collette and how she was going to react, and of telling Jacob that I'd be going the day after tomorrow. Mr Sawyer and his warning of trouble to come flitted through my thoughts.

'Right, Mr French. In that case it only remains for me to administer the affirmation. Would you please raise your right hand and repeat after me: I, Lincoln French, do hereby affirm in law that I will serve the Interplanetary Union as a member of the Union Armed Forces and that I will, at all times, carry out my duties according to the constitution, laws and regulations of the said Union and of the Union Armed Forces.' I repeated it after him and signed a copy. After that he seemed to thaw a little. His mouth twitched and I guessed he was attempting a smile. He stood up and shook my hand. 'Thank you, Mr French. You are provisionally a member of the army. Congratulations. I wish you all the best for the future and thank you on behalf of the president.' He almost made it but that smile never really materialised. I walked out of there in a daze but did see, as I was leaving, that the reception area was filling up with men and women, all come to sign up.

'Lincoln,' boomed Jacob as I walked through the door of the *Mockingbird*, 'You're back for more. I guess your first day couldn't have been that bad.'

'Hi, Jacob. My first day was fine thanks but I need to talk to you rather urgently.'

'Talk away.'

'I…I've joined the army…the infantry. I have to report to the base at Black Tree Canyon the day after tomorrow.'

Jacob was silent for a few seconds then put his hand on my shoulder. 'Well done, Lincoln. Would a done the same at your age. Well done. This aggression needs to be stopped in its tracks and that's only gonna be done by force. Good luck, Lincoln, you're gonna need it.' He looked around. There were a few clients but it was not busy. 'Don't worry about doing your shift today. You go and get your head around what lies ahead. And you better tell that girl of yours sooner rather than later. Am I right in thinking she doesn't know yet?'

'You're the only one who knows,' I said. 'Maybe I should've…it's just that I saw those people in the Protectorate…desperate, asking for help and felt I should be doing something. I still can't believe I've done it, I'm provisionally a soldier. I must say I don't feel like one.'

'I don't know. Get your hair cropped and you could very well pass for a soldier. A coupla' weeks training and you'll be an infantryman through and through. I'm prouda you, Lincoln, and can see you kicking Imperium ass.'

I laughed nervously. 'I'm not really an aggressive type and I'm secretly still hoping that the whole thing gets sorted out without any further violence.' I shook my head. 'Can't see it happening though. It seems that the Imperium is hell bent on trouble.'

'Yeah. Looks that way. They need their asses kicked from here to Andromeda and you guys are the ones who are going to do it. I'll see you later, Lincoln.'

I sat down outside another café, got a sandwich and a coffee and thought carefully about what I had just done. Surprisingly, once I got over the initial shock, I found that I felt quite positive, even excited about what lay ahead. I wasn't worried about the training. I was fit and strong and could look after myself. When I thought about possible action involving fighting and killing, though, that was a different matter. I was, by nature, not aggressive and I knew it would take a huge effort on my part to actually do harm to a fellow human being. But I reckoned I'd cross that asteroid belt when I came to it. Right now, I had to let Collette know and I wasn't looking forward to that. I figured I'd do it face to face rather than remotely and so headed for the tram stop. I knew she was at home. I messaged Cisco and told him what I had done. He replied immediately, telling me that he was still at the base and that he hoped to see me Fiveday. I also sent Collette a message, telling her I needed to talk to her and that I was coming to her place.

She was waiting for me at the tram stop and I could tell from her face that she knew what was coming. She didn't say anything, just put her arms around me and I did the same. We stood there in silence, holding each other for dear life, neither wanting to let go. Quietly, without moving, she asked, 'When are you going?'

'Day after tomorrow. I have to report to the infantry base at Black Tree Canyon for basic training. Eighteen weeks.' We both sat down on the bench, holding hands. 'I...I just felt that I had to do something. I saw those poor people begging for help…maybe I should've spoken to you first…it just seemed the right thing to do at the time. Now I'm not so sure. Seeing you again…I'm going to miss you so much.'

'Oh, Lincoln, it's going to be so awful here without you. I'll miss you more than I can say even though I know I would have done the same if I wasn't still at school. Can we go downtown? I don't want to let you out of my sight and I want to see as much of you as I can before you go.'

We spent the rest of that day and most of the evening together. I rode the tram home with Collette and kissed her goodnight at her door. We agreed to meet the next day and I told her I'd like to say goodbye to her family. They were the only people I knew in Dakota, apart from Jacob, and they had been very kind to me the day I had come to their house. The next day passed far too quickly. I went to Collette's place to pick her up. Her parents were there although Gabriel was back at uni. Her dad came over and shook my hand. 'Well done, Lincoln. I know Collette is upset but I think you've done the right thing. I wish you everything of the best for the future and want you to know that you're welcome here any time.' Her mom too wished me luck and gave me a cake to take with me. I was deeply touched by their sincerity, and Collette and I left for town. I wanted to go and see the city authorities to make sure that I kept the apartment while I was away. I thought it important to have a place to come back to. I finished my business and met Collette at a coffee bar downtown. She arrived just after ten, looking as beautiful as ever. She turned quite a few heads when she walked in and I once again found myself standing helpless, not quite believing how the relationship between the two of us was developing. For a few seconds it felt like a dream but then she had her arms around me and I felt her against me. 'I've missed you, Lincoln. I've missed you so much.' She sat down and ordered a drink.

'You okay?' I asked.

Collette leaned over towards me, looking really serious. 'I'd like to go and see your apartment,' she said. She kept looking at me over the top of her glass. 'Now.' I just nodded, my heart hammering.

'Sure. I'd like that too,' was all I could manage. We left the drinks and made our way to my apartment. I closed the door behind us and it was pretty clear that we weren't going to stay dressed for long. 'You sure you...?' I began but Collette silenced me with a kiss and, without another word, stood looking at me as she pulled my tee-shirt over my head and then started unbuckling my belt while I pulled her gently towards the bedroom, walking backwards.

That afternoon and evening were as passionate and intense as could ever be. At times I felt as if my heart would burst and, as I lay enveloped in Collette's nakedness, I wanted to stay right there for the rest of time. I had never felt such piercing happiness, such deep contentment. We didn't say anything, just lay there in wonder, enjoying the silence of the passing time and happy in each other's company. After a while Collette stirred. 'That was too wonderful for words. I'm dazed by the way I feel about you, Lincoln. It's like...I don't know...it's like you have permeated every fibre of my being.'

'Love at first sight.' I looked at her. 'Like the flying spaghetti monster, I've heard of it but never come across it. Until now. I reckon that's what it must be – for me, anyhow.'

'Do you think so? I've always scoffed at that sort of thing. It...it just seems too unbelievable that two people can meet and fall in love like this. It feels too good to be true but I don't mind admitting that I feel scared at the same time...as if it'll all come crashing down...as if it shouldn't really be happening. I mean, I'm only seventeen and you...how old are you, eighteen, nineteen?'

'Nineteen. And this situation is as surprising to me as it is to you. I've also had my doubts, wondered whether you would change your mind. I reckon the only way we can go through with this is to be completely straight and open with each other. I can start now by telling you that I am in love with you. Head over heels. I can't think of any other way to describe it. I also promise that I will let you know the minute that changes, although right now I doubt that's going to happen.'

Collette lay there looking at me, tears welling in her eyes. 'I'm in love with you too, Lincoln. It seems crazy, more than crazy, only having met a few days ago but I have no doubt. I know that I love you and I think we have struck something rare and precious that we need to handle carefully. I promise to be completely truthful about my feelings for you too and, like you, I can't see them changing any time soon.'

She looked at me in that earnest way of hers. 'I love you...I always will. I...I know we're going to be away from each other for quite some time but I promise you that I'll not stop loving you. You know that don't you?'

'I do because I feel exactly the same about you. I don't want you to go anywhere,' I said. 'I want you to be here with me forever.'

'I will be.' She kissed my throat. 'No matter what you have to go through, remember that.' She kissed me again.

The time came, all too soon, for her to leave. 'I want to say goodbye here, Lincoln. I want to remember our time here. Is that okay?'

'Yes,' I said. 'I'd like that too. I don't want to stretch this out any longer than we have to. Here's a key to the apartment. Feel free to use it anytime you want. I promise I'll get out to see you just as soon as I can. In the meantime I'll keep in touch as best I can. I've no doubt there are going to be some restrictions.' We got dressed and kissed goodbye outside the apartment. She reached into her bag and drew out a small package, beautifully wrapped.

'This is for you, Lincoln. Think of me when you wear it.' She had given me a gold locket in the shape of a heart containing her image. She fastened it around my neck and kissed me one last time. I watched her walk to the tram stop in Euclid Square, which was still crowded with people. Dakota was a city that literally never slept. I found a bar, had a drink and then walked home, shot through with longing and loneliness. My band buzzed. 'My darling Lincoln, I'm at home in bed wishing you were here beside me. I LOVE YOU TO BITS XXX'

Part 2

Gone for a Soldier

Chapter 1

I reported to the Black Tree Canyon army base the following morning, together with hundreds of others. We were a mixed bunch, all shapes, sizes and colours, standing in lines on the parade ground, facing a raised dais and a tall flagpole. The Union flag fluttered from the top of the pole and the dais was occupied by an officer in an immaculate uniform. He spoke, or rather barked, at us. 'My name is Colonel Lesch and I am the officer commanding this base. You have been provisionally accepted into the army and you are about to undergo basic training. Those of you who make it through the training will become soldiers. Ready for combat. And make no mistake, combat is what's coming. Our Union has been attacked without provocation. It is our job to repel this attack and make that attacker pay. And that is exactly what we are going to do. That is what we are here for. If you have any doubts, if you don't think you can do that, now is the time to speak. Once you are assigned to your platoons, once training starts, there will be no turning back. Understood?'

We all mumbled 'Yes.'

'When I ask if you've understood I want to hear you all say out loud "YES, SIR". TOGETHER. UNDERSTOOD?'

'YES, SIR.'

And so my time in the army began. Sergeants took over, our names were called and we were each assigned to a platoon under the supervision of one of the sergeants, who were carved from the same hard rock as all the others I'd seen so far. We marched (well, sort of) to a barrack room and formed up outside.

'I am Sergeant Faber and I am in charge of this platoon. You are Platoon 57 and you will address me as 'sergeant'. Do not address me as 'sir' or salute me. That is reserved for officers. Your rank for the present is recruit. UNDERSTOOD?'

'YES, SERGEANT.'

'Good. The barrack room behind you will be your home for the duration of your time here and when I dismiss you, go and find a bunk, leave your belongings, and then come back out here, all within five minutes. Understood?'

'YES, SERGEANT.'

'Fall out.' We made our way inside and I felt quite at home. It wasn't that different to the bunkrooms at the orphanage. I found a suitable bunk, put my bag on it and made my way outside. When we'd all fallen in again we were marched to the canteen where we enjoyed a pretty good breakfast. It was the first time we were able to talk to each other and I joined in the general conversation at our table. As was to be expected, we came from a variety of backgrounds, with the majority of the recruits from Dakota. There were some from outlying towns and districts and two others from Ironmarsh, but not Oasis. Everybody was receiving messages from friends and family and one came through from Collette. 'Hi Lincoln. Just a quick note to say that I am missing you so much and love you more than I can say. Good luck with you training and please don't forget me xxx'. That message sure shook me around a bit. I sat and stared at my band for a few moments. 'Hello Collette. I love you too far more than I can say and could never forget you. Take care angel and I'll try and keep in touch as best I can xxx'.

After breakfast we again fell in outside the barrack room and were taken off to have our hair cut and to be fitted for uniform, which consisted of several sets of training fatigues, physical training gear, boots, plimsolls and a formal uniform, to be used when we went into town. I learnt that we were not allowed off the base for the first twelve weeks and that communication with friends and family was to be restricted for security purposes. I informed Collette before handing in my wristband. We were kept pretty busy that first day and at the end of it I was still wondering whether I'd done the right thing. I started unpacking and chatting to one of my neighbours who introduced himself as Danny Wallace. While we were busy Cisco walked in. 'Hi, Lincoln. Welcome to Black Tree Canyon.' We hugged each other.

'Cisco, good to see you.' I shook my head. 'Never expected to end up here with you. How are things?' I introduced him to Danny.

'You guys gonna join me for a coffee?' asked Cisco. 'There's a half decent coffee bar for recruits near the canteen. Not a bad place to spend some time in the evening.' We agreed to go and the three of us made our way there. It was pretty crowded but we managed to find a table outside and I ordered an iced tea. I gave Danny a short summary of how Cisco and I knew each other. 'How about you?'

'I'm originally from the Shanghai system in the Protectorate and came to Dakota to complete my post graduate studies. The university here is one of the best in the Union for advanced mathematics, which is my field. I got a message from my folks – I'm their only child – telling me about the threat to their system and how these people are hell bent on eradicating most of the freedoms we all take for granted. Then I saw those people begging for help and figured it would be best if I did something. I couldn't think of anything else to do except join up. You guys?'

'I've always wanted to join,' said Cisco. 'Got here a few days ago. Never expected to see you here, Lincoln, but am real glad you are.'

'I'm like you,' I said to Danny. 'Saw those people and am worried about this thing spreading. I like the Union and the Protectorate just the way they are and certainly wouldn't want to live in a system run by those imperial nutcases. It just seemed the right thing to do. Are your folks staying put or do they intend to move?'

'I'm quite worried about them. Dad is determined to stay and 'keep the Union flag flying' but I'm trying to persuade them to join me here on Proserpine. Those Imperium people don't seem particularly sane to me.'

'I agree,' said Cisco. 'Their ideas and their intolerance would force our society back to an age I don't want to see again. And to tell the truth, I'm kinda looking forward to taking them on. I also saw those desperate people begging for help and I'm more than ready to kick ass. Wouldn't mind sorting that Supreme Leader out personally.'

Danny looked nervous. 'I wish I were that confident. I feel really scared about the whole thing, including the training. I just hope I'm up to it. You two look like you'll have no problem but I've never been the physical type. I just hope I can make it 'cos I do want to take part in the fight against this aggression.'

'Half the battle is really wanting to do something,' I said. 'You'll be fine. I don't think it's going to be easy but you'll make it. Cisco and I will make sure of that. And that's not a promise, it's a threat.' Danny smiled although he still looked uncertain. We finished up and made our way back to the barrack room where I promptly fell into a deep sleep, dreaming about Collette.

Chapter 2

Our training started in earnest the following morning. We were woken at four thirty and sent on a five kilometre run, led by Sergeant Faber. He was as fit as a flea and he ran us pretty hard that morning. Quite a few of the recruits, including Danny, quit along the way, collapsing by the roadside, some retching, others doubled up with cramp. A few of us made it all the way, with me way ahead of the rest, and I found myself back at the barracks, alone with Sergeant Faber for a few minutes. 'Well done,' he said. 'You're obviously in training. What's your name, recruit?'

'French, Sergeant. Lincoln French.'

'You ran very well, Recruit French, and I like the way you tried to help some of the others. I am appointing you platoon leader. That means you are the spokesperson for the platoon. You will also have other duties which I'll outline as we go on. Understood?'

'Er, yes, Sergeant,' I said, 'but I'd prefer it if the others had a say in the appointment of their spokesperson.'

'Nice thought but no. I do the appointing roun' here and you're it. I'll inform the platoon as soon as they're all here. Understood?'

'Yes, Sergeant.' They all eventually arrived and we fell in and faced Sergeant Faber.

'Not good. In fact, NOT GOOD AT ALL. I can see that most of you need to shape up in a major way if you are going to succeed with your training. You're flabby, outa shape and most of you are about as fit as shit in a sack. But don't worry. That's what I'm here for. I'm an expert at getting the likes of you up to speed. Believe me, by the time I'm finished with you you'll be doing 20 kilometres in your sleep. One more thing – we will be constantly in competition with the other platoons at the base and I DO NOT INTEND COMING SECOND AT ANYTHING. DO I MAKE MYSELF CLEAR?'

'YES, SERGEANT.'

'Recruit French, fall out and face the platoon.' I went and stood beside Sergeant Faber. 'I have appointed Recruit French here as your platoon leader. He will be your spokesperson and it is to him you will turn first regarding any problems or other matters. He will be the go-between between the platoon and me. He will also be given duties by me from time to time and will be expected to lead the platoon in the performance of your duties and in the competition with the other platoons. I suggest you get to know him. Your first duty, Recruit French, is to ensure the platoon is here in PT kit ready for physical exercise at oh eight thirty.'

'Yes, Sergeant.'

He turned to the platoon. 'Listen carefully. I am going concentrate on getting you all as fit as possible over the next twelve weeks. That means a complete change of lifestyle for most of you. I want you to all get mentally prepared and to be ready for hard times. Fall out.' We all went inside and quite a number of my colleagues flopped out on their bunks. Danny looked like he'd been shot. He just lay there with his eyes shut.

'You okay?' I asked.

'Never been better. It's a bit disheartening to realise that you're about as suited to running as a pregnant fish. Can't wait for the exercise regime to start after breakfast and sooo looking forward to the next twelve weeks. "Get prepared for hard times." That sounds ominous.' He smiled. 'Well done on your appointment as platoon leader.'

'Yeah, thanks.' I thought I'd better explain to the platoon how I came to be in this position and turned to the room. 'I suggested to Sergeant Faber that everybody have a say about who becomes the platoon leader but apparently that's not how things are done around here, so I'm it. Hope you're all okay with this.'

Danny laughed. 'Just as long as all this power doesn't go to your head. Don't want to see you strutting around shouting at us, kickin' ass, barking 'UNDERSTOOD?'...' Some of the others joined in, giving me a bit of stick but all in good humour.

'I'll try not to let it,' I said. 'I will say, though, that I'm quite happy not coming second at anything. Just so you all know where I stand, I am with Sergeant Faber in this and will do my best to ensure we come first in any inter-platoon competition. I hope that's not going to be a problem. First off, can we please make sure that we're back from breakfast in good time and that we are outside, in PT kit, by eight twenty five. I don't think it would be a good idea to turn up late for our first session.' I figured the best way to be an acceptable and successful platoon leader was to lead by example and to be as supportive as possible. There were clearly quite a few who were going to need a lot of encouragement and help to get through this basic training.

We duly formed up outside the barrack room at eight twenty five and spent the rest of the morning tackling the assault course which was one of the most strenuous things I'd ever done. I managed to get through and then went back to help and encourage the others. Danny and some of the others were really struggling and I helped them as much as I could. Some of the fitter ones also helped where they could. We all eventually got through and formed up in front of Sergeant Faber.

'Absolutely hopeless,' he said. 'Jesus, you're in worse shape than I thought. Let's do that again. GO.' This carried on until it was time to break for lunch. 'Well done, all of you,' said Sergeant Faber. 'I like your attitude and the way you stuck at it. I also like the way you all helped each other get through this. That was undoubtedly difficult and not something you're used to but you can bet it'll be easier next time. At the end of your training here I want to see all of you get through this assault course on your own without any help from your comrades. Recruit French, please make sure the platoon is formed up and ready for drill instruction at oh fourteen thirty sharp. All to be in tee-shirts, trousers and boots. Enjoy your lunch.'

We made our way back to the barracks where we all collapsed on our beds. I lay on my back, eyes closed, relaxing before going to lunch. As always, Collette entered my thoughts and I found myself longing to see her again. Being away from her like this was becoming unbearable although I knew that I had no choice. I had elected to be here and I would be able to see her again after twelve weeks but that didn't make it any easier. I had never missed anybody before, not really, and the feeling was new to me. I imagined her missing me as much as I missed her and found some comfort in that thought.

Danny and I walked down to lunch where we met up with Cisco and some of his platoon. 'Hey guys, how are things? We saw you all heading for the assault course this morning. How'd it go?'

'Just great,' said Danny. 'It's been the best day of my life so far. First, we're woken at four thirty and sent on a five k run and then we spend the morning tackling the assault course from hell. Lincoln here strolled through the whole thing like he was born to it but yours truly has found out he is about as fit as an asthmatic tortoise. I ache in parts I didn't know I had.' There was general laughter at Danny's description of the day's activities.

'Don't worry,' said Cisco. 'It'll get easier each time you do it and Lincoln here is a helpful kinda guy.'

'He's also our esteemed platoon leader. Appointed by Sergeant Faber,' said Danny.

'That right? Well, congrats ol' buddy. The first step on the ladder to greatness. It so happens that your humble servant Cisco has been appointed to a similar position and I am here to inform you officially that Platoon 56, led by Sergeant MacLean and my good self are going to win the inter-platoon competition.'

I laughed. 'Yeah right. Well, that could only happen if we pulled out of the competition altogether. Your default position is going to be second or even further down the list. Both Sergeant Faber and myself are determined we're not going to come second at anything, which means we're going to come first.' The other platoon leaders joined in. Recruits started betting on the eventual outcome and the competition, so beloved of the platoon sergeants, got into full swing.

We all formed up at two thirty and Sergeant Faber addressed us. 'We will be attending the camp commandant's parade twice a week, Twoday and Fourday, at the start of the day. This means the whole camp marches onto the parade ground and we are formally addressed and inspected by Colonel Lesch and the Regimental Sergeant Major. This also means that you have to know how to drill correctly and that is what we are going to spend the rest of the day doing. I do not want this platoon arriving on the parade ground looking like you've just shuffled out of some back alley somewhere. We are going to look smarter than the other platoons and that means getting our drilling correct in all respects. UNDERSTOOD?'

'YES, SERGEANT.'

The rest of that day was spent learning how to march in step, halt, right turn, left turn and all the other manoeuvres required for correct parade ground drill. On top of that, I was required to get to know the commands and towards the end of the day I had to drill the platoon under the watchful eye of Sergeant Faber. Again, it was strenuous work but I found myself enjoying it and I liked being in charge. 'Good work, everybody. You're starting to look like soldiers although there's quite a way to go. Our first parade is on Fourday and I want you all to remember what we've practised here today. You've had a pretty full day and you can expect more of the same over the next few weeks. Recruit French, I want you to take over and march the platoon back to the barracks. I also want you to ensure that the platoon is formed up ready for a run at oh four thirty tomorrow morning. Carry on.' I marched the platoon back to the barracks and dismissed them.

'I've never been so hungry in my life,' said Danny. 'And everything aches. A run at four thirty tomorrow morning? Kill me now and get it over with.'

I smiled. 'You'll feel better after a good dinner and a night's sleep. I also feel like I've been through it today. Let's get cleaned up and go and have something to eat. I'm starving.'

Chapter 3

Most of the platoon, including Danny, fared better during the run over the next few days. By the end of the week all made it without actually collapsing and we formed up outside the barrack room. 'Getting better,' said Sergeant Faber. 'A definite improvement over the first day. After breakfast we will be going to the gymnasium where we will be boxing against Platoon 56. We will also start learning the basics of self-defence during the rest of the morning. Recruit French, have the platoon ready for PT at oh eight thirty sharp. Fall out.'

We all trooped off to breakfast and were in pretty good spirits. While we were sitting eating, Colonel Lesch, accompanied by a lean, grizzled individual who turned out to be Regimental Sergeant Major Relwana, came in and wandered between the tables, chatting to the recruits and enquiring as to the quality of the food. As far as I was concerned the food was first class and I had no complaints. There was plenty of it and it was well prepared. That seemed to be the general consensus.

'Well done, Danny,' I said. 'You ran well this morning.'

'Yeah thanks,' he said. 'Mind you I still had to walk for a lot of it.'

'Yes, but you didn't stop moving and that's progress,' I said. 'How are your boxing skills?'

'Non-existent. I've never been in a fight in my life and can only hope that I'm up against someone similar. If I get into the ring against some street fighter I'm done for. What about you?'

'I learnt to box at school and took part in inter-school competitions. It's been a while since I put on any gloves, though. I guess I'll be okay, a bit rusty maybe. I'm going to try and get matched against Cisco. He's also an ex-school boxer and last time we fought we were pretty evenly matched.' I looked around to see if I could see him. He was over the other side of the dining hall, sitting at a table of female recruits with some of his platoon but I managed to catch his eye. He came over.

'Hey guys, how's it going?'

'Great,' I said. 'Did you know that we're up against each other at boxing this morning?'

'We were told about it but not which platoon. So it's you guys? We'll have to get paired off, Lincoln. I recall you beat me narrowly last time we met and' – he struck a pose – 'I will have my revenge.'

'Yes, now I remember. At school. Yeah, good idea. We'll pair up, show the rest of them what a good fight looks like. Revenge? In your dreams pal.' He laughed and went back to his table.

'Wow, this is going to be something worth seeing. Two old school pals squaring up to each other and both boxers,' said Danny. Other members of the platoon sitting at the table also showed an interest and there was soon a buzz among the two platoons. Again bets were taken and the competition between 56 and 57 rose to new heights.

After breakfast we formed up and marched to the gym. Platoon 56 also filed in and we were seated around the boxing ring, looking up at a PT instructor who seemed to have been carved from even harder rock than the rest. He had a cleanly shaven head, flattened nose and was built like the proverbial brick outhouse. When he spoke, we all listened. 'Good morning. My name is Sergeant Sharpton and I am your PT instructor for this session. This morning you are going to have your first session of milling, which is a form of boxing but without any of the skills. Basically, you will don a pair of boxing gloves and a head protector and slug it out toe-to-toe until one of you falls down or I call a halt. No kicking or head-butting allowed. Just use your fists. Any questions?' Both Cisco and I stood up. Sergeant Sharpton looked from one to the other and settled on Cisco. 'Speak up,' he said.

'Thank you, Sergeant. Recruit Gonzales. I'd like to be paired with Recruit French over there. We go back a while and the last time we fought he beat me. I'd like a chance to get my revenge. Also we're both platoon leaders.' He smiled.

'Aha, two trained fighters. One out to even things up. Should be good. You okay with this, French?'

'Yes, Sergeant. Can't wait to beat him again.'

He laughed. 'That sure of yourself huh? Okay. We'll do it differently for the two platoon leaders. We'll do three two minute rounds and I'll decide the winner. After that the rest of you will continue with the milling exercise. Right you two, into the ring.'

The rest of the crowd started shouting and calling either 'Lincoln' or 'Cisco'. There was a tremendous buzz around the ring as the two of us climbed in and got togged up. A member of my platoon, called Andrew Somerhill, who had also boxed a bit, came up to help me with my gloves. 'He may be a friend of yours, Lincoln, but you're fighting for the platoon. Remember that. Don't be nice to him.'

'Don't worry. Our friendship has been suspended until this bout's over. He'll be thinking the same. You can be sure neither of us is going to give an inch. And you can spread the word – I mean to win this.'

'Good man. We're going to be rooting for you. Give him hell.' He climbed out and I stood there working my neck and shoulders, knowing that I would need all my skills as a boxer if I was going to win this one. Cisco may have joked about getting his revenge but I knew him better than anyone and he was deadly serious. It's the same in all sport I guess. Even being up against a friend doesn't stop the competitiveness. It's more acute in boxing though because it's a sport specifically designed to cause hurt and I, for one, had to work hard to put friendship aside. But I knew what I had to do for the next quarter of an hour. The rest of the platoon didn't care about the fact that Cisco and I were friends. All they cared about was that I won and I had no doubt that Cisco's platoon felt the same about him. I briefly thought about Collette and wondered what she would make of this situation. The thought of her spurred me on in a way. I imagined telling her about the fight later and knew that I couldn't lose. There was no way in the world I was going to see her only to say that when it counted, I wasn't up to it. She was my secret weapon.

Sergeant Sharpton brought the two of us together and we touched gloves. 'Right, usual rules apply. This'll be three rounds, each two minutes. Let's have a clean fight. Come out fighting on the whistle.'

We went back to our corners. Andrew was there and fitted my head protector. 'Okay, Lincoln, this is it. He's the one looking for revenge and that might make him too keen, open to mistakes.'

'Yeah, I thought about that but don't underestimate Cisco. He's a good fighter and when we were at school we were pretty evenly matched.'

Sergeant Sharpton called 'Ready?' and blew his whistle. There was a tremendous shout from the onlookers and then Cisco and I were warily circling each other in the centre of the ring looking for the opening that would allow one of us that crucial advantage. We spent the first couple of minutes jabbing at each other and each of us landed some good punches. I certainly felt a couple of Cisco's, especially one to the head that really jarred. I staggered back but I managed to block two follow up punches and then hit him in the ribs twice which made him pull back. I tried to follow these up with a haymaker to his head but he ducked just in time and landed two well-aimed punches to my body. They really hurt and it was all I could do to defend myself against further damage. The whistle sounded and I went back to my corner, where Andrew was waiting with a towel. 'Not bad, Lincoln, not bad. Those two shots to the ribs were good and if that one to the head had landed it'd all be over by now. Try and up your aggression, Lincoln. So far I'd say you're both pretty even but it's this round that counts. Get the better of him in round two and the last round will become that much easier.'

'Okay, round two.' Sergeant Sharpton looked at both of us and blew his whistle. Cisco came out of his corner a lot faster than the previous round and before I knew it he was right there, in my face, punching for all he was worth. I was forced to give ground, desperately defending and found myself against the ropes. The onlookers were screaming and shouting while Cisco, using both hands, tried to land that knockout blow. He nearly succeeded, too, and it was only by keeping my cool that I survived that flurry of punches. Some of them found their target and really hurt but I managed to parry most of them. I slid sideways and away from the ropes. He came after me but for a split second he left himself open and I hit him hard on the right side of his head, which knocked him off balance. It was my turn to pile in and I managed to hit him a couple more times. I realised that the shot to the head had stunned him. I moved forward and aimed another punch at his head which he managed to block but this left him open and I landed a really hard right to his ribcage. He gasped and reeled backwards. I pushed aside any lingering thoughts of friendship and went after him, intending to finish the fight there and then. He was against the ropes, arms up in defence. I kept him there with a series of well-aimed punches and believe I would have finished it if the whistle hadn't gone. My platoon were cheering wildly as I made my way back to the corner, believing that the fight was as good as won. I knew Cisco, however. He was as tough as they came and would certainly want to even up the score in the next round. 'You okay?' said Andrew as I sat down. I nodded. 'Pity the bell went. You coulda finished it. You gotta keep up the pressure now. When the whistle goes get out there faster this time. Don't allow him to settle. Go after him.' The platoon were shouting my name and urging me on. Collette popped into my head and again strengthened my desire to win. I stood up and made ready to get on with the fight.

'Ready? Final round.' Sergeant Sharpton blew his whistle and this time, spurred on by Collette, I moved into the ring at speed, clashing with Cisco as he moved forward. We slugged it out toe to toe in the centre of the ring. Punches from both of us were finding their target and I really felt some of Cisco's. I could see that he really wanted to make up for the previous round. It was vital that I kept my cool and outfought him in this final round. I stepped back, keeping my guard up, inviting him to follow, hoping he'd be too keen and it worked. He came after me, believing that he'd got the better of the slugging match and getting ready to pile into me. In doing so, however, he opened up a bit and I was ready for him. I sprang forward and planted a left fist straight in his face. I followed up with two more punches to the head and then an uppercut to the body. He staggered backwards and I went after him. With that adrenaline rushing through me I believe I would have punched him until he dropped if Sergeant Sharpton hadn't come between us. 'Okay, okay, enough. Back to your corner French. It's all over.' I turned and went back to my corner, relieved that I had been prevented from hurting Cisco any more. The platoon were going wild, jumping up and shouting my name but all I wanted to do was go and see if Cisco was alright. I went over to his corner and we both hugged each other. 'Nice one, Lincoln. You got me that time. Well done. I'm sure gonna be hurting for a while.'

'Thanks, Cisco. Yeah me too. I'd forgotten just how hard you can punch.'

We both went to the middle of the ring where Sergeant Sharpton stood between us and held our arms. 'The winner of this bout is Recruit French,' he said and held up my arm. There was cheering from my corner and clapping from the other platoon. 'Well done, French, and well done to both of you for a good, clean, entertaining fight.' He spoke to the onlookers. 'Okay, we'll give these two a few minutes to cool down and then the rest of you will get on with the milling. We'll have two pairs in the ring at one time. You don't move around too much, you just stand toe to toe and slug it out. The one who quits or falls down first is the loser. Understood?'

'YES, SERGEANT.'

'Good. French, Gonzales, you can help me here in the ring. Keep an eye on each pair. They'll fight for a minute and then stop. If one of them is getting too much of a hiding, stop the exercise. Okay?'

'Yes, Sergeant.'

He turned to the two platoons. 'The object of this exercise is to get some aggression into all of you. I don't want to see anyone standing there like you don't mean it. You are all to try and beat the hell out of your opponent. IS THAT CLEAR?'

'Right, you two and you two.' He picked out two from each platoon. 'Into the ring. Gloves and head protection on. French and Gonzales will tell you when to start and finish.' One of the combatants happened to be Danny and he was paired against a much bigger recruit from Platoon 56. Sergeant Sharpton was obviously not worried about mismatches in size and just expected everyone to get on with it. Danny was looking genuinely nervous when I walked over.

'Right guys, you heard Sergeant Sharpton. You stand here facing each other and battle it out, being as aggressive as you can.' While I helped them with their gloves and head protection, I winked at Danny and formed a fist, urging him with my eyes to be as aggressive as possible. He nodded back and they squared up to each other. 'Go,' I said. Danny really surprised me. The bigger guy landed a few good punches but Danny didn't flinch. He gave as good as he got, punching away for all he was worth. He did very well considering his size and the fact that he had never done anything like this before. After fifty seconds, a particularly well aimed punch from his opponent landed Danny on his backside on the canvas and I called a halt. Sergeant Sharpton came over.

'Well done, you two. That's exactly what I was looking for.' He looked Danny over. 'You okay?'

Danny smiled, real relief and happiness on his face. 'Yes, Sergeant.'

'Good. Shake and back to your platoons.' The others patted Danny on the back as he sat down. Everyone was impressed with his effort and I could see that he felt pleased with what he had done. After the milling exercise, we were shown basic self-defence moves that we then practised until it was time for lunch. 'Good work, everyone. There'll be more of this before we're finished. Recruits French and Gonzales, please march your platoons to the barracks and dismiss them for lunch.' Once back at the barracks, most of us went inside and collapsed onto our beds. I lay down quite gingerly as Cisco's punches were starting to hurt. I knew I was going to feel pretty sore for the next few days and that all activities were going to be difficult. Danny was lying with his eyes shut, a quiet smile on his lips. 'Well done, Lincoln. Impressive. Would definitely want you on my side in a fight.'

'Thanks, Danny. It could have gone either way but I'm glad I won. You were pretty impressive yourself by the way.'

'I was wasn't I?' He laughed. 'I was really scared about this morning's activity,' he said. 'I was dreading the milling bit. I've never been in a fight in my life, never even raised my fists in anger. And when I saw that big fella in front of me... I nearly ran up my own ass. I can't tell you how good I feel, that I got through without making a complete fool of myself. I reckon we both deserve a good lunch after that. I'm ravenous.' We made our way to the dining hall where we met up with Cisco and other members of his platoon. There was a good atmosphere among the recruits and Cisco and I made a point of sitting together for lunch.

'What are you gonna do this afternoon?' asked Cisco.

'I don't know. I notice there's an opportunity to do some archery. Thought I might give it a try. Amazing to think that was the main weapon all those thousands of years ago. Yeah, let's go and try that. Should be fun. You up for that?'

'Yeah, good idea. Anyone else want to go and shoot some arrows?' said Cisco.

'Definitely,' said Danny. 'After this morning that sounds just the ticket. Count me in.' Some of the others also said they'd be interested.

'Okay,' said Cisco. 'We'll come and collect you from your barrack room in about an hour. Til then.'

Danny and I made our way back to the barrack room, grabbed a couple of chairs and sat outside, enjoying the sun. It felt good just to sit there and enjoy the sunshine after the exertions of the last few days. We had been worked pretty hard and it would no doubt continue for the time we were under training. I dozed off, dreaming about Collette. She was standing at the far end of a burning field calling to me. I was trying desperately to get to her but she seemed to just move further and further away. No matter how hard I tried I couldn't reach her and she seemed unable to see me. I woke with a start, feeling a bit shaken and overwhelmed with longing. I just sat there staring into space. 'You okay?' asked Danny. 'You woke with a jolt and seem a bit upset.'

'Yeah, I'm okay,' I said. I hesitated, kept staring ahead. 'Missing someone though…more than I thought possible.'

'Back in Oasis?'

'No, met her on the shuttle. Name's Collette.' I told him about our meeting and how, against all the odds, we seem to have found something special. 'Unbelievable really. I mean, what are the chances of that?'

'She's here in Dakota? What does she do? She in the military?'

'No, going into her final year at school.'

'That's great, Lincoln. If you really have found something special together, that's fantastic. What does she look like?'

I opened the locket she had given me and her head and shoulders appeared in 3D. 'She's beautiful, Lincoln, really lovely.' He smiled. 'No wonder you're missing her. I bet she's missing you just as much. Keep that thought in your head.' He looked concerned. 'You're not thinking of going AWOL are you? You know, sneaking out to go and see her without permission.'

'The thought had crossed my mind but no. I mean to do well here and don't want to do anything stupid. Deep down, I don't think Collette would be too impressed either. Can't wait to see her again though. What about you?'

'My ex-partner's name is Marcus and he works at the university back on Lindfield. He's a maths lecturer and I met him when I was an undergraduate. We were together, on and off, for about four years. When I decided to come to Dakota we ended it. He didn't want to move and, anyway, it wasn't going that well. Now, with this war on and me in the military, I think I'll stay single. I'll find it easier.'

Just then I heard Cisco behind me. 'Jeez, Lincoln, who's *that*? She's gorgeous.'

I laughed. 'Her name's Collette.' I told him briefly about her.

'Well, well – you sure kept that quiet,' he said. 'If she were mine, I'd be missing her too. In fact, I'd be tempted to go AWOL to see her.' He looked serious. 'You're not thinking along those lines are you? It's not worth it.'

'Don't worry, I've already assured Danny that I'll be staying here until we're allowed to leave camp.' I closed the locket. 'You guys ready? Let's go shoot some arrows, make believe we're back on earth fighting for king and country.'

Chapter 4

The following morning we were drawn up on the parade ground in front of the flag and dais and were addressed by Colonel Lesch. 'This war has taken a turn for the worse,' he began. 'News has come through of the Lindfield and Jerendasien systems being overrun, with Union casualties and the loss of most of the military bases in the area. Various ships of the Union space-navy have also been captured or destroyed. We are pulling out of the systems around Halcyon, Jerendasien and Lindfield while we regroup and build up our forces. This affects you in that we need to speed up your training. Instead of waiting until next week, you will begin weapons training today. Be assured that the president is determined that this attack will not succeed. She has asked me to thank you all for volunteering and for your commitment to the Union. All over the Union the response to the president's appeal has been overwhelming. Here at Black Tree Canyon we are expecting a large influx of volunteers throughout the coming weeks. We are going to make sure we play our part in defeating the enemy. Thank you.' He nodded to the sergeant major who took over.

'If anyone here has family or is any way connected with the systems mentioned or the Protectorate in general, please report to the main office after the parade.' He dismissed the parade and we marched back to our barracks. Danny was really worried about the news and immediately left for the office. The rest of us found ourselves waiting around for the musketry instructors to turn up. Danny came back after a while, telling us that the news from the Shanghai system was okay so far. 'Their part of the Protectorate has been unaffected up to now although the federal forces are pulling out. I can only hope that the imperial forces don't get as far as Shanghai before we are able to get there.' He shook his head and smiled. 'This has made me more determined than ever to succeed in getting through this training.' He laughed and flexed his muscles. 'I'ma be the meanest bastard ever put on this uniform. Mr Supreme Leader I'm coming for you, you imperial sonofabitch and when I find you I'm gonna…'

'TENSHUN.' We all jumped to our feet and stood at the end of our beds. Two musketry instructors stood just inside the door. They were dressed completely differently from the rest of us and each carried a type of helmet that I hadn't seen before. One looked at Danny and smiled. 'Hope you get a chance to kick his ass,' he said. 'At ease everyone. Please be seated. My name is Warrant Officer Sparrow and this is Corporal Usher. We are going to be your weapons training instructors and I need to have a short chat before we go up to the firing ranges. You will find things at musketry a little different to the rest of the base. We don't stand on ceremony too much and very seldom shout at anybody. Your safety and the safety of those around you and the correct use of weapons and related equipment is what we regard as important. Most of you will not have handled any type of firearm before so it is vital that you obey instructions at all times. I can't emphasise this enough. The weapons you will be using are of the most up-to-date technology and wrong use can be very dangerous. I repeat – please ensure that you obey instructions at all times. Any questions? No? Okay. Platoon leader, march the platoon over to the ranges. We'll lead the way.' We followed the two instructors over to the far side of the base and on to the musketry area which lay adjacent to the base itself and consisted of an administration block, various different firing ranges and a mock-up town used for urban warfare training. We filed into one of the classrooms and sat down. 'Welcome to musketry and please make yourselves comfortable,' said Warrant Officer Sparrow. 'Now you will have noticed that I am dressed somewhat differently from the rest of the instructors on the base and that is because I am wearing a smart suit. Basically a modern suit of armour that will protect me from a lot of incoming. I also have here a smart helmet, an advanced AIU designed not only to protect my head but to connect with any weapons system I am going to use to improve accuracy and deployment. It is also designed to enhance my senses so that I am much more aware of what is going on all around me when I am in a combat situation. And let's face it that is now a certainty. The first thing we are going to do is to get you all kitted out. Once you have got your suit and helmet, they will be yours to keep as long as you are in the army so please look after them. The same applies to your rifle and sidearm. I'd like you now to follow Corporal Usher to the armoury stores and I will see you back here when you have finished.'

We made our way to the stores and spent a good hour or more being carefully fitted with a smart suit and various other items of equipment we needed for combat. We were issued with a rifle and a pistol and, finally, a close fitting helmet which we were not to put on until given permission. I stood there, pistol strapped to my side and rifle in hand, and realised that I'd taken a giant step away from the person I'd been just the previous week. I was now an old fashioned warrior, armed and with the power to do some real damage. I was surprised at how easily I handled the weapons, even how good they felt in my hands. I still baulked at the idea of shooting a fellow human but started to understand how some people came to be interested in firearms.

I walked back to the classroom deep in thought. The training became a lot more focussed now that we were armed. Our reason for joining the army became clear. We were here for only one reason – to face up to the enemy and defeat them by force. That meant, when devoid of all euphemisms, killing as many of them as we could to force them to surrender. I also feared that countless civilians would be wiped out as the war machine the Union was unleashing got into full swing. The president was determined to win this one and, given the size of the Union and the resources available to it, I was in no doubt that in the end we would prevail. There was a new determination among the recruits too, especially now that two more systems had been overrun, with deaths among military personnel and fellow citizens. The imperial leaders must have been mad to start this. Surely they didn't think the federal government would just roll over and accept such a violation of their territory and principles. Maybe they had been fooled by the thought that the Union, for so long a beacon of peace, would somehow fail to react. As far as I could see the only hope the enemy had in the long term was to call off their occupation and retreat before any further damage ensued. All the indications, however, pointed to them doing the opposite. No doubt buoyed by their initial successes they seemed determined to continue on the road that could only lead, in the end, to their defeat. It was the collateral damage, caused in bringing about the defeat, that worried me. A lot of innocent people were going to be killed or injured before this was over.

We all resumed our places in the classroom and it looked as if a new species had taken our place. All of us looked totally different, dressed all in black, carrying a sidearm, our rifles racked and our helmets on the desk in front of us. Nobody spoke. Warrant Officer Sparrow walked in and motioned for us to remain seated. 'Okay people, you're all suited up and ready for combat. Before we do anything else, you need to get to know your suit and helmet. They are basically indestructible and will be your best friends and companions in any combat situation. The helmet is an advanced AI Unit that will not only protect your head, but link to any weapons system you use and ensure that your smart suit is, at all times, doing its job of protecting you. Additionally, the helmet will be wirelessly connected to your brain so that all your senses become greatly enhanced while you are wearing it. It is voice controlled but is backed up should you find yourself unable to speak. I want you now to put the helmet on and give the command 'fix'. There is no need to shout or speak loudly.'

I tentatively put the helmet on and quietly said 'fix'. I had the feeling of cool, soothing gel forming perfectly around my head and the really weird sensation that the helmet had somehow become more alert as if it was springing to attention. Within a matter of a second or two my helmet was sitting perfectly around my head with the visor down, strap secured under my chin, and feeling incredibly light and comfortable. My suit too had subtly changed and seemed to fit me better. A voice inside my head startled me. 'Is that comfortable?' it asked. I looked around and found the others doing the same as I realised the helmet had actually spoken to me. I said 'yes' softly and then tried 'visor up'. The instruction was immediately complied with.

We all spent the next hour or so getting to know those helmets. I realised that this piece of equipment was going to be vital in keeping me safe and in improving my combat readiness. It was partially sentient and was part of the AI that was spreading rapidly through our society. I thought of the robots that were increasingly performing tasks in inhospitable environments, like mining, and felt sure that many were going to be reprogrammed and put on a war footing. I could imagine AIUs playing an ever greater role in this war and while they weren't yet comparable with humans in decision making, I felt sure that as the war went on the manufacture of these units would improve immeasurably.

After becoming thoroughly familiar with the helmets we were taken out to the firing range and started what became days, and then weeks, of shooting with machine guns, rifles and pistols, throwing grenades, firing grenades and using anti-armour weapons. These activities included firing at static targets and simulated house to house fighting in the mock urban environment that had been built for that purpose. We went on manoeuvres in the countryside where we fought simulated battles, platoons up against one another as we learned the skills required to be an infantryman. It was gruelling work and continued relentlessly through those first twelve weeks. At the same time, we continued with our running and assault course training as the army believed we had to become as fit and healthy as possible before starting our off-surface training. Towards the end of our first twelve weeks I saw a noticeable difference in Danny. He was a lot fitter than when he started and could now run ten k's without stopping. He was also a lot better over the assault course and could complete it without any help from anyone. There was a steely determination to succeed. He really wanted to get at those enemy troops.

At the end of the twelve weeks we finally completed the initial on-surface training and were drawn up on the parade ground before the Colonel Lesch. He stepped forward and spoke to us. 'Good morning, recruits. You have all successfully completed the first part of your basic training and you are about to embark on the next stage. Congratulations to all of you. If the next phase goes as well as this one, then I believe the Union has nothing to fear for the future. I wish you well with your off-surface training and feel sure that you will all pass with flying colours. We are not going to waste any time. Your leave has been postponed and I can tell you now that you will be embarking aboard a navy cruiser at 1800 hours today and your training will commence as soon as the ship has reached the required destination in space. Make sure you spend the rest of the day packing up and report to the admin block no later than 1600 hours. That is all.' He nodded towards us and stepped back.

The sergeant major dismissed us and I spent the rest of that day packing up and chatting to the rest of the platoon. We had all become close friends over the twelve weeks and were pleased that we would be embarking on the next phase of our training together. I called Collette as soon as I could. 'Hi, angel, you okay?'

'Lincoln! How lovely to hear from you. I was just sitting here wondering what you were up to. I'm really missing you, Lincoln.' Her voice started to rise and falter. 'I'm having a hard time getting through this, Lincoln. It's getting to me. I don't want to be too much of a drama queen but…'

'Hey, you're not being a drama queen. This is difficult and I feel exactly the same. All I want, all the time, is to be with you. I…I am about to start on the next phase of my training and just wanted to speak to you while I could.'

'Where are they sending you?'

'I don't know but we're shipping out later today. As far as I know we're staying here within the system. I love you, Collette, always will. Please keep remembering that. I promise I'll be back as soon as I can.'

'Take care, Lincoln. Please, please take care. I love you more than I can say and I just want you to come back to me alive and unharmed. Bye, Lincoln, bye…'

We shipped aboard the *USS Zodiac*, a vast, sleek, dark cruiser that looked as if it had been built for speed and for the second time in my life I found myself in space. Unlike my previous trip there was no human standby pilot and no time for any sightseeing. The ship was fully automated and heavily armed, and crewed by about twenty space-naval personnel. We were welcomed aboard and briefed by the ship's captain. 'Good evening, ladies and gentlemen, and welcome aboard the *Union Star Ship Zodiac*. We are travelling to the Armstrong Space Station, the destination for your off-surface training. Please help yourself to food this evening and don't hesitate to ask a crew member for any assistance you may require. Thank you.'

Cisco, Danny and I sat down to a very good meal and then spent a while chatting before we went our separate ways. I felt tired and was soon in my bunk and fast asleep with Collette, as usual, the last thing on my mind. I slept very well and was up at five the next morning and put in an hour in the gym, joined by Cisco and Danny. While we were there an announcement came through. 'This is a wakeup call for all military personnel. You are to report for breakfast no later than 0700. I repeat no later than 0700. After that you are all required to report to Musterbay A7 at 0830, I repeat 0830, when your off-surface training will commence. Please report for duty in combat suits without firearms, I repeat without firearms.'

'Here we go,' said Danny. 'No doubt they're gonna invent new ways to make sure people like me end the day in pain.'

I laughed. 'You're over that now,' I said. 'Look at you. You're a thousand percent fitter and stronger than you were twelve weeks ago. I saw you going through that assault course recently. You didn't seem to have any problems.'

'I guess,' said Danny. 'Nevertheless, I'm still wary about any new training we're about to embark on.'

'I'm pretty excited about this off-surface stuff,' said Cisco. 'I mean, a space-station. How cool is that. Always wanted to visit one. I hope we get the chance to look around the thing.'

I went back for a shower and breakfast and then joined the rest of the recruits in the musterbay where we stood facing a raised area. An officer, who introduced himself as Brigadier Ferrario, spoke to us. 'Good morning, ladies and gentlemen. Please be seated. As you've been informed you are about to start the final stage of your training and this will take place here on the ship and around the Armstrong Space Station. You are no doubt aware that space stations and asteroids are important scientific and military installations and I have to tell you that quite a number have fallen into enemy hands. We need to recapture them as soon as possible and prevent others from suffering the same fate. Therefore, it is necessary for you to learn how to attack and capture a space station or an asteroid and how to operate in space outside of a ship, using specially designed suits and weapons. You will also learn how to attack and capture a ship. This is what we are going to be concentrating on over the next four weeks. And you heard right. It is four weeks, not six. Because of the war situation, the powers that be have decided to cram your six week programme into four weeks, after which you return to Black Tree Canyon and from there to war.

'Just before we get down to it, I would like to bring you up to speed on the progress of the war so far. The Union government has decided to pull back from our positions in the Protectorate until we have built up our forces and I have to report that the Imperium has taken advantage of this decision and advanced further into the Protectorate.' The names of thirteen systems and a 3D map appeared on the stage next to him. 'They now control these thirteen systems inside the Protectorate, with Shanghai being threatened. So far, they have not actually encroached on Union territory itself but that remains a possibility at the present time and your own Zardogan system, here, has been talked about as a possible target.

As you can appreciate we need to get this training done as soon as possible so we can start the fight back. Good luck to you all. Company commanders, please take over.'

We moved to a smaller bay and there we began the second phase of our training by getting to know how to use a special suit that operated as a mini space vehicle in its own right, was connected to our helmets and answered to voice commands. It could change shape to suit the environment. Designed to be used in space outside a ship, it carried an array of weapons and we spent the first two days in a simulated space environment within the ship familiarising ourselves with this new equipment. By the end of the second day I was utterly exhausted but pleased with my progress. I had full control of the suit and although I was nervous, I felt fairly confident about trying it outside the ship the following morning.

I joined the others in the dining hall for dinner. All of us were really tired and we were starting to feel the effects of the training being cut down to four weeks. 'You guys ready for your space walks tomorrow?' I asked.

'I am,' said Cisco. 'These suits are something else aren't they? I can't wait to see it working out there.'

'For the first time since I joined the army I've found something I'm completely at home with,' said Danny. 'I've loved working with this suit and feel confident about tomorrow. Actually looking forward to it and also think it'll be a fantastic experience. Right now though, I'm ready for bed. If you guys'll excuse me, I'll see you all tomorrow.'

The following morning we assembled in the musterbay and got ready to leave the safety of the ship. Now that we were on the verge of actually doing this for the first time it was nerve-racking. The musterbay was depressurised and an outer hatchway opened. Commands were given to the suits and the next thing I knew I was outside the ship and moving through space under my own steam. The ship was stationary and flying away from it was both the scariest and most exciting thing I'd ever done. We spent half a day just getting used to being out there and controlling the suits, and then we learnt to use the weapons, which included automatic rifles and small cannon. At the end of the first day's training we were all on a high and trooped into the dining hall in tremendous spirits. Nobody had been lost in space and we all felt that we had moved onto a higher level in our training.

'That was outa this world,' said Danny. 'I'm definitely going to be looking for an off-surface job when this war is over. I loved it. And using those weapons...'

We all agreed that it had been an exhilarating experience and I for one felt much more confident than at the start of the day. Mind you, I could see how, in a combat situation, with ships on the move, and in the confusion of battle, you could get lost in space. That would be unbelievably frightening and not something I wanted to think about too much.

Over the next few days day we took part in simulated attacks against the ship, which at first was stationary and then on the move, blowing open hatches, getting inside and fighting our way to the bridge. Companies took turns at being attackers and defenders and by the end of it we were thoroughly familiar with the ways in which a ship could be attacked or defended. The inter-platoon competition remained in place and at the end of this phase of the training our platoon remained ahead of the others, with Cisco's in second place.

The next phase involved the simulated attack and capture of the Armstrong Space Station which was basically the same as taking a ship but on a larger scale. The Armstrong was about ten kilometres across and hugely complex once we got inside. A detailed plan of the whole place had been downloaded to our helmets before we started the exercise but it was still a massive task. It took four weeks of intensive training and practice but at the end of the time we were ready for anything. We practised exiting from a fast moving ship and landing on an asteroid and finally, at the end of an unbelievably intense training period, we turned for home, our training complete. The return trip to Dakota was uneventful and we landed at Black Tree Canyon ready to go to war.

Danny and I were lying on our beds when a recruit walked in and shouted 'Bands'. She handed us our wristbands and I immediately activated mine. I found that Collette had sent me a message for every day that I had been away in space. I couldn't believe how lucky I was meeting her like that…on that shuttle. What's more, we were beginning three days leave the following morning and I was going to see her again. I also thought the platoon could do with having a celebration together.

'Listen guys, we've got three days leave so let's organise to meet up and have a drink the night before we're due back. There's a great bar called the *Mockingbird* in Euclid Square. What say we meet there for a celebratory drink? I reckon we deserve it after the last sixteen weeks.' They agreed and said they'd try and get there.

'TENSHUN.' We all scrambled to stand at the foot of our beds. Sergeant Faber walked in. 'Good afternoon, gentlemen. You will be going on leave tomorrow and I don't want to hear reports of any wrongdoing by anyone in this platoon. You will be in uniform and you must conduct yourselves in an exemplary manner at all times. There will be a barrack inspection tomorrow morning at oh eight hundred and I want to see this place looking perfect. Understood?'

'YES, SERGEANT.'

'Well done so far. I can tell you that your training has been a success and that Platoon 57 is in first place in our inter-platoon competition. I'll see you tomorrow morning. At ease.' We all cheered and then made our way, in high spirits, down to the dining hall. The other platoons were drifting in and we soon caught up with Cisco.

'Hey, Lincoln, Danny. How are things guys? You ready to hit Dakota tomorrow?'

'You bet,' said Danny. 'I can't wait to get outta here for a while.'

'Same here,' I said. 'It'll be great to be back in the city. What about you?'

'Got plans, pal, got plans. I'm hooking up with Segolene from Platoon 28. We've become pretty friendly over the past few weeks and we're planning to meet up in town and take it from there. She doesn't really know

Dakota that well so yours truly will be showing her the sights.' He put his arm around our shoulders and winked at Danny. 'That girl of yours still want to see you, Lincoln, or has she come to her senses?'

I laughed. 'She still wants to see me. Yeah I know – unbelievable. Listen, Cisco, our platoon is meeting the evening before we're due back at *The Mockingbird*, Euclid Square. Why don't you guys from 56 join us? And 28 for that matter. The more the merrier.'

'Sounds good. I'll spread the word and we'll see you there. Until then, have fun. What are you doing, Danny?'

'I've arranged to meet some of the people from the faculty who think I'm some kind of hero. Don't quite know how I'm going to live up to that but I aim to have a good break. I'll definitely see you guys at the *Mockingbird*.'

Chapter 5

When I walked out of that gate and saw Collette waiting for me, an indescribable feeling of happiness and relief overwhelmed me. We both hesitated for a moment and then fell into each other's arms and for those first few minutes I was unable to let go of her. We just stood there pressed against each other and I couldn't recall ever feeling so happy in my life.

'You look even leaner, somehow,' she said after a while, standing back to look at me. 'And fitter, if that's possible.'

'I probably am,' I laughed. 'These past sixteen weeks have been pretty intensive.' Out of the corner of my eye I saw Cisco and Danny loitering nearby. They were obviously curious about Collette. I held her hand and walked over to them. 'Collette – Cisco, Danny.'

'Hi, Collette. Pleased to meet you,' said Cisco. 'Heard your name mentioned a couple of times.'

'Hello, Collette. Likewise,' said Danny. 'Lincoln has mentioned you once or twice. Good to meet you.'

'Hello, nice to meet you both. I know a bit about you Cisco. Danny, I guess you and Lincoln met here at the base.'

'Yes we did. And very pleased, too, to have met him. He's helped me get through this training. I don't know if I would have made it otherwise.'

'I'm sure you would have,' I said. 'Anyhow, let's get that train into town. You two guys coming?' The four of us rode the train to the spaceport where we went our separate ways after agreeing to meet at the *Mockingbird* on the final evening.

'My folks and Gabe want to see you, if that's okay with you. They've laid on a bit of a homecoming on our boat but I told them that could only happen after I've had you to myself. It's so wonderful to see you again, Lincoln. I really want to make the most of these three days. Who knows when we'll be together again.'

I put my arms around her and kissed her lightly on the forehead. 'I love you, Collette. Always will. No matter where I have to go or what I have to do. Over these three days I don't want to let you out of my sight. Not for a second.'

'Let's go to your place, Lincoln. Right now, I don't want to do anything else but be alone with you. Everything else can wait.' We made our way to my apartment and spent the rest of the day there, deeply, passionately in love and blissful in each other's company, knowing that our time together was limited and determined to make the most of that limited time. Collette had made sure the apartment was appropriately stocked and around mid-afternoon we were lying on the bed sipping champagne, enjoying the moment.

'What's this about your parents laying on some sort of homecoming?' I asked.

'Mom's idea actually. She figured we were the closest thing you had to a family and insisted on arranging this get-together for you this evening on the boat, which is moored on the river near our place. She said she'd understand if you didn't want to come and I said I wouldn't try and force you…'

'I'd love to come along,' I said. 'Your mom's right. You are the nearest thing to a family I've ever had and I really appreciate the gesture. If it's anything like the barbecue, it'll be great. Will Gabriel be there?'

'Yes, he will. Also there'll be some friends and neighbours, all of whom are looking forward to meeting you.'

'You know me,' I said, 'just love to be the centre of attention. By the way, I'll be sticking to you like a limpet.' I stroked her cheek and she took my hand and kissed my fingers.

'I'll make sure you do. I won't allow you more than a centimetre away from me at any time. In fact,' she continued, taking my glass and putting it on the bedside table, 'let me show you just how close I'd like you to be.'

We eventually left the apartment toward evening time and made our way to the boat. Dakota looked lovely in the evening sun as Collette and I walked hand in hand to the river. I was quite saddened to see that the streets were full of men and women in uniform, a manifestation that the Union was at war. I could also see preparations underway for the defence of the city against aerial attack. Proserpine was in the firing line and had been mentioned by the imperial leadership as a system that needed to 'return to the fold'. I felt distinctly uneasy. 'You'll take care won't you, Collette?' I said. 'All this preparation for war. Proserpine could be attacked.'

'I know. I heard what that ghastly Supreme Leader said about us. Who does he think he is? He'll have a fight on his hands if he comes here. '

'Nevertheless, I want you to be careful. A surprise aerial attack would be devastating and I can't bear to think of anything happening to you. These people would use nuclear weapons if they were desperate. They're as crazy as drunk rats.'

Collette put her arms around me. 'I promise I'll take care. I won't do anything stupid. But it's you who we should be talking about. You'll be going who knows where and facing all sorts of danger. I…I try not to think about it too much or I find myself becoming really anxious…panicky. I can't imagine life without you Lincoln. You promise me you'll take care, won't you? Don't be a hero, just come back and we'll look after each other for the rest of our lives.'

I kissed the top of her head. 'I promise.'

We rode a river taxi upstream to her parents' boat which, like their house, turned out to be luxurious. The party was a quiet, sober affair. Everyone was preoccupied with the war. Gabriel had tried to join up but had been rejected as the government wanted him and his mathematical talents for some highly secret work that he couldn't discuss at the time. I guessed it was something to do with the development of Artificial Intelligence but didn't pry. Some neighbours' sons and daughters had joined the armed forces and I chatted to a couple of space-sailors who, like me, were undergoing basic training. I invited them to join us at *The Mockingbird* and they accepted.

Collette's parents were concerned about my safety even though they had only just got to know me. Collette was pretty open about her feelings for me and I suppose her parents just came to accept me as part of their family. I felt flattered and was determined to live up to their expectations. This was my chance to become part of a family and I wasn't going to blow it.

I went for a run the next morning and looked in on Jacob who invited me in for a coffee. I told him that I'd taken the liberty of inviting all these people to his place the following evening. He roared with laughter. 'Great. My place is going to be filled with army and navy types. Sounds good. You know how I feel about those pricks who have attacked the Union. It'll be a pleasure having you all here.' He looked me over. 'How's the training going? Told you it wouldn't take much to turn you into a soldier. You certainly look the part.'

'Thanks, Jacob. The training has been fine. In fact, I've enjoyed it so far. How have things been here at the bar?'

'Usual. The war hasn't really touched us yet except for the defences being erected around the city. The planet and system defences are also being beefed up but I hope we stay clear of any trouble.'

'I hope so too but you never know what these people are going to do next.' I finished my coffee and said goodbye. 'I'll see you tomorrow.' I made my way to my apartment where I had a shower and breakfast and waited for Collette to arrive. We headed for the beach. I had grown up on a sea free orbital and I stood on that beach and stared spellbound at the ocean, constantly moving and seemingly infinite. I walked into the sea, water swirling around my waist, holding Collette's hand. We stood in silence for a while. 'Growing up in Oasis on the orbital, I used to gaze up at Proserpine and marvel at the blue of the oceans. Now, to actually be standing in the sea...' I looked at Collette who laughed and hugged me. We had a fantastic day together, swimming, lying in the sun, eating, drinking and just enjoying being there with each other. The weather was perfect and the sea was warm and I was like a kid out on his own for the first time. It was unforgettable.

We left the beach in the late afternoon and went back to the apartment and from there to Collette's place. I spent the evening there and then returned to the apartment where I slept like a baby. After a run and breakfast, Collette and I met in town and spent a lazy day together, having lunch in Collette's favourite restaurant, going to a movie and spending time together in the apartment. Towards the evening we made our way to *The Mockingbird* to meet the others. Quite a crowd had already gathered by the time we got there and more were arriving all the time. Jacob was in his element, chatting to the clients, roaring with laughter and shouting orders to the bar. Cisco was there with Segolene and Danny arrived with a couple of university colleagues. There were soon over two hundred soldiers, sailors and others in the place and the atmosphere was electric. None of us knew what the future held and in the back of our minds was the thought that we could well die in the coming conflict. A kind of recklessness pervaded the assembled company with alcohol and assorted narcotics flowing in torrents. The bar staff were kept pretty busy and Jacob had his hands full making sure all the orders were handled correctly. Anyone with less experience or personality would have crumpled under the pressure but he was magnificent. He was everywhere and he ensured that the atmosphere remained positive and friendly.

'Hey guys, having a good time?' said Cisco, making his way through the crowd. He had his arm around Segolene. 'We're thinking of heading on to a club. Interested?'

Danny shook his head. 'No thanks, Cisco. Gonna stay here for a while longer and then home for me.'

'Me too,' said Collette. 'Don't feel like clubbing at the moment and am happy just being here.' I agreed.

'Okay, in which case I'll see you two back at camp and Collette – it's been great meeting you. Hope we see you soon.'

'Bye, Cisco, and take care,' said Collette. 'You too, Segolene, be careful.'

Collette and I eventually said our goodbyes and I took her home to her place. We held hands and spoke to each other all the way back and found ourselves at her house all too soon. We exchanged gifts, held each other tight, whispered endearments, promised to love each other for the rest of time, then kissed each other one last time and I waved her goodbye and headed back home. Once again I felt wretched and lonely and fell into a fitful sleep, drifting into a world in which everything was badly distorted and nothing was as it should be.

Part 3

Fighting and Killing

Chapter 1

Our final parade took place on the morning of our return to the base. We donned battle dress and marched onto the parade ground where we were addressed by the camp commandant. He congratulated us on successfully completing our training and wished us well for the future. We were being sent into battle against a fanatical enemy and there was no doubt that some of us would not come out of this conflict alive. He personally handed us our 'Infantry ID', a black metal badge that was worn on the left collar and denoted that you were a member of the Union infantry. I was called out and went up to the dais to receive the inter-platoon trophy on behalf of the platoon. We had won the competition and I saw Sergeant Faber beaming with pleasure as he stood next to the platoon. We marched back to the barracks and were told to remain drawn up in formation outside. To my surprise the colonel himself came over. 'Congratulations again, Platoon 57. You can be very proud of what you have achieved over the past sixteen weeks. I am also here to inform you that as of today you have a new sergeant in your ranks. Private French, I'm pleased to tell you that you have been promoted to sergeant with immediate effect. Your name was put forward by Sergeant Faber and seconded by your company commander Captain Molyneaux. The Union needs good leadership at this time and you have stepped up to the mark. Congratulations. I hope this promotion is the first of many. Good luck to you all. It's been a pleasure knowing you.'

The platoon gathered around and congratulated me and then Sergeant Faber came over. 'Congratulations, Lincoln. I saw from day one that you had the potential to go far. I'm really pleased for you and wish you well.'

'Er...thanks, Sergeant, and thank you for putting my name forward for this promotion. I hope I live up to your expectations.'

'I'm sure you will and feel free to call me Nick. By the way you're taking over this platoon as you'll be going off to war together. I have to stay here and train the new recruits taking your place. '

'Okay...er...Nick.' I shook my head. 'That's going to take some getting used to.' He laughed and walked away and I went and sat on my bunk, dazed at being promoted so soon after joining the army. Because of the emergency things like this were bound to happen but I looked at the chevrons I'd been given and had to admit that I felt really good, especially as I was to stay with Platoon 57. I was already platoon leader and so becoming their sergeant wasn't going to present much of a problem. Nevertheless I needed to know and so gathered them around and spoke to them. 'Just to let you know I am to take Sergeant Faber's place in charge of this platoon. Things won't be very different from when I was platoon leader but I am aware that my promotion does change our professional relationship and if any of you are uncomfortable with that and wish to deploy to another platoon, please feel free to put in a request.' None of them wished to change but a couple of those congratulations weren't too heartfelt. I realised that being favoured like this could cause some upset among my peers and that I was going to have to deal with it up front as and when it arose. Also, I reckoned that as long as I lived up to any promotion I received, things would be okay. It's when a person is promoted above their abilities or uses the position in a negative manner that problems arise. I felt confident that I could lead people in a positive and supportive manner.

We were all called to a special assembly after lunch. 'The powers that be have decided the time has come for you to join the first counter-attack against the Imperium and you will be leaving this system first thing tomorrow to join the 15th Army, which, together with the 33rd and 42nd Armies, has launched an attack to retake the Jerendasien system. We will be shipping out at 0600 so please spend the rest of the day ensuring that you are ready when the time comes to leave. All officers and NCOs please remain behind for a further briefing. That is all.' I joined the officers and non-commissioned officers in the rows of chairs immediately in front of the platform.

'At ease, ladies and gentlemen,' said a brigadier togged out in combat gear. 'I don't want to keep you long. My name is Freeman of the 15th Army. You are now part of that army and we are engaged in fighting to recapture the Jerendasien system. The attack against the capital city, Adrendakon, has stalled and we have sustained heavy losses. General Bullen, however, is determined that this first counter-attack against the Imperium will succeed and so you are being sent to reinforce the division attacking the city. You will be involved in heavy fighting as soon as we get there and I want you to make sure those under your command are fully prepared for this. Please spend the rest of today getting everything and everybody ready. All weapons and equipment must be checked and all personnel must be left in no doubt about what they're going to face once we leave this base tomorrow morning. I also want all troops to be carrying grenades and I want each platoon to be equipped with anti-armour weaponry. My staff and I shall be coming round during the day to carry out random checks so please make sure everything is in order. Any questions? Okay, deployment as follows...' Platoons 56 and 57, renamed Platoons 3 and 4, became part of Bravo Company, 707th Infantry Regiment, 15th Army.

'Right, you heard the man,' said Captain Molyneaux, the commander of Bravo Company. 'You are to ensure that there is absolutely nothing out of place by the time we go. All your weaponry and other equipment must be in tip-top order. Anything defective, get it reported and get it fixed. If any of you need any help don't hesitate to call me or Lieutenant Regan. I'll be in the company office for most of the day. Carry on.' We saluted and I joined the platoon.

'Okay guys, gather round. At ease everybody.' I repeated the brigadier's message to them and we agreed that we would be completely ready with no hitches by

1830 when we would be ready for inspection. I appointed Danny and Mollie as the anti-armour personnel, which meant they had to carry the required weaponry between them. We got to work. After sorting out my own stuff, I went round helping the others and making sure all their weaponry and equipment was in working order and that nobody was missing anything. We also made sure that we all drew grenades from the armoury and I told the platoon to make time to contact friends and family before we left that night. By 1830 we were finished and I was satisfied that Platoon 4 was as ready as they'd ever be for what we were about to face. There was a tense nervousness about the place but also a quiet determination to see this task through. After all, we had all volunteered to fight in this war, most of us for sound reasons, and we had come too far to have any doubts now. The platoon had bonded well as a unit throughout the training and I was happy to be going to war with these guys on my side. They in turn seemed happy to have me lead them and I was determined not to misplace that trust. We were inspected by one of the 15th Army officers who had accompanied the brigadier and she could find no fault with our preparation.

'Good turnout, Sergeant French, and everything seems to be in order. Well done. You're all on downtime until reveille when you will assemble on the parade ground in full kit and with weapons. Carry on.'

'Yes, ma'am,' I said and saluted.

I immediately called Collette. Now that the time had come for me to go to war, I felt a hollowness inside me whenever I thought about her. If there was any reason for me not to go it was the thought of not being near her.

'Lincoln, where are you, how are you, can I see you?' Collette was squealing and I laughed.

'Hey, angel. It's so good to see you and hear your voice. I'm at the base, I'm fine but I can't get out. Where are you?'

'I'm at school. When you came up on the band I ran out of the class. I'll explain to the teacher later. It's wonderful to be speaking to you. When am I going to see you again?'

'Er...that's the thing. We're shipping out in the morning. I've no idea how long I'm going to be away. All I know is that...is that we're heading to a combat zone. We...'

'Lincoln, nooooo. Oh, Lincoln, you...you're going to war. I don't know how...if...Lincoln, I don't know what I'll do if anything happens to you.' Her voice had risen and she was now openly crying. 'Don't be a hero, just be as careful as you can. Promise me that. Promise me you won't...oh, Lincoln, what am I going to do?'

'Okay, okay, take it easy. I promise I won't do anything stupid, I'll be as careful as I can. I'm going to come back to you. I want to spend my life with you, remember that. I love you, Collette, more than I can say.'

'I love you too, Lincoln, and always will. Wherever you are or however long it takes, I'll wait for you. You're in my thoughts always.'

That farewell call was the hardest thing I'd done and for a few minutes it wouldn't have taken much for me to go AWOL. In the end we said our goodbyes and I spent some time on my own gathering my thoughts and pulling myself together. After all, I was about to lead troops into battle for the first time and needed to have my wits about me. Sitting there, I made up my mind to concentrate fully on the task in hand. Any thoughts of Collette would have to be pushed to the back of my mind and it certainly was going to be of no use whatsoever moping about being away from her. Easier said than done, mind you, easier said than done...

I joined the others for coffee, helped Captain Molyneaux with admin, lay on my bunk and read and slept fitfully. Then it was 0500 the next day and we were getting ready to assemble on the parade ground. From there we shipped aboard shuttles that took us to a vast transport vessel on station just outside the planet's atmosphere. Once aboard we found that the ship had already picked up troops from other systems and so there were about 10,000 of us in total. We were ushered to a massive hangar to be addressed by the officer in charge of the 15th Army. Her name was General Pauline Bullen and even in the short time we had been in the army we had heard of her. There was a platform at the back of the hangar and behind it a vast Union flag had been projected onto the wall. A sergeant major marched onto the platform and barked 'TENSHUN'. We all jumped to our feet and General Bullen walked onto the platform. She looked the part and, when she spoke, she sounded it as well. A real kick-ass individual if ever I'd met one. 'AT EASE, BE SEATED,' barked the sergeant major, who saluted and marched to the back of the platform. The general took over, striding to the front of the platform in a perfectly ironed dress uniform, full of stars and decorations, with four stars gleaming on each collar and across the front of her helmet. She carried a swagger stick which she tapped against her highly polished boots.

'You are soldiers of the Interplanetary Union and you are about to go into battle for the first time. No doubt some of you are feeling nervous at the prospect but I want you to dispel all those thoughts from your minds. You are now part of the 15th Army and in this woman's army there is no room for nervousness or any other affliction that will, in any way, diminish your capability as a fighting soldier.' She looked out over the assembly facing her. 'We have been accorded the honour of being the first federal force to go on the attack and we are going to retake the Jerendasien system as a first step in putting an end to this war.' She pointed the swagger stick at us and spoke out in a clear voice. 'There will be no room for failure. I wish to make it clear from the outset that I do not want to hear any excuses why something cannot be done. We are going to go through those imperial sonsofbitches like a rat through cheese and we are not going to stop until they are all dead or have surrendered. And I mean unconditional surrender. There is to be no negotiating with the enemy.' She strolled from one side of the stage to the other. 'I want you to remember that we did not start this conflict. But I want you to be in no doubt that we are going to end it. This war has been forced upon us and we have to see this through. I want the Jerendasien system recaptured and I want no pussyfooting around while we're doing it. I expect you to engage with the enemy and to defeat them. I want you to keep advancing until we are victorious. Nothing else will do.' She walked back to the centre of the stage. Speaking more quietly she said. 'I have no doubt that's exactly what you will do and I am proud to lead this army into battle. Carry on.'

We broke into our different groups and we joined others who, like us, had been assigned to the attack on the capital, Adrendakon. A number of battalions were fighting their way to the centre of the city and all had suffered grievous losses. The attack against the city had become bogged down. Our company was assigned to reinforce one of these battalions who were finding it difficult making any further headway without their losses being replaced. We had badly underestimated both the enemy numbers and their determination not to give the city up to our forces. General Depardieu who had led the original attack against the city had been replaced by a General Hani who addressed us on a giant screen. He was quietly spoken but he left us in no doubt that he meant to shift the operation up to a higher gear and that failure to take the city was not an option. It sounded like we were heading for hell itself. I felt sorry for the civilian population, caught up in the middle of this madness because it didn't sound as if General Hani was going to be too careful while carrying out his orders.

I couldn't help thinking that the Union had gone on the offensive too soon. We should have waited until we had built up our forces sufficiently but it was too late for that. Here we were and I couldn't see General Bullen even contemplating any kind of retreat. She would rather we all died on this planet than abandon what we had started. No doubt she had made that pretty clear to General Hani too because he sounded just as determined to succeed. We were going to make the best of what we had and take this city and this planet or die in the attempt.

Captain Molyneaux called the company together. 'Communications lockdown is lifted for five hours and so mail should be coming through. Any outgoing mail must be sent through the usual official channels. We're on downtime until further notice so relax because it doesn't sound like we're gonna have much R and R where we're going.'

'Sounds like we're headed for a fun time,' said Danny. 'Gonna make the training seem like a party.'

'Yeah,' said Cisco. He looked like he was actually looking forward to it. 'This is gonna be some fight.'

'That General Bullen is something else isn't she?' said Danny. 'I sure wouldn't want to get on the wrong side of her.' He started strutting up and down. '"We gonna go through those sonsabitches like a rat through cheese." Jeez, can you imagine how General Depardieu got replaced: "Depardieu, you useless prick, I told you to take that shithole called Adrendakon and you're still fucking around on the outskirts. This bag a donuts coulda done a better job. You're fired, numbnuts. Gonna find me a real soldier."' We all fell about laughing as Danny did a great send up of General Bullen. He sounded just like her as he carried on. "Hani, get in here. I want you to capture that place and I want it done NOW. I catch you pissing around like that bastard Depardieu I'ma hang you up by your ankles, cut out your nuts and feed them to you through your nostrils. You fucking got me?"' Again we roared with laughter. Danny's impersonation of General Bullen worked wonders on our morale. We all went off feeling good and ready for whatever we had to face in the coming days.

'I'm going to try and get some sleep,' said Danny after a while. 'I reckon we're going to need it.'

'Yeah, okay. See you later, Danny. Sleep tight,' I said.

On the morning of the second day, we transferred to the *USS Andromeda,* a troop transporter which was to take us to Adrendakon. I gathered the platoon around me. 'Stay together, stay with me and follow instructions. Don't try and be too much of a hero and never underestimate the enemy. As we've heard they're very good fighters and there is no-way that this is going to be easy. Remember what you've been taught and put it into practice. Good luck.'

The Jerendasien system lay on one of the outer spiral arms and the trip required hyper-travel, the discovery that had allowed humanity to leave their original solar system and engage in interstellar travel. We were strapped in in our full battle gear so that we could be ready for action as soon as possible after reaching our destination.

We all felt pretty nervous. What we didn't want was the ship being attacked while we were travelling or just as we emerged from hyper-travel, when our protective shields were down. Danny looked around. I could see he was really nervous and I knew exactly how he felt. Although rare, things did go wrong with hyper-travel and I wouldn't feel happy until we had reached our destination and were sub-hyper again.

We strapped ourselves in and remained there while the ship went through a series of space-jumps until we found ourselves in orbit around Jerendasien. We touched down just outside Adrendakon and our division was stationed to the rear of the besieging force, waiting for orders that would send us into the thick of the fighting. And I was in no doubt we were going to be needed before this operation was over. General Hani had been joined by General Bullen herself, determined to ensure that we succeeded in defeating the Imperium here at Adrendakon. News had come through of a space-naval battle in the Deutschland Gap where a federal fleet had defeated a much larger imperial force resulting in the gap once again being in Union hands. The Deutschland Gap, an area of space containing millions of asteroids rich in elements, had been one of the first areas taken by the Imperium and it was good news to hear that we had taken it back. It also provided a boost to our forces waging the war here in the Jerendasien system. We were more determined than ever to succeed – especially as we didn't want the navy having one over us! – and the renewed attack against Adrendakon started early on the morning after we arrived. It was old fashioned fighting, one army against another because we didn't want to destroy the city or the civilian population inhabiting it. Unless the enemy surrendered, we were going to have to take this city street by street, building by building. We sat there quietly, waiting to be deployed, and knowing that not all of us were going to get through this alive.

The call came soon enough, about two hours after the start of the battle. The voice of Captain Molyneaux came through the headphones. 'Bravo, fall in. We're about to move out towards the city. Platoon commanders make sure all personnel are ready for action. Troops, keep all comms channels open and listen out for orders. Good luck everyone. Let's look out for each other. We're going to be fighting in a built up area so try not to become isolated.'

I got my platoon together. 'Right, you heard. We're going to be fighting in an urban area. Cisco, you lead section one, Andrew, section two and Mollie, section three. Make sure you don't become isolated. Radio contact at all times. Let's go.'

Each company was assigned to an attack shuttle. They were compact and designed to be virtually undetectable by enemy radar. We climbed in and sat in two rows along the length of the vehicle facing each other, securely strapped in. Captain Molyneaux stood at the end nearest the pilot. 'Okay, this is it. As you know we're heading for Adrendakon and some heavy fighting. Both General Bullen and General Hani have made it clear that the city has to be taken. That means fighting to clear it of imperial troops without causing too much devastation to the civilian population who are our allies and friends. As soon as we stop, I want us out of this vehicle and getting into position. We'll be reinforcing a battalion commanded by Colonel Matfield, who will brief us when we get there. Listen out for instructions and good luck to you all.' He took his seat and the shuttle moved out onto the airfield. We took off suddenly and with nerve-shredding speed, climbing vertically for what seemed an eternity before eventually levelling out, heading towards our destination. It was impossible to see where we were going and we had no choice but to sit quietly and trust the pilot. I didn't know if the pilot was human or AIU but fervently hoped that he, she or it knew what they were doing. There was no denying that I felt scared while experiencing a sense of elation as well. I glanced over at Danny, who was sitting next to me. He was staring straight ahead with a tight grip on his rifle. I patted him on the shoulder. 'Okay, mate?'

He nodded. 'Bit jumpy, that's all,' he said with a nervous grin. 'I don't want to make a fool of myself out there.'

'You won't,' I said. 'You've been brilliant through the training, have made unbelievable progress. You're going to be just fine. Let's make sure we all stick together.'

'Yeah good idea. I'd like that,' he said. I looked across at Cisco, who gave me the thumbs-up, and gave Segolene a wave. She and Cisco were sitting next to each other and I hoped that nothing happened to either of them or Danny. The shuttle made a sharp turn to the right and then a steep dive before levelling out. It was impossible to know whether we were descending or ascending but the next thing I knew we were shuddering and bouncing along. It was a really rough ride and I sat there bouncing around like flotsam in a rough sea. I just closed my eyes and hoped for the best. There were suddenly multiple explosions all around us and the shuttle lurched sickeningly, listing to the left before righting itself. The explosions continued and I realised we were under fire. Suddenly there was a violent explosion near the rear of the shuttle and we started losing height rapidly. We had been hit. The cabin started filling with smoke and a claxon went off, adding to the feeling of terror building up inside the shuttle. Our helmets and suits saved us from the effects of the smoke but we were strapped in and just had to sit there hoping for the best. A voice came over the intercom. 'CRASH LANDING, CRASH LANDING. BRACE POSITION. BRACE POSITION.' I stiffened and felt the straps tightening around me. My suit too tightened around my body and my helmet did the same around my head. The next thing I knew we were down, hitting the ground with a tremendous jolt and bouncing and shuddering and slewing to the right until with a shattering crash we finally came to a halt, half-tilted over with the rear at 45 degrees to the ground. The rear doors sprung open and Captain Molyneaux was shouting 'OUT,

OUT. QUICK AS YOU CAN. GET UNDER COVER.' It was difficult, climbing up the shuttle to the doors and I stayed and helped the men and women get out. Most of us were dazed and confused but we finally made it out into a built-up area of the city. The shuttle had come to a stop against a warehouse. We were in a street, surrounded by damaged buildings and the sound of gunfire, and by sheer good fortune or pilot skill, I still don't know, we were within federal lines so had time to run for cover. An officer, all dusty and looking like he had been in the thick of things, appeared from one of the buildings and shouted for us to take cover. We all did as he told us and just in time because heavy firing started from up one of the streets towards our position. Three of our company were hit but we managed to drag them inside with us and then started returning the fire. After a while things started quietening down and the firing stopped. The officer whom we had seen initially gathered us together. His face was grimy with dirt and he looked like he needed some sleep. Most of those who we found there looked the same and I realised that they had been holding their position with great difficulty and real bravery.

'Right, listen up people. I'm Colonel Matfield and this is my temporary HQ. There's a battalion of us scattered through this part of the city with the enemy up the road there. We've succeeded in holding on here but it has been a close run thing at times. However, now that you've joined us things should be a whole lot easier and we can start advancing into the heart of the city until all these imperial pricks have been cleared out of the place.' He beamed a map onto one of the walls and a 3D model of a part of the city sprung out towards us. He pointed to the model. 'We're here and up that road about a kilo and a half there's a sprawl of buildings and a tower on an extensive site where a large force of imperial troops are concentrated. The place is surrounded by a high fence and there are other buildings all around it and narrow streets. I'd like your company to capture that site and as much of the neighbourhood around it as possible and hold the place while the rest of us advance through this area here. Once you secure the complex and the residential area we'll call it a day and plan any further advance from there. I don't know whether any civilian staff are still on site but they could be in place and being used as cover. However, we need to keep advancing into the city if we are going to succeed in taking it. This will mean civilian casualties but we're gonna keep doing our best to keep these to a minimum. We've had a few getting this far but the population is on our side and pleased to see us.' The model and map changed and now the whole of the city was projected. It was also in two colours, green in a thin band around the outskirts and orange for the rest. 'The green area represents the area already in Union hands. As you can see we're still really on the outskirts and we need to start making progress towards the centre. We still have a lot of work to do and the imperial troops are refusing to even consider any suggestion of surrender. We've tried talking to them, especially as regards the civilian population, but they don't want to know. So we're gonna play hardball. We're not going out of our way to take prisoners but I leave that to you. Keep your suits on high alert for drones and armour. We've knocked some out but there are always more. Let me know when you are in complete control of your objective. Good luck.'

Captain Molyneaux went up to the map. 'Okay, this is how we're gonna do it. Lieutenant Regan, you are to take half the company and proceed up the left side of this street and clear the enemy from all buildings and properties, advancing up to the complex. Don't attempt an attack on the site until we're all in position and have assessed the situation on the ground. Make sure that all the buildings in this area leading up to the site are completely clear of enemy troops and wait for further instructions before we take any action at the complex itself. I'll take the other half of the company and do the same up this side of the street. Sergeants French, de Villiers, Tsukadi and Kandoria you're with me. Sergeants Redding, Ahmed, Dela Rosa and Ndlovu you're with Lieutenant Regan.' He turned to Colonel Matfield. 'If any of them surrender, I'm gonna send them back here.' I was pleased to hear that. I wasn't happy with a policy of not taking prisoners. There was no way I was going to cold-bloodedly shoot someone who had surrendered. If I had to, I'd rather just let them go. I wanted to get through this war with as clear a conscience as possible.

We started out towards the site and arrived at the perimeter fence without incident. It seemed that all the defenders had withdrawn from their previous positions and were regrouping in this complex. This was confirmed a few minutes later. No sooner had we cut our way through the fence than heavy firing from one of the buildings, a single storey office block, started up. Captain Molyneaux was hit immediately and although his suit stopped him from being killed outright, it was clear that he was badly wounded and unable to carry on. He lay crumpled on the tarmac and our attack started to falter. Without thinking I took over. 'Platoons 3 and 4, move right and keep up continuous answering fire into that building. Platoons 1 and 2 move to the left. Follow me and don't stop until we get to the corner of those buildings on the left. GO, GO.' I stood up firing and started running diagonally to the left. 'LET'S GO. GET OFF THIS

EXPOSED GROUND.' The two platoons followed me and the firing from the barrack room hesitated as our company split up. Our guys in Platoons 3 and 4 poured a withering fire into the building while the rest of us ran like mad for the shelter of the other buildings. We suffered more losses but suddenly found ourselves behind a building and out of the line of fire. I knew we needed to get to that office block as soon as possible before the guys in Platoons 3 and 4, still out on exposed ground, were wiped out. 'Platoon 1, move round to your left towards the building. We have to stop that firing. Platoon 2, follow me.' We moved towards the firing from the side, although some of the defenders guessed our intentions and were there to meet us. I stood up and fired towards them, saw two go down and kept moving towards them. All of us were now firing at them and they were firing back. Whoever blinked first was going to lose. Just then Platoon 3 and 4 stood up and charged towards the enemy while Platoon 1 appeared behind them. All of us were now shooting towards the defenders in a frenzy of fire that soon wiped them out. They didn't have a chance to surrender before we burst in on them and shot them all. I didn't have time to think about how I'd feel shooting another human, I just did it in the fury of the moment. 'Okay, block secure. Let's make sure about the other buildings.'

We secured the two remaining office blocks without any resistance and I then called for medical backup for the dead and wounded. I called Colonel Matfield and told him what had happened. 'Well done, French. Stay in charge. Let me know when the whole complex has been taken.'

We could see there was a lot of fighting going on around the large building and tower where Lieutenant

Regan had arrived with the rest of the company. It seemed that the majority of the defending force had deployed there and were spread out through the upper floors. They were defending the place with everything they had and our attack had stalled. The radio tower was surrounded by buildings of various shapes and sizes and the enemy were intent on denying us any kind of victory there. Our guys had managed to take a couple of smaller buildings by the time we got there but we were mainly hunkered down, trying to avoid getting shot. The main enemy resistance was coming from the main building and an adjacent building and it seemed that we were unable to storm these two positions. It was clear that we had tried a frontal assault but this had failed. Quite a few of our dead and wounded lay on the ground between our position and theirs. An image of General Bullen floated into my mind. I could imagine her telling us to 'stop pussyfooting around and get that tower block secured.' Maybe you could come over here and show us how, I thought. Nevertheless, I knew we couldn't stay cowering forever and the arrival of our platoons had at least added to our numbers.

We were pretty green at that stage and had underestimated enemy numbers and determination. We were also not tooled up enough. We only had light assault weapons and grenades. Some heavy artillery would have come in handy but I knew we had to make do with what we had. There was nothing for it but to get this done, I thought. Lieutenant Regan was pinned down but that wasn't going to dislodge the enemy from their positions and they seemed to be getting bolder, firing at will towards us, causing mounting casualties. I decided to take the bull by the horns, figuring that if I survived this it wouldn't do my prospects any harm. After all, I thought, I'd been told to 'stay in charge' and it wouldn't hurt to use that bit of authority to take this tower. I could see that another frontal attack would be suicidal but I noticed that to our left lay a derelict building that could offer some shelter. Opposite the building was a metal door in the wall of the building complex containing the tower, about two metres up from the ground. If we could get to the derelict site and blast open that door we may have a chance of fighting our way up through the building to the tower and the enemy positions. It was a long shot but better than no shot. We were best placed for this assault as we had taken up positions to the left of rest of the company.

'Platoons 1, 2, 3 and 4, we're going to move left into that derelict building. It means a sprint of about 150 metres across open ground but we can't stay here. I'll stay here with Platoon 1 and give covering fire. We'll then come and join you. I'll explain when we're all there.'

'What if you don't make it?' asked Sergeant de Villiers.

'Oh yeah, that's a thought,' I said. 'Okay, I figured we could try and blast open that metal door and get up to the tower from the inside.'

'Good idea,' he said. 'Let's do it. GO, GO, GO.'

The three platoons started running towards the derelict building while we began firing furiously at the enemy positions in the radio tower. The rest of the company saw what we were doing and joined in the covering fire. It meant exposing ourselves and a number of us became casualties. I also saw, out of the corner of my eye that a few from our platoons had been hit while running towards the building but most of them got there.

Sergeant de Villiers yelled to me. 'Okay, Lincoln, we're here. We'll give you what covering fire we can.'

'Okay, Platoon 1, let's go. MOVE IT.' We scrambled up and started sprinting towards the others. I can tell you that was the longest 150 metres I'd ever run. The noise of the firing all around us was unbelievable. I was at the rear of the section, turning round every few steps to fire at the tower, and after what seemed like a lifetime, I dived over a low wall and out of the line of fire. All in all we had lost nine members of the platoon. 'Right,' I said, 'we need to blast open that door opposite us. Hopefully it'll give us access to the tower. Danny, Cisco search this building and see if you can locate a ladder of any kind. Segolene, Mollie, Juan – concentrated fire onto the lock of that door until it gives way.' I went around and made sure everyone was okay. We were all pretty shaken up but the adrenaline was running through us and everyone was raring to have a go at that tower. Cisco and Danny came back with a rickety ladder that would just have to do. I checked on the door. It had been blasted open and was hanging at an angle. 'Okay, listen up. I'm going to get into that opening and see what's inside. Listen out for further instructions.' I grabbed the ladder and ran to the building and climbed inside. I found myself in a small room that had clearly not been used for a long time, at the bottom of a spiral staircase that disappeared into the darkness overhead. Night vision revealed that the stairs ended at another door about ten metres up.

I started up the staircase and tried the door at the top. Surprisingly it was unlocked and I quietly gave instructions to the others to follow me. Within minutes the others were crowded into the room and up the staircase behind me. I cautiously opened the door and looked down a corridor that turned sharply to the right about ten metres further on. I signalled to the others to wait while I went and took a look around the corner. I almost stopped breathing. Coming towards us, and totally unprepared for our presence inside the building, was a squad of enemy soldiers, probably just looking for a better firing position. They saw me just as I rolled out into the corridor, firing at them. Some of the others joined me and we shot most of them. Five of them surrendered. I left one of our guys to guard them and we moved forward quickly now as the rest of the defenders must have heard the skirmish and realised we were in the building. The corridor ended at a stairwell and we heard voices coming towards us down the stairs. We flattened against the walls and started inching forward, firing towards the stairs. I started firing up the stairs and ran up to the first landing. Two or three enemy troops came down the stairs but by this time Cisco and Danny had joined me and we managed to clear the next landing before heading up there ourselves. The rest of the company came piling up behind us and when we reached the top of the stairs we fanned out into a vast storeroom stacked with old furniture and other items. They were stored all over the place and afforded great cover which was just as well because, at the same time, a considerable number of enemy troops entered the room from the opposite side. An old fashioned, close quarter fire fight ensued. We all dived for cover and shot it out as best we could. It was ferocious fighting and included quite a few hand-to-hand battles. I was involved in one and to this day I look into the eyes of my attacker before shooting him through the mouth with my pistol. I had no time to feel anything at the time because of the savagery of the fighting.

We were suddenly reinforced by Lieutenant Regan and the rest of the company. The remaining enemy troops started falling back with us hot on their heels. We soon reached the main body of enemy fighters and after a short fight they started to surrender. They were throwing down their weapons and raising their hands. 'Cease fire,' I shouted. 'Stop shooting.' That took some doing, I can tell you. I saw at least two enemy combatants shot down after raising their hands. In the fury of the fighting and with the adrenaline running through us it took a while for our guys to stop shooting. It was touch and go for a few seconds and it wouldn't have taken much to have killed them all whether they had surrendered or not. The tension in the room was sky high. Lieutenant Regan stepped forward.

'Okay, let's calm down. They've surrendered.' He turned to the captives. 'Sit down, all of you. Keep your hands on your heads and remain silent. Sergeant Ahmed, sort out a detail and keep these prisoners secure. Sergeant French, take two platoons and work your way through the rest of this complex, including the tower. I'm going to do the same with the rest of the site. Let me know when the whole building is secure.'

'Yes, sir,' I said and led the troops through the rest of the building and then up the tower. It was nerve-racking work as I expected to be ambushed at every turn but the rest of the building turned out to be empty. We had killed, wounded or captured the whole of the enemy force and a palpable feeling of relief ran through all of us as we visibly relaxed. We went back to where the fighting had taken place and I stood there looking at our captives. They looked stunned and many had a look of disbelief on their faces. Others just looked dejected. One or two showed defiance. I turned to the window and saw the medics busy with the dead and wounded outside. An ambulance had arrived and the wounded were being carried aboard. The dead, too, were being removed from the battlefield. I had come through my first experience of war unscathed but felt pretty shaken up by what had happened. In the wider scheme of things this battle for this complex had been a minor affair but for those of us who took part it was gargantuan. This had been our first experience of war and I realised with a jolt that I had killed and wounded several of my fellow humans. During the fighting I hadn't given it a thought. The successful capture of this tower had been all consuming. Nothing else had mattered.

The prisoners were led off to be taken into captivity. Cisco and Segolene came over. We were relieved that each of us had got through without being killed or wounded. I found Danny sitting on his own, head back against the wall with his forearms resting on his drawn up knees. He was holding a water bottle in his right hand and his rifle was leaning against the wall next to him. I walked over and he smiled a weary smile.

'Hey, Lincoln, you okay?'

'Yeah, kinda.' I gazed out of the window. 'I don't know...maybe not. I can't believe what we've just been through.'

He closed his eyes. 'Me neither. I've never been so scared and so hyped up at the same time in my life. I'm just glad to be alive right now.'

'Me too. I didn't think we were going to get out of that storeroom in one piece.' I turned and stared out of the window. 'I...I actually shot someone at close quarters…looked into his eyes just before…Jesus, I don't want to do *that* too often…'

He took a sip at his water bottle. 'Don't beat yourself up, Lincoln. Just remember that he'd have had you given half the chance.'

'Yeah, I guess. Nevertheless, I can't say that I'm ever going to feel good about killing or wounding anybody, enemy or not. I just want this to be over so I can live a normal life again.'

He closed his eyes. 'Same here. I'll do what I have to while this war is on but even after this first fight I have made myself a promise – to find a quiet place when it's over and live the rest of my life in peace.'

I continued to stare out of the window. 'That sounds good…a quiet place…the rest of my life in peace.' I was thinking about Collette and what it would mean just to hold her hand at this moment, to hear her say that things were going to be okay, that together we could spend the rest of our days in peace. A deep sense of desolation swept through me, to such an extent that I wondered for a few seconds whether I'd be able to carry on. The feeling passed but I stood there still missing her desperately and trying to imagine a life together after this war was over.

Word came through via Lieutenant Regan that Colonel Matfield and the rest of the battalion had moved forward and captured a large area around the complex. We were now in control of much more of this part of the city and one step further on our way towards the centre. We were told to dig in and to ensure that we weren't surprised by any retaliatory attacks. 'Sergeant French, please report to Colonel Matfield's new HQ in the high school immediately.'

'Yes, sir,' I said and made my way over to the school. There were signs of fighting all around the area, which was mainly suburban residential, and it must have been quite a struggle taking this from the enemy. I found Colonel Matfield in a classroom poring over a map of the city.

I saluted. 'Sergeant French reporting, sir.'

'Sergeant French, come in, come in.' He came round the table and shook my hand. 'Lieutenant Regan has told me about your role in capturing the complex and I want you to know that I am going to be putting your name forward for promotion. I for one don't want to see your natural abilities wasted.'

'Thank you, sir. Much appreciated.'

'Coffee?'

'That would be good right now.'

'Captain Molyneaux won't be back with us for the foreseeable. Unfortunately he needs major surgery and repair but the good news is that he's likely to make it through. I have no bodies to spare and Lieutenant Regan has requested that you act as second-in-command of the company until a more permanent arrangement is in place. That's okay with me. I'll let the others know. Between you, you can appointment a suitable trooper to take over your platoon. In the meantime, we need to make sure this area is secure. I don't want any retaliatory attacks to take us by surprise. Liaise with Lieutenant Regan and I'll be in touch soon about our next move into the city.'

'Yes, sir. Thank you.' I finished the coffee and made my way back to the company deep in thought. For someone who never thought about joining the military I wasn't doing too badly. First promotion to sergeant and now acting second-in-charge of Bravo Company. However, underneath it all I was still a reluctant soldier. The more I thought about it, the more horrified I was about the killing and wounding I'd done. I wasn't going to need therapy or anything like that but it was going to take a while to get used to it. I thought again how good it would be for this war to be over and to be living a normal life. I reported to Lieutenant Regan who confirmed that I was to be his second-in-command.

'Thank you, sir. I'd like to recommend that Cisco Gonzales takes charge of the platoon. I've known him all my life and he is as sound as they come.'

'That's fine by me. You can let the platoon know.' He turned to where a part of the city was projected into the room. 'I've been looking at this projection and we're vulnerable here. I'd like you to take half the company and plug the gap at the top of this boulevard. I'll do the same along this area here. If I'uz planning a counter attack, this'd be where I'd do it. As you can see there's a bit of a rise there so let's get to that high ground as soon as possible. Let me know when you're in position.'

'Will do.' I went out into the street. 'Okay, Platoons 1 through 4 with me. We're going up that avenue and we're going to take up positions at the top of the rise. I want you to be under cover and to stay alert for any enemy counter-attack. Cisco, take charge of Platoon 4. Let's go and keep your eyes peeled.'

We made our way up to our allotted position and I made sure that the four platoons were spread through the buildings and under as much cover as possible. It was a good position as we could also move forward from here and further into the city when given the word by Colonel Matfield. I didn't think there would be a counter-attack as we had made a thorough job of taking this part of the city and we were well dug in. I went to find Cisco. 'Hi Cisco, you okay with the platoon?'

'Hi, Lincoln. Yeah, no problems so far. You reckon they'll try and take this area back again?'

'Nah, don't think so but you never know. There could be someone out there desperate for glory. Also, I reckon they know that if they lose here it'll mean the beginning of the end for them. Keep alert and remember to do it to them before they do it to you.'

He smiled. 'Sounds like a distortion of old Sawyer's golden rule that we got at the start of every lesson. I liked him. A really straight guy who practised what he preached.'

'Yeah, he's one of the good guys. He came to see me off at the station and mentioned the possibility of trouble coming. He sure got that right. If I get back to Oasis I reckon I'd go and say hi to him.'

'Same here although I hadn't planned on going back to Oasis any time soon. I know it's my hometown and all but Dakota's a whole heap better and there's the rest of the galaxy to see first. I still want to stay in the military when this is over so who knows where I'll end up.'

'Not me. I'll be a good soldier while I have to but I haven't changed my mind. It's back to civvy street for me when this is over and I wouldn't mind settling in Dakota. It's a great place but I suppose it depends on what Collette and I do with our lives. I still have no idea what I want to do except that it's not soldiering.'

'You that serious about Collette? You reckon you're gonna spend your life with her?'

'Yeah – against all the odds but it seems we are the real deal. I know the chances of this happening between two people are negligibly small but it's happened to us. I...I can't even begin to think of a life without her and she feels the same. It's weird, I know, but barring any accidents, I think we're genuine.'

'Good for you, pal. I wish you both well. In the meantime, let's get through this in one piece.'

'Yeah. See you later. Keep your eyes peeled and keep me in the picture.' I was just turning to go when there was a tremendous explosion to our left, followed by heavy small arms fire. 'What the fuck...?' I looked towards the noise and saw a large body of enemy troops heading towards us, firing as they came. They had decided to counter attack after all. 'HOLD THE LINE, HOLD THE LINE.' I shouted. 'PLATOONS 1 THROUGH 4 MAINTAIN YOUR POSITIONS. GET THOSE MACHINE GUNS WORKING.' I realised immediately that we were outnumbered and that we had a desperate fight on our hands if we weren't going to be overrun. Lieutenant Regan's voice came through.

'Hold your positions, French. We must not allow this attack to succeed. Battalion are sending what help they can and we're trying to get some armoured support.'

I ran from platoon to platoon making sure that they stayed steady but it was hard work as the incoming fire was becoming a crescendo. They were pulling out all the stops and had thrown all they had into recapturing our position. We fought like crazy, shooting at the oncoming troops in a frenzy of fire that finally caused them to falter. I saw them starting to move sideways to try and escape our fire and urged our guys to even greater efforts. I reckoned that if we hit them hard enough and quickly enough we could turn this attack to our advantage. If they found us moving against them from a defensive position instead of retreating they might decide to call it a day. It was dodgy but I had enough faith in our troops to give it a go. 'THEY'RE WAVERING. KEEP UP THE FIRING.' Two platoons were over to my left. 'PLATOONS 2 AND 3, START TO PUSH FORWARD AND CLEAR THOSE TWO BUILDINGS AHEAD OF YOU. DON'T LET UP, DON'T STALL. THEY WON'T BE EXPECTING US TO GO ON THE OFFENSIVE. USE THE FLAMETHROWERS AND GRENADES TO GET THEM OUT OF THERE.' I spoke to the remaining platoon sergeants. 'We're going on the attack. Platoon 1, I want you to move along the back of the buildings to the right of the boulevard and surprise these bastards by coming out behind them. Attack them immediately with everything you've got. Platoon 4, we'll stay here and keep their attention focussed on us. Go.'

Platoon 1 scrambled out and keeping low made their way along the backs of the buildings. I was hoping they didn't run into any enemy troops before we had a chance to surprise them. We stayed put and fought it out with an enemy who were just starting to regain the initiative. They realised we were outnumbered and they were limbering up for an all-out attack on our position when Platoon 1 came out behind them and opened fire. At the same time we went on to the attack, using all the firepower at our disposal and even though they outnumbered us they didn't stand a chance. The slaughter and carnage was something I won't ever forget and those that weren't killed or wounded fled into the surrounding streets in complete disorder. I reckon some of them are running still.

'Cisco, Gina, what's happening?'

'Still busy clearing these buildings. Some fierce resistance here. Could do with some help,' said Gina against the noise of battle.

Lieutenant Regan broke in. 'We're on our way to help you. Sergeant French, are you okay?'

'Yes, sir. Platoons 1 and 4 have just cleared the enemy from this area. I don't think they'll be back.'

'Okay, have them hold their position and secure that area. I'm sending Platoon 8 over to reinforce you. I'll be with you just as soon as we've secured these two buildings.'

'Okay, Lieutenant. Thank you.' I deployed the two platoons and saw to the dead and wounded. We had sustained a number of casualties and we made them as comfortable as possible until they could be shipped back for treatment. I saw Danny helping one of them and went over to lend a hand. Danny was talking to him as I got there.

'Easy, fella, you gonna be just fine. Lucky we got these suits or you'd be in more than one piece. Just lie still and wait for the medics to arrive. You'll be outa here in no time.'

'Danny, you okay?' I asked.

'Oh hi, Sergeant. Yeah I'm fine. Managed to get through that lot without any serious mishap but Christoph here wasn't so lucky. He's gonna be okay though.'

I looked at Christoph who seemed to be in a bad way. It was true that his suit had stopped it from being worse but he had taken a shot to the chest and he looked a mess. I reckoned it was touch and go but out loud I agreed with Danny. 'Yeah, you gonna be fine. The medics'll be here any minute now and you'll be shipped out and fixed up.' He was taken aboard an ambulance shuttle after a while and shipped out. I heard later that he didn't die but needed some major repair and never rejoined the war.

'Jeez, Lincoln, this has been some baptism of fire. I thought for sure I was a dead man when that lot attacked us.' He shook his head. 'I fried a few with that flamethrower. This is gonna be something to tell our kids huh?'

'Yeah..."What did you do in the war, Dad?" Guess I'll say that I just did my best if it ever comes up.'

Danny smiled. 'Your best hasn't been too bad so far, Lincoln. Platoon leader, sergeant and now second-in-charge of the company. You were born to soldiering. A round peg in a round hole here in the army.'

'Yeah maybe but the more I've read about war throughout the history of humanity, the more I'm convinced that war has mostly been a manifestation of human idiocy. If you look at the reasons humans have gone to war, whether it be tribal leaders, kings, emperors or political leaders, it was invariably to claim dominion over people and land where those claiming the dominion were not wanted and where the population on the receiving end was never consulted. Like this invasion by the Imperium. Or some inbred thought he should wear a crown instead of another inbred, or some equally ludicrous excuse. And often backed by some god or other because the tosspot in question heard voices in his head.'

'You're right,' smiled Danny. 'And back in earth-time this sort of thing was looked upon as some kind of heroic activity with parades and commemorations. I'm sure I read that somewhere.'

'Definitely. I just hope they're not thinking of reviving that sort of thing here. I can tell you now that I won't be taking part in any unnecessary parades.'

'Me neither. Can't think of any reason why I would.'

Just then a call came through from Lieutenant Regan. 'Sergeant French, could you please join Colonel Matfield and me for a debrief at the school up the road. We'll meet in 15 minutes.'

'Yes, sir, will do.' I turned to Danny. 'Got to go. See you later.' I made sure that all the platoons were in place and alert and then made my way to the school. It was situated on our front line and had taken quite a battering during the battle for this part of the city. I found the two officers who had been joined by others. I was the odd one out as far as rank was concerned but that didn't last long.

'Sergeant French.' Colonel Matfield greeted me as I came in. 'I've been hearing good things about you and how Lieutenant Regan here wants you to stay on as second in command. You guys did a great job in taking that industrial complex and then in repelling the counter-attack. Well done. I've been in touch with General Hani and he has been pleased to promote you both. Field promotions. As of now you are Captain Regan and Lieutenant French. Congratulations.' He shook our hands and the other officers present came over and did the same. 'You keep this up, Lieutenant French, and I'll be saluting you soon,' laughed Colonel Matfield. 'Well done to the rest of you as well. We would not have been as successful if we hadn't all pulled our weight and I'd like you to pass that on to your troops. They've done a magnificent job. We have managed to penetrate further into the city than the rest of the division and I want to keep it that way. We want to be the ones who take the enemy surrender and I see no reason why that shouldn't happen. That means pushing on as quickly as possible. We'll rest here tonight and then move out at first light.'

He rummaged in the bags behind him and produced two bottles of whisky. 'Before we disperse, I'd like you to join me in a drink. I've managed to bring along a few bottles of whisky and I'd feel privileged to share some of it with you.'

That whisky, drunk from an army beaker, was better than anything I'd ever tasted before. It slid down my throat with a wonderful burning sensation, initially causing my eyes to water slightly. It was out of this world and each time my beaker was refilled it tasted even better until I felt decidedly fuzzy round the edges. After a while we all said goodnight and Captain Regan and I walked back to our positions. I noticed Captain Regan was walking quite carefully and hiccupping. He looked at me and smiled. 'Guess I drank too much too fast,' he said. 'Any more and I'da been truly fucked by now.'

'Me too,' I said. 'I'm feeling pretty wobbly as it is. Don't normally make a habit of drinking that much, certainly not in one sitting. I'm going to quietly crawl into my pit and get some sleep.'

'Good idea. I'll see you at oh four thirty and we'll get ready to move out. Til then.'

'Night, Captain. Sleep well.'

Chapter 2

I was up at four the next morning, doing the rounds and making sure the company was ready to move out when the order came. Most of the troops had had a good night's rest and were eager to move further into the city. I was hoping that with one effective push we could take the place within the next couple of days but knew that it all depended on the ferocity of the imperial troops and how much they wanted to defend the place.

Captain Regan returned from his early morning briefing. 'Morning, Lieutenant French. All ready to move out?'

'Yes, sir. The company's ready. Just awaiting further orders.'

'Good.' He projected a 3D map into the room. 'This is where we are at the moment and our company is to advance through this district here and clear the enemy as far as this road system here. As you can see it's a large area and it's mixed industrial, commercial and residential. I reckon we'd better split it up as follows. Your four platoons cover this area here while I move in this direction. We will stay in touch the whole time and rendezvous at this junction here at a time agreed by the two of us as we move nearer. That okay with you?'

I studied the projection and agreed with the captain's assessment of how to tackle our objective. I copied the projection onto my helmet's computer and went to brief the platoon leaders. 'Keep together and make sure nobody gets isolated in this urban environment. Stay alert and try and keep any civilian casualties to a minimum. Remember these people want the Imperium out of here as much as we do. Keep the company comms channel open at all times and listen out for any change to our plans. Any questions?'

Cisco piped up. 'Lieutenant, we gonna get to the centre first? Take the surrender?'

I smiled. 'We're sure going to do our best. Don't want anybody beating us to it. Stay alert people. Remember your urban warfare training. Let's go.' We moved out carefully in the first light of the morning, keeping to the sides of the streets and doing our best to present the enemy with as small a target as possible. At first the going was slow as we made sure all the buildings on the way were clear of enemy troops. We were also nervous, moving from building to building, not knowing whether we would be surprised by an attack or a sniper at any moment. It was nerve-racking work but after a few hours we suddenly found ourselves in a purely residential area with houses and gardens. There was some damage to some of the houses and it was clear that there had been some fighting here. We were cautiously moving forward when the front door of one of the houses opened suddenly and we dived for cover. A woman came out shouting, 'Don't shoot, don't shoot, only civilians here, women and children'.

I shouted back at her. 'Stay where you are and keep your hands where I can see them. Don't come any closer. Who else is in the house?'

She stopped moving and put her hands up. 'My father, two neighbours and their children. There are no soldiers here.'

'Were there any soldiers here?' I said.

'Yes, soldiers from the Imperium but they left a few days ago. I don't know where.'

I told my troops to stay hidden and got up slowly, hoping she was telling the truth. I felt jumpy standing there facing the woman, half expecting gunfire to erupt from the house behind her. 'We're Union troops. You sure there's nobody in that house about to shoot me?'

'No, no, please believe me. I'm so glad to see you. It's been awful, I can't tell you...it's just me and my neighbours in the house.'

'What's your name?'

'Emma Mayfield. I live in the house with my father and my two children. I'm a widow.'

I spoke to the company. 'It looks like this area has been evacuated by imperial troops but we need to make sure. Platoons 1 and 2, fan out left and make sure this residential area is safe. Platoons 3 and 4 do the same to the right. Look out for any booby traps. Report back ASAP.' I turned back to the woman. 'Okay if I take a look inside? Just want to make sure.'

'No, not at all. Please come in. Everybody will be so pleased to see you.' I followed her inside, still on high alert but it turned out she was right. They were very relieved that we had finally shown up and I started getting reports of our troops being welcomed all over the place. People were coming out of their houses now, with food and drinks, some even hugging our soldiers. They told us that they had tried to reason with the Imperium but it had backfired and quite a few people had been killed. A large number of people were desperately upset. At least a hundred men and boys had been rounded up and taken away and had not been heard of since. They were clamouring for answers and asking us if we knew anything. Of course I had to tell them that we had not come across any civilian prisoners. It was becoming clear that living under Imperium rule had been very unpleasant. I reported to Captain Regan, who was moving through a commercial area where a few civilians were also happy to see him. I asked him if he had come across any large group of male prisoners but he hadn't.

'Probably don't need to tell you, Lieutenant, but stay on high alert. I don't believe all imperial troops have left the city or that we're gonna have it this easy all the way. This seems like a good place for a rest and for us to plan our next move.'

'Yes, sir. Platoon sergeants, stay fully alert. Let's not be taken by surprise. We're going to stop here for a while but I want forward posts set up and staffed on a two hour rotating shift basis. You can stand the rest of your troops down for now.' As usual, I went round making sure everything was okay and checking on the pickets we'd posted. The troops were mingling with the civilians and hearing stories of how they'd been in a lock down situation under the Imperium. I met with Captain Regan at one of our lookout posts.

'So far so good,' he said looking around, 'but I won't rest easy until we get to the centre, meet up with the rest of the division and declare this city free of imperial troops. I've reported to Colonel Matfield who wants us to wait here until the rest of the battalion are level with us. Don't see why we should wait for the slowcoaches but orders is orders as they say. I also have to go for a briefing so you'll be in charge here.'

'I reckon I'm going to get these civilians back into their houses. There could be a drone strike or a counter-attack which would be disastrous at the moment,' I said.

'Good idea. Tell 'em the party's over for the time being. Our troops, too, need to stay awake even though we're resting here. Let's get it done.'

I got it all organised and then went on my rounds again. I came across Cisco and Danny, sitting at the corner of a property, leaning against the wall. 'Hey, you two, how're things?' I said.

'Howdy, Lincoln...I mean Lieutenant,' said Danny with a smile. 'Great to see you moving up the ladder at such speed.'

'Yeah,' said Cisco. 'And thanks for recommending me for promotion. Really appreciate it.'

'No problem, Cisco. You were the obvious choice. Thanks, Danny. I sure didn't envisage being an officer quite yet but…you'll get your turn before this lot's over.' I said.

'No, not me,' said Danny. 'I want to stay exactly where I am. I'd be no good leading anyone anywhere. We'd only end up getting lost or going round in circles. I'm quite happy being a private and when this is over, I'm quietly going to go back to academia.'

'Good for you,' I said. 'I still don't know what I want to do. You still planning on staying in the military, Cisco?'

'For sure, especially now that I've got my first promotion. I'm going to apply for officer training. I've never really wanted to do anything else.'

Just then an urgent message came through from one of the pickets. 'Lieutenant, sniper fire. Two of our lookouts down, the rest of us under cover. It's coming from that high-rise further up the road.'

'Okay, try and pinpoint the location and don't fire any rockets at the building. There may be civilians in that block. I'm coming to join you.' I turned to Cisco. 'We've got a sniper to deal with. Cisco, deploy your platoon along the leading edge of this housing area. We may need to storm the building.' I sent a message to the other platoon sergeants to get their troops under cover and to be prepared to move further up the road.

Using the houses for cover, I joined the lookouts who were crouching behind a low wall. 'There's a high-rise further up the road in an area we haven't cleared yet and I reckon that's where this fucker is,' said Private Adams.

'It's a fair distance up the road so he or she must be a good shot. Took out Privates Thokozile and Silk when they weren't presenting much of a target at all.'

'Where are they?' I said.

'Back in that house. We managed to drag them there and we've called for medical backup. They're both in a bad way.'

'Well done, Adams. Okay, let's try and pinpoint this sniper and then flush him out. Do we know if there are any civvies in that building?'

'No, we don't know,' said Adams. 'I don't even know if it's a residential building or commercial.'

'Or how many imperial troops are in there,' I said. 'We have no choice but to go up there and take a look. But first, let me see if I can get any info from any of the people around here. Sergeant Gonzales, get ready to move out. I need you to clear that building up the road.'

I dodged back to the nearest house and made some enquiries about the building in question. It turned out to be a high-rise office block but it hadn't been in use for about two years and so was probably unoccupied at the moment. I crept back to the wall and used a spare helmet as a decoy to draw more fire from the building. A single shot rang out and the round struck the helmet. We did this a few times at different places along the wall and I was pretty sure that we were dealing with a lone sniper up on the ninth floor. He or she would have done better to have moved around the building and given the impression that there were more of them but maybe they hadn't thought of it. Sending a rocket in there would certainly have sorted the problem out but the damage would have been extensive and if any civilians were in the building, the loss of life would have been unacceptable.

'Okay, Sergeant Gonzales, I want you to clear that high-rise up ahead. As far as I can tell there is a lone sniper up on the ninth floor, about half way across. There may be others so watch out. Take care 'cos he or she is a good shot and using a long range weapon. Use a grenade launcher if you have to but be as accurate as you can. We want to minimise civvy casualties.'

'Understood, Lieutenant. Will report back ASAP.' I watched as Cisco, Danny and four others moved off. We waited behind the wall, keeping out of the line of fire. I felt tense as I waited for Cisco to report back. This was dangerous work and I could only wait and hope nothing happened to him or Danny. I didn't want anything to happen to any of them but these two were my best friends and I could imagine continuing our friendship when the war was over. Suddenly, Cisco was talking to me. 'Lieutenant, we've managed to get pretty close to the building but I need to see where this guy is exactly. Can you get him to start shooting?'

'Okay, will do. Here goes.' I again moved the helmet across the top of the wall. Immediately a shot rang out and this was followed a few seconds later by a tremendous explosion up the road.

'I think we got him,' said Cisco, 'but I'm going in to make sure.'

'Take care, Sergeant. There may be others.' I cautiously looked over the wall and saw a gaping, blackened hole in the centre of the building where the sniper had been.

'Lieutenant, building safe,' said Cisco, his voice sounding strained, 'but you need to come and have a look. I think we've found the missing civilians. Looks like they've been executed. The sniper is dead.'

I made my way to the building and followed Cisco down into the basement. It had obviously been used as a storeroom but now it was filled with the bodies of men and boys. It was clear that they had been herded in and then murdered in cold blood. The bodies were everywhere and in various postures as they had tried to hide or protect themselves and the smell was awful. It must have been truly horrific. It looked like grenades had been used as well and some of the bodies were too damaged for any visual identification. I went upstairs and inspected the sniper who had been killed by a grenade. He had been blown back into the building and was draped across the rubble like a broken ragdoll. His weapons included an automatic rifle and a long range sniper rifle. I reckoned that he and his mates had done the killing before taking up his sniper position. I felt only contempt for him, as I did for all snipers. Basically, I regarded them as the lowest of the low and cowardly with it, shooting from hidden positions without their victims having much of a chance to fight back. 'Fucking hell, what a mess. What the fuck made them do something like that?' said Cisco.

I stood there and shook my head. 'Who knows what goes through the minds of men sometimes. Put a guard on the doorway to that basement. Nobody in until the medics and the MPs arrive. I'll call the captain. He'd better come and have a look.'

'I guess you're right,' said Captain Regan, who arrived a few minutes later. 'Looks like those imperial bastards decided to clean up before skedaddling up the road, leaving this turd behind as a sniper. We'll have to inform those residents down the road. These must be their missing menfolk. I'll get the medics to lay the bodies out for identification, try and clean things up a bit.' He looked round. 'Fuck me, I'm not looking forward to this.'

'I'll go and tell them,' I said. 'I've kinda got to know one of the women down there. She seems pretty steady. I'm sure she could help me get word to the others.'

'Okay, see what you can do. I'll wait here. I'd better let the colonel know too.'

I made my way back to the first house I had gone into and knocked on the door. The woman answered it. 'Oh hello, Lieutenant. Come in. Excuse the mess but we're trying to get back to normal.'

'Hello, Mrs Mayfield. Thank you.' I stepped inside. 'I wonder if I could have a word with you in private.'

'Sounds serious.'

I nodded. 'It is. Very.'

She led me through to the kitchen where we were alone. 'I...I think we've located the missing menfolk that were rounded up a few days ago.' I looked at her. 'I'm really sorry but they are all dead. We found the bodies in the basement of that disused block up the road. They've all been executed and left there.' I looked down. 'It's a real mess. I'm sorry...'

She gripped the kitchen table and then sat down slowly. 'Oh my God, how dreadful. I mean, who would...? Those poor families. Oh God, how awful...'

'I know. But I've come here to ask for your help. We need to get those bodies identified and buried as quickly as possible and I was wondering if you knew any of the families involved. I have to get word to them.'

She stared at me for a few seconds, her face pale with shock, and then seemed to snap out of a daze. 'Wha...? Yes, yes of course. The families. I do know two of them, they live just down the road. Of course I'll help.' She stood up. 'Just let me get the kids organised. I'll get my dad to look after them. Please come through to the front room. I'll be with you in a sec.' She stopped and looked at me, tears welling. 'It could have been me,' she whispered. 'I don't know how they missed dad.' She hurried out and I heard her getting the children and her father organised. A few minutes later she came into the front room. 'Okay, let's go.'

'I'll tell them if you like,' I said. 'Just show me...'

'We'll go together. I'm fine, I promise you. I'm not going to faint or get hysterical.' She smiled at me. We reached the first house and knocked on the door. I had never done anything like this before and felt nervous and tense as we waited for the door to be opened. We were about to tell someone that her husband/son/father had been brutally murdered. That she needed to come up the road and identify the body, or what was left of it. Bloody hell... The door opened and a small woman wrapped in a shawl stood before us. She looked concerned as if she knew that we were the bearers of bad news.

'Hello, Emma, Lieutenant. Can I help you?'

'Hello, Aishah,' said Emma. 'May we come in?'

Aishah suddenly looked stricken. 'Have they found...?'

'Aishah,' said Emma taking hold of her hands, 'we need to come in, darling. We have some bad news.' We moved inside where we were joined by a young girl of about sixteen. She put her arms around her mother and I then told them that we had discovered a number of bodies who could be their missing menfolk and they were required to come and identify them.

'I'm really sorry,' I said. 'I wish I had better news.' By now all three women were openly weeping and it wouldn't have taken much to get me going as well. Just then a neighbour arrived. Her son and husband had been taken and I explained the situation to her. She had to be helped to a chair but she gave us the name of someone who would be able to get the news to all those concerned. Emma and I again expressed our sorrow and went off to find this person who turned out to be the head teacher of the local school. Although she herself had not lost anyone, she was prepared to act as a spokesperson for the group and undertook to inform all those who needed to come and identify their loved ones. Emma Mayfield said she would stay and help.

'I'd better get back,' I said. 'I'll be up at the site. Please don't hesitate to get hold of me if I can be of any further assistance.'

'We'll be fine,' said Emma. 'And thank you for all you've done, Lieutenant. No doubt we'll see you later.'

I made my way back to the high rise where a lot of activity was going on. Searchlights had been switched on and the medics were busy cleaning up the bodies as best they could and laying them out for identification on the ground floor of the building. Some ID cards and other documentation were laid out on a table and I found that Colonel Matfield and a military police captain had joined us. 'Evening, Lieutenant. A bad business.'

'Yes, sir.' I said. I gave him and the captain a rundown of what I had been up to and told them to expect the relatives within the next half hour. 'Emma Mayfield is going to call me when they start out.'

'Okay, thank you, Lieutenant.' He turned to Captain Regan. 'We have two doctors and some nurses joining us who are trained in this sort of thing and I'd like you to take charge of the security arrangements. Make sure this area and this building are one hundred percent secure from any enemy attack. It's unlikely but you never know. I want the company deployed through this area and on maximum alert. Lieutenant French and I will be here with the bodies.'

'Yes, sir. Immediately.' I glanced at Captain Regan who looked decidedly relieved at not having to stay there, especially as the relatives and loved ones of these dead men were about to arrive. I felt my stomach tightening up.

This was going to be deeply traumatic but I had no choice. Orders is orders as they say so I was just going to have to do the best I could.

'I'd like some of my troops here with us, sir,' I said to the colonel. 'We're going to need some help with people who faint or collapse and I know those who would be good in this situation.'

'Good idea, French. Get 'em here ASAP. At least four or five.'

I called up Danny, Segolene, Mollie and two others and briefed them when they arrived. We stripped down to shirts and trousers so as to look as unthreatening and non-military as possible and waited. A few minutes later Emma called. 'Hello, Lieutenant. There are thirty-seven of us and we're just coming up now. Is that okay?'

I turned to the chief medic who gave me the thumbs up. 'Yes okay, Emma. Come on up.'

I often think about that night when I'm alone and it's quiet, and that scene is one that will be seared into my mind until I die. Those people went to the far side of hell and back in that building and I cannot ever forget the wailing and the look of horror and despair I witnessed on all those faces. We all worked like mad comforting the grieving, helping the helpless but I knew that nothing was really going to help except time which, they say, heals all things. The two doctors and the nurses did sterling work, as did Emma. She was everywhere and it was obvious that her presence was a great comfort to those who knew her. She also acted as a spokesperson for the group, liaising with the medical staff and the army. At the end of it all I wandered outside just to get some fresh air and to put some distance between me and the horror I had witnessed. Danny and some others joined me and we stood there in silence while groups of people, supporting and comforting each other, shuffled home, their lives blighted forever. After a while Emma joined us as well. She looked drained. 'Well done, Emma,' I said. 'You did an amazing job in there.'

'Thank you and I'd like to thank you all as well. It is not something that any of us could have envisaged. I know I certainly never dreamt I'd ever be involved in anything like this.'

'No, none of us did,' I said. 'I feel sorry for those relatives and family members who are going to have to live with the memory of this night. I know they say that time is a healer but it's going to take some time before any of them are anywhere back to normal.'

'I know. As a community we are going to have to do our best to support each other and get through this as best we can,' said Emma. 'Right now I need to get back home and see to the kids. The army have been great and are going to help with the burials.' She turned to me. 'Would you mind walking back with me? I don't feel like walking home on my own at the moment.'

'Of course,' I said. I turned to the others. 'Thanks for everything guys. You did a great job with those people. Go and get some sleep and I'll see you all later. Okay, Emma, let's go.'

We walked back to her house slowly while she told me something of her life. She had been born and raised in

Adrendakon, had married and had two children. Shortly after the birth of her second child, her husband had been killed in an industrial accident and she had lived with her father and her two children ever since. Her mother had died when she was very young and so she never really knew her. I told her about my life and how I happened to be there fighting with the Union forces.

'You're a natural leader, Lincoln,' she said. 'I know you didn't envisage joining the military but you look and act like you were born to it.'

I smiled. 'I must admit I have found it easy, natural even. Who knows, I may decide to stay in the army when this is all over. I guess I'll make my mind up when the time comes.'

'Just make sure you get through this war alive and come back and visit us under better circumstances. And bring Collette with you. Here, please take my contact details and let me know if you have any luck finding these people.'

We hugged each other. 'I will. Let's hope the circumstances are better next time you see me. Take care, Emma and all the best. Hope to see you again in the not too distant future.'

Chapter 3

We moved out early the following morning and made our way cautiously towards the centre of the city. My half of the company had to negotiate some tricky territory with narrow streets and clusters of buildings and we fought two or three skirmishes along the way. We also had to deal with two more snipers but it seemed that the fight had gone out of the enemy and they didn't put up too much resistance before falling back. On the morning of the fourth day after leaving the site of the massacre we found ourselves on the edge of Reunion Square where we remained under cover and surveyed the situation. It was huge, bigger even than Euclid Square back in Dakota and was surrounded by classically designed buildings which included the city hall, other civic buildings and a railway station. I saw that there was just one imperial soldier standing in the centre of the square with a large white flag on a pole. He just stood there not moving and it seemed rather odd, maybe even some sort of trap. However, after a few minutes I decided to get things moving. 'Okay listen up. I'm going to see what this guy is up to. Keep me covered. If things go squonk shoot anything that moves.'

I stood up and walked into the square, towards the lone soldier, beckoning him to move towards me at the same time. I was tensed up and half expected a round to slam into me at any moment. However we met without any mishap. 'Do you speak Galactic Standard?' I said.

'Yes,' he said. 'I will be able to talk with you.'

'Good,' I said. 'Tell me your name and why you're standing here on your own with a white flag.'

'I am Trooper Usagu. The others are afraid they will be killed if they surrender. There are at least two thousand of us in these buildings and streets around here but that is all that's left of our command. We wish to surrender and I volunteered to wait for you here. Also I speak your language and do not believe you will kill me.'

'Who's your commanding officer?'

'Commandant Zamtra. Don't tell him I said so but he is worse than useless. He will act all brave when I assure him he won't be harmed.'

'Okay, Trooper Usagu. I am Lieutenant French. I will give you ten minutes to communicate with your comrades. They are to leave their weapons at the edge of the square and then walk into the square and sit down in rows. No one is to run. Walking only. Also, and this is very important, anybody who brings a weapon into the square will be shot. That understood?'

'Understood, Lieutenant.'

'One more thing. I'll be waiting here and I want you personally to bring the commandant to me. He too is to be unarmed.'

'Very good, Lieutenant. I will be back as soon as I can.' He saluted me and then walked away towards the far side of the square, where he disappeared into a side street. I reported to Captain Regan who told me that he would be there with the rest of the company in about fifteen minutes.

After about five minutes groups of imperial soldiers started appearing at different entrances to the square, dropping their weapons and walking into the square with their hands on their heads. They seemed very docile and quietly sat in rows. Very soon the trickle turned into a steady stream as up to two thousand troops came into the square and surrendered.

I spoke to the company. 'Stay alert, people. Platoons 1 and 2, I want you to move over to the far side so that we have these prisoners surrounded. We must make sure that no one escapes. The rest of the company will be here shortly to assist us. Don't hesitate to act if any prisoner steps out of line. Shoot anybody coming into the square armed.'

Trooper Usagu came up to me accompanied by the commandant. 'This is Commandant Zamtra,' he said. 'He cannot speak Galactic Standard so I will translate.' The commandant barked something at him and then stood waiting while Usagu translated. 'The commandant says that we are surrendering but he demands that...'

'Trooper Usagu, please tell your commandant that he is surrendering unconditionally. He is in no position to make any demands. Also inform him that I am placing him under arrest for a war crime committed in the Mirendajar area of the city four to six days ago. Up to one hundred and twenty unarmed men and boys, all civilians, were murdered by imperial troops and I am holding him responsible. He will be handed over to our military police for any further judicial process. You got all that?'

Usagu nodded and then spoke to the commandant. He actually seemed to be taking pleasure in telling the commandant what I had just said. I watched the commandant's face carefully and it was as clear as day that he knew nothing about the massacre. I wasn't surprised. I doubted that he had any real control over his troops and I would have been even more surprised, given Usagu's attitude, if any of them respected him. He spluttered that he knew nothing about any massacre and that he was disgusted at being placed under arrest. 'He says that you have no right to treat him in this way,' said Usagu.

'Yeah, whatever. Just tell him to quietly accompany the sergeant here or he will be removed by force. I have neither the time nor the inclination to stand here arguing with him.' I turned to Cisco. 'Sergeant, take this officer back and present him to Colonel Matfield. If he gives you any trouble, sort him.'

'With pleasure', said Cisco. 'C'mon you. And no funny business. I'm not as nice as the lieutenant.'

I reported to Colonel Matfield and told him that Zamtra was on his way. Trooper Usagu stood looking at me. 'Something you want to say to me?' I asked.

He stepped closer. 'I know who carried out the massacre but you must promise that I will not be linked to their arrest. These are hard, dangerous men and I will certainly be killed if they know I am telling you this.'

I looked at him. 'And I'm just supposed to take your word for this am I? How do I know you weren't involved and that you're trying to shift the blame?'

'Lieutenant, believe me I would never be involved in anything like that. I am happy to undergo any DNA test and you're welcome to check my rifle against any ammunition found at the scene. Also, I could have kept quiet.'

'So why are you telling me?' I said.

He shrugged. 'There are some things that should not be, even in war. And this crime taints us all who wear this uniform. More important, when this war is over I wish to live at peace with myself and with your Interplanetary Union.' Just then we were joined by Captain Regan. I related Usagu's story to him and after questioning Usagu some more we were satisfied that he was telling the truth.

'Okay, Lieutenant. Get these men arrested and I'll get on to the military police and get them to meet you there.'

'Yes sir. Trooper Usagu, let's have the information so that we can get these men into custody. You will be kept separate from the other prisoners and act as an interpreter for our army. Understood?'

'There are five of them, sitting apart from the main body of prisoners, by the clock tower. One of them is wearing a woollen hat, the type that is worn under our helmets. As I said they are dangerous and are feared even by our own side. That is why they are sitting apart. They may well put up a struggle.'

'Thank you. We'll find them and arrest them. They'll never know that you gave us this information. You go with Private Wallace here. He'll take you to our HQ.' He walked off with Danny and I sensed that he was relieved that his war was over. I then spoke to the company. 'Sergeant de Villiers, you guys are nearest the clock tower. Don't let them know you're onto them, but there are five men sitting on their own by the clock tower. Do you see them?'

'Yeah, Lieutenant, I can see 'em. They're just sitting there, not doing anything.'

'Good. These five have been fingered for the massacre in Mirendajar and we need to arrest them. Keep an eye on them without arousing any suspicion on their part. I'm coming over to join you.' I walked around the prisoners until I reached Sergeant de Villiers. 'Hi there. Right, let's have ten of your guys. I want us to move in hard and fast so that they don't have a chance to resist in any way. All five are to lie face down until the MPs can get to them and 'cuff them. Are we ready?'

'Yes, sir.'

'Right, go, go.' We moved in swiftly and took the five suspects completely by surprise. One of them started to half rise from his sitting position but he was smartly hit with the butt of a rifle and joined the others spread-eagled on the ground. We shouted at them to remain still and even if they didn't understand Galactic, the meaning was clear. They lay without moving until two military police officers joined us and handcuffed them all behind their backs.

'Thanks, Lieutenant. If it's them we shouldn't have too much trouble tying them to the scene of the crime. However, I need to read them their rights. Anybody round here able to translate?' We asked around and one of the prisoners volunteered to be an interpreter. The military police captain read them their rights and they were led away.

'Captain, can you keep me posted regarding this case? It's just that I'd like to inform the families of the dead how it pans out.'

'Of course. Give me your details and I'll let you know the outcome. See you later.'

I contacted Emma and brought her up to date with the case, telling her that I would contact her again with the final outcome. A message came through from Colonel Matfield, requesting all officers to attend a briefing at HQ in half an hour. I slowly made my way over to the city hall where the officers were gathering, sincerely hoping that we'd get another taste of that whisky that the colonel carried around with him and I wasn't disappointed. This time we drank it out of glass tumblers and it tasted even better. The battalion had secured our part of the city and we were waiting on the arrival of two more battalions. A rota was worked out, giving each company some downtime and I gratefully downed one last slug of whisky before going out to join the troops. Captain Regan and I set up Company HQ in a disused office in one of the side streets. Bravo Company was to remain on duty until the following afternoon, when we could enjoy our time off. I sat in our HQ and sent a message to Collette, telling her that I had survived the campaign and was now waiting for some time off. I really missed her and would have given anything to have been with her at that time.

We stayed at our posts until midday the following day when we were relieved and we could at last relax. One of the other battalions had joined us by then and there were a lot of troops in the area. The third battalion had been diverted to another part of the city. I called on Cisco, Danny, Segolene and some of the others to join me in one of the cafés that were slowly reopening in the area and we all sat down for our first real rest in quite a while. 'Cheers, everybody. Here's to a job well done. The city's taken and I've no doubt General Bullen is as pleased as punch with us all.' Again Danny did an impression of the general that had us splitting our sides. I could feel the tension ebbing out of me and was starting to feel wonderfully mellow when a grating voice cut across our conversation.

'Well fuck me sideways, if it ain't mister goody-fucking-two shoes French. Didn't think I'd ever run into you again but they say the galaxy's a small place.' I looked up and saw a large body in a marine's uniform, swaying slightly, standing in the middle of the road. 'And whaddaya know, there's his fucking sidekick too. Mister prick features Gonzales. Large as life.'

I stood up and faced him and Cisco did the same. 'Hello, Dixter. How you doing?' He looked at me, baffled hatred in his bloodshot piggy eyes.

'How you doin', Dixter?' he mimicked in a sneering, sing-song voice. 'Don't try get friendly with me, French. You know I never liked you. Always thought you wuz a fucking creep and now...' He noticed my Lieutenant's bars for the first time. 'See you've schmoozed your way to Lieutenant. You want me to call you 'sir'?

'Dixter, you're drunk. I suggest you go back and sleep it off and then come and talk to us.'

'Do you now? Fucking... Do you now? You hiding behind your rank trying to tell me what to do, you fucking prick. Always with the words huh, French? Always in the good books at the orphanage, at the school. Couldn't do nothin' wrong. Fuck.'

'Listen, Dixter, I am who I am. I don't try to please people or displease them. I'm just myself, always have been. If that pisses you off, too bad. Now fuck off and leave us alone.' I stepped towards him. 'And don't worry about me being a lieutenant. You want some action, go ahead. I'll bust you in half you vacuous tosser.' He lunged at me but I sidestepped him and landed two good punches to his ribs. He managed to stay on his feet, staggering a bit and then Cisco came past me.

'My turn,' he said and flew at Dixter with a flurry of punches that floored the drunken idiot. Blood was pouring from his nose and his mouth. I could see that Cisco was getting ready to give him a good kicking and do some real damage so I pulled him back.

'That's enough,' I said. 'At the moment it's self-defence but if we start kicking him on the ground it becomes more serious.'

'It'd be worth it,' said Cisco. 'Just to put that gormless barstard in hospital for a while.'

Dixter was moaning and trying to get up. He sat up but he couldn't stand. Cisco had hit him really hard and he couldn't speak. Just then the military police arrived. It turned out to be the same guys who had helped us arrest the murder suspects the day before. 'Afternoon, Lieutenant. What's happened here?'

'This here's Dixter. We go back a ways. He's had too much to drink so the two of us had to restrain him.'

'You wanna press charges?'

'No, just lock him up. I'll come round and have a word with him later, after he's sobered up.'

'Okay. You heard the lieutenant. Load him up and throw him in the can. Thank you, sir. Enjoy your drink.'

'Thank you, Corporal. I certainly will.' I watched them load Dixter into their vehicle and then joined the others at the table.

'Who the hell was that?' asked Segolene.

'Name's Dixter, Olaf Dixter. He grew up with us in Oasis,' said Cisco. 'Always was a piece of work and always had it in for Lincoln and me.'

'And everybody else at the orphanage,' I said. 'We had a few run-ins with him over the years. Obviously things haven't changed.'

'What's going to happen to him?' asked Danny.

'Nothing,' I said and shook my head. 'I feel sorry for him really. Poor Dixter doesn't have much going for him. He has an unfortunate character trait that puts him on a permanent war footing against the rest of society. He's always just been really angry. He needs treatment but it looks like he hasn't had any so far. Anyhow that's enough of him. Let's relax and enjoy ourselves.' But as we sat there enjoying our drinks, I couldn't help thinking about Dixter and how he needed help. Later that evening I went round to the lockup to see him. He had sobered up but his face looked a mess. He was sitting on a bench but stood up as I walked in. 'Lincoln...er...Lieutenant...'

'Call me Lieutenant or Sir, Dixter, and be thankful you're not on a charge. Sit down, I want to have a word with you.' He sat down, trying to look defiant but failing miserably with his puffy mouth and blood-clogged nose. His cheek was cut and one eye had swollen shut. 'What the hell did you think you were doing, Dixter? Behaving like that and trying to assault an officer?'

'Dunno...I was drunk...I saw you sitting there...just...dunno...just...'

'Just thought you'd try it on, maybe thought we were still back at school.'

'Listen, Lincoln...'

'I told you to call me Lieutenant or sir.'

'Yes, sir.'

'I've had a word with your commanding officer, Dixter. Seems that you've been in the shit for inappropriate behaviour quite a lot since you joined up. Is that right?'

'Yes, sir.'

'In fact, Major Loewann tells me that she's kinda sick of having to deal with you and now wants you out.' His expression changed immediately. He looked stricken and shifted around on the bench.

'Please, Lincoln...Lieutenant. The marines are the best thing I've ever done...I really like it and when...when I do things right...they go well. The major will tell you I've fought well...'

'Yes, she told me that when it comes to combat and carrying out your normal duties there's nothing wrong with you. So what's the problem?'

'I dunno...*you* know...I've...I've always been in trouble...getting into fights...I dunno...I just feel angry a lot of the time...can't make no sense of it. This feeling seems to take over. It gets worse when I drink...and I drink because I'm always so mad at everything and everybody...it's all...it's all a mess really. Look, I'm sorry about what happened earlier, Lieutenant...I...I genuinely wanted to hurt you and Cisco. I don't know why because I don't want to now. I know we've never been buddies but...I'm just sorry.'

'Okay, Dixter, here's the deal agreed between Major Loewann and myself. You take it or leave it. Either you voluntarily go for treatment, you hand yourself in to the medical authorities, or you're out. If the major gets rid of you I can't see any other unit taking you in.'

'Treatment?'

'Yes, treatment. I'm not a medical expert Dixter but I reckon there's something that can be done for you. It's worth a try and you have nothing to lose. It'll mean you're away from the fighting for a while but you can't carry on like this. You'll end up in a ditch before your time.'

He hung his head. 'I guess.' He looked up. 'Not being funny, Lieutenant, but why do you care? I mean…it's not like we ever got on…or that I'uz ever kind to you or anything.'

'I don't know, Dixter. I remembered all those times when we were kids – how you were constantly in trouble, always madder'n hell about something or somebody and then I saw you lying there on the road, bleeding and about to get a kicking from Cisco and…I don't know…it just seemed to me that nothing had changed. I also remembered you were often sorry about your behaviour afterwards, a bit like now. I guess we all need to be cut some slack sometimes, especially when we're struggling, so I had a word with Major Loewann and we agreed that you need some help.'

'I dunno what to say…I…'

'You don't get to say anything. You're staying here for the night. Get some sleep. You get yourself cleaned up and I want you to report to me at oh seven hundred tomorrow and we'll take it from there. Is that clear?'

'Yes, sir. How will I find you?'

'I'll leave details at the front desk. Pick them up on your way out. Don't be late, Dixter, and don't even think about sneaking off. I'll have you up for desertion.'

'I'll be there, Lieutenant. And say sorry to Cisco. I didn't mean nothin'.'

'Okay. See you in the morning. Get a good night's sleep.' I left there feeling a lot better. Maybe, just maybe, something could be done for Dixter, to cure him of his affliction. The medical profession had made great strides in the treatment of mental problems. There was a chance that the good qualities he possessed could become dominant and he could find some peace at last. Maybe even lead some kind of productive life. It was certainly worth a try. I called the medical centre and spoke to one of the doctors who had helped us at the scene of the massacre. 'Hi, doc. He's agreed to come in for treatment. I didn't actually give him much of a choice but there you go. I'll bring him in tomorrow morning and make sure he signs the consent forms.'

'Okay, Lieutenant. See you tomorrow morning. I'm on early shift so ask for me when you get here.'

'Thanks, doc, will do.'

Dixter, cleaned up, was standing to attention in front of my desk at seven the next morning. I could see that he was ill at ease and nervous. 'Sit down, Dixter. Just relax. Remember we're trying to help you. You agreed yesterday that you'd go for treatment. That still the case?'

'Yes, sir. Dunno if they'll be able to do anything though. I've been like this all my life.'

'I've spoken to a Doctor Olomu who is confident that your condition, your anger is treatable. It may require an operation but we'll leave that to them shall we? I need you to sign these consent forms and then I'll take you over to the medical centre and hand you over. That okay with you?'

'Yes, sir. And…and…thank you.'

'No problem. Okay let's go.' We walked over to the medical centre and I sat with Dixter while Doctor Olomu explained what was going to happen.

'We're going to take you back to the military hospital in Dakota where you will be scanned and then undergo any necessary treatment. At this stage I can't say how long you'll be off. When you return, you will hopefully be free of these uncontrollable bouts of anger and be able to lead a more normal life. Okay?'

'That would be great. Thank you, Doctor.'

I shook Dixter's hand and wished him everything of the best. 'Keep me posted, Dixter. Let me know when you're back in the firing line. Major Loewann will know how to get hold of me.'

'Thanks, Lieutenant. I will. And thanks again for what you've done here.'

'Glad to help. I hope it all works out. Thanks very much, Doctor Olomu. Much appreciated.'

Chapter 4

My darling Lincoln, you cannot imagine the relief I felt when I heard you were alive, unhurt and safe. I couldn't stop crying for hours and contacted all my friends to tell them the news. And I'm so proud of you. Lieutenant French! It has a nice ring to it. I just know you'll be an outstanding officer and an inspiration to those you lead. I can only imagine what it must have been like fighting to take the city of Adrendakon. The news from the rest of the Jerendasien system is generally good, with our forces gaining the upper hand, although it doesn't sound as if it has been easy. Life here in Dakota goes on much as usual. I go to school every day and do my best to study but I have to say it's not easy with you being away at war. I sit and think about our lives sometimes and still find it hard to believe what's happened. The danger to the Zardogan system seems to have receded a bit now that the Imperium are on the verge of losing in Jerendasien but they still have a tenacious hold in other parts of the Protectorate and seem far from beaten. In fact there is a rumour going around that the Sylvan Moons have been captured. Those poor people. All they wanted to do was live in peace away from everybody else. I can only hope that you're not involved in much more fighting. I want you home now. Life is awful without you, Lincoln, and it's so much worse thinking that you could be killed at any time. Please promise me you will take great care and that you'll come

home safe to me. I love you to bits and the thought that
you feel the same way about me keeps me going. Take
care, gorgeous. My parents and Gabriel send their love
and, as usual, I send all of mine, Collette xxx.

I sat at my desk and read that letter a few times and experienced that same old hollowed out feeling I got every time I thought about Collette. There were times when I wanted to go and personally kill the leader of the Imperium for starting this war that had interrupted our lives in this fashion, while knowing how ridiculous such a thought was. In reality, all I could hope for was to get through this alive. I hadn't heard about the Moons being captured, although I did know that the campaign here in the Jerendasien system was going our way. I was busy daydreaming when Captain Regan came in. 'Howdy, Lincoln, how're things?'

'Okay I guess. I've done the rounds and everything is in order. The city council is ready to resume their duties and the handover is on schedule for tomorrow morning.'

'Good, 'cos the colonel wants to see us, ten hundred in his office.'

'What for?'

'Dunno. I've just been told.' He shrugged.

'It's almost that now. Let's take a stroll around there.' We left the office and ambled over to the city hall where we found Colonel Matfield sitting behind his desk, talking on the phone. He waved us to a chair and we sat facing him while he finished.

'Captain Regan, Lieutenant French, good to see you again. Seems a while.' He leaned over and shook our hands. 'By the way the MPs have just informed me that those five you arrested for the Mirendajar thing have been linked to the crime scene and will stand trial. They'll no doubt spend the rest of their lives in prison. You'd better let those people know, Lieutenant.'

'Yes, sir, will do. Glad we got the right guys.'

'Are you ready to hand this city back to the civilian authorities?'

'Yes, sir,' said Captain Regan. 'We're ready to hand over tomorrow morning.'

'Excellent. Now, first things first. Captain Regan, you are to remain here and become part of battalion staff – strategy group. Lieutenant French, you are to take over command of Bravo Company and it's back to fighting for you. General Hani, no less, has requested that you lead a company to recapture a space-station that's still in enemy hands. It's in orbit around the planet Greywynne, two out from here, and was taken at the beginning of hostilities. The Imperium obviously didn't expect us to go to war over the Protectorate so they've been quite happy to sit on the thing. Now it appears they're getting ready to fly it back to their territory and we can't allow that. It's very hi-tech and up-to-date apparently and we can't afford to lose it or for them to find out too much about it.'

'Bit late for that, I'd have thought,' I said. 'They've occupied the thing for the past few months so probably know quite a bit about it. Why don't we just blow the thing out of the sky and have done with it?' I said.

He shrugged and chuckled. 'Yeah you'da thought, but ours not to reason why... Be ready to move out at fourteen hundred. Assemble in the main square and you'll be taken to the *USS Grey Wolf* from there. By the way, your second-in-command will be Company Sergeant Major Gonzales. He's promoted as of now. You can inform him and give him these badges of rank. I'll leave it to you to promote someone to take his place as platoon sergeant.' He looked at me. 'Just get the job done, Lieutenant. I've every confidence in you.'

'Thank you, sir. I'll get it done.' I turned to Captain Regan. 'Congratulations, Captain. Good luck with your new position.'

He gripped my hand. 'You too, Lincoln. You take care and I'll see you when you get back.' I went back to the office and set about getting everything in order so that we assembled in the main square on time. The last thing I wanted was for this whole operation to start by being late. I called Cisco and asked him to come over to the office.

'Hi, Cisco. Bit of a change for both of us,' I said. 'I have been given command of Bravo. Captain Regan is now on battalion staff.'

'Wha...? You serious? Jeez, Lincoln, that's fantastic. Well done. You'll be a great CO.'

'Thanks, Cisco. That's not all. As of now you are Company Sergeant Major. Congratulations, buddy. You deserve it.' I handed him his badges of rank. He just stared at them for a few moments.

'Thanks very much, Lincoln. I…I don't know what to say.' He looked at me and smiled. 'Company Sergeant Major…sounds good.'

'Yeah, it does. And I wouldn't want anybody else as my second-in-command. Who do you think should take your place?'

'Andy Somerville. He's well respected in the platoon and has proved himself in combat.'

'Good choice. We'll let him know when we assemble.'

'Assemble?'

'Yes. You'd better put those badges on 'cos you need to perform your first duty. It's back to combat for us and I want the company assembled in Reunion Square at thirteen thirty in combat gear, fully armed and ready for inspection. We're shipping out at fourteen hundred and I don't want any hitches. Okay?'

'Yes, sir. Thirteen thirty it is.'

I was nervous as I went to collect my own belongings. This was my first solo command and I wanted things to go well. I had a fleeting vision of reporting to General Bullen, telling her I'd failed. I'd rather have shot myself.

At the appointed time I was standing in front of the company, who were drawn up in platoons. 'Good afternoon, everyone. I want, first of all, to inform you of some changes to the command structure within the company. As of today, I am the new officer commanding

Bravo Company and my second in command will be Company Sergeant Major Gonzales. Private Somerville will take over as sergeant in charge of Platoon 2. Captain Regan has joined the staff of the battalion.

'We are about to go into combat again and I expect all of you to be as professional as you were in the taking of this city. When you are dismissed make your way to the shuttle for the trip to the spaceport, stow your gear and make yourselves comfortable. Fall out.' There was a buzz of excitement among the troops as they made their way to the shuttle, standing on the far side of the square. Within a short time we were aboard and making our way to the spaceport. Once there, we transferred to the *USS Grey Wolf*, a sleek, matt-black cruiser that looked threatening, just standing there. All the gear was stowed and I waited while the troops took their seats and strapped themselves in.

The pilot introduced herself. 'Good afternoon, ladies and gentlemen. You have a human crew for this trip. I'm Captain Jane Kyle and the second officer is Flight Lieutenant Max Kindle. On behalf of the crew I welcome you aboard. We are heading for the *USS Constitution*, at present being used by General Hani as his HQ. Our journey time will be about twenty-seven hours and although we are assured the transit route is in Union hands, we are not taking any chances. The ship will be battle ready throughout the journey and you are all to remain in full battle gear. Your battle suit will keep you alive outside this ship for at least fourteen hours should the unthinkable happen. You will be free to unstrap and move around once we're at cruising speed but please stay away from the restricted areas. They are clearly marked. Flight crew, battle stations please. Maximum alert. Ship ready for take-off. Lieutenant French, please join us on the flight deck. Thank you.'

I made my way forward and entered the flight deck, an area filled with computers, screens and a million blinking coloured lights, and occupied by two crew members in navy uniform who came forward to shake my hand and introduce themselves. 'Welcome aboard, Lieutenant French. I'm Captain Jane Kyle and this is Flight Lieutenant Max Kindle. We're your flight crew for this trip and we'd be happy for you to join us here on the deck for the lift off and for as long as you like after that.'

I shook hands with both of them and was struck by their easy manner and their friendliness. 'Thank you, I'd like that very much. It's not often you get this kind of opportunity. I've watched a commercial take-off from a viewing platform but I guess this will be different.'

'Yes, just a bit. We're in a war zone so the take-off will be much faster than any commercial craft and we will be climbing vertically almost immediately. Hence the need to strap ourselves in. If you could sit in that seat over there. It is voice controlled so just say 'strap me in' and the seat will do the rest. Keep your eye on the screen in front of you for flight info like speed and distance from the surface.' She smiled and turned to the Lieutenant. 'Okay, Max, we good to go?' They took their seats and the captain started to issue a string of commands. I heard the words vertical, full speed and a series of numbers and then we were lifting off and heading for space. I was tilted right back, facing upwards, with my seat automatically adjusting itself to compensate. I was thrust back into the seat and watched, fascinated, as the screens, dials and lights came to life all around me. All the time the two flight crew were talking to the spacecraft and to each other and I had the sensation of travelling at tremendous speed by the way I was being pushed back into the seat. This was confirmed by the numbers on the screen. In no time at all we were travelling at well over fifteen thousand kilometres an hour and that number just kept on climbing. We cleared the atmosphere in seconds and were in space, heading for the *Constitution*. The automatic gravity kicked in and after a while the ship levelled out, enabling me to resume some sort of normality. I was able to unhook myself and sat while the flight crew continued to issue commands. After a while Max said 'full auto' and turned towards me. 'You okay?' he asked.

'Yes, fine thanks. Glad I was allowed to be here during that take-off. That's something I'll remember.'

'No problem. We're gonna have a coffee. Care to join us?' said Max.

'That sounds good,' I said. 'Hope I can repay your hospitality some time.' I stayed there talking to those two for quite a while. They were interesting characters who had crewed together for some considerable time. In fact Max had twice turned down promotion to stay as a co-pilot to Jane. She had been born and raised in the Protectorate and had joined the navy straight from university. She was married and had two children. Max originated from the Kepler system in the Union and had been a navy man all his life. He was a few years older than Jane and very laid-back. He was married to Andrew, a doctor, and they had one child. After a third cup of coffee and far too many snacks, I decided it was time to rejoin the troops and see how they were getting along. 'Thanks very much for your time,' I said. 'It's been great getting to know you. I'd better get back and show my face, see how everybody is doing. See you later.'

'Pleasure,' said Jane. 'Pop back any time and don't hesitate to ask any crew member if you need anything.'

I made my way back and found Cisco and Danny sitting chatting, each nursing a hot drink. 'Howdy, fellas, how things going?' I said.

Danny looked around to see that we were alone. 'Hi, Lincoln. Come and join us. Forget you're an officer for a while.'

'Gladly,' I said. 'I'd like to think the three of us are friends first and ranks second. I hope you stay in touch when this war is over Danny.'

'Of course,' said Danny. 'You two aren't going to get rid of me that easily.'

'Good,' said Cisco. 'I'd hate to think we'd just drift apart after all we're going through.'

I looked around. 'Where's Segolene?'

'Yeah, well, talking of drifting apart, we've decided to cool it for a while. Mutual decision,' said Cisco.

I nodded. 'You feeling okay about it?'

'Yeah, I'm fine. We're heading for more combat and I've got more responsibility now so that'll take my mind off things. And don't worry, Lincoln. This ain't gonna affect my combat readiness in any way.'

I smiled. 'Glad to hear it. Not like Shalaka then.'

Danny's ears pricked up. 'Who's Shalaka?'

Cisco shook his head. 'Some chick I fell for in senior school. Jesus, head over heels and when she dumped me I didn't eat, sleep or drink for weeks. A real pain in the ass. Mind you, I don't recall you being too happy when that Romina told you to get lost, Lincoln. You were moping around for a long time, like your dog had been shot.'

We laughed. 'Yeah I remember. Jeez, she was gorgeous. I couldn't believe it when she told me it was over. She went off with that Dwyer kid as I recall. Talk about humiliation. Didn't you threaten to beat the shit out of him?'

'Yeah,' said Cisco. 'I figured it might make you feel better but it never happened. By the time the opportunity presented itself there seemed to be no point. She'd dumped him as well and moved on to someone else.'

I smiled at the recollection of it. Oasis and the orphanage seemed such a long time ago. We continued chatting for a while and then I went to get some sleep. It was only when I lay down that I realised just how tired I was. The last few weeks had been non-stop and now we were heading for more action. I couldn't even remember going to sleep.

I was awakened a few hours before we were due to rendezvous with the *Constitution* and met with the troops. 'Okay, guys, we're about to go aboard the *Constitution*,

General Hani's HQ, and get briefed about the mission. I want you all to remember that we've been specially chosen for this task because of the way we conducted ourselves in Adrendakon. I expect you all to be at your professional best in whatever we're required to do. As far as I know, we're being sent to recapture a large space-station so that means off-surface combat. Remember your training and remember, above all, that each one of us is dependent upon everyone else in the company. We have to fight as a unit and look out for each other. Sergeant Major take over please. I want you to carry out a final inspection. Make sure we have no faulty gear and that everything is as it should be.' I left them and made my way to the flight deck where I greeted the two pilots.

'Hi, Lincoln,' said Jane. 'Take a seat and watch as we dock with the *Constitution*. It's all automatic, of course, but still an experience.' I took my seat and was strapped in. An announcement went out instructing everyone to do the same as we were about to dock with the *USS Constitution*. As with the take-off, Jane and Max spoke to the ship and each other as we approached the other ship, which I now saw ahead of us. It was a great deal bigger than the *Grey Wolf* and as we got nearer I felt we were travelling far too fast to be able to stop in time. I didn't say anything as the two pilots and the ship knew what they were doing but it was pretty nerve-racking watching the *Constitution* looming up ahead, getting closer by the second. Suddenly the *Grey Wolf* braked hard and rotated to the left, bringing it parallel with the other ship. I saw the docking area on the *Constitution*, one of four or five, lit up and ready to receive us. Moving sideways, we slid smoothly towards the *Constitution*, slowing all the time until with a sigh the two ships docked and locked together.

'Will all army personnel please make their way to the gangway by following the instructions displayed throughout the ship. We hope you had a good flight and we wish you all the best with whatever you now have to undertake.' Jane and Max turned towards me. 'Nice meeting you, Lincoln. I guess you're about to embark on a combat mission. I wish you all the best and hope to see you again sometime,' said Jane.

'Ditto,' said Max. I shook their hands and wished them well, hoping, too, to see them again. I joined the others and walked through the airtight passageway, or 'gangway' (I couldn't imagine where that word had come from) that had formed between the two ships. We formed up in platoons on the other side and were welcomed aboard by a naval officer. He led us to a moving walkway that took us up thirty five floors and into a large assembly room.

'Please be seated, ladies and gentlemen. General Hani will be with you shortly.' I took my seat in the front row. After about two minutes a sergeant major strode onto the stage.

'Tenshun,' he barked, and General Hani strolled onto the stage behind him.

'Thank you, Sergeant Major,' he said. 'At ease everybody, please be seated. Welcome aboard the *USS Constitution*. I'll cut to the chase and tell you that you have been selected to attack a space-station which we need to recover from the Imperium as a matter of urgency. We believe that this space-station, the Yang Liwei, is about to be removed to the Imperium and we can't allow that to happen. It contains the latest computer technology, something light years ahead of anything the enemy possess at the moment, but it appears that the Imperium has been unaware of just what they've got their hands on. It may have dawned on them lately though because, as I said, they appear to be making plans to take it back to their territory. Under no circumstances will that happen. We are on standby to destroy the thing if we have to, even if you are still on board. Hopefully that won't be necessary.

'You will be accompanied by a team of scientists and others who know about these computers. You will be ready to move out at twenty two hundred local time, which means in exactly two hours from now. When you are dismissed I'd like Lieutenant French and Private Wallace to remain behind. Okay, let's look at a plan of attack.' A computer image of the space-station was projected into the room and we went through the best way of securing the thing. It looked pretty daunting and part of me wished that the authorities had decided to destroy it. General Hani finished up. 'As you can see this is not going to be easy but I want you to know that destroying the space-station is not the government's preferred option. We have to capture it with as little damage as possible. Good luck. That's all.' Danny and I remained where we were while the others filed out. 'Good evening, gentlemen,' said General Hani. 'At ease. I've been hearing good things about you, Lieutenant. Well done so far. I have the greatest confidence in you and know you'll recapture this goddam thing. Private Wallace, a Professor Dooley of the University of Dakota has requested that you join the scientific team who are accompanying this mission. Seems you're a maths wizard and she thinks your presence will enhance their team.' He looked at Danny. 'I'm impressed. That means you only get involved in any combat if you have to. Stay in your gear just in case but regard yourself as a part of the civvy team for this operation. You can join them immediately. That's all, gentlemen. Lieutenant French, all the best.' He shook our hands and left.

'Wow, Danny, impressive. Who's Professor Dooley?'

'She's the head of the maths faculty at the university. I can't believe she's singled me out for this operation. Does wonders for the ego. I'd better go find her and see what we have to do on this space-station.' He hesitated. 'Lincoln, I'm still part of Bravo. If things get rough I'm not just going to do nothing. I'll join in any fighting if I have to.'

'Yeah, I know. Stick with the civvy team for now though and play it by ear. Keep your comms open and listen out for any commands. Having you with that lot could be handy. I guess they'll need a bit of shepherding and you'll be the one to do that. I'll come with you and introduce myself.' Danny and I made our way to a conference room where we found the scientific team. There were seven of them and to my amazement Gabriel was one of them. I couldn't believe it when I saw him standing there. He was just as surprised to see me and for a moment we just stared at each other. 'Gabriel, what are you...?'

'Lincoln, why...?'

We shook hands and hugged each other. 'Great to see you again, Gabriel. What a surprise.'

'Absolutely,' said Gabriel. 'I certainly didn't expect you to be here. Fantastic. Lincoln, this is Professor

Dooley.' A tall, slim middle aged woman stepped forward and shook my hand. I was introduced to the rest of the team, who all seemed to know Danny. Gabriel said he had seen him around the university.

'Glad to meet you all,' I said. 'As you know Danny is to be seconded to your team so he will remain with you until the space-station is secured. If you don't mind he will remain in combat mode and I'd like you to follow his instructions until you are safely aboard the space-station.' Gabriel and I walked off to one side. 'I still can't believe you are here,' I said. 'Does your family know?'

'No, it was all very hush-hush. Not a word to anyone we were told. And then we were whisked off, hyper travel and all, and deposited here two days ago. We now know what we have to do once we're aboard the space-station but that seems the easy part. You have to capture it first.'

'Yeah, but I guess that's what we're here for. Gabriel, I have to know how Collette is. Have you seen her lately?'

'Yes, I saw her towards the end of last week and she's missing you like mad. There's no hiding that. She's putting a brave face on it but...I take it you still feel the same?'

'Without a doubt. What I wouldn't give just to see her right now.'

'I can imagine. I suppose we can only hope this war doesn't last too long. Are you likely to get some leave soon?'

'I don't know,' I said. 'There was some talk about me attending an officer's training course at Black Tree Canyon but with this new operation...'

'You've done very well, Lincoln. You're already an officer. I never dreamt it would be you leading this mission. I'm glad it is though. It's good to see you again and I have great faith in your abilities.'

'Thanks, Gabriel. I'd better go and get the thing underway. I'll see you on the space-station. Promise I won't touch anything until you guys get there.'

We all transferred to a transporter and set out on our journey to the space station. During the trip I made sure the company was as ready as they could be for what lay ahead. We practised exiting the ship and revisited our off-surface training until I was satisfied we knew what we were doing to the best of our ability. We were nearing our destination and I was sitting preparing an interim report for Colonel Matfield when the message came through. 'Urgent, priority one. Bravo Company to assemble immediately in Musterbay 4. The Yang Liwei space-station is on the move. It has left its geo-stationary position and is moving away from planet Greywynne. Bravo Company to Musterbay four immediately.'

'Danny, assemble the civvy personnel and join us in Musterbay 4. Cisco, get all troops to Musterbay 4 immediately. We're leaving in fifteen minutes. Confirm receipt of this message.' I ran to the musterbay where the troops were congregating and falling in. All eight platoons were there within minutes and I relayed the news. 'Slight change of plan people. The station is leaving its geo-stationary position and building speed. We want to get there as soon as possible and stop it in its tracks. That means attacking a non-geo-stationary target so don't forget the drill. We'll be dropped ahead of the station going forward, a lot nearer than originally planned. We'll probably come under fire but we'll stick with the plan of attack. Platoons 1 and 2, open Port 4 and get to the computer room ASAP. Platoons 3 and 4, Port 6 and then the bridge. Platoons 5 and 6 secure the docking area, including the docking pad and hangars, and Platoons 7 and 8 stay in reserve and give covering fire. The original occupants are still on board as far as we know so look out for them. Professor Dooley, Danny will liaise between you and the squad. Please follow his instructions until we are securely aboard the station. Let's go.'

Chapter 5

We donned our assault suits and boarded the attack shuttles for our first off-surface combat mission. Everybody was ready and the whole company was buzzing, fearful and excited at the same time. The thing that worried me most was becoming isolated and lost in space. It could happen and I would only feel at ease when I was aboard the space-station. The plan was to exit the fast moving shuttle near the space-station and then attempt to land and blast our way inside. A detailed plan of the whole space-station had been downloaded to all of us so once we were inside getting to our target areas would be relatively easy. We had to make sure we had complete control of the thing as quickly as possible in case the imperial troops on board decided to destroy it, something we had to prevent at all costs.

The two shuttles floated free of the ship, the rockets kicked in and we were heading towards our target. Cisco was in charge of one and I was in the other. The two hour ride was uneventful and then the red light came on. The troops stood up and checked the equipment of the person opposite them, making sure they were ready to leave the shuttle safely. We stood waiting, the light changed to green and I stood at the doorway and supervised the jump, two at a time. After the last two had left, I jumped myself and found myself out in space with the company spread out ahead of me. I homed in on the space-station, which was five kilometres away and moving towards me. 'Ok company, to me. Platoons 1, 2 and 3 to my left, 4, 5 and 6 to my right. 7 and 8, keep behind us and be ready for deployment where you are needed. I'm facing the thing so spread out either side of me. Remember the drill. Danny, you okay back there?'

'Yes, Lieutenant. Just waiting for the word.'

'Okay, I'll let you know as soon as we've secured the space-station. Ready? Let's go.'

We spread out and started to move forward. It was a sizeable structure, 38 kilometres long, 15 wide and about 500 metres deep with a complex superstructure and various structures that had been added over the years. It was moving towards us at an ever increasing speed and we soon came under sustained fire, small arm and cannon, and I saw one of our troops crumple and spin off into space. We weren't presenting much of a target so our losses remained low and then before we knew it we were alongside and heading for the target areas. Platoons 7 and 8 started firing back, flying alongside and raking the structure with cannon fire and small arms fire. I was everywhere, exhorting our troops, making sure that the platoons reached their objectives. Platoons five and six reached the docking area and were immediately in the middle of a firefight with a large body of defending troops. I joined them and we buzzed around shooting at anything that moved. Those imperial troops gave as good as they got and for a while it was touch and go whether we were going to be able to secure the objective. We were outnumbered and when we finally managed to get onto the station and find cover we were pinned down and taking losses. 'Platoons 7 and 8, you're needed at the docking area. Urgent. Come in shooting. There's a large enemy force here, mainly around the docking pad itself.'

'Gotcha, Lieutenant,' said Sergeant Ahmed. 'We're on our way.'

We kept on fighting, desperate not to be dislodged from our tenuous position but our losses were heavy. Of the sixty who had originally fought their way onto the station, we had 24 dead or wounded and were about to get kicked off the station when Platoons seven and eight came in shooting. That turned the tables and slowly but surely we pushed the defenders back, killing or wounding most of them and forcing the remainder to surrender. In the meantime messages had come through that both ports had been opened and that our troops were involved in heavy fighting inside different areas of the space-station. The station contained a complex system of passageways, corridors and walkways and we needed to clear them all and make sure that no enemy troops were left to surprise us as we made our way to our target areas.

I left four troopers to guard the prisoners and split the rest of the troops into two groups, each assigned to help inside the station. I downloaded the map onto my visor and made my way towards the group fighting to get to the bridge. We had to stop this thing as soon as possible and make sure nobody was making any plans to destroy it. I also wanted to find the original crew and just hoped they were still alive.

'Lieutenant, we've secured the computer suites,' said Cisco. 'Nothing seems to be too badly damaged. All enemy troops in the vicinity either dead, wounded or surrendered.'

'Thanks Cisco,' I said. 'Leave a squad there and work your way through the station, secure sections X through Z and make sure all enemy troops are disabled.' I joined the fighting in the area of the bridge, which was being fiercely defended. In the end our greater numbers forced the imperial troops to surrender and we made our way onto the bridge. The imperial crew, seven of them, all stood up as we entered. 'Anybody speak Galactic Standard?' I asked.

A tall man with silvery hair stepped forward. 'I speak your language,' he said. 'I am Flight Captain Massini and I am in charge of the personnel on board this space-station.'

'Flight Captain Massini, I am Lieutenant French. I want you to instruct all your troops throughout the station to surrender immediately to avoid any further bloodshed or damage,' I said. He looked at me for a few moments and then spoke through the station intercom, telling all the imperial troops to lay down their arms. After five hours of heavy fighting, the space-station was ours.

'Thank you, Captain,' I said. 'Now, there are two things I need to know as a matter of urgency. Firstly, are any plans in operation to destroy this space-station?'

'No Lieutenant. We have taken no steps to destroy the station.'

'Good. I'm glad to hear that. Secondly, I need to find the original crew. Are they your prisoners and are they still alive?'

'They are aboard and alive. They are in sector G, confined to quarters. They have not been harmed in any way.'

'Captain, can you please instruct all imperial personnel to make their way to the docking area where they are to join the other prisoners.'

'Lieutenant,' said Cisco, 'we've secured the whole station and all enemy action has ceased. Also, we've found the Union crew. There are 48 of them and they appear to be okay. The captain and flight crew are coming to the bridge.'

'Okay, thanks, Sergeant Major. Place troops strategically throughout the station and ensure we remain on maximum alert. I don't want to be surprised by an imperial warship. Sergeant Somerville, head for the docking area and help with the prisoners. Sergeant Ahmed post two guards outside of this bridge area. Captain Massini, stay with us please and turn this thing around. I want us back in geo-stationery position. The rest of you, join the prisoners on the docking bay.' One of the two shuttles docked with the space-station and we transferred our dead and wounded, as well as half of the prisoners onto it. The scientific team and Danny landed and immediately got to work on the computers they had come to save. The second shuttle was scouring the area for dead and wounded that had floated off into space and managed to recover most of them. However, there were five whose receivers were no longer functioning and they were lost.

We couldn't spend too much time searching for them and after a while I called the shuttle to come and pick up the rest of the prisoners.

Our numbers were somewhat depleted. Of the 246 troops who had taken part in the attack on the space-station, 129 were either dead or too badly wounded to carry on. We were thinly spread and I just hoped that we didn't come under attack from an enemy warship. I sent a message to the *Constitution* telling General Hani that we had successfully captured the space-station but we had sustained heavy losses and we would be hard put to repel any counter-attack. I received a return message informing me that the *Grey Wolf* had been dispatched to ride shotgun and that she would be bringing replacement troops. That was a relief, I can tell you.

The Union crew appeared on the bridge and the captain came forward and introduced himself. 'Lieutenant French, am I pleased to see you. My name's Alok Magata, Captain, Union Navy, and I am commander of this vessel. These are my flight crew,' he said, indicating towards the others, who all came forward and shook my hand.

'Pleased to meet you, Captain,' I said, saluting him. I nodded a greeting to the crew. 'Captain Massini here has been in charge while the Imperium has had this station. You might want to have a word with him and acquaint yourself with what has gone on here while you have been held captive. He speaks perfect galactic and I expect him to co-operate fully. Any problem with that Captain Massini?'

He sighed. 'No, Lieutenant, no problem.'

'Good. You will remain aboard the station as a prisoner of war for the present and then be transferred to a prisoner facility at our convenience.' I turned to Captain Magata. 'I do need to know that you have been treated in accordance with the rules of war.'

'Yes we have been treated well. All my crew are accounted for and all are in good health, even if our nerves are a little frazzled by the experience.'

'Okay. I'll leave you to it. We have a cruiser, the *Grey Wolf*, arriving shortly to ride shotgun in case of a counter-attack so we should be okay until we get to Union held territory.' I left two troopers to watch Massini and to escort him to his quarters when Captain Magata had finished with him, and called Cisco. 'Everything okay, Cisco?' I asked.

'Yeah. Troops posted and all prisoners on their way to the *Constitution*.'

'Great. Members of the crew are coming around to assess any damage. Make sure they get all the assistance they need. They might want some troops to help them with repairs.'

'Okay. I'll sort that out.'

I went to find the scientific team. They were all in the computer suite, huddled around a bank of screens when I walked in, with Danny talking about quantum something or other, and pointing to a stream of figures that filled the screens. I didn't even pretend to understand.

'Lieutenant, good to see you again,' said Danny.

'Hi Danny, hi everyone. Everything in order?' I said.

'Hello, Lieutenant,' said Professor Dooley. 'Yes, not too much damage, although it seems that they have tried to access these programmes and some repair work will be necessary. And well done in successfully capturing this space-station. I hope you didn't suffer too many losses.'

'Thank you professor. The losses were heavier than we had anticipated but we're just glad it all ended okay. Take all the time you need. The *USS Grey Wolf* will be accompanying us until we are safely inside Union held territory, and the station has a long ride ahead of it. We are returning to the Zardogan system. The authorities figure it's the safest place to be at present.'

'Really?' said Gabriel. 'Back home. Sounds good.'

'Yeah it does but it could take a few months. This thing can do point two five percent hyper at most and at the moment they're not even sure about that. Anyway, I'll leave you to it. Danny, give this task priority. You won't be needed for combat until your work here is completed.' I left them to it and went back to the bridge.

'Just had confirmation from the *Grey Wolf* that they're 50 minutes out. I'll be glad when they arrive,' said Captain Magata. 'I feel a bit jittery out here on our own.'

'Yeah, me too.' I said. 'We wouldn't stand a chance against an enemy warship intent on destroying us. Have we managed to turn around yet?'

'Just about to start the manoeuvre. Just to let you know that Captain Massini has been most helpful and has co-operated fully with us.'

I nodded. 'Glad to hear it. Let the guards know when you no longer require his presence here.' I went off to meet with Cisco and work out a duty rota. We were all dead on our feet and I wanted the troops to get some rest as soon as the *Grey Wolf* arrived. In fact, I found one of our soldiers asleep at his post and shook him awake. 'Stay awake Private, you may well be needed to defend this thing against attack. You'll get some rest soon enough.'

'Sorry sir...just kinda nodded off...didn't mean...' he slurred.

'No problem. Keep moving around. Don't sit down. You'll be relieved as soon as we can arrange it.' I found Cisco, who was going around checking on the troops. I went with him and found all the surviving soldiers to be in good spirits even though they were dog tired. We got back to the bridge in time to see the *Grey Wolf* approaching. That was a welcome sight and I breathed a quiet sigh of relief. With a fully armed cruiser for company we were practically out of danger from any counter-attack and the troops could get some well-earned rest. I also wanted to get Captain Massini transferred onto the *Grey Wolf* where he would be out of my hair and away from the space-station. He had co-operated so far but I was aware that his mission had been to take the space-station to the Imperium and I had no doubt he would try and sabotage our mission if he got half a chance. Having him in military custody would bring a further sigh of relief as far as I was concerned. I contacted the *Grey Wolf* and found myself talking to Max.

'Lincoln, great to see you again. Didn't think we'd meet up again so soon.'

'Hi Max. Yeah, good to see you too. It's a relief having you guys here riding shotgun. I don't think we would have been able to hold off a serious counter-attack.'

'No problema compadre. Always glad to help the army out of a tight spot.'

I smiled. 'I'll remember that when we're saving your asses one day. I'm on my way to the docking bay so I'll be with you in a few minutes.'

'Ok, we'll be fully locked onto the space-station in about ten minutes.'

'I'm going to head for the docking area,' I told Cisco. 'When I send word, I want you to personally escort Massini for transfer to the *Grey Wolf* and make sure you search his quarters thoroughly. I don't want him pulling a fast one on us.' I made my way to the docking bay in time to watch the *Grey Wolf* dock with the space station. The airlocks opened and two naval crew came through followed by the new troops. I sent them to the far side of the hangar and was pleasantly surprised to see that four of the troops who had been wounded and taken away by shuttle were with the new lot. 'What are you guys doing back here?' I asked.

'Couldn't keep away, Lieutenant,' said Victor Edelstein. 'I got patched up and wanted to get back to Bravo.' The other three had similar stories.

'Great to see you guys again,' I said. 'You can help Cisco get these new guys settled.' Cisco arrived and I accompanied Captain Massini onto the *Grey Wolf,* where he was placed in custody under guard. I went forward to the bridge and spoke briefly to Jane and Max, telling them I'd come and have a longer visit once I had sorted everything out. I returned to the station and went to have a word with Cisco. 'After I've spoken to them show them their quarters and then get them to take over from the others who can get some rest.

'Also, I don't want any of that infantile bullshit where the veterans give the new guys a hard time. These new guys are as much part of Bravo as we are. Get them sorted into platoons and make sure each new trooper is paired up with one of the experienced guys so they get integrated quickly.'

'Good idea,' said Cisco. 'I'm with you on that one.'

We went over to where the troopers were waiting. They looked nervous.

'Tenshun,' said Cisco.

'Welcome aboard guys and welcome to Bravo Company,' I said. 'I am Lieutenant French, CO Bravo, and this is Company Sergeant Major Gonzales. I am going to leave you with the sergeant major who will show you to your quarters and explain your duties to you. I'll see you all here at ten hundred tomorrow. Okay, Sergeant Major, carry on.'

I then called the platoon sergeants and got them to assemble the other troops in the hangar area. 'Ok guys, stand easy. Have a seat if you wish.' I said. 'I want to congratulate you all on a job well done in taking this space-station. That wasn't easy and we sustained heavy losses, with five of our comrades lost in space. You've all done a fantastic job and you are now on well-deserved downtime. You've been assigned quarters in sector G so go and find a bed. The medical team is on standby in the hospital area should any of you want to go and see them and I'll be in my office near the bridge if any of you want to see me. You're back here tomorrow morning at ten hundred. Until then relax. By the way, Edelstein, Patel, Holomisa and Kirkham are back with us. Fallout.'

I went around and checked on the new troops. They were at their allotted stations and getting used to being on active service. I returned to the bridge and ascertained that we had begun the long journey to the Zardogan system but wondered whether we were going to remain with the space-station all the way. The speed with which we had received replacement troops made me think that we were destined for combat sooner rather than later.

I found the scientific team hard at work in the computer suite. Danny and Gabriel were sitting at a table poring over figures and I went and slumped down next to them. 'How're things going guys?' I said.

'Lincoln, you're looking worn out,' said Gabriel. 'Coffee?'

'That would be good,' I said. 'Strong and sweet.' Gabriel got up to make the coffee. 'You seem to be in your element Danny.' I looked at the reams of figures. 'Needless to say, I can't make head or tail of this lot.'

Danny laughed. 'Knowing you Lincoln I'm sure you'd get the hang of it if you were shown the ropes.'

'Thanks for the vote of confidence but somehow I doubt it.' Gabriel came back with the coffee. 'Thanks Gabriel, I owe you one.'

'Think nothing of it. I could do with a break anyway. Going cross-eyed here. How are you Lincoln? You seem to be rushing around doing a thousand things. I hear we have a warship for company and more troops.'

'Yes, we have the *USS Grey Wolf* for an escort until we're safely inside Union territory and for that I am very grateful. And yes, replacements have arrived that has brought the company up to full strength. Call me cynical, but I reckon that means we're heading for more combat. We wouldn't have been brought up to strength just to accompany you guys back to Zardogan.'

'If that's the case, I want to be a part of it,' said Danny. 'I reckon a couple more days here and my work will be done. What do you think Gabriel?'

'Yes, that would be fine. Your input has been invaluable but you're right. Once we crack this problem here, you'll be free to go. Better make sure with Prof Dooley first though. She's in charge, not me.'

'I'll leave you to it,' I said. 'Danny, you're more than welcome to join us but, as Gabriel has said, I need it cleared with Professor Dooley first. You know how it is – chain of command and all that. I'll see you guys later. Just call if you need me.' I made my way to my quarters after doing another round and checking on all the troops. Cisco looked worn out and I told him to go and get some sleep. I'd take the first shift in charge and he could relieve me in six hours. I sat down to complete my report of the action for General Hani and Colonel Matfield. That report, together with another inspection of the troops and a visit to the bridge took up most of those six hours and then Cisco was there and I collapsed onto my bed and fell asleep, dreaming of Collette.

Chapter 6

We spent a week on the space-station, during which time Cisco and I made sure we got Bravo working effectively as a unit. We devised a programme that included a daily keep-fit routine and we kept them busy with simulated combat, inside and outside the space-station. By the end of the week I was satisfied that Bravo Company was once again a fit and effective fighting force, which was just as well. On the morning of our eighth day I was instructed to rejoin the battalion which was being rushed to the New England region, consisting of five solar systems, to stem a dangerous counter offensive by the Imperium. The message came through from Colonel Matfield. It was good to see him again. 'Lieutenant French, Bravo Company is required to re-join the battalion and to rendezvous with us as per the co-ordinates now on the screen. The Imperium has launched a major counter-offensive in the Medway system which needs to be stopped. The *Grey Wolf* will transport you and I'll see you in a couple of days. You will be fully briefed when we meet.'

This was the first time that fighting had actually spilled over into the Union itself and it came as a tremendous shock. The Medway system, which had only recently joined the Union, was of strategic importance in that two of the planets, Chatham and Rochester, were rich in minerals and metals needed for the production of weapons and AIUs.

By this time the space-station had entered Union held territory and I went to find the scientific team to say goodbye and to find out whether Danny would be joining us.

'Hello, Lincoln,' said Gabriel, 'how are things with the army?'

'Hello, everybody,' I said. 'The army's on the move I'm afraid. I've come to bid you farewell as we're required elsewhere. The *Grey Wolf* will be transporting us as you no longer need an escort. It's been great working with you guys and I wish you all the best for the future.'

'Thank you, Lincoln,' said Professor Dooley. 'You and your staff have been most helpful and I certainly hope we'll see you again in Dakota when this war is over. We'll also be saying goodbye to Danny who has expressed a wish to rejoin his army unit.' She turned and hugged Danny, as did all of the team. 'Bye, Danny and look after yourself. Thanks for all you have done here with us and see you back at the university when this is all over.'

'Goodbye, everybody,' said Danny. 'It's been fantastic working with you and I'll definitely be seeing you again when I return to the university. Until then, take care.'

Gabriel and I walked off to one side. 'There's a message on here for Collette,' I said. 'Please give it to her as soon as you see her. Tell her I can't wait to see her again and that I'll get to Dakota just as soon as I can.'

'I will,' he said. 'She'll be very pleased to hear from you, Lincoln. I just hope this war ends soon so we can all be together again.'

'It can't end soon enough for me,' I said. 'Give my regards to your parents and to Rachel. It'll be good to see them all again as well.'

'Look after yourself, Lincoln. I'll see you back home.'

I turned and walked out of the room with Danny. 'Good to have you back, Danny,' I said. 'Bravo hasn't been the same without you.'

'Good to be back,' he said. 'I couldn't let you guys go off without me.' He struck a pose. 'I mean, where would the company be without my fighting skills?'

I laughed. 'Where indeed? You can rejoin your platoon. Cisco's now CSM and Andrew Somerville is your platoon sergeant.'

'Wow, good for Cisco. I'll congratulate him when I see him. And Andrew. I'm more than happy to serve under him. See you later.'

I found Cisco on the bridge. 'Hi, Cisco, we're on the move. The Imperium has attacked the Medway system inside the Union. We're to rejoin the battalion and I'd like you to get the company together in the hangar where we'll transfer to the *Grey Wolf.* More combat, buddy. Here we go again.'

'Yes, sir,' he said. 'More than happy to oblige. I'll get it organised immediately.'

'Okay. Also Danny's back with us. I'm really pleased.'

'Yeah me too. That's great news. I'll see you in the hangar in thirty minutes.'

I said goodbye to Captain Magata and his crew, collected my stuff, donned my combat suit and made my way to the docking area. The troops were assembling and after about half an hour we were all ready, drawn up in platoons. Cisco marched up and saluted. 'Company ready for transfer to *Grey Wolf*, sir.'

'Thank you, Sergeant Major.' I stepped forward. 'Good morning, people. Congrats on a fine turnout and well done for the way you have conducted yourselves while we have been aboard the space-station. Now, though, it's back to action for the company. The Union itself has been attacked. The Imperium has captured sections of the Medway system in a major counter-offensive and it seems we are going to go and stop them, turn back the attack. We'll be fully briefed once we re-join the battalion but I expect each and every one of you to conduct yourselves as you have up to now. When you are dismissed, please make your way to the *Grey Wolf*.' I nodded at Cisco, who took over.

Once again we found ourselves aboard the *USS Grey Wolf* heading towards a combat zone with all the nervousness and excitement that entailed. Half the company hadn't been tested in battle before but I was quietly confident that with the help of the veterans, the new troops would be fine. Like us they were volunteers and were committed to the preservation of the Union and the relationship that existed between the Union and the Protectorate. None of us said it out loud but there was an underlying anger at what the Imperium had done and a determination to prevent it succeeding. Now that the Union itself had been attacked that determination deepened. I for one wanted to finish the job we'd started and to make sure the Imperium was in no position to cause any trouble again for a long time.

I made my way aboard behind the last of the troops and went to the bridge where Max and Jane greeted me like a long lost friend. I was glad to see them again as well. During the week we'd been on the space-station I hadn't had a chance to visit the *Grey Wolf* although I had of course spoken to them. Face to face is different however and we hugged each other, glad to be in each other's company again. Being at war heightened the feeling of friendship as we had no idea when or if we'd see each other again. I stayed on the bridge while we decoupled from the space-station and chatted to the two of them for quite a while.

The *Grey Wolf* was heading into inter-stellar space and travelling towards enemy-held territory so we were on full alert right from the start. The naval crew were at battle stations and we were instructed to remain combat-alert for the duration of the journey. I'll certainly give the navy their due; that ship ran like clockwork and it would have taken a lot for the Imperium to have carried out a surprise attack against us. Nevertheless, we were jumpy, expecting the ship to be attacked at any time. Cisco and I worked out a rota whereby a third of the company were resting at any one time while the rest of us remained ready for anything.

We rendezvoused with a transporter so as to transfer the prisoners and then continued with our journey. After about three hours the instruction came through for us to strap ourselves in and to prepare for a multiple space jump. That was nerve-racking as I thought of the stories I'd heard of things going wrong, of ships lost in space or damaged. I knew that we would have to switch off our protective shield before the jump could be made and that meant we were vulnerable immediately after returning to sub-hyper speed and until the shields were back up again. However, I felt sure that Jane knew exactly what she was doing and strapped myself into the seat on the bridge. I could see that Jane and Max were tense and so I sat quietly and let them get on with it. Again they were talking to the ship and each other and before I knew it they were counting down from five and the stars ahead of us became streaks and we were jumping through space-time. After the third and final jump we were on the edge of a planetary system, hiding inside the comet cloud. 'Activating shields, sector reports please, maintain battle stations,' said Jane. 'The Imperium has managed to capture the two inner planets of this system so keep your eyes glued to those screens people. We don't want any nasty surprises.' I could see her and Max relax a little. Max turned towards me and smiled. 'No damage reported and no sign of enemy shipping so we're okay for the present. It'll be more difficult to spot us here in the comet cloud. We're waiting for word from the 21st Battle Group which is transporting the rest of your battalion and other elements of the 15th Army. Until then we just have to sit tight.'

'I think it would be a good idea for us to get into assault suits,' I said. 'If we are attacked I'd want us to be able to operate outside the ship.'

'Yes, just what I was thinking,' said Jane. 'In fact, have your troops move to the shuttle Bay. That way we can deploy them fast if need be. Feel free to carry out a practice run if you want to. I'll get three shuttle pilots to help. They'll meet you down there.'

I found Cisco and together we got the company into assault suits and down to the shuttle Bay where the pilots were waiting for us. They introduced themselves as Flight Lieutenants Tony Fisher, Marisa Ruiz and Caroline Ghali. 'I want us to be ready for any eventuality if we are attacked out here,' I said. 'We're going to practise getting those shuttles out of here as fast as possible. When I give the word, I want you to board the shuttles and strap yourselves in, ready to move out. Platoons 1, 2 and 3 shuttle 1; 4, 5 and 6 shuttle 2 and 7 and 8 and shuttle 3. Cisco, you take charge of shuttle 3, Andrew shuttle 2 and I'll take shuttle 1. Any questions? Okay go, go.' I had made sure that the attack shuttles were fully armed with some heavy armaments and mines that would cause major damage to a ship. I couldn't help feeling on edge and the others detected it. I knew we were right at the limits of the system and hiding in the comet cloud but we were nevertheless on our own and a large Imperium force was operating within this system. They could have ships out here as well. It turned out they did.

We exited the ship and I led the way to a comet about the size of a large mountain, which would afford a good place from which to spring a surprise. The operation went smoothly and we were just about to make the return trip to the ship when an emergency sounded through the shuttle; 'Emergency, emergency – three suspected enemy vessels approaching bearing two zero two – ETA three minutes and thirteen seconds – lock down for action. Bravo Company remain where you are and try and remain hidden.' Jane's voice came through my earphones. 'Lincoln, stay away from the ship. Luckily they're approaching from the opposite direction to you so you may not be detected. Good luck.'

'Okay, Jane. Good luck to you. Tony, Marisa, Caroline, did you read?'

'Loud and clear, Lieutenant. What do you want us to do?'

'We'll stay hidden and see what happens. We don't know yet what size these ships are or what their firepower is. Sit tight behind this ice cube and let's see how this pans out.' We sent out a micro-drone which gave us a clear view of the *Grey Wolf*. The ship was moving away from us on a bearing towards the oncoming enemy ships, which came into view a few seconds later. A full-scale naval conflict started with the *Grey Wolf* putting up a tremendous fight but she was outnumbered by three larger ships and didn't stand a chance. After about fifteen minutes, she was overpowered and virtually destroyed. There was no chance that anyone on board had survived and I felt sick to my stomach thinking about Jane, Max and the rest of the crew. They had been really good to us and we had built up quite a friendship with them. I knew we all would be feeling the same and thirsting for revenge but I needed to think clearly because any rash, vengeful action on our part would lead to our destruction as well. I sent a message to all the pilots: 'Sit tight. We cannot take on these three star ships right now and I don't want them to know we're here. Do not move until I give the order.' I realised that Jane had purposefully moved away from our position to give us a better chance of remaining undetected and I proposed to make the most of that. I just hoped the three ships didn't come nosing around and find us but they seemed content to stay near the wrecked, burnt out hulk of the *Grey Wolf* and they eventually moved off in the direction from which they had come.

Chapter 7

I gave them half an hour and then we made our way over to the *Grey Wolf.* I tried calling the ship but received no reply. There was no sign of life, just a smoking shell. 'I'm going to take a look,' I said. 'Stay alert.' I left the shuttle and slowly made my way through what remained of the ship. It was a shocking sight, seeing the scale of the destruction close up. Whatever weapons had been used had done the job and I knew I had been right in not trying to take on those imperial warships. We would have been no more than dust within a very short time. I searched but could find no recognisable crew members, just charred remains of bodies scattered throughout the ship. I made my way to the bridge area and found Jane still in her seat, burnt almost beyond recognition. There was no sign of Max so I guessed he must have been obliterated. 'Tony, Caroline, Marisa – I have found some bodies, including the captain. I'm really sorry. There's nothing we can do and I don't want to hang around here any longer. Let's work out where we go from here.' I made my way back to the shuttle in a state of shock after seeing what remained of Jane and I sat quietly gathering my thoughts. I asked Cisco and the shuttle pilots to join me, and while I was waiting for them more bad news came through from Colonel Matfield.

'Lieutenant French – scheduled rendezvous not possible. Unable to contact *Grey Wolf* but battle group attacked and forced to retire to Union held territory. Warn *Grey Wolf* Imperium seems to know of our plans. You need to be on full alert. Confirm receipt of this message.'

The pilots and Cisco arrived and we sat together on the bridge. I first spoke to the pilots. 'I'm sorry about your comrades on the *Grey Wolf*. I know this must be hard for you but we have to survive so that we can continue the fight against the Imperium.' I showed them the message and Cisco went as white as a sheet.

'Fuck sake, the *Grey Wolf* and the battle group. I can't believe we're still alive. I wonder what's left of the battalion.'

'Good thing is the Imperium don't know about us and we want to keep it that way. I'd like to jam a rocket up the fuckers who did this.' I turned to the pilots. 'How long can we survive on the provisions in the shuttles?'

'We're okay for two weeks although I reckon we could push it to three if we're careful,' said Caroline. 'We're lucky in that these three shuttles are of the latest design. They can't space jump, though, so we're stuck here until help arrives.'

I sent Colonel Matfield a return message.

'Colonel Matfield – the *Grey Wolf* destroyed with total loss of life by three imperial star ships. Bravo Company and pilots intact in the three attack-shuttles at present in hiding. Provisions for three weeks.'

'Lieutenant French – bad news about the *Grey Wolf* but pleased Bravo survived. Best stay where you are and await orders. Will try and get a rescue together.'

'Colonel Matfield – message received.'

I turned back to the group. 'I have no intention of just sitting here waiting for a rescue mission that may or may not turn up. I want to go after those three ships and destroy them. I noticed they returned on exactly the same bearing they arrived on and it's my guess that they have some sort of base in that direction. If that's the case we might just get the jump on them. They certainly won't be expecting us and I reckon it's worth the risk.'

Marisa spoke up. 'We're with you, Lieutenant. I for one would do anything to avenge my dead crew mates.'

'Glad to hear it,' I said. 'I can assure you we feel the same. Also, the *Grey Wolf's* a wreck but we may be able to top up our provisions. I don't know the ship as well as you three and I know this is a big ask, but would you be prepared to go and see what you can find?'

'I'm okay with that, Lieutenant,' said Tony, 'but I request that we give what remains of the crew some kind of decent burial. I don't mind organising that and it won't take long. These shuttles contain self-destructing body bags.'

I nodded. 'Yeah, that would be a good thing to do. Okay, let's get it done. Cisco, Tony, organise a burial detail. We'll do this properly.'

'Caroline and I will go and see about finding any extra provisions on the *Grey Wolf*,' said Marisa.

'Okay,' I said. 'Let's give it two hours to complete everything. In the meantime, I'm going to talk to the company and let them know how things are with us here.'

That was a busy and nerve-racking two hours. At any moment those ships could have returned to the scene of the battle, although the detection systems in the shuttles were ultra-modern and would have warned us in good time. Nevertheless I was mighty relieved when it was all over and we were back in the shuttles. In the end there had been five bodies which we sent off into space. We had formed a Guard of Honour and released the bodies from a hastily constructed platform. The body bags were timed to self-destruct an hour after leaving the *Grey Wolf*, when the remains would be turned to a fine dust.

Caroline and Marisa had managed to secure enough provisions to give us an extra week if need be and I called a council of war which consisted of Cisco, the three pilots and me. Sending Jane off into space had strengthened my resolve to get those ships. We thrashed out a battle plan based on the weapons at our disposal and after informing the troops and ensuring everyone knew exactly what was required of them we set out, following the path the three ships had taken after their destruction of the *Grey Wolf*. We crept forward at a snail's pace, our detection equipment (the most modern in the Union) at maximum level. Because of our size, we would have been very difficult to detect and in stealth mode virtually invisible, but I was taking no chances. Every time something suspicious showed up on the screen we stopped and examined it before creeping forward. Eventually our strategy paid off. After 28 hours a large object appeared on the screen, 1500 kilometres ahead of us, cylindrical in shape. We stopped dead and I felt my excitement rising.

'That ain't no comet,' said Tony, 'and there ain't no Union settlement out here, that's for sure.' I nodded.

'It looks huge,' said Marisa. 'How could they get away with building something like that inside the Union? It couldn't have been assembled in a few days.'

'I don't think it was that difficult,' I said. 'This system only joined the Union recently and our eyes were on the Protectorate in the months leading up to the war. Also, this new system is right on the edge of the Union. Why they chose this place I'll never know but it's our job to destroy that thing. First of all, though, we need to find out exactly what this 'thing' is. Get Danny up here, see if he can shed any light on the matter.' Danny joined us and stared at the screen but just shook his head.

'The only thing I can say is that it is a human construct,' he said.

'I'm going to have a look using an assault suit,' I said. 'That way, there's very little chance I'll be spotted.'

'I don't think you should go, Lieutenant,' said Cisco. 'You're needed here to lead this mission and to make sure it is a success. I'll go and have a scout round and report back.'

'I agree,' said Danny. 'You'll have to lead the attack and we're also counting on you should things go wrong. You shouldn't risk your life on a scouting mission. Also,

I request that I accompany the CSM. Two pairs of eyes are better than one.'

They were looking at me pretty intently and I could see some sense in what they were saying. 'Okay, Cisco, Danny, you're it. Make sure your suits are on stealth mode and get a good look at this structure. Bring back as many images as you can. Take care. Look out for anti-personnel mines strung out around the thing. Maintain comms silence and we'll crack open the champagne when you get back.'

The two of them set out and we watched them disappear into the dark. That was a long wait, I can tell you, not knowing whether we would see Cisco and Danny coming back, or have an enemy warship shooting at us. We were hidden among a cluster of comets but the thought of those three ships returning and finding us there had us sweating. I moved between the three shuttles, chatting quietly to the troops and found them to be in good spirits, everything considered. They were more than ready to attack whatever lay ahead and I was confident in our ability to overcome any reasonably sized force that stood against us. But first we had to destroy those ships because no matter how brave or competent we were, we were no match for them.

After an eternity of waiting and worrying, Cisco and Danny returned. The relief among us was palpable. Both were in high spirits as Cisco projected the images onto a desktop. 'Lieutenant, they are there for the taking,' he said. He pointed to the images. 'They're not taking any precautions or maintaining a proper watch. I reckon they've been here quite a while undetected and have become over confident that nobody's going to find them.'

I looked at the photos and saw a large donut shaped space-station with the three ships attached at different docking stations. Lights were blazing and Danny and Cisco reported that he had seen no patrols and had encountered no minefields. Maybe they had become blasé. After all, the Imperium had captured the system, the *Grey Wolf* had been destroyed and the battle group turned back. They had no idea we were in the vicinity and so it made sense they were relaxed about their position. That meant striking while the iron was hot and I got down to planning immediately. After a discussion with Cisco and the three pilots, I gave the order for the attack. 'Okay this is how we're going to do it. Segolene, Danny and Cisco are going to approach the station in assault suits and plant three mines apiece on each of those ships. We know that ships attached to a space-station cannot activate their shields. Once they have placed the mines, they will come back here and then we'll make our way openly towards the base, forcing the ships to respond. When they leave the station and are on their way to meet us we remotely trigger the mines, disposing of those ships. We go in using the shuttles as gunships and attack the space-base itself. Shuttle 1, concentrate on this sector here, shuttle 2 here and shuttle 3 here. After softening up the place, the troops will exit the shuttles and finish the operation by capturing this station. Cisco, you take Platoons 5 through 8 and attack this docking station here. I'll take the other four platoons and do the same here. Once we get inside make the attack as ferocious as possible. We want to capture this thing real fast. We may be able to use it to get back to civilisation. Any questions?' I looked around the bridge. 'Okay let's do it.'

The three of them set out towards the imperial base and very soon were up to maximum speed. Once again we waited, sweating with anxiety, while the three of them were away. They eventually came back and Cisco gave his verbal report, telling us that the mines had been successfully planted and that the rest of the operation could go ahead as planned.

'Well done, all three of you. Fantastic job. My report will include bravery citations for the three of you,' I said. We set the attack in motion. I used the radio to call the other two shuttles and we moved forward, making as much of a show as possible. We switched off the stealth mode and chatted over the radio as much as possible. Danny, who had been watching the screen, came through my earphone. 'They're on the move, Lieutenant. Three objects have separated from the base and are now approaching us. ETA nine minutes.'

'Okay, Danny. Keep monitoring their approach. When they are five minutes out, trigger the limpets. Pilots, let's get to that base ASAP after the limpets have been triggered.'

'Limpets triggered, Lieutenant,' said Danny. 'Christ, the three ships have disappeared from the screen. Success.'

'Great. Let's go. Bravo, prepare to jump as soon as green light shows. You okay, Cisco?'

'Rarin' to go, Lieutenant.'

We were now speeding towards the imperial base and came across what was left of their warships. They had been shredded and were floating in pieces as we passed them. There was no sign of life but we couldn't have stopped anyway. I wanted us at the base before they could organise their defences properly. By the time they realised their ships were wrecked we were upon them, swooping out of the dark and raking that structure with cannon fire and machine gun fire. The attack went off like clockwork, with each shuttle attacking their designated part of the base. There was some ragged return fire but they had been caught completely by surprise and were no doubt in a state of panic and confusion. 'One more drive-by and then we'll go in,' I said. 'Troops, prepare for the jump. Red light on.'

We made one more pass along the structure and then the green light came on and we out in space, heading for the docking area. We arrived shooting at anything that moved and soon gained entry into the base itself where we encountered very little resistance. They had had the fight knocked out of them and we ranged through the base with relative ease and soon secured the whole structure. 'Cisco, let's get all prisoners into one place. There's a large area near the dock we attacked. Make sure they keep their hands on their heads. I don't want anybody sending any signals anywhere. I'll meet you there.'

'Okay, Lieutenant. Will do.'

I started herding our prisoners towards the holding area, their hands on their heads. We came round a corner and I heard loud music blaring from behind a door. I nodded to Sergeant Ahmed to carry on with the prisoners and kept Danny and three troopers with me. We went in fast and I got the surprise of my life. This was clearly the officers' mess and we had interrupted what looked like a great party. There were about twelve men and women there, all looking dishevelled and quite a few of them very drunk. It was clear that they had hastily got dressed and one of the women was lying half naked passed out across a sofa.

'Fucking hell,' said Danny, 'looks like we've spoiled the party.' He walked over and turned off the music.

I stepped forward. 'Anybody speak Standard Galactic?' They all stared at me. Someone stumbled and another hiccupped loudly. I raised my voice. 'I said, does anybody speak Standard Galactic?'

A woman stepped forward, shock all over her face. She tried to pull her skirt down and stretch her skimpy top but without much success. 'I speak little. If you...um...speak slowly I understand.'

I spoke slowly and she nodded as I spoke. 'I am Lieutenant French, Union army. We have captured your station and destroyed your ships. Understand?'

She nodded vigorously. 'I understand but...how...where you from?'

'Never mind that. Who is in charge here?' I said. She turned and pointed to a short round individual, uniform awry and so drunk he could hardly stand. 'Him? You sure?'

'Yes, he commandant here. He...er...how you say...er...in charge. But now I...um...think he drink too much.' She shrugged. 'Is party here...every night.'

'And you,' I said, 'what's your position?'

'Some missionary, some doggy style, I reckon,' said Danny, which made us laugh. She looked at me quizzically.

'Who are you, what is your job here?' I said.

'Oh...oh yes, I understand. I am Private Lagota, Makreet Lagota. I...um...work in...um…make food. I am at party always for...er...please officers.' She shrugged again looking sheepish.

'Fuck sake, this is some way to run a ship,' I said. Just then the commandant lurched forward and leant on Makreet. He looked at me bleary eyed and shouted something. I looked at Makreet, who moved sideways, causing him to stumble. Two troopers caught him and held him upright. 'What'd he say?' I asked.

'He want to know how you...er...get here, where you...um...come from,' she said. 'He very...um...surprised to see you here.'

'I bet he is but he's no good to me in this state. You two, can you take this prick to the medics and have them sober him up please. Keep him under close guard. I don't want him touching anything or communicating with anyone.'

'Yes, sir,' they said and dragged him away.

I turned back to Makreet. 'Do you want a coat?'

'Please...yes. The officers like me dress...er...like this but I not really like it...please.'

'Can somebody please find a coat for Makreet. And the same for that woman lying on the sofa. I don't think she intended to be half naked in front of enemy troops.' Coats were found and Makreet looked grateful. 'Makreet, can you tell everyone here that they are prisoners of war. The station belongs to us and the ships are destroyed. Nobody will be harmed if they obey our orders. You understand?'

She nodded and relayed the message to the others in the room. One of the women burst out crying and crumpled onto the floor. She was wailing, her head in her hands. I looked at Makreet and mouthed 'what?'

'You must excuse. She son on ship. Is dead?' she asked.

I nodded. 'They are all dead,' I said. 'Tell her I'm sorry.' Makreet put her arms around her, whispering something. They both stood up and I signalled to one of our troopers to go and help her. Makreet walked back to me. The rest of the crowd were looking sober now and stunned with shock. Not in their wildest imaginings did they ever think they'd be prisoners on their own station. Another officer stepped forward and said something to Makreet.

'This Captain Kahorra. He now in charge. He want know what to do now.'

Danny came up to me. 'Lieutenant, I've rigged up an instant translation system on this terminal. When anyone speaks, the transcript will appear on the screen.'

'Well done, Danny. Let's get started.' I spoke into the mic. Immediately the transcript appeared on the screen in their language. 'Captain Kahorra, you are all prisoners of war and so are the rest of the personnel throughout the station. The three ships that were based here have been destroyed with total loss of life. The first thing you have to do is to speak to the personnel on the station and inform them that no harm will come to them provided they obey orders and behave themselves. I'd like you to do that now please. I imagine some form of intercom exists on this structure.'

Captain Kahorra read the transcript and nodded. He proceeded to speak to the station and repeated what I had said. He switched off the intercom and stood looking at me. He looked terrified and so did Makreet. I had a feeling they wished to speak to me alone so had the others removed from the room. 'You two want to say something?'

The captain stepped forward. 'Sir, we are now prisoners and we must remain prisoners. For any officers to go back to the Imperium would mean death by firing squad. If it ever got out that the officers were at a drunken party when the station was captured and the ships destroyed, we would be shot for treason. Other personnel, like Private Lagota, could also be shot or sent to a penal colony, something worse than death. Because of that I want to give you some information now that will help you and us. I know Private Lagota and trust her.'

Just then the door opened and a sorry looking commandant was escorted into the room. I didn't know what those medics had done but he was completely sober and trying to salvage what was left of his dignity. He glowered at the captain and Makreet and snapped something at them. They both stood to attention, looking scared. I couldn't have him strutting around here like he was still in charge so I decided to cut him down to size.

'Welcome back, Commandant, and glad to see you're able to stand. I've decided that you are of no further use to me and so you are going back to the Imperium with a full report of how this station was captured including details of the party. I'm sure you'll be welcomed with open arms by the authorities there.' He read the transcript and gripped the table.

'Lieutenant, I never meant any disrespect. I...I was drunk and didn't know what I was saying. Please you must believe me. I...I cannot go back after what happened here. I will be executed or worse, spend the rest of my life in a penal colony. Of that there is no question. I am your prisoner and I beg you not to send me back. Please...'

He looked like he'd been shot so I let him stew for a while. 'Okay, Commandant, you will remain a prisoner of war. But I want you to remember that I now run this station and what I say goes.' He stared at me, decided I was serious, and allowed the relief to flood through him.

'Thank you,' he said, shoulders slumping, 'what are your instructions?'

Captain Kahorra asked if he could speak to the commandant.

'Go ahead,' I said.

He spoke to the commandant, gesticulating wildly, his voice low and urgent. I looked at Makreet, who nodded imperceptibly. When Captain Kahorra had finished speaking the commandant turned to me. He hesitated and again turned towards the captain, who made a gesture urging him to speak. He sighed and looked at me. 'Lieutenant, I am Commandant Foskatch and I have to tell you that because of the temporary lapse of discipline that occurred here today we ask for your understanding.' He suddenly looked mad as hell. 'We thought we'd be involved in the capture of this system but it turned out they didn't need us. Not even any acknowledgement that we had been sitting out here for months, just some junior officer telling me to "await further orders"'. He glowered at me. 'Await further orders. I ask you. Me, a commandant with over thirty years' service and I'm told to await further orders. Which never came by the way. And so we have been sitting here getting bored for months now. What I am telling you does not make me proud. However, it is true. Discipline has been very lax and I have not run this station as I should. Even the security on the ships was slack and so you have captured us with ease. I can tell you now that the Imperium has no idea what has happened here. You are free to check our outgoing log but you will not find any message to the Imperium telling them of our capture. The reason is simple. We were drunk at a party and nobody has thought to send anything. Do not allow any of our personnel near a terminal. They do not have personal devices. The authorities regard them as dangerous and potentially subversive.' I sent a message to Cisco reminding him to make sure nobody went near any computer. He was to also carry out a search for any personal devices just in case.

'Okay, carry on,' I said.

'I understand that there cannot be many of you, Lieutenant, perhaps a company. Otherwise the officer in charge would be of higher rank. I also suspect that you are survivors from the Union warship that was destroyed two days ago and that you arrived here in attack-shuttles. If that is the case then you are going to need a way out of here as I know the shuttles will not get you very far.'

I studied the commandant's face but he was just being straight with me as far as I could see. 'You're very perceptive, Commandant,' I said.

He shrugged. 'I have been a soldier for more than thirty years and an officer for more than twenty.' His voice turned bitter. 'I was a very good officer, Lieutenant, and destined for high office until I got on the wrong side of a particular political faction. Now look at me, sitting here in this backwater, going nowhere, my life in danger from my own side...' He sat there staring into space. I just sat quietly until he shook himself out of daydreaming. He looked at me. 'I can see that you are an excellent officer, Lieutenant, and if I am to be a prisoner of war then having you as my captor is at least bearable.'

'Thank you, Commandant, but I need that information you mentioned,' I said.

'Of course. A ship, the *Wawrthk*, carrying supplies and provisions will arrive here in about six hours. If they do not think anything is wrong they will dock as normal.

If on the other hand they suspect something they will contact the Imperium who would send more warships. You would certainly be defeated and we would end up being executed.'

'A supply ship?' I said. 'Give me the details.'

'It arrives every six weeks or so and brings us supplies. There is a seven man crew, well known to us. We need them to dock as normal, Lieutenant. That ship can get us to Union held territory where I shall sit out the rest of the war as a prisoner. I am not that much of a fool to believe that we have any chance of winning this war anyway. I just hope the idiots who started it get what they deserve.'

I looked at the three of them and decided that they were speaking the truth. They were as frightened as hell and I could imagine what end they faced if the full story of the capture of this station got out. Danny turned off the mic. 'Well, they say fortune favours the brave...maybe we'll be able to destroy this place and get back home after all. Well done, Lincoln, you made this happen. I know you'll talk of teamwork and all that but you initiated this attack. There are plenty of officers who would have sat back and waited for a rescue which would probably never have come.'

I smiled. 'Thanks, Danny. But I was beginning to wonder where we'd go from here with only three shuttles and forty prisoners. We are going to have to nail this one. That ship must dock and shut down without the crew suspecting anything. By the way, you believe these guys? They seem genuine to me.'

'Yes I do. I've been watching them closely and they're terrified of being sent back home. Also, this commandant is extremely bitter about his treatment at the hands of the authorities.'

I turned the mic back on and spoke to the three imperial crew. 'Okay, we're going to have to work together on this. I don't want anything going wrong. I have to tell you this though. If there is a hint of betrayal by any of you I will personally shoot you in the back of the head. Is that clearly understood?' One look at my face convinced them I wasn't kidding and they all nodded vigorously. I turned to Danny. 'Okay, I'm going to check on the security situation and make sure the troops and the prisoners are being properly cared for. Keep these three here. I'll be back within the hour and we'll get down to working out a plan.' I went and found Cisco. 'Hi, Cisco, how are things?'

'Everything ship-shape, Lieutenant. All prisoners secured, watered and fed. I've kept the officers separate from the rest.' We wandered down a passageway until we were on our own.

'Well done. Make sure you are looking after yourself as well. How are the troops?'

'Morale is good. They're stationed throughout this thing and they too have had food and drink. Half the company are on downtime. I've got them working on four hour shifts.'

'Sounds like you've got everything sorted. Thanks, Cisco. Let me bring you up to date on things at my end.'

I told him about the officers' mess and the subsequent conversations with the three crew members.

He started laughing. 'So you walked in on an orgy in the officers' mess?'

'Well, just after I think. They must have heard the attack and wondered what the fuck was going on.' I started laughing too. 'I can only imagine them all trying to get back into their clothes...one woman with hardly anything on had passed out...the others were standing there smashed as fucking rats...the commandant shouting incoherently...it was some fucking sight I can tell you.'

Cisco was rocking with helpless laughter. 'I can just imagine them trying to unhook themselves...blokes... fumbling around...trying to get their cocks back in their pants...pissed outa their heads...shouting 'what's that fucking noise?'...trying to get dressed...fuck me, that must have been some sight...maybe Danny could give us an impression.' He roared with laughter. 'Jesus, Lincoln, you get all the luck...and now they want us to save their sorry asses.' We were laughing hysterically and it felt good as the tension of the last few days drained out of us. We ended up sitting against a bulkhead, our legs stretched out in front of us.

'Yeah, and save ourselves I guess. This station is pretty basic,' I said. 'It can't move anywhere and we can't stay here much longer. The Imperium is going to figure something's wrong sooner rather than later so I reckon we're gonna have to grab that supply ship and get back to friendly territory.'

'Sounds like a good idea. I'll leave the planning to you,' he said. 'I'll keep on looking after the station and the prisoners. Just let me know what you want us to do.'

'Okay,' I said, standing up. 'Make sure that every prisoner is under close guard. I'll go and get this thing done and get back to you. Take care, compadre.'

He looked around to make sure we were alone. 'You too, pal. I'm real pleased you're the CO here, Lincoln. Not many officers would have got us to this place and destroyed those ships. I'll wait to hear from you.' He patted me on the shoulder. I went off to get a bite to eat and to plan our next move. I was starting to feel edgy and wanted to get off this structure. We'd had our share of luck up to now, even made some of our own, but that never lasted. I was counting on that supply ship but anything could happen. I called the three pilots and asked them to meet me in the officers' mess. 'Hi, guys, how are things?'

'Okay,' said Tony. 'We've just finished checking the shuttles and they're in excellent shape. Trouble is, as you know, they're way out of their league here. We're at least a light year out from the Medway sun and the shuttles are far too small to get us anywhere near there. They certainly can't get us to another system.'

'Yeah I know but there may be a way out.' I told them about the supply ship, how I planned to capture it and use it to get us all away from here. 'We're going to need your flying skills for the operation. In the meantime I want to be extra vigilant. Anything could turn up here before that supply ship arrives so I wondered if you could work out a rota whereby at least two of you are on patrol all the time over the next eight hours or so. Keep up a 360 degree spherical full depth scan as well. The supply ship mustn't be aware of the shuttles before it docks and shuts down. I don't want word getting back to the Imperium until we are safely away. On the other hand, if something goes wrong and the supply ship tries to make a break for it, I'd like you to be close enough to intercept and to stop it.' I smiled. 'Not much to ask but hey...'

'No worries. We'll organise something and keep you posted,' said Caroline. 'Those three shuttles are still lethal weapons and we should be able to take on any single ship.' I left them to it and returned to the room where Danny was waiting with the three imperial crew members.

'Right,' I said, 'let's get down to planning. Danny, Makreet, I'd like your input so please stay with us. Let's make sure we get this right.' The five of us spent the next hour or so planning the capture of the *Wawrthk* down to the last detail. By the time we'd finished I knew all about the ship, where it came from, how it docked, what happened during and after docking, how we were going to bluff the crew, seven of them, into thinking all was normal on the space station, including a viable explanation for the visible damage and the fact that the three warships would not be present. We covered everything more than once and in the end I was satisfied that we had covered all exigencies. The commandant shook his head ruefully. 'What's the problem?' I asked.

'Nothing,' he said. 'I am impressed with your eye for detail and the way you plan your next move. I used to be...should have run this station like that...'

'Yeah, you probably should have,' said Danny, 'but it's too late for regrets. We are where we are and if you want to get out of here safely we'd better stick to this plan.' They nodded their agreement.

'Thanks, Danny. Okay, everyone, I suggest you get some rest. The two of you will remain here under guard but feel free to ask for refreshments. I'll be back in a while,' I said. 'Makreet, you will also be under guard but in a room on your own. I have arranged for you to be taken there. Like these two you will not be allowed out but can ask for refreshments. You must change into your uniform as you are a prisoner of war.' I switched off the computer and turned to the two troopers guarding the door. They had just arrived. 'Okay, guys, this is very important. These two are to be under close guard in this room. We've done a thorough search of the place. It's clean and as you can see there's no other way out. They have toilet facilities en suite. You can get food and drink for them but under no circumstances are they allowed out. Understood?'

'Loud and clear, Lieutenant,' said one of them. 'They won't be going anywhere.'

Two more troopers turned up. I gave them the same orders I'd given the other two, thanked Makreet for her help, and they made their way to Makreet's room. 'That's that,' I said. 'Danny, thanks for your input here. You were a great help and I'd like you to stick around. I'll let Cisco know. Let's go and get some coffee, strong and sweet for me. I don't think I'm going to get much sleep over the next few hours.'

After snatching a quick cup of coffee and a few cookies, I made my way to the docking area where one of the shuttles was moored and found Caroline on board, getting ready to take over from one of the others. 'Hi, Caroline. Okay if I use your comms facilities? I need to try and contact my battalion commander, let him know how things are here with us.'

'Sure go ahead. I'll give you a hand if you like,' she said. We went to the bridge where I sent a message through to Colonel Matfield, hoping he would still be able to receive it. I sent it twice, telling him what had happened and how I proposed to get us out of this situation after destroying the space station. I waited for some time but received no acknowledgement. 'Let me know if anything comes through, Caroline,' I said. I made my way back to the officers' mess a bit worried about the situation in the Medway system. I didn't know whether the Imperium had conquered it completely or whether our forces had started fighting back. What if the battalion had been wiped out or captured? What was happening to the 15th Army? Then I had a thought. Maybe the commandant or the captain could tell me. They would be able to call their command to find out. I decided to wait until we were safely aboard the supply ship before trying anything like that though. I didn't want to draw attention to this space station in any way. We would just have to sit it out and hope for the best.

I made another inspection of the station, ensured all prisoners were safely under guard, chatted to the troops and checked with the pilots. I spoke to Cisco. We went over the intended capture of the crew of the *Wawrthk*. 'There are seven of them. Make sure that all seven have exited the ship before you jump them. I don't want anyone left in there getting a message to the Imperium.' A call came through saying that Makreet wished to speak to me. I told her guards to bring her to the room Danny and I were in. We were joined by Segolene and a few minutes later Makreet walked in. She was in her uniform, had obviously had a shower and removed all traces of the party, and looked very different from the last time I had seen her. She stood looking down, her hands clasped in front of her. It was clear that she was nervous. I stood up and walked over to her. 'Come in, Makreet. Please sit down,' I said, leading her to a chair. 'You wanted to talk to me.' She looked nervously at Danny and Segolene. 'Don't mind Danny and Segolene. They are friends of mine and anything you want to say to me you can say in front of them.' I smiled broadly at her. 'Can I get you anything to eat or drink?' She shook her head and smiled back at me. I placed the terminal on the table. 'You can speak Imperese, Makreet. This terminal will pick it up and translate it.'

'I don't want to take up too much of your time Lieutenant. I just want to tell you that I am grateful for the respect you have shown me and I want to thank you for the way I have been treated. You have not judged me. I am not used to being treated in this fashion by army officers. I am also here to say that I am willing to help you in any way I can. I know it's difficult for you but I promise you can trust me,' she said.

'Thank you, Makreet. I shall bear in mind what you have said and if there is any way in which you can help I'll let you know.'

'One more thing, Lieutenant. I know the commandant and Captain Kahorra are assisting you out of fear for their lives but please be careful. If they think they can get away with it they might turn on you. I know you are no fool but just be careful when dealing with the likes of them.'

'I will, thank you. Believe me, I know they are only acting out of self-interest. I'll keep a close eye on them.' She smiled and stood up. Just then Cisco walked in and stopped in his tracks when he saw Makreet. He quickly recovered but I had no doubt he liked what he saw. 'Makreet, this is Company Sergeant Major Cisco Gonzales. He is second in command here. Cisco, Makreet.'

'Er...pleased to meet you, Makreet. Er...' She smiled at him which seemed to make him worse. He turned to me looking flustered. Danny and Segolene were smiling. 'Lieutenant, I've...er...got those...er...we're ready to receive that ship.'

'I...go back my room,' said Makreet extending her hand. 'Thank you, Lieutenant.' I stood and shook her hand.

'I'm...uh...going that way,' said Cisco. 'I'll see she gets back okay.' He took her gently by the arm and led her out of the room before any of us had a chance to say anything. The three of us looked at each other and burst out laughing. 'Christ, he's gone and fallen for a prisoner of war,' I said. 'I hope he doesn't do anything stupid.' I decided to leave him be and to trust his common sense. He knew that fraternising with the enemy was not allowed, no matter how beautiful they were.

It was Marisa who first alerted me to an object approaching the space station from about 1000 kilometres out, bearing 140 degrees. Commandant Foskatch, Captain

Kahorra, Danny and I assembled in the communications suite. Three troopers stood guard. Captain Kahorra volunteered to communicate with the *Wawrthk* and all communication between the space station and the ship was instantly translated onto a large screen facing us. I stood behind him with my pistol in my hand. He knew – one word out of place and I would shoot him in the back of the head.

Thankfully it didn't come to that. The ship docked and shut down, and the crew walked off and into captivity without a hitch. They were stunned and just stood there when Cisco and twenty soldiers suddenly surrounded them. They separated the pilot and first officer from the rest and brought them to the communications room where I was standing, pointing my pistol at the commandant and the captain. I indicated to the two new arrivals to join us and to read the screen where I informed them that they were prisoners of war and that I was taking their ship.

I was in a hurry to get away from that space station. The place was starting to give me the creeps but it took another sixteen hours or so before we were finally ready to leave. Our pilots had to familiarise themselves with the ship, we had to load the ship with extra provisions, fix up suitable accommodation for a company of soldiers and some forty prisoners and carry out a final check of the station to ensure that nobody was being left behind.

'We gonna booby-trap the place?' asked Cisco.

'No,' I said. 'I thought about it but there's a chance that another civilian craft could dock here. Also, I think most of these imperial troops are conscripts and they don't deserve to die like that.'

257

We found that the rear loading bay of the ship could accommodate two of the shuttles and after flying them in we had to improvise and secure them properly. We tied the third shuttle to the outside of the ship, using structures already in place for holding different types of cargo. Finally we were ready. I was on the bridge with the pilots. Caroline assumed responsibility as captain, with Tony and Marisa as her first officers. Danny had worked feverishly so that all commands were instantly translated into Imperese, meaning the ship could respond to voice control and I had Makreet with us to act as translator and interpreter if need be. After my talk with her I trusted her more than the others and Marisa gave her a five hour crash course in pilot-speak in case we had to communicate with any enemy ships. I also wanted to keep her away from Cisco as much as possible which was proving difficult as he suddenly had numerous excuses for being on the bridge. I don't know what he had said to her but it was clear that she perked up whenever he appeared. Christ, that was all I needed; a growing attraction between my second-in-command and a member of the imperial armed forces.

I switched on the intercom. 'Listen up, everybody, we are about to leave the station. I want you to be in assault suits at all times and ready for action. Although this system is within the Union we have to assume it is in enemy hands and so we will operate as if we are in enemy territory. Stay alert and be ready for anything.' Tony was in the shuttle attached to the outside of the hull. 'Tony, you read that?' He affirmed that he had. On the bridge they were all looking at me. I switched off the intercom and nodded to Caroline. 'Let's go.'

Chapter 8

We disengaged and crept away from the dock, Caroline still nervous at the controls. I watched as the station grew smaller and smaller and started to breathe a sigh of relief although I knew things go your way for only so long. We set a course for the centre of the system and started picking up speed. My plan was to get nearer to the sun and then try and find out what the situation was. If it was bad we would try and jump our way out of there and deeper into the Union. I was hoping that our forces had at least started to retake this system and that we could rejoin the campaign. We had a fourteen hour journey at sub-hyper ahead of us before we reached the co-ordinates from which we could make a space-jump. The detection systems in the ship and shuttle 1 were on full alert but space all around us was empty except for the comets. I was fervently hoping it was going to stay that way. I told Cisco to take over on the bridge (both he and Makreet looked as pleased as punch) and told them I was going to take a rest. I wanted to be on my own for a while. I had commandeered the captain's cabin and flopped down on the bed. I couldn't remember how long I'd been awake, relying on coffee and sugar to keep me going but it was in excess of 24 hours and I figured I'd get some rest while the going was good.

My thoughts turned to Collette. The last communication she'd had from me was the letter I'd given to Gabriel. I hoped that nothing had happened to the space-station to prevent her getting it and flipped open the locket she had given me. There she was, as gorgeous and radiant as ever. I stared at the hologram, at that unbelievably beautiful face, those large, sparkling green eyes, that dark hair, the dusting of freckles and the perfectly formed neck and shoulders, and yearned to see her again, to be with her and to see her smile. A feeling of dread swept through me as I briefly imagined dying out here without seeing her or hearing her voice again. I snapped the locket shut and forced myself to concentrate on the present. I was still alive, I told myself, and I was going to do my damndest to stay that way. I lay there staring at the ceiling, a jumble of thoughts running through my mind, and slowly drifted off to sleep.

'Lieutenant, you're needed on the bridge – urgent.' Cisco's voice came through the intercom and woke me immediately. I checked the time and realised I'd been asleep for four hours.

'On my way,' I said, and headed for the bridge. It sounded bad – Cisco's voice had been strained and I made my way there as quickly as possible. 'What's up?'

Cisco pointed to the screen, which showed three objects still some distance away to our left but on a converging course. Everyone was quiet, eyes glued to the screen. I studied the images. 'My guess is that we have three warships for company,' I said. 'The question is; are they ours or theirs and, if theirs, can we give them the slip?' I kept my eyes on the screen. Somebody handed me a cup of coffee.

'If we've seen them chances are they've seen us,' said Caroline, 'and if they are warships we won't be able to outrun them.'

'Steady as she goes, Caroline,' I said. 'Let's just carry on as if we're completely legit. If they turn out to be imperial, Makreet will give them the story. Hopefully they'll fall for it. Tony, you with us?'

'Sure am. I've got them on the screen and I agree with you – they are warships and moving at quite a lick. From their direction I'd say they are imperial.' That's what I was thinking. There was no good reason why any Union ships should be coming from that direction.

'Makreet, can I have a word please?' I said. We moved to the rear of the bridge away from the others. I spoke slowly and quietly. 'I just want to know I can trust you, Makreet. I don't really want to stand behind you with a pistol in my hand ready to shoot you.' I looked at her intently.

She looked straight back at me spoke earnestly. 'Lieutenant, you can trust me...er...complete. I...I... am...never go back to be...um...pleasure woman for officers...never. Also I be shot or...er...go in prison colony if I go back or...er...commandant and captain they have me killed to...to...er...keep secret how they behave. I...er...not trust them. I...am...your prisoner but you can trust me.'

I believed her. I nodded. 'Okay, that's good enough for me. You stay with Caroline and you speak to those ships if they call us. You understand?'

She smiled and nodded. 'I understand. Thank you, Lieutenant.'

Cisco came up to me. 'Unless you want me for anything else I'll be back with the troops,' he said. 'We may be involved in more fighting.'

'Good idea,' I said. 'I'll keep you in the loop. Be ready for anything.' I was pleased that Cisco had shown he was still fully committed. I had never really doubted him but this thing between him and Makreet was unusual, to say the least. I went back to the screen and saw that the three ships were maintaining their direction of travel and their speed. Maybe, I thought, they would choose to ignore us, regard us as insignificant. Things don't work like that of course. It wasn't long before they contacted us and they turned out to be imperial alright. They wanted to know who we were, where we were heading and why – everything I didn't want to tell them. I turned to Makreet and smiled. 'Okay, Makreet, your turn in the spotlight.'

She was brilliant. She sounded like she'd been flying ships all her life, very professional and utterly convincing. She gave them the information they wanted, telling them that we had been diverted to Rochester, the planet at the centre of the fighting, and that we were carrying extra supplies for the army. We gave them the co-ordinates where we were going to make the space jump towards the centre. She even asked them to identify themselves and ended by praising the 'glorious Imperium'.

They came back saying that they were a flotilla consisting of two troop transporters and a cruiser, carrying another 30,000 troops to the battle front on the planet

Rochester. They were heading for the same space jump co-ordinates as us and would reach it about an hour behind us. The commander of the group was very loquacious and full of himself, telling us that with the addition of these troops, the advances the Union had made would be stopped in their tracks and the 'glorious Imperium' would finally be victorious here in the Medway system. He bid us farewell and hoped we had a good journey.

'Thank you, Makreet. That was brilliant,' I said. I turned to Caroline and Marisa who looked at me and were thinking the same thing as me.

'We have to try and stop those troops reaching their destination,' said Marisa, 'or at least delay them.'

I nodded. 'We also have to warn the Union command somehow. They have to know about this force heading their way.' I called Cisco and asked him to join us on the bridge, and got Tony to join the conversation. Makreet indicated that she wanted to have a word with me.

'Lieutenant, I…er…now with you. I…er…not want to go back…er…to be prisoner. I stay…um…here and help.'

'You sure, Makreet? We are going to fight these ships, understand?' She nodded. 'Maybe kill some soldiers of the Imperium. You still want to help?'

'Lieutenant, I…er…not going to shoot anybody. I…er…not want to kill anybody but I…um…help you here in ship.'

'Okay, Makreet, you stick with Caroline. She will need your help.' Cisco arrived on the bridge and once again Makreet looked like the sun had just come out. Cisco, too, looked pleased to see her but it didn't detract him from his work. We got down to planning a course of action that would stop those transporters from getting near the battle zone. We had to hit them before any space jump, while they were still relatively isolated. Once they got nearer the centre of the system it would undoubtedly be more difficult.

'Once again we'll have surprise on our side,' I said. 'These guys obviously know nothing about the space station but this time we're hopelessly outnumbered, and outgunned by that cruiser. However, we can do some damage. I reckon we use the shuttles to first attack the two transporters and try and disable them. Bravo Company then continues the attack against the transporters while the shuttles do their best against the cruiser. Caroline, you move this ship away from the battle. If any of us survive we may need it.' We worked out the details and came up with a credible plan of attack.

'I reckon that's the best way to do it,' said Cisco. 'That cruiser won't want to shoot towards the transporters so we'll have a few minutes leeway while we're busy with the transporters. After that, well, who knows...?'

'I want to talk about the prisoners,' I said. 'This ship may be destroyed or at least disabled. They are under lock and key. They could be burnt alive in their cells or freeze to death without being able to get out. I don't think that would be right.'

'I agree but what are we going to do with them?' said Tony. After some discussion we decided we would disarm one of the shuttles, strip out any technology that might be useful to the Imperium and disable the comms, give them some provisions and give them a chance to get back to the space station. As the meeting ended I pulled Cisco aside.

'Cisco, Makreet has told me she wants to stay with us but I'd like you to tell her what we are doing with the other prisoners. It's only fair and from what I've seen, it'll be better coming from you. She needs to know she's taking a real risk staying here with us. If she is captured by the Imperium she'll be treated as a traitor. Maybe it would be better if she was in one of our uniforms and didn't say anything.' I smiled at him.

'Thanks, Lincoln,' he said softly. 'I owe you one. If we get out of this in one piece we'll celebrate in style.'

Tony came aboard and he and Marisa, with the help of the troops, set about stripping out the shuttle and stacking it with provisions. I sent a message to Colonel Matfield, General Hani and General Bullen, giving them information about the imperial reinforcements and what we were about to do. I gave them information about the *Wawrthk* and our position, and hoped the message reached at least one of them.

I had Danny bring his translation tool and we went to speak to the prisoners. I decided not to tell them about the intended attack on the flotilla. If they didn't know of the flotilla's existence they wouldn't be tempted to try and sabotage our plans. 'We are heading towards the fighting here in the Medway system and I cannot guarantee your safety as I have no idea what the situation is on the planet

Rochester. If this ship is attacked and you are trapped in these cells there is no telling what might happen to you. For this reason I am giving you a chance to return to the space station where there is every likelihood you will be rescued by your own side. We are putting a shuttle at your disposal. It is carrying provisions and has enough software to guide you back to the station. For obvious reasons it is unarmed and the communications software has been stripped out. You will not be able to contact the Imperium until you get back to the space station. Any of you who wish to remain prisoners of war are free to do so but as I have said, I cannot guarantee your safety.' They stared at me and then started talking amongst themselves. In the end sixteen, including Commandant Foskatch and Captain Kahorra, elected to remain as prisoners of war.

We took the rest to the shuttle and Marisa gave the captain of the *Wawrthk* a lesson in how to fly the thing. Before long they were gone and we could concentrate on stopping those reinforcements from reaching the war zone. I started by speaking to the troops. 'We have encountered a flotilla of two troop transporters and a cruiser heading for the combat zone on Rochester. They are carrying an extra 30,000 imperial reinforcements to add to those already fighting against the Union and it is our job to try and stop that from happening. We are going to attack that flotilla just before they make their space jump but I have to tell you that this time we will be heavily outnumbered and also outgunned by that cruiser. Nevertheless, when we attack those transporters I want us to cause as much death, damage and destruction as we can. I cannot say how many of us, if any, are going to survive this operation but our primary purpose is to prevent those troops from reaching their destination.

Platoons 1 through 4 with me in shuttle 1, 5 through 8 with CSM Gonzales in shuttle 2. Good luck everybody.'

We hit them hard and fast, and at first things went according to plan. The shuttles attacked the two transporters, repeatedly raking them with fire, until they were left hanging in space, unable to move. It was when we jumped and the shuttles turned on the cruiser that things began to go wrong.

The captain of the cruiser, rather than trying immediately to shoot down the shuttles, concentrated on fully activating his protective shields so that the shuttles were useless when they turned their fire on the cruiser. The fire from the cruiser, on the other hand, was devastating, and I saw shuttle 2, piloted by Marisa, fragment into dust a few seconds after the cruiser opened fire. At the same time, the surviving imperial troops inside the transporters started pouring out to meet us and although we had a technological superiority over them, there were, in the end, just too many of them.

'We've stopped them,' I said to Bravo Company. 'They won't be going anywhere so now we just fight like hell.' A hearty cheer came back through my earphones as we tore into them as best we could. I knew it was hopeless but I wasn't prepared to surrender to the Imperium at this stage. In any case it didn't seem that they were in the mood to take prisoners. It was a desperate fight. The firing from the cruiser was becoming more accurate and if it hadn't been for Tony's act of selfless bravery, Bravo Company would have been wiped out.

The *Wawrthk* had been hit and was drifting away from the fighting, badly damaged, and I was desperately fighting off three or four imperial troopers when I saw shuttle 1 head straight for the cruiser at high speed. The cruiser's shields could protect it against incoming fire but they were no match for the shuttle, which burst through and rammed into its side, ripping open the fuselage and causing it to spin away from the battle scene, its guns firing wildly but no longer a threat to us. We now had to contend with the imperial troopers who slowly but surely were whittling our numbers. I heard Cisco exhorting the troops and then felt a tremendous pain in my right side. I managed to start turning to my right and then there was another searing pain in my back and something slammed into my helmet and I had the sensation of spinning head over heels, out of control, my rifle flying loose. I was in pain and starting to lose consciousness, but before I blacked out completely, somebody was cheering and I thought I heard Colonel Matfield's voice but couldn't be sure...

Chapter 9

There are a few awakenings that stay with you all your life and this was one of them. I opened my eyes, gradually focussed, and found myself lying on my back looking up at a white ceiling and hooked up to various screens and items of medical equipment. I slowly inspected my surroundings. I was in a comfortable bed on crisp white sheets with others covering the lower half of my body. There were two tubes going into my left arm and an armband on my right. I looked at it more closely and read 'Captain French, 3rd Battalion, 707th Regt.' in Standard Galactic. The script on the machinery too was in Galactic so I figured I was, somehow, in a Union hospital and either someone was mistaken or I had been promoted. I tried moving but that was painful so I stayed put. Memories started coming back in snatches. The imperial troops pouring out of the damaged transporters, the supply ship, holed and drifting away from us, shuttle 1 flying into the cruiser, and me, back in the blackness of space, in tremendous pain, fighting going on all around me, spinning, head over heels, losing consciousness. I tried putting things together after that but nothing came. It was a blank until now, lying here in this hospital bed. I thought of Cisco, Danny and the others and wondered what had become of them. When I blacked out we were losing the fight, badly outnumbered and heading for annihilation but somehow…

A nurse appeared at the door and smiled at me. 'Hey, you're awake,' he said. 'How you feeling?'

'Okay, I think,' I said. 'Hurts a lot if I try to move.'

'Figures,' he said. 'You been damaged some. Gonna take a while.'

'Where am I?'

'City Hospital Dakota,' he said.

'Dakota? What, Dakota, Proserpine?'

He nodded and smiled. 'Yeah, welcome home.'

'How long have I been here?'

'Three days,' he said. 'Four days on the *Constitution* before that. You were picked up drifting in space and you're real lucky to be here.' He reached over and pressed a button. 'Doc better take a look at you before we let the army in.' He gripped my hand. 'Honoured to meet you, Captain.' He smiled and moved towards the door just as the doctor arrived.

'Captain French,' he said in a booming voice, 'you're with us again.' He shook his head. 'Had us all worried there for a while, pal. We wondered whether you were going to make it after drifting in space for so long but from the look on Nurse Corand's face it seems you're okay.' He came over and shook my hand. 'Doctor Benning. Glad to make your acquaintance.'

'Pleased to meet you, Doctor, but what do you mean drifting in space for so long?' I said.

'You were adrift in your assault suit for twenty-three hours before you were found. Those suits are meant to keep you alive for up to seventeen, eighteen hours but somehow you held on. Hypothermia nearly got you but you're obviously a tough customer, Captain, because you had also been wounded. That assault suit saved your life. You were hit in three different places and would have been in three different pieces if it hadn't been for that suit. Really glad to see you awake. I'm just going to take some readings and then the army can see you. Make sure you lie still. Don't try and move too much.'

I lay there while he took the readings. I was back in Dakota and thought immediately about Collette. Had she been in to see me? Did she even know I was here? 'Er, Doctor Benning, apart from the army, have I had any other visitors?'

'You sure have,' he said. He looked at the pad at the end of the bed and then back at me, a grin on his face. 'Collette came when she got the news and has stayed for the duration. She'll be back in a couple of hours apparently, or sooner if she hears you're awake.' He smiled and winked at me. 'You're a lucky man, Captain. The rest of us are as jealous as hell.' He laughed, a great booming laugh, and walked towards the door, calling for Nurse Corand, while happiness flooded through me. I shut my eyes and said her name quietly to myself two or three times. It was better than good, knowing I was with Collette again and that she obviously still felt the same way about me.

Footsteps sounded in the corridor and the next second Colonel Matfield came into the ward. He shook my hand. 'Glad to see you're back in the land of the living, Captain French,' he said. 'Thought we'd lost you for a while there.'

'Morning, Colonel,' I said. 'Glad to be back, sir but...how come I'm here and why captain? Last I remember I was a lieutenant and Bravo company was about to be annihilated.'

He smiled. 'We got your message and General Hani ordered a force to be put together to go and help you. We got there just in time but I have to tell you that Bravo has been decimated. We finished off the imperial cruiser, which had been badly damaged by the shuttle, and killed or captured the rest of those replacements. We found that supply ship, damaged and drifting, and I'm pleased to tell you that Caroline Ghali survived and is fine. So is that prisoner who was helping her – Makreet Lagota. The other prisoners didn't make it – they took a direct hit, all died instantly.

'General Bullen promoted you to captain and I have a list here of those who survived the fighting.' He handed me the list. There weren't many names on it. Most of the company had been wiped out, including Andy Somerville, Mollie and Segolene. Cisco and Danny were among those who had made it, however, and that was some relief but it hit me hard knowing most of the company were dead. I lay there, not able to speak. 'I know how you must be feeling,' said the colonel, 'but you guys did one hell of a job in stopping those replacements. We were holding out on Rochester but our position was still pretty ropey. If that lot had arrived on schedule, we would have been in real trouble. Bear that in mind. Those guys in Bravo didn't die in vain.' I nodded. 'We found everybody by the way. Did a wide sweep and the rest of Bravo refused to leave until we had found everyone, including you. We found you drifting about fifteen kilometres from the battlefield and were surprised you were still alive. Took you to the *Constitution* and here you are. General Bullen ordered that the survivors be brought to Dakota, thought it'd be good for you guys to be back home for a while. She then ordered the rest of the battalion to join you. We were due some leave, been in the thick of things non-stop, so here we all are, based at Black Tree Canyon. We have two weeks but I reckon you might have a bit longer.'

I managed a smile. 'Welcome to Dakota, Colonel. I hope you like it here.'

'It seems a fine place,' he said. 'To tell you the truth, anywhere away from the fighting is good right now. As you know, the battalion has seen its fair share of action and overall our losses have been heavy. But I reckon we've turned a corner. Slowly but surely the Imperium is being pushed back all over the Protectorate and apart from Medway, they haven't got into the Union.'

'How are things in Medway?' I asked.

'Better,' he said. 'They haven't penetrated any further and on Rochester they're retreating, thanks in no small measure to you. They threw everything at the system but we've managed to stop them. Your CSM, Gonzales, has submitted an interim report which includes the attack on the space station and the destruction of those three warships, and how you then got hold of the supply ship. He has also detailed the action of Flight Lieutenant Tony

273

Fisher, who flew his shuttle into the cruiser and how a prisoner of war, Makreet Lagota, helped with the attack on the flotilla. Your name, and that of Fisher, have gone forward for a Star of Honor and Bravo has been awarded a Gallantry Star, decoration to be worn by all members of Bravo, past, present and future. Helliva job, Captain, helliva job. Well done.'

'Thank you, Colonel. I'm glad about Tony's name going forward. If he hadn't knocked out that cruiser I don't think you would have found any of us alive. And Makreet – her contribution needs to be recognised.'

'Yeah and talking of being recognised, the president and General Bullen are going to be in Dakota to attend a memorial service for those from this system who have perished in the fighting, including Bravo, twelve days from now. President Joyce will also be awarding decorations and you are up for the Star of Honor and the Gallantry Star. If you are up and about by then you will be required to attend. You may invite guests.'

He got up and I noticed for the first time how tired he looked. His face was gaunt and there were dark shadows under his eyes. He'd been through it alright. 'You take it easy now, Captain and just get better. That's an order.'

'You too, Colonel. You look like you could do with some downtime.'

He smiled, patted me on the shoulder and left. I closed my eyes and thought about all we had been through and how Bravo Company had ceased to be. There were only 28 survivors, 17 of us wounded, out of a company of 240. I was pleased that all of us, living and dead, had been found after the battle, and promised myself that I would personally get to see all the survivors as soon as I was able. I would also try and visit the families of the dead if I could, or at least send them a letter of condolence.

I drifted off to sleep and was back in space, the dead and dying all around me, shouting at me, begging me to help them. Jane and Max appeared, badly disfigured and reaching out to me with burning hands and dripping flesh while Collette, unable to hear me or see me, drifted among the dead calling my name over and over again.

I awoke with a start and lay there, confused and pretty shaken by the nightmare and feeling utterly miserable, and just about to call for a nurse when Collette appeared in the doorway. For a second or two I thought I was seeing things, maybe the nightmare was still going on and she would be surrounded by the dead of Bravo Company. But she was real and, unable to speak, I reached out towards her, my eyes filling with tears. She came and sat on the bed, kissed my hands and then leant over, cupped my face in her hands and smothered me with kisses. 'Lincoln, you're awake, you're going to be okay,' she said. 'I've missed you so much and when they told me you were…you were…' She couldn't finish, just buried her head in my neck and sobbed. I managed to croak her name and held her as tightly as I could with the tears rolling freely down my face and my spirits starting to soar. I had to tell myself this was real, no longer the dream it had been for so long. Collette was here in my arms and I was content to stay right there for as long as the universe lasted.

After a few minutes she sat up and we dried our tears and smiled at each other. We sat there holding hands. 'I've missed you too, Collette, much more than I can say. All through the fighting you were in my thoughts and the one thing I dreaded was not seeing you again. I don't want to think about that now. I'm here with you and that's all that counts.'

She kissed me. 'I know. I'm not letting you out of my sight again. They came to the house and told me you were back in Dakota, in a coma in the hospital. I'm afraid I didn't behave very well. I just screamed and mom had to come and finish speaking to those poor soldiers standing at the door. They managed to calm me down and mom brought me here and you were lying unconscious. That nearly set me off again but thankfully I didn't have a second bout of hysterics.' I smiled and squeezed her hand. 'I told mom I was staying here with you. The hospital has been marvellous. They've kept me fed and watered and moved the spare bed in here where I've slept. It's so good to see you awake, Lincoln, and on the mend. I can't tell you how awful it's been, not knowing where you were or even if you were still alive.'

'I can imagine,' I said. 'I'm sorry, angel, didn't mean to put you through it.'

She smiled. 'It's not your fault. And there are those who are going through much worse. The city's in mourning. Most of the dead of Bravo Company came from Dakota as you know. The school has closed for the rest of the week and a lot of other places are staying shut as well, out of respect. The exploits of Bravo Company are all over the news – how you destroyed three enemy warships and the attack on that flotilla that stopped those replacements from reaching Rochester. You're mentioned as well. Your promotion to captain and your name being sent to the president for a Star of Honor. Also, everyone is talking about your humanity, how you gave those prisoners-of-war a chance to live.'

'How does anyone know about that?' I said.

'They were recaptured on the way back to their space-station and the story got out. Mom just burst into tears. We're so proud of you, Lincoln.'

'They were the lucky ones. Those that chose to remain as prisoners were all killed.' I shook my head. 'Let's talk about you. You must be near to your final exams. How have things gone at school?'

'School has been difficult,' she said. 'It's been hard to keep my mind on my studies with this war going on and you in the thick of the fighting. Just did my best I guess. Exams start in three weeks. I'm as ready as I'll ever be. Because of all that's happened, I may end up having to repeat some of them in about three months.'

I squeezed her hand. 'I can't imagine trying to study under these circumstances. I think you've been marvellous. What about your mom and dad? How are they getting on?'

'They're fine thanks and want to come and see you when they can. Dad has been incredibly busy and is hardly ever at home. Cameron sends his regards and Gabriel is back at the university, working on some top secret project. He also has been working long hours and I don't see a lot of him these days. It's been mom and me really and she's been wonderful, a real friend and someone I have been able to turn to when I have been down. She'll be here to pick me up a bit later. You're looking tired, Lincoln. When mom gets here I'll let you get some sleep.'

I smiled and stroked her face. 'I'm fine. You've got a great family. I liked them from the moment I met them. I got to know Gabriel a lot better while we were busy with the space station. He's one of the good guys and everyone was very impressed with his knowledge of maths and computers. How are your girl friends?'

'They're all well thanks. We have been to the *Mockingbird* a few times and Jacob refuses to let me pay for anything. He's looking forward to seeing you again.'

'It would be good to see him again as well. I like the thought of sitting at the *Mockingbird* again, having a drink with you. By the way, I've decided to stay in the army after the war. I know I didn't plan on it but I've kind of fitted in pretty well and wouldn't mind spending my life as a soldier. You don't mind?'

She smiled. 'Of course not. I'm not surprised and neither will anyone else be. Gabriel wondered why you would even consider any other career after being with you on the space-station.'

'Yeah, that operation went off pretty well. And they obviously got back here. However, being in the army could mean me getting posted anywhere in the Union or the Protectorate. Are you okay with that?'

'I'll have to be,' she said. 'I want to spend my life with you, Lincoln, so we'll have to deal with any challenges that come our way. I need to stay in Dakota for the next eight to ten years, for example, to finish my degree in architecture so we'll just have to play it by ear.'

I squeezed her hand. 'I'll do my best to get stationed here for as much of that time as I can.'

She bent forward and kissed me on the forehead. 'That's settled then,' she said. 'You just make sure you get through this war alive and we'll have our future together.' I told her about the memorial service and how I'd like her and her family to be there. While we were chatting Georgia arrived.

'Hello, Lincoln,' she said, 'how are you feeling?'

'A lot better thanks, Georgia. How are you? It's good to see you again,' I said.

'I'm fine and pleased to see that you're awake and starting to feel better. We were all rather worried. I bring greetings from Stanford and Gabriel. They're both going to try and get here as soon as they can. Are you okay, Collette?'

'Never felt better but I think Lincoln's looking tired.' She turned to me. 'I think it's time you got some sleep. I'll be back later. Is there anything you need?'

I shook my head. 'Nothing right now. I look forward to seeing you later.'

She leant over and kissed me. 'Get some rest. I love you.'

'Bye, Lincoln. Hopefully I'll see you again soon,' said Georgia. 'Take care.'

After they had gone I drifted off to sleep but this time there were no nightmares, just a peaceful glide into a deep sleep, dreaming about Collette and a life together. When I awoke it was dark and a glance at the time told me I had slept for fourteen hours. I shifted around and found that the pain had eased a little. There was a note on the bedside table: *Came back but you looked so peaceful I didn't want to disturb you. Did kiss you tho - Will be back tomorrow. Love you to bits, C xxx.* I smiled and lay there, at peace for the first time in a long time. I tentatively contemplated a future in which I survived the war and embarked on my career with Collette as my life-partner, realising with a profound sense of satisfaction that I didn't want anything else, that my life would be fulfilled. My thoughts returned to the present and the war loomed large. I thought about the dead of Bravo and found some relief knowing that Cisco and Danny had survived – Cisco uninjured and Danny only slightly wounded.

I drifted off to sleep again and woke a few hours later feeling refreshed, the ward bright in the morning sun. The pain had eased further and I was able to slowly get myself into a sitting position with my legs over the side of the bed. I stood up, gripped the drip-feed frame and took a few tentative steps, wheeling the frame with me. A nurse appeared in the doorway of the ward and leant against the door frame with her arms folded watching me. 'I suppose I'd be wasting my breath telling you that you shouldn't be doing that,' she said.

I smiled and nodded. 'Just thought I'd try and get moving again,' I said.

'All very well unless you decide to faint,' she said. 'But, you seem okay to me. Would you like to go out on the terrace? I'll walk with you.' I could only move slowly but we both walked through the outer door and onto a sunlit terrace. Having the warm sun on my face was too lovely for words. 'Let's walk for a bit,' she said, 'and then you can sit in one of these chairs and enjoy the sun. I'll tell Doctor Benning you're out here.' We walked slowly around the terrace and then I was ready to sit down. I found a comfortable chair, my face turned towards the sun, eyes closed, letting the light and the warmth flood over me, through me. That's where Cisco and Danny found me. Danny's left hand was bandaged but he and Cisco were in excellent spirits. I felt better just seeing them again. They were in civilian clothes so we could forget about ranks and just be the friends we were. They told me how they had both resigned themselves to dying out there on the outskirts of the Medway system but then the Union force had arrived and turned the battle in our favour. Cisco, who had assumed command of what was left of Bravo, insisted that all living and dead be found before leaving the battle area and so I had been located, still alive, and treated aboard the USS Constitution. There was unspoken relief that we were alive and the three of us talked and laughed for the next half an hour, and at the end of it I felt emotionally and mentally very much better.

'What's happening about Makreet?' I said.

'She's been moved from the prisoner-of-war camp outside Dakota while they consider her application for Union citizenship,' said Cisco. 'She's being held at Black Tree Canyon. Caroline and I have put in statements supporting her application and we need one from you when you are ready. I've tried to get to see her but I have to wait until I get special permission. Probably think I'm going to try and elope with her.'

'Yeah, we all fell about at your reaction to seeing her for the first time. Talk about head over heels,' said Danny.

'I guess I did make it quite obvious,' said Cisco. 'I dunno, I saw her and she just blew me away. I felt like a bit of a dick in front of all of you but couldn't help myself.'

'And she feels the same way about you. She certainly seemed to be happier whenever you appeared. Good luck to both of you. I hope it works out,' I said. 'I'll get my statement off today. She was adamant that she wasn't going to return to the Imperium. If she wants to take out Union citizenship, that's fine by me.'

'Thanks, Lincoln, appreciate it,' said Cisco. 'I've no idea how it's going to work out. All I know is that I'd like to see her again. Talking of which, look who's here.'

I turned around and saw Collette walking towards us. That familiar feeling of complete happiness overwhelmed me. She leant down and kissed me. 'Lincoln, you're looking so much better and you're up and about. Hi, Cisco, Danny, really pleased to see you both. How are you guys?'

'Hi, Collette,' said Danny, 'nice to see you again too. Me, I'm just glad to be alive. Didn't think I was going to be for a while out there.'

'Hey Collette, good to see you,' said Cisco. 'Like Danny says, glad to be here. Also good to see Lincoln making such rapid progress.'

'Actually, we can thank Cisco that I'm here at all,' I said. 'He insisted that all of Bravo were found. Certainly owe you one buddy.'

'Nah, nothing more than you would have done,' said Cisco. 'Anyway, gotta go. We'll leave you and Collette in peace. Be back to see you tomorrow. Collette, we're going to be in the *Mockingbird* this evening if you want to join us.'

'That sounds good,' said Collette. 'Probably see you there.' Cisco and Danny got up, said their goodbyes and left. Collette and I stayed out on the terrace for another hour and I felt at peace with the world. We both looked at the universities offering degrees in architecture in Dakota, discussed which of these would suit her best and we familiarised ourselves with what was required for a successful application. Collette was fairly confident that her final grades would be good enough to secure a place at one of the universities, and her final hurdle would be an interview to test her suitability – this was a requirement at all the architectural schools – but she was sure that she would be able to get through that without too much difficulty. I found it really exciting going through this process with Collette. It felt as if we were adding some sort of reality to our future, that we could, provided I survived the war, have a great life together.

After she left, the nurse returned and we walked back to the ward. I was worn out and slept again for hours. The following day I was checked over by Doctor Benning and he was more than satisfied with my recovery. 'You're healing a lot faster than I thought you would,' he boomed. 'Like I said, you're one tough customer, Captain. You can come off that drip and I recommend that you do as much walking over the next few days as possible. I'll have the physio look in on you and give you the once over. She'll give you an exercise regime to help you.'

I wanted to get out of the hospital as soon as I could and spent a large part of each day walking and exercising and visiting the other wounded of Bravo Company. A number of them were not going to take any further part in the war, being too severely injured but the others were making progress and would be out within days. After a week and a half Doctor Benning pronounced me fit enough to be discharged and, accompanied by Collette, I made my way to my apartment. I didn't have to report back at Black Tree Canyon for another five days, which coincided with Collette's break, and we were going to make the most of that time. There was every chance that I would be ordered back into combat and although we didn't speak about it a lot, we both knew, having come close to dying once, that I might not make it back.

We spent a lot of the time in the apartment being as close to each other as is possible for two people in love to be, but we also spent some time clubbing, visiting places of interest, going to the beach and the cinema. I joined her family at their house and once more that was a comforting experience. They all welcomed me like some long lost son and it was good to see Gabriel again and catch up. We met up with Cisco, Danny and some of the other Bravo survivors at the *Mockingbird*, where we were joined by some of the team from the University, who had been with us on the space-station. Jacob put his great hairy arm around me. 'Lincoln,' he roared, 'fantastic to see you again. Heard all about your exploits. You and your pals are not going to pay for a thing. It's on the house for you guys.' The place was crowded as usual and the other clients cheered and clapped.

'Thanks, Jacob, good to see you too. Hope you're keeping well,' I said.

'Better by the day,' he laughed. 'We've started to get the better of those imperial bastards. You guys'll soon have them on the run. Only a matter of time. Enjoy yourselves.' And we did. The drink tasted special, reminding me of the whisky I had shared with Colonel Matfield in Adrendakon, and I felt decidedly unsteady on my feet by the end of the night.

The evening before I was due to report back we were lying on the bed, music playing softly in the background. 'Promise me you will take care, Lincoln. I can't bear to think about you drifting in space, almost dying of wounds and hypothermia. Please look after yourself.'

'I will, I promise,' I said. 'I won't do anything stupid and I'll try and keep in touch as best I can. It's not always easy. Anyway, I might be around here for a while. I'm not necessarily going to be shipped out immediately. As long as I'm here at Black Tree Canyon I'll get to see you as much as I can.'

She smiled and reached out for me. 'You make sure you do,' she said.

I reported for duty the following morning and was met by Regimental Sergeant Major Faber. He saluted smartly and smiled broadly. 'Morning, Captain,' he said, 'and welcome back to Black Tree Canyon.'

'Sergeant Major Faber,' I said, returning his salute, 'good to see you again. And congrats on the promotion. I can't imagine anybody more suited to making sure the base runs efficiently.'

'Congratulations to you too, sir. Glad to see you've done so well,' he said. 'Must have had a good instructor to start with.'

I laughed. 'Certainly did, Sergeant Major, had the best. From that first morning run to the end of off-surface training. How have things been going here?'

'Same as always sir, although the intake is now about ten times as big. The base is far busier than when you were here but I like to think we maintain the same standards.'

'I'm sure you do.' I looked around. 'Everything certainly looks shipshape.'

'If you would accompany me, sir, the colonel would be pleased to see you right away.'

'Certainly, Sergeant Major.'

We made our way to HQ and he saluted and shook my hand. 'Great to see you again, Sergeant Major, and see you again soon I hope.'

'Sir.' He saluted and marched off. When I got to the office I removed my cap, knocked and entered. Colonels Lesch and Matfield were there.

'Captain French reporting for duty, sir.'

'Captain French,' said Colonel Lesch, leaning over his desk and shaking my hand. 'Welcome back. You left here a sergeant and have come back a captain. Very well done. It's good to see you again.'

'Thank you, sir. Good to be back.'

'Morning, Captain French,' said Colonel Matfield. 'I trust you are feeling better and on the way to a full recovery?'

'Yes, sir. According to the doctors I am virtually back to normal although I have to report for a final check-up tomorrow morning', I said.

'Good, we could do with you back in the battalion,' said Colonel Matfield. 'We're here for two more days and then we're shipping out to help with the recovery of the Medway system. Bravo Company is being brought up to strength here at Black Tree Canyon and Lieutenant Cheney will be taking over from you. You will be joining Battalion HQ as part of the Strategy Group, reporting directly to me and responsible for co-ordinating and planning. We could do with your skills to ensure the battalion operates as an effective fighting force.'

'Thank you, sir,' I said.

'One more thing, Captain. We assemble in Federal Square at thirteen thirty, dress uniform, tomorrow. The rest of the regiment already know about the parade. Any questions?'

'Er...no. Better go and find my quarters and see to that uniform,' I said.

'Okay, Captain and once again, well done,' said Colonel Lesch.

'I'll walk with you,' said Colonel Matfield, 'give you the rundown on your new responsibilities.' We started walking towards the officers' quarters. 'Basically I want you to have operational charge of the company commanders. An overall company commander if you like. I want you to make sure that they are doing their thing to the best of their ability at all times. Some of the older ones might take exception but I'm sure you'll handle that. In any case they'll hear it from me by tomorrow.

'One last thing. I need your full report, from the destruction of the *Grey Wolf* to the attack on the flotilla. On my desk tomorrow morning would be good.'

'Yes, sir.'

I found my room, where all my gear had been hung, packed and laid out appropriately. There was a desk with a computer and I got down to producing the report. It took about two hours to complete and after checking it carefully I forwarded it to the colonel. I then called Collette.

'Lincoln, I've been thinking about you all day and wondering what you've been up to. Are you calling from the base?'

'Yes, I'm at Black Tree Canyon. I'm on duty until six but am free until the memorial service tomorrow afternoon so wondered whether you fancied going out for dinner.'

'Of course I would but I'd prefer to go for a drink and then something to eat at your place. I'd like to cook you a meal.'

'That sounds even better,' I said. 'I'll come by your place around six thirty and pick you up.'

'Can't wait. See you then.'

We spent a great evening together. After about an hour in a pub near her house, very different to the *Mockingbird*, much more traditional, where once again the drinks were on the house, we made our way to the apartment where Collette put together a great meal of fillet steak, chips and salad, washed down with cold beer. Towards the end of the evening we were lying together on the bed. 'I don't want you to go,' I said.

'Just as well,' said Collette. 'I told my parents I wouldn't be back until tomorrow. I have my toothbrush and change of clothes in my bag and the school is closed tomorrow because of the memorial service.'

'That sounds good. My hospital appointment is at eleven thirty. We can have a lie-in.'

Collette laughed. 'Knowing us, we're going to need one.' And we did.

I was given the all-clear by Doctor Benning and I bade farewell to the staff at the hospital as well as the remaining members of Bravo who were still too ill to be released. Collette was waiting for me when I returned to the apartment. She had changed into a shimmering dark blue dress for the service and my heart nearly stopped at the sight of her. She looked as elegant and beautiful as I'd ever seen her, those gorgeous, sparkling eyes smiling at me. 'You look out of this world, Collette,' I said. 'You are indescribably beautiful and I am truly, madly, deeply in love with you.'

She put her arms around me and kissed me. 'I'm in love with you too, Captain French. Truly, madly, deeply. Have been since I met you and always will be.'

'You've no idea how good that makes me feel,' I said. 'I'd better go and get changed.'

I put on my dress uniform; cap, gold buttons and gold braid, highly polished shoes and belt, and we made our way to Federal square in the centre of the city, where we met Collette's family and Rebecca, Gabriel's girlfriend. Collette joined them as they took their seats and I went off to join the troops. Colonel Matfield came straight to the point. 'What did the doctor say, Captain?'

'I'm fully fit and ready for duty, Colonel,' I said. 'I have a dose of painkillers just in case but don't think I'll be needing them.'

'Excellent news,' he said. 'Captain French, meet Lieutenant Cheney, the new CO Bravo.'

We shook hands. 'Pleased to meet you, Captain, and honoured to make your acquaintance.'

'Thank you, Lieutenant. Welcome to the regiment and to our battalion. I wish you well as CO Bravo.' We took our seats at the head of the regiment and after about ten minutes President Joyce and General Bullen, who by now had been promoted to a seven star general and was in overall charge of the Union armies, appeared together on the dais in the middle of the square. They were accompanied by the provincial governor and the mayor of Dakota, who spoke first.

'President Joyce, General Bullen, Governor Kouvaras, members of the armed forces, ladies and gentlemen. It is a great honour for me to welcome you all here today although the occasion is one of profound sadness. We are here to pay our respects to the dead of the Zardogan system and beyond, and I would ask all of you who are able to do so, to stand and join me in a two minute silence for those who have perished in this conflict.' I stood with my head bowed and thought of the dead of Bravo company, not only those who died in the attack on the flotilla but also of those who had died before that, in Adrendakon and in the attack on the space-station. We had sustained heavy losses in this war and it was still far from over. 'Profound sadness' exactly described my feelings as the tears rolled down my face and dropped silently to the ground.

'Thank you,' said the mayor at the end of the two minutes. 'Please be seated as I invite President Joyce to address you.' He turned towards her. 'President Joyce.'

She stood there and seemed overwhelmed for a second or two. She looked tired and careworn, and it was evident that the events of these past months had taken their toll. But she remained popular with the general public and had announced her intention to stand for a second ten year term in the presidential election scheduled for four months hence. She had refused to abandon her strong liberal beliefs, that human rights are universal and eternal, even though the opposition had urged her to do so, citing the war as an excuse for the suspension of some civil liberties. She had adamantly refused to do so, saying that civil liberties could not be protected by suspending them, and had enhanced her standing among the general populace as a result. Strict instructions regarding the treatment of prisoners of war and the high standards of conduct expected of the Union armed forces had been issued from the Office of the Presidency early on in the war and repeated recently, and some Union troops who had flouted the rules had been severely punished. I was pleased that she had been in office at the outbreak of hostilities.

She spoke clearly and concisely. 'Thank you, Mayor Zelaya. I am honoured to be here in Dakota, capital of the Zardogan system, a city and system whose sons and daughters have played such a crucial role in the present conflict. It is with great pride, and immense sadness, that I stand here in remembrance of those who have given their lives for the Union and our friends in the Protectorate, and I offer my condolences to all those who have suffered personal loss. I am strengthened, however, in the knowledge that their lives were not given in vain. We in the Interplanetary Union have much to protect. Over thousands of years we have created a society based on tolerance and mutual respect, a society based on an unshakeable belief in the universality of human rights and the belief that any society so constituted is worth preserving. This belief is underlined by the fact that we have not had to resort to conscription. Our armed forces, now greatly augmented, are made up solely of volunteers, with no shortage of those coming forward all the time, and I am immeasurably proud of the way you have conducted themselves during this conflict. With very few exceptions you and your colleagues have maintained the high standards upon which our society is based. That we will be victorious I have no doubt and when that time comes let us not forget who we are or what we stand for. Let us ensure, through magnanimity in victory, that those who have perished have not done so in vain, and that our Union continues to be a shining beacon throughout the galaxy. Thank you.'

Those of us receiving awards and stars then assembled and we were called forward one at a time to receive them from the president. The survivors of Bravo went up first and I received the Star of Honor, and then the Gallantry Star on behalf of the company. I saluted and shook hands with both the president and General Bullen, who spoke to me briefly. 'Congratulations, Captain French. You can be proud of your achievements and I am pleased to see that you are on the mend.'

'Thank you, General,' I said. I saluted, left the dais and resumed my seat. When it was all over I said goodbye to Collette's family and then spent time, with Collette, meeting the families of those who had died, offering my condolences and giving support where I could. Collette was magnificent and those we met warmed to her immediately. She turned out to be one of those rare people who offered genuine compassion and comfort, and those on the receiving end took her to their hearts. I was deeply impressed by the way she handled the whole situation. At the end of it all we made our way to a coffee bar where we sank down, mentally and physically drained. Various people came up to me and shook my hand, expressing their appreciation for the job we were doing, all hoping I would see the war out safely.

'You were fantastic with those people,' I said to Collette. 'A natural when it comes to comforting the afflicted.'

'I found it really upsetting,' she said, 'but realised it wouldn't do for me to break down. Those poor families. I can't begin to imagine what they're going through. I don't know what I'd do if anything happened to you, Lincoln. I don't think I'd cope.'

'Let's not think about that now. We're living through difficult times and we have to take each day as it comes. I'm unbelievably happy just thinking about the time we've had together so far and I live in hope that we'll be able to spend our lives together.'

'Me too,' she said. She leant over and kissed me. 'I love you Lincoln and will be forever thankful that we ran into each other on that shuttle.'

After spending the evening with Collette and her family the time came, once again, for us to say goodbye. It seemed to get harder each time and I felt as if I was being wrenched apart when I finally left her and made my way back to Black Tree Canyon. I knew I was heading back into danger and dreaded the thought that I may never see Collette again. It was all very well talking about taking each day as it came, but being apart from Collette under these circumstances wasn't easy at all.

Chapter 10

We shipped out the following day and headed straight for the Medway system. I learnt that the imperial space-station we had attacked had been occupied by Union forces. It was being updated and modernised, and was going to be a permanent part of the system as a Union space-naval base, the *USS Bravo*.

'Hey, how cool is that,' said Danny. 'We have a naval base named after us. Mind you, whenever I think about the place I can't help but remember that orgy we interrupted.' We burst out laughing.

'Yeah, wish I'd seen that,' said Cisco, 'or maybe best I didn't, given that Makreet was involved.'

'I don't think she had much choice at the time,' I said. 'Her circumstances have sure changed for the better since then. I understand her application for citizenship is going through the system at the moment.'

'Yes,' said Cisco, 'I finally got to see her a couple of days ago. I think they got sick of me pestering them. Anyhow, they've told her it'll take a few months. They've had so many prisoners of war applying for citizenship that the process is taking a bit longer than was initially thought.'

'That's great,' said Danny. 'What happens while she's applying? Do they release her?'

'Apparently,' said Cisco, 'although she's been told she will be required to work for the Department of Defence directly supporting the war effort for at least a year. She's fine with that.'

'Fair enough I guess,' I said, 'and a year is not very long. Does she have any idea what she wants to do after that?'

'Not really except that she wants to educate herself. She tells me that she only received a very basic education where she came from. She reckons she can't be a proper citizen without being fully educated so she's going back to school as soon as she can.'

'Good for her,' said Danny. 'I hope it all works out for her and for the two of you.'

'Yeah, me too,' I said. 'Sounds like she's got her head screwed on the right way.'

'Thanks, guys,' said Cisco. 'In the meantime, we're heading for some fun again.'

We landed on the planet Rochester and were immediately involved in the fighting. The battalion formed part of an offensive to clear the imperial forces across a wide front around the city of Dickens and three companies, Bravo, Easy and Foxtrot, were given the task of capturing the strategically important small town of Eynesford. I spoke to the three company commanders before the attack. 'It's vital we take this place if this offensive is to succeed,' I said. 'We're going to use the three companies in a pincer movement so once the attack starts you must keep moving forward until the town is taken, understood?' They all nodded.

'The enemy knows that the loss of Eynesford means they have little chance of holding their line so resistance will be stiff but I want this attack to succeed. Stick to the battle plan we have worked on and you'll be okay. Good luck. Listen out for the signal to start the attack.'

I went back to my position and gave the signal for the attack to start. I was also in touch with the other company commanders, making sure that the whole battalion was engaging as planned. I turned back to the attack on Eynesford and noted that the three companies seemed to be moving forward. Surprisingly, there wasn't any sign of any resistance from the enemy. As the three companies moved forward Eynesford seemed eerily quiet. I had expected us to meet some sort of resistance by now and became alarmed. I wondered whether we had walked into a trap and was answered within the next second as the place exploded with the sound of heavy artillery and armour. This was accompanied by small arms fire and it became clear in a split second that we had badly under estimated the enemy's determination to hold onto this place. The three advancing companies of infantry were facing a concentration of armour and artillery and were in danger of being wiped out.

'Bravo, Easy, Foxtrot, get out of there NOW,' I shouted. 'Get back, get back. There's no way we can take the town on our own.' I watched as our troops started running back the way they'd come, with explosions all around them. We had been well and truly caught with our pants down and the dead and injured were starting to litter the fields around the town. And then I watched in horror as my best friend Cisco died there on that battlefield. He and two others had stopped and turned around to give covering fire. They had an anti-armour weapon and were firing towards the town when an armoured vehicle raced towards them and fired at point blank range. The explosion blew all three of them up into the air and Cisco landed some distance away, his head missing and his arms and legs at crazy angles to what was left of his body. I couldn't believe what I was seeing and screamed 'Nooooo, nooooo, not Cisco, please, not Cisco.' Colonel Matfield, who had come up beside me grabbed me and held me close to him while continuing to give orders to the retreating troops who were now piling into their foxholes and turning their anti- armour weapons towards the advancing enemy.

'Give them everything we've got,' he said. 'Keep firing until we stop them. I'm going to get air support.' He held me by the arms and forced me back away from the fighting. Eventually he sat me down against a tree. 'Don't move, Lincoln. You sit there. You're in no fit state to do anything at the moment. You hear me? Don't move.' I nodded dumbly, tears running down my face, unable to speak or think straight. All I could see, over and over, was Cisco, headless, hurtling through the air and landing in a crumpled heap. In the background I heard Colonel Matfield calling for air support, giving our position and our situation. He came back to me, knelt down and held me by the shoulders. His face appeared blurred through my tears which just kept flowing. 'Listen Lincoln, stay here until I get back, you hear? Don't move until I return. You hear me?' Again I nodded. He patted me on the shoulder and was gone, back towards the fighting which sounded like it was reaching some kind of crescendo. Our guys had obviously got themselves organised and were fighting back, using what we had, which included anti-armour weapons and rocket propelled grenades.

I dried my eyes and stood up, forcing myself to think straight. I shook my head to clear it and put my helmet back on. There's no way, I told myself, that Cisco would want to see me moping behind the lines while the rest of the regiment was engaged in a life or death struggle. There'd be plenty of time for tears later and I forced myself to head back to my position on the ridge where the fighting was taking place. Colonel Matfield saw me and started to shout something but I waved him down and joined the fight. I saw that we had knocked out quite a few of their armoured vehicles but our position was still precarious. They had concentrated a huge amount of firepower in this place, determined to stop us from taking the town. The only way we were going to succeed was with the help of air power and that meant doing something we had been trying to avoid – blowing the town and its population to pieces.

I ran from foxhole to foxhole, helping the troops and firing at the enemy whenever possible. I landed in a foxhole next to Danny and we blasted away at anything that moved in front of us. 'Jeez, Lincoln, this is some fucking fight,' he shouted. 'Those guns firing from inside the town need to be silenced somehow.'

I nodded. 'Colonel Matfield has called up air support. I just hope they get here before it's too late.' He obviously didn't know about Cisco and I didn't enlighten him. He needed all his powers of concentration at that moment.

The fighting kept me from thinking about Cisco too much. We had taken a fair number of casualties and were being subject to increasingly accurate artillery fire when the navy arrived in the form of five attack shuttles. They proceeded to take the enemy apart in spectacular fashion but their attack left Eynesford a shattered, burning wreck. The civilians, citizens of the Protectorate, suffered grievous losses and even though I was grieving for Cisco, I felt sorry for the survivors and what they were going through.

After the imperial forces had surrendered, Colonel Matfield came up to me. 'You okay, Captain?'

'Yes, sir,' I said. 'Sorry I lost it for a while back there but...'

'No need to apologise, Captain. It's perfectly understandable. I'm just glad to see you're back on an even keel. I know Gonzales was a good friend of yours and I know how hard this is for you. If you want some time off...'

'No thank you, sir,' I said. 'I'd rather carry on as normal and keep busy. I would like a few moments, though, to say goodbye if you don't mind.'

'No problem,' he said. 'Take the time you need. The dead are being bagged up and laid out over there. Report back to me when you're ready.'

I was making my way to where the body bags had been laid out ready for transfer to an ambulance shuttle when Danny came running over. 'Is it true...?' he began.

I nodded and pointed to the body bag containing Cisco's name, lying neatly next to the others, at the end of the line. I removed my helmet, bowed my head and stood there, while my tears flowed uncontrollably, Danny quiet next to me. After what seemed like an eternity the tears stopped and I said a quiet goodbye to the friend and comrade I had known all my life and whose passing drove a black hole right through me. I was going to miss him terribly. (I still do, by the way, all these years later. Not many days go by without me thinking about him, the times we had together and what might have been had he lived).

'I only just heard,' said Danny. 'I'm completely devastated and I can't imagine how you're feeling, Lincoln. I'm so sorry.' He shook his head. 'And Makreet…'

'Thanks, Danny. Yeah, I'll let Makreet know. I reckon she's going to be wiped out by this.' I looked around. 'We need to carry on as normal. It's what Cisco would have wanted.'

That evening, after I had completed all my duties, I sent a message to Collette, giving her the news. I also wrote to the orphanage and finally sent a letter of condolence to Makreet.

Cisco and the rest of the dead were buried with full military honours in the town cemetery at Eynesford and Danny and I spent some time standing at his grave after the others had left. We both stood in silence, wrapped up in our own thoughts. After about ten minutes I patted Danny on the shoulder. 'Time to go, Danny. We can't stay here forever.'

'Yeah, I guess,' he said. 'Won't forget this for a while though.'

'Me neither,' I said. 'I'm going to miss him more than I can say but he wouldn't want us to stand here moping. Let's get going.'

The regiment moved on to other offensives. We fought all over Rochester and the other inhabited planet in the system, Chatham, and my last battle occurred right at the end of the Medway campaign when the regiment was required to capture another small town as part of the advance towards the capital. Four companies were chosen for the operation and I briefed the company commanders beforehand.

'Okay people let's get this done. We need to boot the enemy out of this place. It seems that this group of desperados has decided to make a last stand here. We've tried talking to them, telling them that it's basically all over for the Imperium here on Chatham but they refuse to listen. They want to go out in some blaze of glory so we're going to oblige them. I want two companies to attack from here while the other two come in from this direction. That'll force them to fight on two fronts and should make it easier for us. Listen out for the signal to start the attack.'

I took up my position and gave the signal for the attack to start. The companies started moving forward and were immediately met by fierce small arms resistance. Those defenders meant business and suddenly Bravo Company stopped, leaving themselves very exposed. 'Lieutenant Cheney, what's happening? Your company is being exposed to enemy fire. Keep moving forward.' I got no answer and immediately became alarmed. I moved to higher ground and surveyed the battle scene through the viewfinder. The other three companies were making good progress even though the enemy were putting up a fight, but Bravo had come to a stop and Lieutenant Cheney was crouching behind a low wall. He didn't appear injured so I called him again. 'Lieutenant Cheey, why aren't you moving forward? You cannot stay there, you'll be wiped out.'

This time he answered but it was jumbled. 'I can't…Christ, all this shooting…we're all…going to be killed.'

'Lieutenant Cheney, you have to move forward. Foxtrot will be isolated in the town and Bravo will be shot to pieces if you stay where you are.'

Danny spoke to me, sounding desperate. 'Captain, Lieutenant Cheney has lost it. He won't move and we can't stay here.'

Just then Colonel Matfield came through. 'Captain French, what the hell is happening? Foxtrot aren't getting any help from Bravo and can't make any headway.'

'I'm going to take over from Lieutenant Cheney,' I said. 'He won't go forward for some reason.'

'Okay. I'll take over the co-ordination. Get that company moving.'

I raced to where Lieutenant Cheney was crouching behind the wall. The rest of the company had taken what shelter they could although quite a few lay dead or wounded out on the field. 'Listen, Cheney,' I shouted,

'I'm taking over. You're no longer in command.' I took his rifle from him and got two troopers to take him back towards HQ. 'Okay, Bravo, let's move out. We've got some ground to make up. GO, GO.' I spoke to Lieutenant Bukayo, the CO Foxtrot and told her we were back on track. Leading from the front, I took the company towards the objective and after three hours of fierce fighting we forced the defenders to surrender. The town was in our hands and we set about tending to the dead and wounded. Colonel Matfield commandeered an office in the town hall for his HQ and asked me to join him there.

'Well done once again, Captain French. You sure rescued the situation there this morning. I've had word from army HQ. We have pushed forward across a wide front and the enemy is definitely on the run here on Chatham. I don't think it'll be too long before we kick them out of this system completely.'

'Thank you, sir. That's good news. I'd like to think that this incursion into the Union is their first and last. By the way, Colonel, what's the news about Lieutenant Cheney?'

'I don't know yet but I've asked the MPs to bring him here as I'd like to have a word with him, assess the situation.'

A few minutes later there was a knock on the door and two military police officers brought Lieutenant Cheney into the room. He looked a mess and had clearly been crying. His hands were shaking and he couldn't stand still. The colonel was surprisingly gentle with him. He walked over and took him by the arm. 'Come and sit down, Lieutenant. You don't look well.'

I handed Cheney a cup of water. He grasped the cup like a dying man and clung onto my arm with his other hand. 'I'm…sorry…so…sorry…don't know…what… just…move… couldn't…move…never happened before… so sorry…'

'Take it easy,' said Colonel Matfield. 'It could happen to any of us at any time. I'm aware of your record, Lieutenant, and it's a good one. You've been an outstanding soldier, seen your fair share of action and been cited for bravery.' He patted Lieutenant Cheney on the shoulder. 'I've arranged for you to be flown back to the hospital in Dakota where you'll receive the best treatment available. I've no doubt you'll be as right as rain in no time. You okay with that?'

He sat there with his head bowed and nodded. 'Thank…thank you, Colonel…and I…I…just want to thank you, Captain…for…for what you did out there…I…I…'

'That's okay,' I said. 'You just go and get yourself better.'

He nodded again and then the two police officers led him out of the room. It was clear he would be out of action for a while. 'Poor bastard,' said the colonel. 'Hope they can do something for him. I was impressed with Lieutenant Bukayo. She did a great job out there, kept a clear head while Bravo sorted themselves out.'

After three months the Medway system was back in Union hands, the Imperium having been completely defeated there. The system, however, had suffered damage on a monumental scale, with most major cities

306

very badly damaged and many residential and industrial areas utterly destroyed but that's what it took to get the Imperium out of there. This had been their only foray into the Union itself and they had been determined to make a success of it. To get them out of there had taken a massive effort and the civilian population had paid a heavy price. I looked at the devastation and realised, with a shudder, that this was what Dakota would have looked like if the Zardogan system had been attacked. I tried to imagine Collette caught up in something like this but it was too dreadful to contemplate.

Once again the battalion's losses had been heavy but I was pleased that Danny had come through unscathed. Both of us had been cited for bravery and decorated accordingly. Colonel Matfield was also decorated for bravery and promoted to brigadier, now on the staff of the division, while I was promoted to major, second-in-command of the battalion under Colonel Parton. Danny, too, became an officer. At the end of the campaign he was required to transfer to 15th Army Headquarters, given the rank of captain and told to join a team, military and civilian, working on AIUs.

'Congrats, Danny,' I said. 'The powers that be obviously are impressed with your maths and computer science skills. AI troops are the future and you're going to be right there. I'm going to miss you when you go. Let's stay in touch.'

'I'm going to miss you and of course I'll stay in touch. After all, I'll be at Regimental HQ so should be able to see what you are up to. In the meantime, let's try and stay in one piece until this is all over.'

The regiment was taken out of the front line at the end of that campaign for a week's downtime. We were billeted in a small seaside village on Chatham. Except for a brief occupation by the imperial army, the place had been largely untouched by the war, and I found myself sitting at a pavement café with Danny, the warm sunlight on our faces, pizza and cold beer on the table in front of us, after having gone for a swim in the sea. We sat in silence, taking in the view and enjoying the peace and quiet. It was a relief to be out of danger and among friendly people who were pleased to see us.

'Jesus, that was some three months,' said Danny after a while, munching on pizza. 'Don't know if I'm in a hurry to go through that again.'

'Me neither,' I said. 'Mind you, when you see what these civilians have gone through…'

'Yeah, I know,' he said. 'Months of living under the Imperium and then all this devastation. I thought Adrendakon was bad but this is so much worse.'

'I hear the marines and the navy have mounted a full scale attack against the Imperium in the Lindfield system,' I said. 'Good luck to them and rather them than me right now.'

My band buzzed and I got a message from Collette. She expressed her shock and deep sadness at the news about Cisco and hoped I was coping. She had passed all her final exams and was now out of school, had got my birthday greetings and had gone out with a couple of friends for a quiet drink. Although she had gone to Black Tree Canyon to volunteer for the army they couldn't accept her as there was now a waiting list and they were going to get back to her within the next six months. As a contribution to the war effort, she was doing voluntary work at the military hospital in Dakota.

'Nice one,' said Danny. 'Things have changed a bit since we joined. They couldn't get you into the camp fast enough then. Six months waiting list? Let's hope it's over before that.'

'Yeah I hope so,' I said. 'Joining the army now would just disrupt her life for very little reason. The end is in sight at last. The news from the Protectorate is mostly positive and we've now kicked them out of Medway. The only thing the government has to decide is whether we take the war into the Imperium or stop at the border. The navy has apparently given their capital city a real pasting and done some lasting damage to several of their border systems recently so we may stop short of actually going into their territory.'

'We want to make sure that the Imperium are in no position to start anything like this again,' said Danny. 'I reckon we should at least occupy their capital system for a while and teach them how to run their part of the galaxy.'

'That would be good,' I said, 'except that it's very difficult to impose a system on top of an existing culture. However, we should ensure that they stay militarily weak until they figure out some form of democratic system for themselves. Either way the Union military is going to be kept busy for a long time after this war is over.' I tipped back my head and emptied the bottle of beer, signalling to the waiter for another

The week passed all too quickly. I spent a lot of it swimming in the sea and lying in the sun and returned to duty looking tanned and feeling relaxed and ready for whatever was in store. Danny and I said our goodbyes as he went off to Regimental HQ and I returned to duty with the battalion. I was sitting at my desk at HQ when Colonel Parton walked in. I had only met him briefly before we went on leave but knew he had transferred in from the 420th Regiment, also a part of the 15th Army and that he had done his fair share of fighting. Like Colonel Matfield he was no desk officer and wasn't scared to get into the thick of things if need be. I stood up and we shook hands.

'Pleased to meet you, Major French, and glad to be working with you,' he said. 'Brigadier Matfield has only good things to say about you.'

'Thank you, Colonel,' I said, 'and welcome to the battalion.'

'I heard about Lieutenant Cheney,' he said. 'Any news on what's happened to him?'

'Last I heard he had been transferred to some rehabilitation hospital where he was making good progress. I don't know whether he'll be back or not.'

He shook his head. 'I knew him before this happened. He was a good soldier and fearless in combat. Just goes to show…'

I nodded. 'As Brigadier Matfield told him, it could happen to any of us. I sometimes wonder how I came through some of the action I've been in.'

'Yeah, I know what you mean. And talking of which, we're off to the Protectorate, to the Maharashtra system to be exact. The navy and the marines are pushing the Imperium out of the place as we speak and we're to take over garrison duty in the capital, Mumbai. I protested, saying I'd rather the battalion was involved in the fighting but garrison duty it is. We ship out at ten hundred tomorrow. Can you ensure everything and everyone is shipshape and ready to go?'

'Yes, sir,' I said. 'I'll report back to you by twenty hundred today.'

'Okay, until then.'

I was glad to be busy again. Missing Cisco and being away from Collette was beginning to get to me and all I had thought about for the previous couple of days was being with her. There was a lot of work to be done getting the battalion ready to move out the following morning and it took my mind off Collette and Cisco. I was also quite happy doing this work. I hadn't said as much to the colonel, but garrison duty sounded fine to me. I wasn't in any hurry to get back to the front. I'd taken part in enough killing and wounding to last me ten lifetimes and was happy to garrison a city, which would include helping the civilians get their lives back to normal. I even toyed with the idea of asking for a transfer to the medical corps but felt a strong sense of loyalty to the battalion and the regiment.

We shipped out on schedule the following morning and arrived in a city that had been blown to pieces. The damage was unimaginable and we were put to work helping the population, who were beginning to get their city back on its feet and restore some kind of normality. I enjoyed the work, which was a mixture of administrative tasks and physical labour and which I found to be so much more positive and constructive than fighting. I got to know many of the local population and was amazed at their resilience and optimism about their future. They had suffered badly under imperial occupation and were unbelievably pleased to have been liberated. They also appreciated the work we were doing and the help they were receiving from us, and the time I spent there was uplifting and positive. After about a month I was called into the office by Colonel Parton.

'Word has just come through from HQ,' he said. 'The Imperium has surrendered unconditionally. Their armies have thrown down their weapons and they're pulling what's left of their armed forces out of the Protectorate and limping home. When they get there they're going to find many of their systems in ruins, destroyed by our navy. Apparently the place is a real mess. The political leadership has been thrown out – and culled as usual. The Supreme Leader is among the assassinated and is not being replaced for the present. A provisional military government has taken over and confirmed the surrender. That's all I've got for now. We're to carry on here as normal.'

More news came through all the time. It was true that the leadership had been culled and replaced by a military government. The difference this time, though, was that for the first time in Imperium history they were talking about installing some kind of democratically elected government when circumstances permitted. It was becoming clear that the military had no desire to continue in government a minute longer than was necessary. They were appealing to the Union for help and President Joyce was going to organise a joint conference with the new Imperial leadership. She had also agreed that the Union armed forces could be used in those parts of the Imperium which were so chaotic that some kind of temporary policing was necessary until order and imperial authority could be restored. The populace of the Imperium were up in arms about the military adventure they had been fooled into supporting. It was evident all that talk about the Protectorate wanting to rejoin the Imperium had been a lie and millions of imperial citizens had been killed and injured for nothing. There was a demand, swelling to a clamour, all over the Imperium for a change to a democratic constitution and the military knew they could no longer run things as they had in the past. The head of the armed forces dropped the title of 'Supreme Leader' for the more moderate 'Acting President', promising to make way for civilian rule as soon as a new constitution was in place and they were ready for democratic elections. This had never been tried before so there were quite a few hurdles to negotiate first.

We were ecstatic about the end of the war and I couldn't wait to get back to Black Tree Canyon. However, one evening I was called into Colonel Parton's office. 'You've obviously made some impression on the powers that be,' he said. 'You are required to report to the Office of the President in Starlight.' He smiled. 'Sounds ominous, Lincoln. I wish you luck.'

It sounded ominous alright. This was obviously no pleasure trip and I had a feeling in the pit of my stomach I wouldn't be going home any time soon.

I was transported to a frigate, the *USS Blue Lightning*, which then took me, via numerous space jumps, to the New Washington system and the city of Starlight, the capital of the Union and the seat of the Presidency. We flew over the place before landing at The Residency, the place where the president lived and worked, and which was situated in a part of the city known as Government Square, modelled on classical lines. All the buildings, housing government departments as well as the Union Congress and the Supreme Court, were white painted, with columns and domes, and the streets were wide boulevards, planted with colourful trees and plants. The area was surrounded by a beautifully laid out park, ten kilometres wide, a mixture of wild woodland, lawns and lakes, with flocks of birds and open to the public. I was familiar with all of it, having visited the virtual model all through my school life, but being here for real took my breath away. The rest of the city, on the other side of the park, was a modern, gleaming mixture of residential and commercial areas, mostly there to support Government Square. By any reckoning, it was the most beautiful city in the Union.

The Residency itself was vast, also domed and columned, and after walking along endless spotlessly shining corridors I was ushered into the president's office by a flunky in a bow tie and white gloves. President Joyce and a man in the uniform of the Imperium, epaulettes full of stars, were standing waiting for me. He was obviously a high ranking officer and I felt that this was going to be more than just a casual meeting. I came to attention and was greeted by the president.

'Major French, welcome to the Residency. Allow me to introduce Space Marshall Bharmaga, the acting president of the Imperium and the person tasked with changing their political system to something more akin to democracy. Space Marshall Bharmaga, please meet Major French.'

He was a tall, lean, tough looking character with piercing eyes and a lined face, the kind of person you wouldn't ordinarily mess with. He stepped forward, shook my hand and spoke perfect Galactic. 'Pleased to meet you, Major. Your reputation precedes you and I offer my congratulations on your excellent military record.' I was taken aback and didn't quite know what to say.

'Er...thank you...er...Marshall.'

'Let's get started, gentlemen,' said the president, 'we have much to discuss.' She led us to a conference room next to her office and we seated ourselves at the table where a map of the Imperium was hovering. The president spoke directly to me. 'I apologise for dragging you halfway across the galaxy without much prior notice but there is an urgent matter I want to talk to you about.

'Firstly, I would like to congratulate you on your war record, Major French, and I am very pleased that you have decided to make a career in the army. Your service has been exemplary and I would like you to take command of the Union garrison in Zangsh, the imperial capital. First of all, though, I want you to help the space marshall with a problem he has on his hands at the moment.' She turned to the space marshall. 'Marshall Bharmaga, can you please enlighten our guest.'

'Certainly,' he said and turned towards me. 'As you are no doubt aware, the Imperium is in something of a mess at the moment. We are working hard to restore it to a fully functioning state, as well as changing the political system, but many parts of the Imperium have become lawless. They remain outside the government's control and we are indebted to the Union for their help as we grapple with these problems. Slowly but surely, with the help of the Union armed forces, we are restoring order but there is one area that has become particularly troublesome. A renegade general has taken advantage of our present state of affairs and, with a band of two to three thousand followers, all of whom are trained soldiers, has been terrorising the inhabitants of a number of cities in the Imperium. He has refused to listen to reason and they are now calling themselves the Imperial Wolves. They have ships and are well armed, and frankly, we are unable at present to stop their murderous activities. They are acting like old fashioned pirates and racketeers, attacking cities within the Imperium that don't pay for protection. The forces at our disposal within the Imperium are very busy dealing with everyday lawlessness and I have asked President Joyce for assistance to deal with this specific problem. I have indicated that I would like a combined force of Union and imperial troops to go after the renegade and bring him to justice and I would like that force to be led by a competent Union officer.'

'Your name has been put forward,' said President Joyce, 'and your record speaks for itself. I would like to know if you are prepared to take on these two tasks.'

I thought fast. I could decline and leave it to someone else but somehow that didn't seem the right thing to do at the time. The president obviously thought I was the one for this job and under the circumstances I found it impossible to refuse. It didn't take more than a second or two before I answered her.

'I'm happy to take on both responsibilities, Madam President,' I said.

'Thank you, Major,' she said. 'I knew I could count on you. First of all you are to hold the rank of colonel with immediate effect, and you will take up your post as commander of the garrison a month after the operation against the renegade has been successfully concluded. You will have a warship, the *USS Theseus*, commanded by Captain Ghali, and a battalion of our troops, at your disposal. A further thousand troops from the armed forces of the Imperium with their own commanding officer will be joining you, but you will be in overall command. You will report to your old CO, Major-General Matfield – yes, he too has had a well-deserved promotion – who will be here later and with whom you can discuss the finer details of the operation.' She looked at me intently. 'I want this man caught and brought before a criminal court, Colonel. Please remember, at all times, who we are and what we stand for. I do not want any unnecessary extra-judicial execution of this renegade or any of his followers. If any of them are killed I want to be able to say with complete honesty we did everything in our power to bring them to justice and that any killing could not be helped. Do I make myself clear, Colonel French?'

'Perfectly clear, Madam President. I happen to hold those views myself. I do not believe in the death penalty – judicial, extra-judicial or otherwise,' I said.

She nodded and smiled. 'I'm glad to hear it, Colonel. Good luck with the mission. You and I will be speaking to each other again soon I have no doubt. Please liaise with General Matfield who will be contacting you when he gets here.'

The space marshal came forward and shook my hand. 'Thank you, Colonel. You will be working with Commandant Shraska and I assure you that all the imperial troops will be among those seeking change in the Imperium. You will not have to work with any of the old guard. Good luck.'

I went and stood outside for a while, thinking about the tasks I had taken on. I had to get my head around the fact that I would be operating with imperial troops but I thought about Makreet and those on the space station and reckoned it wouldn't be too bad, especially if they were modernisers, opposed to the old regime and their way of doing things. As for the garrison command, well, that could wait until the hunt for Hradoshk was over. One thing for certain – I needed to speak to Collette urgently.

A message came through from General Matfield, asking me to meet him at the Starlight military base that evening. I spent the rest of the day having a look at the city. It was a truly wondrous place, designed around wide streets and boulevards, green parks and large pedestrian squares, with architecturally perfect buildings, beautiful fountains and stunning riverside areas. The place was immaculate and made Dakota look shabby. It probably made every other place in the Union look shabby, I thought to myself.

I sat and had lunch at a riverside restaurant and thought about Collette and how it was going to be a while longer until we could be together. Maybe she could spend some time with me in Zangsh. I sent her a message telling her, without going into detail, that I was to carry out a mission for the president and how much I loved her and missed her. I couldn't wait to see her again and hoped it wouldn't be too long before I was back in Dakota, and we could get on with our future together.

I got a heart-warming message back from her, telling me how proud she was that I had been specially chosen by the president and for me to take care of myself. She was still doing voluntary work at the hospital but had decided against deferring her studies and would be heading for university in two months' time to start her degree in architecture. Most important of all she loved me more than ever and couldn't wait until I was back in Dakota, safe and sound. That made me feel a whole heap better and I felt more positive about taking on this mission and seeing it through to a successful conclusion.

General Matfield and I were glad to see each other again and I congratulated him on his promotion. He was looking a lot better and eager to get on with planning how to hunt down and capture this rebel general. We were in a conference room at the Starlight military base and a map of the Protectorate and the Imperium was hovering in one corner. We both walked up to it and General Matfield brought me up to date regarding our quarry.

'The guy's name is Hradoshk and he was a general in the imperial army during the war. He is a hard case and those areas of the Protectorate that came under his command suffered more than most. Seems he has between two and three thousand followers with him, a number of ships, and they are all well-armed and have started causing havoc in this area here. He hasn't actually attacked any Union forces or threatened any Union territory – probably knows he wouldn't get very far. Instead, he has ravaged a number of imperial cities who have refused to go along with him. Seems like he has become nothing more than the leader of a large criminal gang, taking advantage of the chaos within the Imperium. Thousands have been rendered homeless, killed or injured and he needs to be stopped before he causes any further damage.' He turned and pointed to the map.

'This area, known as the Plains of Yandanarra or Sea of Hope, depending where you come from, has not been properly mapped or explored. There are some settlements we know of and the Union started some exploratory missions into the area before the war but it is largely unchartered and it officially doesn't belong to anybody at the moment. We suspect this band of outlaws is operating out of there and it's quite possible they have made their base on a moon or planet somewhere. The president is adamant that we should go after them with a combined force from the Union and the Imperium. She would prefer it if he was actually caught by imperial troops but we cannot guarantee that of course.

'You will command this force. Their commandant, Shraska, equivalent to a major, will be second-in-command and he can apparently speak fluent Galactic. You two will have to work well together if this job is to get done but I'd like you to have one of our guys as an additional second-in-command. Do you have anyone in mind?'.

'Yes,' I said, 'I'd like Captain Wallace to accompany us. I know he is at HQ working with the AI team but he is a first class soldier and we would work well together.'

'Okay, I'll get him here. Anybody else you want with you?'

'Yes, the former prisoner Makreet Lagota. She would be ideal as a liaison between us and them.'

'I'll get them here over the next couple of days. This mission is top secret by the way. We don't want this bastard getting wind of the fact that we're putting a force together to go after him. Let him keep thinking the Imperium, acting alone and busy rebuilding, is going to struggle for years to catch him. That's about it, Lincoln. I wish you all the best. If anybody can get Hradoshk, you can. Keep me informed of your progress.'

Chapter 11

Danny arrived the following morning with some of the battalion and he was followed a few hours later by Caroline. I hadn't seen her since the attack on the flotilla.

'Lincoln, Danny, how good to see you again. And congrats. You've both been promoted since we last saw each other,' she said, giving us each a hug.

'It's great to see you again as well, Caroline,' I said. 'And congrats to you too. A full navy captain. Those gold rings suit you.' I stepped back and looked at her. 'Thanks for joining us on this mission, Caroline.'

'No problem,' she said. 'Wouldn't miss it for the world. It's also an opportunity to put this new warship, the *USS Theseus*, through its paces.'

I smiled. 'Our friend Makreet should be here shortly. She's going to act as a liaison between us and the imperial troops.'

'It'll be good to see her as well,' said Caroline. 'She said she wanted to be a Union citizen. Has that happened?'

'She's working for the Department of Defence, completing a twelve month programme of work directly related to the war effort,' I said. 'This'll be part of that programme.'

Caroline smiled. 'What about Cisco? Are he and Makreet, still...you know...?'

I shook my head. 'Sorry to tell you, Caroline, but Cisco was killed in action during the Medway campaign.'

She put her hand up to her mouth. 'Oh my God, I'm so sorry. Oh God...are you okay, Lincoln? You were boyhood friends...'

I nodded. 'I'm okay thanks, Caroline. It was an awful shock at the time and of course I still miss him but I'm fine.'

Makreet arrived later that day and I barely recognised her. She had had her hair cut and was dressed in a smart suit, every inch the professional. 'Makreet, welcome,' I said. 'You're looking very well.'

'Thank you...er...Colonel...er...Lincoln,' she said, 'it is very good to see you again. And you, Danny. Congratulations, you are an officer.' She turned to Caroline and they hugged each other. 'Caroline, how are you? Lovely to see you.'

'Oh, Makreet, I'm so sorry about Cisco. I've only just found out. How awful.'

'I know. I grieved very deeply for him when I got the news, especially when I thought of what might have been.

He was a lovely person and I think we could have had a life together. However, life goes on and to honour his memory I am determined to continue along the path I have chosen. So, here I am.'

At the end of the five days, a battalion of Union infantry (all volunteers) was drawn up on the parade ground at the Starlight Military Base. The three of us were on the platform in front of the flagpole. I thought briefly how, not too long ago, it had been Danny and me on the parade ground facing Colonel Lesch. Out on the airfield a number of attack shuttles were waiting to transport us to the warship, on station just outside the planet's atmosphere.

I addressed the troops and explained the mission to them. 'At this stage I envisage us playing a support role. It would be better for the Imperium and their efforts at democratisation if these people were captured by imperial troops and tried before an imperial court. However, we may find ourselves in a combat role. Please remember that our primary aim is to bring these people before a court where justice will be served. I want to avoid any unnecessary executions or killings. I will keep you informed as I receive more information. When you are dismissed, please make your way to the shuttles. Once aboard the *USS Theseus* we will be on downtime until further notice. That is all for the present.'

I got together with Danny, Makreet and Caroline on the flight deck of the *Theseus*, where we held an informal chat about the upcoming operation. I included Makreet because this was the first time we would be operating with an imperial force and I wanted her be informed about how we proposed to work with them. She would also be able to advise us where necessary. Her fluency in Standard Galactic had improved beyond recognition and it was obvious to me that she was a highly intelligent, motivated individual, whose intellect would have gone unnoticed in her previous life. I spoke directly to her first. 'Makreet, I asked that you be part of this mission because I would like you to act a liaison between the two forces, as well as being an advisor to us about the Imperium. Do you feel comfortable with these roles and to be working with the Imperium in this way?'

'Absolutely,' she said. 'I have no problem working with the Imperium. As I understand it, they are modernisers who have expressed a willingness to work with the Union to clear up this mess.'

'That's good,' I said. 'You will report directly to me and you will remain a part of this strategy group.' I spoke to the group in general. 'We have to be prepared for any eventuality but I think it would be best if we waited until we've spoken to the imperial commander before going into any detailed planning. He probably has his own ideas on how best to proceed and I'd prefer them to take the lead in this operation. It is their problem after all.'

'I'd go along with that,' said Caroline. 'I was also thinking that most of those who have followed this general have probably done so out of fear or opportunism. I reckon the 'Imperial Wolves' will just disappear if the leader is caught or killed. After all I've been through, I'd like to keep any fighting and killing to a minimum. What do you reckon, Makreet?'

'Yes, I think so too,' she said. 'You will find that most of those who call themselves Imperial Wolves are poor, uneducated and are being seduced by promises of wealth and power. Once the general and his immediate staff have been removed, the rest will cease these activities. I think it would be unnecessary to have to kill thousands of them.'

'Okay,' I said. 'We'll put these ideas to Commandant Shraska and see what he thinks. It would be good to see this operation through without any excessive savagery.'

I was sorting out my equipment when Caroline's voice came through the intercom. 'We are about to embark on a series of space jumps that will take us into the Imperium. Can all personnel please strap themselves in. All personnel into battle suits please and all crew to battle stations. Ship and personnel to be battle ready at all times until further notice. Colonel French to the flight deck, please. That is all.'

I made my way to the flight deck, and sat waiting for the space jump. 'The co-ordinates we've been given will bring us to the rendezvous point with the imperial ship,' said Caroline. 'I thought it best not to take any chances. They might be a bit jumpy.'

'You're right,' I said. 'Let's get Makreet up here too. She can speak to them as soon as we make contact, put them at ease.'

Makreet joined us and I explained the situation to her. 'Apparently Commandant Shraska speaks perfect Galactic but I'd prefer it if we addressed him in his own language initially. It's the courteous thing to do and I reckon he'll feel more at ease.'

After a series of jumps we found ourselves about half a kilometre from an imperial warship, with which we made contact. Makreet, remembering quite a bit from the last time she had contacted such a ship and with some tuition from Caroline, spoke to the crew of the imperial ship and relayed my message. 'Captain Ghali, Colonel French and the naval and army personnel are glad to be here and pleased to be working with you on this operation. We look forward to meeting you personally and hope we can work together harmoniously to bring this issue to a successful conclusion. We cordially invite Commandant Shraska and his staff to join us aboard the *USS Theseus* at their convenience.'

Commandant Shraska came back in perfect Galactic. 'Thank you, Colonel French. We, too, look forward to working together to solve this problem and accept your invitation to come aboard the *USS Theseus*. We will join you within the hour.'

'Cheers, Makreet,' I said. 'Please stay with us. I want everyone to make them feel welcome and to put them completely at their ease. Caroline, can we rustle up some snacks and drinks in the officers' mess? Danny, make sure all the officers, army and navy, are present in the mess within half an hour. Thanks, everyone.'

We watched as a shuttle detached from their warship and made its way over to us. After it had docked, the imperial personnel were shown into the officers' mess where we were waiting for them. They all came smartly to attention and Commandant Shraska saluted. I returned the salute and walked forward and shook his hand, smiling at the same time. 'Welcome aboard, Commandant Shraska,' I said. 'I am pleased to meet you.'

The atmosphere relaxed and there were introductions all round. I asked them to help themselves to food and drink and we spent a good half an hour getting to know each other. I, for one, found it far preferable to shooting them. They were, after all, not very different from us bar language and culture, both of which were worth getting to know. They were all keen to bring about the modernisation of their society and seemed genuinely grateful for our help. Makreet was kept busy and carried out her role as liaison between us very well.

Commandant Shraska and I moved over to one side after a while and began to informally discuss our plans for the operation. I could see immediately why the acting president had chosen Shraska for the job. He was young, highly intelligent, enthusiastic and devoted to bringing about the democratisation of the Imperium. We briefly spoke about the war and I learned he had served loyally right up to the end, while at the same time being aware that they had gone to war on a lie – the Protectorate never had any desire whatsoever of joining the Imperium. He had realised, too, quite early on that the Imperium had no chance of winning a war against the Union but that, with defeat, there would be a chance to change the way the Imperium was governed. 'My generation now has that chance, Colonel,' he said, 'and I am determined to play my part in pushing through permanent change. First though, we have to rid the upper echelons of people like Hradoshk and I am eager to get after him – the sooner the better.'

'Of course,' I said. 'I know I am nominally in command here but Hradoshk is your problem and I would like you to take the lead in tracking him down and capturing him. How do you see that happening?'

'The basis of my plan, Colonel, is to isolate the leadership of this group from their followers so I can avoid any unnecessary bloodshed. I have seen enough killing to last my lifetime and beyond. I believe the majority of those involved in this foolishness will cease their activities if the leadership, including Hradoshk himself, are eliminated or captured.

'And talking of that, I would prefer Hradoshk to be captured alive and brought before a court as that would be more fitting in a proper functioning democracy. However, if we have to kill anyone in the process, so be it.'

I nodded. 'We are going to work well together, Commandant. My thinking exactly. Like you, I would prefer not to have to kill or hurt anyone ever again and I agree that without Hradoshk the whole thing will fall apart. Let's proceed on that basis. What do you know of this area, The Plains of Yandanarra? You ever been in there?'

'No, but that is one area in which the old regime of the Imperium did some good work. They did survey some of that part of the galaxy, apparently with the intention of extending the Imperium, but it came to nothing. However, I have checked the records and I think I know where the general has his base. There is a solar system not too far from the imperial border that has one habitable planet and a habitable moon. And on the moon are remnants of some old settlements, originally built to support gold mining, but long since abandoned.'

'And you think he's there,' I said.

He nodded. 'Unlike the Union, our ships are not capable of supporting large numbers of people so he would need some place from which to operate. These old settlements and mines would be ideal. They would need repair and, of course, there is no climate control or anything like that, but I reckon he could operate out of there.

'In some ways he has been rather stupid but then he doesn't appear to be that intelligent anyway. He could have struck anywhere and kept us guessing but he has operated in one specific area of the Imperium, not too far from the system I am talking about. It seems his imagination, like his intellect, is limited.'

I smiled. 'Plenty of those in the galaxy. Let's hope you're right. It sounds plausible and is as good a place to start as any. It would be great if we could catch him unawares in his hiding place. We need to get down to some detailed planning. Do you have copies of those records with you?'

'They are on our ship,' he said. 'Let's have our first strategy meeting over there. I'd like to repay your hospitality.'

The imperial ship reminded me of the space station we had captured; very basic and not nearly as technologically advanced as ours. I could see why General Hradoshk needed a land base. A Union general would have been able to operate from a ship but these imperial ships couldn't support anything like the numbers Hradoshk had with him. That was fortunate for us, I thought. If he had been able to operate from a ship or ships, jumping around the galaxy and striking anywhere, it would have been much more difficult to track him down.

We got down to business and at the end of the session had agreed a plan of action. We had perused the imperial records and obtained the co-ordinates of the solar system in question. We worked out the best way to approach the target moon and I discovered that there were a number of other settlements on the moon and the habitable planet, people from both the Union and the Imperium who, for one reason or another, preferred to live in this place.

'We'll use the *Theseus* for this operation,' I said, 'only because the technology is superior. I doubt that Hradoshk has any sophisticated tracking system available to him but it will be best not to take any chances. In stealth mode, our ships and shuttles are very difficult to detect and we'll be able to jump him before he knows what's happening. That okay with you, Commandant?'

'Yes, of course,' he said. 'My overriding interest is to successfully complete this mission. Everything else is secondary.'

'Okay, but you are still going to lead the attack when we find him,' I said. 'You must be the one who communicates with these rebels. Makreet can help you but if we are to try and persuade them to give up the fight, it would be better coming from you. Being told to surrender by the Union might make things a bit tricky.'

We finalised the plans. A skeleton crew would take the imperial ship back to base while the rest of their command transferred to the *Theseus*. I felt a lot better with all of us under one roof and went to the flight deck to speak to Caroline. I left Makreet and Commandant Shraska teaching Danny the fundamentals of Imperese.

'Hi, Lincoln, we're getting ready to move out,' she said. 'The flight plan will put us about twenty two million kilometres from the target moon, around one of the planets further out from the sun. From there we can assess the situation and get closer if need be. From what I understand we're still only surmising that they are on this moon. Nothing is known for certain yet, is that right?'

'Yeah that's right,' I said, 'although it's a pretty good bet Hradoshk or someone close to him knew about these old settlements and workings. There would be some kind of infrastructure there they could use as a base. If it turns out to be wrong, well we'll just have to keep looking or apply plan B, which doesn't exist at the moment.'

She smiled. 'Okay, we'll be good to go in about an hour. Sub-hyper for three hours and then a series of jumps to the target area. Battle ready all the way.'

We reached our destination after several hours and were stationed in orbit around a gas giant, the system's sun a bright star in the distance. The habitable planet and moon were about twenty two million kilometres towards the sun and we brought them up on the map hovering above the conference table. Commandant Shraska fed his information into the map and the moon appeared before us with the settlement marked in red. 'That's where we think they are hiding between missions,' he said. 'We think there are between two and three thousand of them but we cannot be sure. We also don't quite know how many ships they have but statements from witnesses and information gathered so far point to two ships of cruiser or battleship size. There may be more. What we need to do is get closer and have a look at this place, see what we can find out.'

I turned to Caroline. 'I'm banking on Hradoshk not having anything too sophisticated as far as radar and tracking are concerned. Let's get closer to that moon, even a geo-stationary orbit on the side opposite the settlements and see what we can see. That okay?'

'Sure,' she said. 'That shouldn't be a problem.' She switched to intercom. 'All crew remain at battle stations. We're moving towards the target in stealth mode. Full battle readiness at all times. That is all.'

We took up station without incident and made preparations to go down and explore the surface. I should have stayed on the ship to direct operations but I gave Danny that job as I wanted to see for myself what was going on down there. Commandant Shraska and I, accompanied by a hundred troops – Union and imperial – boarded an attack shuttle and headed for the surface. It soon became apparent that this was going to be a rougher ride than any I'd taken before. The moon was not climatically controlled and we were bucking around like a cork on a stormy sea within minutes of entering the atmosphere. I was strapped in behind the pilots and could see that they were having to work hard to keep from losing control altogether. We were descending through thick cloud, freezing rain, hail and continual lightning. None of us had experienced anything like this before and I found it pretty scary.

After a while we found ourselves below the clouds but things hardly improved. We continued to descend through driving rain and lightning, the shuttle bouncing around, buffeted by high winds. Our instruments recorded a breathable atmosphere outside the ship but the weather was horrendous. This is what it must have been like on earth before the advent of climate control I thought. Another reason to be thankful things had moved on.

The surface became visible through the stormy weather and I saw low lying hills and shallow valleys, open ground and forests, and a few large areas of water. We were about thirty kilometres from the settlements and were now skimming along just above the surface, hugging the contours of the land. We were in stealth mode and I doubted that anyone would be able to detect us or know we were there.

The mines and the old settlement lay in one of the shallow valleys and we pulled up behind a ridge. 'Okay wait here,' I said. 'We're going to take a peek over that ridge to see what's down there. Troops, stay alert and ready to respond to any emergency. Ready, Commandant?'

He nodded and we climbed out into the driving wind and rain. Our suits sheltered us from the worst of it but the wind still made the going tough. The temperature was a chilly two degrees centigrade although inside the suit I felt pleasantly warm. The two of us made our way to the top of the ridge and lay there looking down at the old workings. It struck me immediately that the place was again in use. Lights were on and a number of derelict buildings had been patched up. One building stood out from the rest. It was three storeys high and had been extensively repaired. All the windows seemed new and lights blazed on the ground floor. It looked far better than any of the others round about. What we needed to find out was whether this place was being used by Hradoshk or whether these were just innocent settlers. There was no sign of any ships but visibility wasn't great and they could have been further up the valley.

'What do you reckon?' I said. 'My hunch is that we've got the right place but I reckon we need to go and have a better look just to make sure. That building with the lights on looks promising.'

'I agree,' said Commandant Shraska, 'Let's go down and see. Not much sign of life at the moment but there's bound to be someone down there we can talk to.'

'Okay, we'll take your guys with us. The Union troops can stay here on standby. Let's go. Tell your guys to spread out through the settlement and to capture anyone they come across. Let's try and be as quiet as we can.'

The weather was truly awful. The wind was getting wilder by the minute and the rain now included sleet and flurries of snow as the temperature started dropping. The imperial troopers joined us and we carefully made our way, through the storm, down the ridge to the buildings at the bottom. Our suits changed their appearance automatically to blend in with our surroundings so we would not have been easy to see. When we reached the bottom of the hill we spread out among the shacks and patched up buildings that made up the old settlement. The commandant and I crept towards the main building and carefully peered through one of the windows, into a fairly large room where three men and two women were sitting at a couple of tables. A fire was burning in the grate and they were talking and laughing, with glasses of drink and plates of food in front of them. A large banner had been draped across one of the walls with a picture of a wolf's head in the centre and imperese script to either side of it. 'The Imperial Wolves,' whispered Commandant Shraska.

'Great,' I whispered back. 'Nothing like advertising your presence. Makes it easier for us. Anything yet from any of the others?'

The commandant spoke into his mic and then turned to me. 'The rest of the site seems deserted,' he said, 'unless there's something further up the valley.'

'Okay, get ten of your guys to come with us and we'll have a chat to these people. The troopers can search the rest of the building. Make sure the rest of your troops dig in and remain hidden. They need to be on full alert. I'll get the Union guys down here as well.' We were joined by ten troopers. I grinned at Commandant Shraska. 'Okay, Commandant, your show.'

They burst into the room and I followed them. Commandant Shraska shouted at the five people sitting round the table, pointing his weapon, and they immediately sat dead still with their hands on the table in front of them. They were in a state of shock, staring at us wide eyed. The troopers spread through the building, heading up the stairs. The translator in my helmet relayed the conversation onto my visor.

'My name is Commandant Shraska of the Army of the Imperium. From the banner on the wall I assume that you are part of the criminal gang known as the Imperial Wolves. Is this correct?'

They sat there staring at him, disbelief all over their faces. They looked at me, in the uniform of the Union, and were more confused than ever.

'Will one of you answer please?' said the commandant. 'You are members of the Imperial Wolves are you not?'

One of the men nodded. 'Yes,' he said in a low voice. 'We are under the command of General Hradoshk.'

'Where is the general and the rest of your band?' asked Commandant Shraska.

A second man, clearly over the initial shock pointed at me and started shouting at Commandant Shraska. 'We don't have to answer your questions. What's he..?' He reached under the table and produced a pistol but didn't get very far because the commandant, as quick as lightning, lifted his rifle and shot him through the middle of his forehead. The force of the shot blew out the back of his head and he lurched backwards and crumpled across the adjacent chairs and table. The other four screamed and ducked down, cowering. Commandant Shraska turned to them. 'Anyone else want to draw a weapon or talk about traitors? No? Good. I have neither the time nor the inclination to listen to your imbecilic chitchat. I expect you to answer my questions. Do I make myself clear?'

They all nodded vigorously, their hands glued to the table in front of them. That's one way to get their attention, I thought. Commandant Shraska continued his questioning. 'Any more weapons we don't know about?' They shook their heads. 'Where is the general and the rest of your band?'

'They left to go on a raid about thirty-six hours ago,' said one of the women. 'We are expecting them back within the next two days.'

'How many others have been left behind?' asked the commandant.

'There are about twenty troops in the barracks. They are ill and couldn't go on the raid.' She pointed. 'The barracks and the star ship landing area are about a kilometre that way. Because of the weather you can't see them at the moment.'

'Hopefully they haven't seen us either,' said the commandant. 'Anybody else?'

She shifted in her seat and looked at the other three. They were clearly hiding something and seemed reluctant to talk.

'What is it?' said the commandant threateningly. 'Quickly, I don't have time to waste.'

One of the men cleared his throat. 'There are... prisoners...men...and...women. Please don't blame us... we are only the guards here...'

'Prisoners? What prisoners?' demanded the commandant.

'The men work in the mines. The general wants to revive the gold mines. The women do general work around the base and...perform...other...er...duties.'

'I can imagine,' said Commandant Shraska grimly. 'Who is guarding these prisoners?'

'We are the guards,' said the man. 'We are required to check on them now and then.'

The commandant glared at them and they were clearly terrified. Their dead comrade was a reminder that we meant business. He barked at them to remain where they were. He turned to me. 'I think we'd better get those troops into custody and then see to the prisoners.' He turned to one of his lieutenants. 'Take two platoons and make sure you capture anyone you find at the barracks. No one is to escape. This woman will show you the way. Bring them back here please.'

'I'll find the prisoners,' I said. I called Lieutenant Gormley who arrived a couple of minutes later. 'Lieutenant, this man here,' I said, pointing to one of the men sitting at the table, 'will show you where some prisoners are being held. Take a platoon and report back to me when you have found them.'

Commandant Shraska told the man in no uncertain terms what was required of him and he left with the lieutenant. We continued interrogating the prisoners and ascertained that on their return from a raid, the general and his officers usually came straight here to his headquarters while the troops made their way to the barracks. He always radioed ahead to make sure the place was properly prepared for his return – fire going, food and drink available. Any prisoners were taken to their respective quarters. A call came through. 'Colonel French, Lieutenant Gormley here. You need to come and see, sir. Urgent.'

'I'll leave this to you, Commandant,' I said. 'Something urgent apparently. Will keep you posted.'

'Okay, Colonel,' he said. 'I'll wait here.'

I followed Gormley's instructions and found myself outside a derelict building, sleet and snow swirling around me and the wind howling like some demented banshee. The temperature now registered minus three. I followed him through the open doorway and to the top of some steps. A trapdoor stood open and a trooper was standing there looking pretty shocked. 'What is it, Lieutenant?' I said.

'Down there, sir, prisoners, shackled, some dead I think...' he said. 'It's not a pretty sight.' I went down the stairs and the smell hit me first. It was really rank and included the sickly smell of death. The basement was dimly lit, and the sight was sickening. It was a long tunnel with a low ceiling and it contained between a hundred and a hundred and fifty men shackled to a thick metal bar running along the floor for the length of the room. They were filthy and their clothes had become rags. Most of them had a threadbare blanket around them but that was hardly enough to keep them warm in this kind of weather. Several of them, as far as I could see, were dead. There were bowls with the remnants of food and some others containing filthy water lying around, and all these wretches just sat there and stared at me. Eventually one of them spoke. He only managed a whisper. The words 'help us, please help us' appeared on my visor. I nodded at him and patted his shoulder.

'Danny, do you read me?'

'Loud and clear.'

'I need a medical team here double quick, ready to lift about a hundred and fifty sick people. Send Makreet with the team. They are in need of immediate treatment and sustenance.'

'Okay, Colonel. Will get them there ASAP.'

I spoke to Commandant Shraska. He told me that the enemy troops had been successfully captured and brought to him. They were now safely in custody. He also said that his troops had found the women prisoners who were apparently being kept in atrocious conditions.

'We've found the men,' I said, 'and their condition is truly appalling. I think you'd better come and have a look and speak to them.' He arrived after a few minutes and was clearly shocked at what he saw. He spoke to the prisoners and then to me. 'These are imperial citizens, taken prisoner by Hradoshk and forced to work in the mines here. According to this man many prisoners have died but they get replaced each time the general returns from his raids.'

I nodded. 'Lieutenant, arrange for provisions from the shuttle to be brought here. These people need warmth and food while we wait for the medical team. Caroline, do you read?'

'Loud and clear.'

'Hradoshk is out on a raid at the moment but could be back at any time. Please let me know the instant he is spotted.'

'Will do, Lincoln. Good luck.'

'Thanks, Caroline. Danny, I'd like you and all the troops here before Hradoshk returns so that we can secure this place.'

'Okay, Colonel, will do. The medical team has just left. The rest of us will be there as soon as possible.'

'Lieutenant Gormley, wait here for the medical team and give them any assistance they need,' I said. 'We'd better go and have a look at those women captives, Commandant.' We made our way through the worsening weather to where the women were held captive and once again were sickened by the sight. It was slightly better than the tunnel in which the men were kept but not much. We entered a long, low building and found about eighty women in varying states of health. The building consisted of a number of rooms, each with some old mattresses and threadbare blankets, and one of the rooms was being used as a kitchen. The women had done their best to make the place liveable but the conditions were pretty dire. They all looked hungry and there were two lying on the mattresses clearly very ill. The commandant spoke to them and ascertained that they were required to cook and clean for the troops, as well as perform sexual favours as and when required.

The medical team arrived and we spent the next couple of hours getting the men and women aboard the shuttles. Once again Makreet proved her worth. She worked tirelessly, giving help where she could and making sure that the captives were made as comfortable as possible. It was a delicate operation as many of them were very weak, scarcely able to move by themselves, and five were already dead. Makreet got the details of those that had died and Commandant Shraska said he'd do what he could to inform their families. I spoke to Caroline and told her about the human cargo that she would be receiving.

'Okay, Lincoln, they'll be cared for properly once they're aboard the *Theseus*. No sign yet of any returning ships but will keep you posted.'

I spoke to the medical team. 'Thank you for your efforts here today. As you can see these people are going to need some serious care and attention before they're able to function normally again and so I'm going to leave them in your capable hands. I've informed Captain Ghali of the situation so she'll be expecting you. I'll see you back on the *Theseus*.'

Danny and the rest of our troops arrived shortly afterwards and I spoke to him and the commandant. 'We want to isolate Hradoshk and his staff from the rest of his followers if possible. That means staying hidden until he is in his quarters, where we found those five guards. The weather's certainly on our side. I think the visibility has got worse in the time we've been here. Danny, can you see to the main body of his followers at the barracks? I'd like the imperial troops to play the main part in their capture so let's arrange for them to be dug in near the barracks with the Union troops as backup.'

Just then a call came through from Caroline. 'Two ships incoming,' she said. 'ETA four hours. Looks like our man.'

'Thanks, Caroline. Okay, guys, this is it. ETA four hours. Danny, I want a squad ready at the landing site to capture and occupy those ships when all the enemy troops have evacuated and left the site. The rest of the Union troops to act as backup for the imperial guys. Commandant, get your guys entrenched so that they can surround the barracks and make sure that the general and his troops remain sealed off from each other. We'll take a squad with us, Commandant, and wait for the general in his quarters.'

'After what I've seen here I can't wait to get my hands on the bastard.' He smiled at me. 'I still think he should be taken alive but he's going to sustain some injuries resisting arrest.'

'Spoken like a true democrat,' I said smiling back at him. 'Just make sure there are no witnesses.'

We took about half an hour to get everything and everyone in place and at the end I was satisfied we'd done all we could to surprise the Imperial Wolves when they returned to their base. Imperial troops, backed up by Union infantry, were hidden behind the ridges around the barrack rooms, ready, at Danny's command, to surround those barracks and prevent the troops inside from hooking up with General Hradoshk and his staff. Troops were stationed in the tunnel and the building that had housed the women prisoners to capture anybody bringing new prisoners to these places. A further squad of Union troops were ready to storm the landing pad and take over the ships, thus preventing their use by the enemy, and Commandant Shraska and I, together with a squad of imperial troopers, were waiting in silence with the four remaining guards in the general's HQ, hoping he stuck to his usual habit of coming straight here with his senior staff after a mission. The squad were waiting in silence on the first floor, ready to come down and arrest the general and his officers.

I racked my brains to think of anything I'd left out but couldn't. If the general changed his pattern of behaviour, well we'd just have to play that by ear. We certainly had enough troops in place to deal with any contingency. I had a feeling, however, that because of the dreadful weather, the general would head straight here where a warm fire, food and drink awaited.

After a couple of hours a call came through from the general and one of the guards moved to the radio to answer it. Commandant Shraska spoke to her and his words appeared on my visor. 'If you want to live a long and peaceful life, you will answer that call in the usual fashion. If I suspect any false move on your part I will kill you. Understood?' She nodded and looked as if she believed him. I certainly did.

That general sounded like a mean bastard. In a rasping voice, devoid of any humanity, he informed us that they would be landing in an hour and that he expected his HQ to be warm, with enough food and drink for himself and his officers. He then gave an order that set him apart from the rest of us. 'I want you guards to go through the prisoners this time and weed out those who you think are too weak or ill to carry on. Take them out to the garbage dump and shoot them. We need room for forty more prisoners – twenty-five men and fifteen women. And I want no excuses why it hasn't been done. That is all.'

'Nice guy,' I said.

'Yeah,' said the commandant, 'one of the best.' He turned to the woman. 'Have you done that before? Killed prisoners in this way?'

'No, it has not been our job,' said the woman, her face ashen with shock. 'The soldiers have carried out the executions up to now. I don't know why we have been told to do it all of a sudden. I…I don't think I could do that.' The others shook their heads.

'Well, lucky for you, you won't have to,' said the commandant. 'However, I noticed that you didn't care too much about the prisoners living in those appalling conditions, did you?' They all looked down, not saying anything. 'Let me tell you, you are lucky to be alive. After seeing those prisoners I was a millisecond away from shooting all four of you. I still will, if you give the general any hint that we are here. You make sure that he suspects nothing, understood?'

They nodded.

'Are you expected to be here when he arrives?'

'One of us is usually here to serve the officers,' said one of the men. 'We take turns. It is my turn this time.'

'Okay, get this place ready for him. Get rid of that body and clean the place up properly.'

They stoked up the fire and scurried around making sure that everything was as the general expected it. When they were satisfied we took three of them into custody and the commandant and I retired to the next room where we waited in silence. I contacted Cisco and made sure that all the troops were ready and knew exactly what they had to do. The commandant did the same.

'Caroline, do you read?'

'Loud and clear, Lincoln. The two ships have entered the moon's atmosphere and should be with you in about twenty minutes.'

'Okay. If Hradoshk suspects something and tries to make a run for it I want you to destroy those two ships. Do not allow them to escape.'

'Understood.'

The commandant turned to me. 'I hope it doesn't come to that. There are those prisoners on board.'

I nodded. 'Yeah, that's something I'd have to live with. Let's hope it all goes according to plan. The weather's certainly on our side and Hradoshk has no reason to believe there's anybody here waiting for him.'

We waited a while longer and then Caroline told me that they had landed and powered down the ships. I was suddenly feeling pretty tense. Things could always go wrong, I thought, and if things went wrong here the result could be death and destruction on a large scale. It wasn't something I wanted to contemplate.

Danny came through. 'Ships are being evacuated now,' he said, 'and troops are returning to their barracks. So far so good. Will let you know when we have completed our ops here.'

'Thanks, Danny. Speak later,' I said. A few minutes later the door opened and we heard the sound of people entering the room. The wind was still howling outside and it took a couple of minutes for them all to come in. Eventually the door slammed shut and I recognised the general's rasping voice.

'You, pour some drinks and then get out. We need some privacy,' he said. There was the sound of drinks being poured amid general conversation which sounded upbeat and seemed to indicate that the raid had gone well. The guard excused himself and walked into the room in which we were waiting. He nodded to us and held up nine fingers. I nodded, put my finger to my lips and pointed him to a back wall. The commandant grinned at me, signalled to the squad to join us, and we walked into the room, weapons at the ready. The imperial troopers joined us and surrounded the nine people in the room.

The look on their faces has stayed with me all these years. They couldn't have been more surprised if a three-headed monkey had walked in singing opera. There was a stunned silence with everybody standing dead still. The commandant's voice rang out loud and clear. 'Stay exactly where you are. DO. NOT. MOVE. I am Commandant Shraska of the Army of the Imperium and you are under arrest for crimes against the Imperium and its citizens. Keep your hands where we can see them. Anyone attempting to resist arrest will be shot.'

He handed me his weapon and proceeded to pat down the captives, making sure that all weapons were removed. It took a few minutes as he did a thorough job, handing side arms and knives to a trooper. 'Right, I want you all to sit at the tables and to keep your hands on the table top. Do not move from that position.' He took back his rifle.

Once they had sat down they seemed to notice me for the first time and further shock registered on their faces. The general, who had sat apart from the others, now started to look angry. He looked from the commandant to me and back to the commandant and it suddenly dawned that the Imperium and the Union had collaborated in his capture.

The commandant carried on. 'Your troops are being taken into captivity and your ships are now in our hands. All the prisoners, men and women, have been released and are now being cared for aboard a Union Star Ship.'

The general stood up slowly and faced Commandant Shraska. He was shaking with rage. His voice was even more rasping as he pointed to me. 'You...you have collaborated with this...this Union trash in the capture of an imperial general. You are the worst kind of traitor to the Imperium.' He looked around at the troops. 'You all are traitorous scum, you...' The commandant, moving like lightning, flipped his rifle and drove the butt into the general's face. He flew back, hands to his face and howling with pain, and landed in a heap on the floor. The commandant followed him, grabbed him by the front of his jacket and yanked him onto a chair. He jammed his gun into the general's face.

'You listen to me, you gormless sonofabitch. One more word out of you and I'll blow your fucking head off. DO I MAKE MYSELF CLEAR?'

The general, slumped and crumpled in the chair, now looked like a worn out old man. He made a feeble gesture of surrender with his right hand and nodded. He knew the game was up. Blood was pouring from his nose and mouth and his arms were hanging loosely at his sides. Nobody else moved or said anything. Shraska's done it again, I thought – got everybody's attention. He spoke urgently into his mic and stood listening for a minute or so, then turned to me. 'Your guys have got the ships but the troops in the barrack rooms have refused to lay down their arms. They have the prisoners and are threatening to execute them.'

Just then Danny confirmed the situation. 'We're in a standoff situation here,' he said. 'These rebels are trapped inside their barracks but they've got the prisoners and are threatening to shoot them if we attempt to storm the place.'

'Thanks, Danny. Don't attempt to storm the barracks. Just keep the place surrounded and await further orders. If they attempt some sort of breakout you'll have no choice but to start shooting.'

'Okay. Will keep you posted.'

'Commandant, we need to defuse the situation at the barracks. It could turn into a bloodbath in no time if either side makes a wrong move. I suggest you explain the situation to these guys. Tell them that resistance is useless and that one way or another they'll be the losers here. Make sure they understand that we want to avoid needless bloodshed but if we have to we'll kill every last one of these Imperial Wolves. Ask them if they're prepared to go and speak to the troops in the barracks and get them to see reason.'

He glanced at the general and then spoke to the others. He basically repeated what I had said, emphasising the fact that we were prepared to see all of the Imperial Wolves dead if that's what it took for our mission to be a success. They looked at me and it was obvious that I wasn't bluffing. After talking among themselves, one of them stepped forward.

'My name is Ronen. I am prepared to speak to the men in the barracks. I will try and get them to lay down their arms but I cannot guarantee anything.'

I nodded. 'Fair enough but do your best to make them see sense. The alternative is a firefight that they cannot hope to win.' Commandant Shraska translated and we made our way to our lines around the barracks. The weather had eased up considerably. It was still pretty windy but the sleet and snow had ceased and visibility was much better. I found Danny who told me that there had been no movement from within the barracks and no shooting either. As far as he knew the prisoners were still unharmed.

The commandant came up to me. 'Ronen feels it would be best if he went into the barracks on his own and spoke directly with the men. I'm inclined to agree.'

'Okay,' I said. 'That's fine by me. Just emphasise again that we are determined to succeed here whatever it takes and tell him to point out that General Hradoshk is in custody and we have the ships. There's no way out of here. It's all over bar the shouting.'

After listening to the commandant, Ronen gave me a curt nod and, with his hands in the air, started towards the barracks. The tension all around us was palpable. An itchy trigger finger inside the barracks could have set the whole thing off but Ronen made it and disappeared inside one of the barrack rooms. We waited for what seemed like eternity. He reappeared and went to another room and another until he had covered them all, after which he walked back to us.

'They want assurances they will not be executed if they surrender. They wish to speak to the commanding officer.'

'That'll be me,' said Commandant Shraska. He handed me his rifle and pistol and without hesitation walked towards the barracks, stopping halfway between us and them, his hands on his hips. He shouted something at the buildings in front of him and then stood waiting while I felt my mouth go dry. If they shot Shraska, there'd be no holding the Imperial troops back. For an eternity there was no movement from the barracks but then a door opened and two men in ragged uniforms, unarmed, came forward and walked up to the commandant. The three of them stood talking for about five minutes and then the two men returned the way they'd come and I saw them moving among the different buildings that made up the barracks. The commandant didn't move, just stood there waiting until, after a few minutes, the first of the prisoners appeared. They filed out, men and women, holding on to each other and moving towards us as directed by the commandant. They reached our positions and we kept them moving till they were behind us and out of the line of fire.

The first of the rebels appeared shortly afterwards and eventually they were all formed up in lines in front of the commandant who still had not moved. We had overestimated their numbers. There were only about eight hundred and fifty of them, all unarmed, their body language indicating that the fight had gone out of them. They looked ragged, cold and hungry, with threadbare patched up uniforms and shoulders slumped and heads bowed, and I figured most of them were just glad to be going home, even if the future looked uncertain. The promises of riches and gold must have started to look pretty thin in this old settlement. Even the most optimistic among them would have realised by now that they weren't going to find Shangri-La in this godforsaken place.

The commandant came back to us, rattled out some orders and a section of his troops moved into the barracks to recover the weapons. Another section led the prisoners towards the landing site, where they would be transferred to the *Theseus*.

Commandant Shraska stepped forward and shook my hand. 'Thanks for your help, Colonel. I really appreciate all you've done for us.'

'No problem,' I said, 'it's been a pleasure working with you. Standing there unarmed and getting that lot to come out peacefully took some doing. I'll get the *Theseus* down and we can get these people aboard and into custody. The sooner we're out of this dump the better.'

It took the best part of the rest of that day to get all the prisoners aboard and properly accommodated, while the weather deteriorated again. Makreet was wonderful. She never stopped and at the end of the operation she came and flopped down next to me. 'That's that, Lincoln,' she said. 'All the prisoners and rebels have been properly fed and the rebels are in secure custody. The sick and injured have been cared for and I don't think there is anything more we can do for anybody at this time.'

'Well done, Makreet. Great job. I noticed you went out of your way to calm some of those rebels. A lot of them seem convinced we were going to execute them.'

'Yes, it's the way we were brought up. In the old Imperium, executions, even mass executions, carried out in public, were a common feature of the judicial system. Some of them are still having difficulty believing that the new government has abolished the death penalty or that Commandant Shraska is not going to preside over a mass public hanging when we get back.'

Skeleton crews staffed the two imperial ships, with two of the shuttle pilots given the task of flying them. We were going to the capital of the Imperium, Zangsh, where the general and his followers were to be handed over to the new authorities for trial. Commandant Shraska, Danny and I joined Caroline on the flight deck. 'I guess that's it,' I said. 'I can't think of anything we've forgotten. We're good to go.'

She nodded. 'Okay, we're sub-hyper for ten hours.' She switched on the intercom. 'Crew, ship ready for lift-off. Battle stations until further notice.' We lifted off and I noticed that the howling weather had no effect on the *Theseus* whatsoever. We rode that storm smoothly and in no time found ourselves in the darkness of space, heading for the capital of the Imperium.

I sent a message to Collette, telling her that I couldn't wait to see her again and that I hoped never to be anywhere without her again. I looked at the locket image I had of her as I sent the message and hoped with all the effort I could muster, that she still wanted to see me. I dreaded a message telling me that it was all over between us, that our enforced separation had caused her to change her mind, and I sat there quite despondent at the thought of it.

Part 4

Heading Home

Chapter 1

As we circled over the city, I saw that the place had been razed, with large areas very badly damaged and rubble everywhere. The death toll must have been horrendous and living conditions for the survivors not much better, I thought, as we levelled out and headed for the military spaceport on the outskirts. I looked at Makreet and saw tears running down her stricken face as she surveyed the wreckage that had been her hometown. 'You okay?' I asked.

She nodded and dabbed her eyes and spoke in a whisper. 'I am shocked to see what has happened to Zangsh. I knew it had been bombed but I wasn't prepared for damage on this scale.'

'Have you heard from your family?' asked Danny.

She nodded. 'They have survived the bombing but I have no idea how they are now or what has become of them.'

He put his arm around her. 'I'll come with you. We'll go find them, make sure they're okay.'

There were three or four of our warships berthed at the spaceport, together with commercial and cargo vessels of various shapes and sizes, indicating that we were clearly involved in the repair and reconstruction of the city. The *Theseus*, vast and ultra-modern compared to all the other shipping, was directed to berth some distance from the rest of the traffic, where a long line of black sinister looking prison vehicles were parked, ready to receive General Hradoshk and his band of merry men. There was a reception committee waiting for us, too, and for a moment I felt like some visiting dignitary. As Commandant Shraska, Caroline, Danny and I descended from the ship an imperial guard of honour presented arms and their commanding officer stepped forward and saluted us.

'Colonel French, Captain Ghali, Captain Wallace, welcome to the capital of the Imperium. Commandant Shraska, welcome back. I am Brigade Leader Hamstra and on behalf of the acting president, I wish to convey our thanks and appreciation for what you have done. We are to escort you to the official residence of the president who is awaiting your arrival.'

On the drive through the shattered city there was precious little that had not been damaged by the bombing. The road itself had been patched up but was still full of potholes and the ride was slow and bumpy. Huge piles of rubble had been piled up along the sides of the streets and more than once I saw people poking through the rubble, probably trying to find some personal items. I saw long queues at various temporary food kitchens that had been set up but there was also a bustle about the place as other groups of people worked at clearing the rubble. Some heavy machinery was in use but it was mainly long lines of people passing rubble and other items.

The presidential residence, formerly the palace of the Supreme Leader, stood on a hill above the city. A huge, sprawling place, it too had been extensively damaged and the present incumbent was confined to one relatively small section of the original building. We were shown in and found Space Marshall Bharmaga waiting for us in a large office. I saluted and he came forward and took my hand in both of his. 'Colonel French, I am delighted to see you again, especially in the light of what you have achieved with the capture of General Hradoshk. Welcome to Zangsh. No doubt you saw that we have much work to do.' He turned to Commandant Shraska, his face beaming. He addressed him in Galactic. 'Commandant, so good to see you back. My sincerest congratulations on a successful mission. Together with our federal friends, you have excelled and the Imperium is eternally grateful.'

I introduced Caroline and Danny, who were also thanked profusely, and we were shown to an adjoining room where we enjoyed a very good lunch. While we were there I learned that over eighty percent of the city had been destroyed by the Union navy, and that many other cities throughout the Imperium had suffered a similar fate. Their armies had been defeated on all fronts with a casualty count in the tens of millions and their navy had virtually ceased to exist. Once the Union military machine had got up to speed there had been no stopping us and the devastation to the Imperium was something that had to be seen to be believed. No wonder Hradoshk had thought they'd never get him. Without our help it would probably have taken forever.

The Imperium was gearing up for its first democratic elections and the space marshall was determined that these would go ahead as scheduled, no matter what state the place was in. Once again I was impressed by the acting president. He struck me as highly intelligent and extremely focussed, determined to ensure that the Imperium took a new road and working hard to prevent it from lapsing into its old ways. He wanted to change the name from Imperium to Republic, a move that was to be the subject of a referendum to coincide with the elections. (It happened, by the way. Our neighbours are now fully democratic and are called The Republic).

He had been successful in enlisting the help of the Union and President Joyce was being very generous. She knew, too, that a prosperous, democratic Imperium posed far less of a threat than the old one and so was doing all she could to bring that about. I felt pleased to be playing a small part in that process.

We returned to the *Theseus* while Danny and Makreet set out to find her family. There was no telling what state they were in so we could only hope for the best. I stayed behind and completed a full report of the operation which I sent to General Matfield. He congratulated me on a successful mission and requested we stay in Zangsh for a further three days in case the acting president needed us for anything.

A message from Collette arrived, telling me how she missed me and couldn't wait to see me again. I lay back on my bed and let the relief flood through me. I should never have doubted her but having survived the war, it would have been unbearable to have lost Collette. I received a message from Commandant Shraska as well, inviting me to dine with him and his wife at their home on the military base. It was just what we needed after the strain of the recent operation. He and his wife, Casipa, made me feel welcome and we spent a wonderfully relaxed evening together. The food was delicious and the wine flowed pretty freely. Casipa excused herself and went to bed around midnight but the commandant and I sat up till the early hours, drinking whisky, and I ended up sleeping in a spare room.

The next day, feeling fuzzy around the edges, I met with Danny and Makreet. Her family home had been flattened but her family had survived. They were deep underground in a bomb shelter the night their house had been destroyed and they were now staying with some relatives.

'I'm really pleased, Makreet,' I said. 'I feared the worst yesterday.'

'Thank you, Lincoln, and thank you so much, Danny. I cannot tell you what it means to find they are well.'

The days passed quickly. Caroline, Danny and I spent a bit of time in the city, looking around but there was not much to see. Most places of interest had been flattened or damaged. We took one of the shuttles and explored the countryside around the city. It was a dry place, undulating, with dusty river beds, jagged uplands and endless scrubland. Small towns dotted the countryside. 'These places are dirt poor,' said Caroline. 'Everything looks pretty basic.'

'Yeah,' I said. 'And no doubt the war and the damage to Zangsh is going to make things a whole heap worse.'

'I just hope the recovery doesn't take too long,' said Danny, 'or get bogged down. These people need all the help they can get. I sometimes forget how lucky we are to be citizens of the Interplanetary Union and the Protectorate.' That was true. We took our living standards and our human rights for granted a lot of the time and it needed something like this to remind us just how fortunate we were.

At nineteen hundred hours on the third day the troops were drawn up outside the *Theseus*, ready for embarkation. Caroline had received her orders which were to fly the battalion to Black Tree Canyon, Dakota, where the majority of them would be discharged from the army, their service completed. Commandant Shraska was there and addressed the battalion, thanking them for the service they had performed and wishing them everything of the best for the future. I did the same and dismissed the troops who proceeded to board the ship in great spirits. Commandant Shraska turned to me and shook my hand, looked at me and we hugged each other. 'Thanks for everything, Lincoln,' he said, stepping back. 'It's been great working with you. Casipa sends her love and we look forward to seeing you next month. And bring Collette with you.'

'Alarro, my friend, it's been a real pleasure working with you and getting to know you. Give Casipa my love and thanks again for a wonderful evening at your place. You guys have a massive job ahead of you and I wish you all the luck in the universe. I'll see you as soon as I get back. Until then.'

I joined Caroline on the flight deck. 'Hi, Lincoln, ready to go home?'

'I reckon,' I said. 'Had enough war to last ten lifetimes.' I shook my head. 'Christ, seen some things…'

'I know. Let's hope we don't have to go through anything like this again.'

I nodded. 'I've been really shocked at the devastation the Imperium has suffered. I know they started it all but I reckon most of them were powerless to do anything against the government of the day and were just dragged along. They were taken to war on a lie, like people in ninety-nine percent of humanity's wars, and the general population have paid an awful price. I just hope their path to a democratic, peaceful future works out for them.' I laid my head against the back of my seat and closed my eyes. 'In the meantime I'm going to enjoy my month's leave. What about you, Caroline? What are you going to do now that the war is over?'

'I'm regular navy,' said Caroline, 'so I'll be carrying on with my career. We're committed to helping the Imperium for the foreseeable future so I guess I'll be spending quite a bit of time here. Still, far better than shooting at each other.'

'Much better,' I said. 'They're not that different to us when you get to know them. I just hope Collette isn't too upset about me being stationed here in Zangsh for the next year.'

'I doubt it,' said Caroline. 'She's happy about you staying in the army so must expect this sort of thing from time to time. Anyway, she'll be able to visit you here during her breaks. We're not at war with them anymore.'

'Yeah, that's true. Let's go home.'

Caroline received a call telling her that the ship was ready for take-off. She handed over to the AIU and then broadcast to the ship. 'Ship ready for lift-off. No need to strap in and no need for battle stations. Sub-hyper for seven hours and then three space jumps, which will bring us home to Black Tree Canyon. Enjoy the trip.'

That flight was the most relaxed I had had for a long time and I couldn't believe how good it felt to touch down in the familiar surroundings of Black Tree Canyon, with thoughts of Collette crowding my brain. I spoke to the battalion shortly before touchdown. We ended with a tremendous cheer and I was on the flight deck with Danny and Makreet when we landed.

The battalion marched onto the parade ground and formed up in front of the familiar dais. General Matfield was there, as was Colonel Lesch, and to my amazement so was General Bullen. I marched forward and saluted.

'Please join us, Colonel French,' said General Bullen. 'It's good to see you back.'

'Thank you, ma'am,' I said, stepping onto the dais and standing next to General Matfield.

She walked forward to address the troops, her riding crop tapping against her highly polished boot. She looked exactly the same as when I first saw her. Everything ironed and polished, nothing out of place. 'At the start of the war I spoke to you and said that although we had not started this conflict, we were going to end it. And by God we've done that. The imperial armed forces have been defeated on all fronts and they no longer have a functioning navy. Many of their towns and cities have been reduced to rubble and their casualty count runs into the tens of millions. That defeat was in no small part due to the efforts of this regiment and this battalion and I congratulate all of you on a job very well done. The Union is immensely proud of you and I congratulate you, too, for the task you have just completed. I am proud to have served with each and every one of you and I hope that many of you will choose to remain in the army. Once again, my profound thanks and I wish you all the best for the future.'

The battalion was dismissed and the troops went off in high spirits. Makreet, who was required to report to the authorities so that the details regarding her citizenship could be completed, left us while Danny and I joined the other officers in the mess where a spread had been laid on for us. 'How's the lovely Collette?' asked Danny.

'Fine, thank you. At least I think so. I haven't managed to speak to her yet. I'm hoping to see her as soon as this shindig is over. What about you? What are your plans?'

'Well, I'm off to see my parents for the next week or so as I have two weeks leave and then it's back here for me.'

'Back here?' I said. 'What do you mean, back to the university?'

He shook his head, smiling. 'You're not going to believe this, Lincoln, and I've kept quiet about it, but I've decided to stay on in the army as well. I've signed on for another five years,' he said. 'They want me to continue working on their AI programme and I'm more than happy to do so.' He laughed. 'Your face is a picture.'

'I have to admit that came out of the blue,' I laughed. 'You, staying in the army. I'm pleased for you, Danny. Army life has come to suit you down to the ground.'

'Yeah, especially now that I'm an officer. I'm to be based here at Black Tree Canyon as the work includes collaboration with my old department at the University of Dakota. I couldn't ask for more really.'

'That's fantastic, really good news, Danny. I was worried we'd lose touch.'

'No chance, compadre. We'll be seeing a lot of each other.'

I stayed at the function and made small talk with the other officers but my mind was on Collette and seeing her again. The time crept by until eventually General Bullen took her leave and shortly afterwards Danny and I excused ourselves.

'I'm off now,' said Danny, 'so I'll get in touch when I get back. Give my love to Collette and see you soon.'

'Thanks, Danny. I hope your folks are okay. Enjoy your break and I'll see you when you get back.'

I wasn't required to stay at Black Tree Canyon and planned to go back to my apartment. I called Collette.

'Lincoln, you're back home. What's happening?'

'I'm back home for a month,' I said. 'It's so great to hear your voice again. I can't wait to see you, Collette. Where should I meet you? I'm not required to stay at the base and actually want to get back to the apartment.'

'I'll come and fetch you,' she said. 'I'm leaving right now and will let you know when I get there. Oh, Lincoln, I've missed you so much. I'll see you in a minute.'

Chapter 2

I sit here decades later writing this memoir and still remember as clearly as yesterday the feeling that swept through me when I walked out of that gate and saw Collette. Everything and everybody around me ceased to exist. Nothing mattered. I saw only her, smiling through tears, arms outstretched towards me and I walked towards her as I had so often in my dreams. To have her in my arms again, to feel her softness, breathe in her perfume, hear her softly saying my name, to kiss those beautiful lips and run my fingers through her hair, to say her name and to tell her how much I missed her, to hear her say she loved me and she always would, to hold each other, not wanting to let go – these things I remember. They have stayed with me all my life and if I close my eyes and sit quietly I can relive them even now.

She stepped back after a while and held me at arm's length and gave me one of those magical smiles that have always rendered me helpless. 'I can't believe you're here, alive and well. It seems you've been away forever, and in the midst of all that fighting.'

'I know. There were times when I wondered if I was going to make it,' I said, 'and I dreaded the idea of not seeing you again.'

'I've just realised you said something about being here for a month. Are you being sent away again?'

'I'm afraid so,' I said, and told her about the mission to the imperial capital and how I found it impossible to decline the president's request. 'You don't mind do you? I'd hate to think I've done anything to upset you.'

She kept her arms around my waist. 'A part of me is upset that you're going away but I'm really proud of you, Lincoln. Your war record, holding the rank of colonel at your age and being singled out like this by the president – I mean that doesn't happen to just anyone. I imagine she can be pretty persuasive and, I must admit, you look the part in that uniform.' She laughed. 'All my friends think I'm the luckiest girl alive.'

'Would you come and visit me there? I want to see as much of you as I can,' I said.

'Just try and stop me,' she said.

We hopped the train back to the city and spent the rest of that day and night totally wrapped up in each other without a care for the first time since the start of the war. We were in love and utterly content with each other's company. After spending the afternoon closeted in the apartment we went out for a drink and something to eat. Euclid Square was returning to normal. The military structures that had been erected for defence against possible attack were being dismantled and the crowds were out again. Collette and I strolled hand in hand around the square, looking at shops, visiting galleries, real and virtual, and generally browsing, and found our way to *The Mockingbird*, where Jacob was in great form.

'Lincoln,' he boomed, giving me a bear hug, 'you're back. Told you you'd kick their asses from here to Andromeda and you sure did. Hi, Collette, how are you? On the house guys, what you having?'

'Hi, Jacob,' I said. 'That's very kind of you. It's good to see you again. I'll have a cold beer please.'

'Hello, Jacob. I'll have the same,' said Collette.

'Coming right up,' he said. 'Sit here at the bar so I can chat to you. Be great to catch up.' We sat at that bar, chatting to Jacob and to quite a few others who recognised me and came up to shake my hand and wish me well. We moved on to a restaurant and then returned to the apartment where we both slept until late the following morning.

'How about getting away somewhere?' I said as we sat on the balcony having a leisurely, late breakfast. 'I'm on leave for the rest of the month and you don't start uni for another three weeks.'

'What a great idea. I wouldn't mind getting away from Dakota for a while. What were you thinking of? Somewhere on Proserpine or something further afield?'

'I don't mind,' I said. 'Tell you what. Because you've been stuck here all these months, you choose. I'm happy to go along with whatever you want to do.'

In the end we decided to rent a holiday cottage for a week in one of the small, beautiful coastal villages situated about seventeen hundred kilometres to the south of Dakota, a favourite holiday destination for a lot of Dakotans. Two days before leaving we were at Collette's house and enjoying a drink in the garden. Gabriel and Rebecca were there and I was reminded of the first time I had visited the place.

'I'm glad that you survived the war, Lincoln,' said Georgia. 'All through the fighting I couldn't help thinking that something dreadful was going to happen.'

'Yes, there was a definite sense of doom and gloom about the place,' said Stanford. 'It's very good to see you alive and well, and congratulations on being so successful. It's hard to believe you didn't really want to join the military in the first place.'

'I had the privilege of seeing Lincoln at work,' said Gabriel, 'and I'm not at all surprised at his rapid promotion or his popularity with the president.' He raised his glass. 'Cheers, Lincoln. Glad to see you back.'

'Thanks everybody, but it was really a team effort and when I look at the whole picture, I played a very small part in the war. I also cannot forget all those who gave their lives and those whose lives have been blighted. It is good to be back, though, and it's great to see you all again. The best thing for me is that the fighting is over and we can get on with living normal lives again. In fact,' I said, raising my glass, 'let's drink to that.'

'Cheers,' said Rebecca. 'Let's hope we never experience anything like that again. I found it unbelievably frightening and I wasn't even involved in the fighting. I can't think how you did what you did, Lincoln.'

'Nor can I,' I said smiling. 'I just did what needed doing at the time but if I'd had time to reflect I probably would have crawled into a dark room and stayed there.'

'I don't believe you,' said Collette laughing. 'You are the last person in the galaxy I'd expect to find hiding in a dark room.' She squeezed my hand. 'And now you're going to command the garrison at Zangsh, at the personal request of the president.'

'Yes, Collette told us about that,' said Georgia. 'All the best with that posting, Lincoln. I imagine it's going to be quite difficult.'

I nodded. 'It's not going to be easy. The devastation caused to the Imperium has to be seen to be believed and it's going to take a massive effort to get the place back to some sort of normality. We're there to help but they are essentially going to have to do it themselves. I'm glad to be doing my bit though as I much prefer that to being at war with them.'

'Nice one, Lincoln. And in the meantime have a good break. You deserve it,' said Gabriel.

'Thanks, Gabriel. I'm looking forward to it.'

'It's a lovely part of the coast,' said Georgia. 'We've been quite often and I always enjoy it.'

'I agree,' said Stanford. 'It's a great place to unwind and relax. The two of you will have a great time. Now, drinks anyone? Collette, do the honours while I go and sort out some supper. You all okay with a barbeque?'

'More than okay,' I said. 'I'll come and give you a hand.'

Part 5

Aftermath

With the successful campaign against the Imperial Wolves and the capture of Hradoshk my war against the Imperium came to an end and I took up my post as commander of the Zangsh garrison while Collette went off to university. I remained there for eighteen months, working closely with the remodelled, modernised army of the new Republic in the reconstruction of Zangsh and the surrounding towns and villages. In the years that followed my initial posting, I returned to the Republic on several occasions and spent a lot of time there while they were rebuilding after the war. For my work I was awarded one of their highest peace time decorations which I wore proudly on my uniform all my working life and, most importantly of all, I was there to witness the demise of the old Imperium and the birth of a new democratic republic. Like all such change in the affairs of humans, it was not without its problems. There were many hurdles to get over and they stumbled along the way but the basic idea took hold and they have been working hard at it ever since. Nobody wants to return to the days of the old Imperium and slowly but surely great progress has been made. The Republic is now a functioning democracy and a staunch ally of the Union.

Collette completed her studies and has, for many years now, been a successful and well-known architect. Her work is greatly admired and she has found herself in demand in different parts of the Union, the Protectorate and the Republic. Because of our careers we have spent fairly long periods of time apart during our lives but the spark that flashed between us on board the shuttle between Ironmarsh and Proserpine became a flame that has burned brightly up to the present time, and through the years we have remained devoted to each other. Her smile still works its magic on me and those eyes have lost none of their sparkle. We have remained together and have two beautiful, successful daughters. I am now the proud grandfather of five grandchildren, and I am constantly being reprimanded for spoiling them too much. Not that they mind, of course. They know a soft touch when they see one and I have no intention of changing.

Collette's parents are no longer with us but we see Gabriel regularly. He is still in Dakota and working at the university with Danny. He and Rachel have three children, two boys and a girl, also successful and living in different parts of the Union.

Danny enjoyed a career in the army for a further fifteen years after the end of the war and was instrumental in the development of AI units within the military. The advance of robotics and other AI development has moved forward at an unbelievable pace and our army is now mainly made up of AI Units commanded by human officers and NCOs. It is unrecognisably different to the human army that fought the war against the Imperium. The robot has come of age and they are now employed in every walk of life imaginable. Many of them are constructed in human form and it is now impossible to tell the difference anymore although they still have AIU printed on their right hand. I can't see that lasting much longer, however, as there is a growing movement among humans to have it removed. More and more people, including me, regard it as discriminatory.

After leaving the army Danny returned to work at the University of Dakota where he has had a very successful career. We still see him on a regular basis. He finally settled down and married one of his colleagues, a lovely guy by the name of Harish, who was originally a prisoner of war, having fought for the Imperium. Like Makreet, he applied for Union citizenship and then proceeded to educate himself and succeeded at becoming a lecturer and then a professor at the university. He and Danny seem happy together.

General Matfield continued to enjoy a successful career in the army and retired as a Lieutenant-general. He and I have been friends for years now.

Makreet has spent many years campaigning and working hard for the rights of women in the Republic, and for human rights in general. The Imperium became a democracy and changed its name to the Republic but some old habits and beliefs remained and one of these was the attitude to women. However, thanks to Makreet and others like her things are very different today and the Republic is a modern democracy and close ally of the Union. Makreet herself has never hooked up with anyone on a permanent basis up to now but the last time we saw her it seemed that there was, at last, someone special she had met. She told us that after Cisco died she had had no interest in getting into a serious long-term relationship with anyone and that her work had kept her busy though all that time. Now, it seems, things might be changing.

And talking of Cisco, I went back to Oasis with Collette and Danny shortly after the war and unveiled a plinth at the orphanage to his memory and that of Olaf Dixter. I had been contacted by Mr Clinton, who informed me of Olaf's death. He had been killed in action in the Lindfield campaign, doing what he loved best – being a marine. The unveiling was a solemn and dignified occasion and I could not help shedding more tears for Cisco. It was good to see everybody again but I was sad to learn that Mr Sawyer had died, in a flying accident of all things, and I went and visited his grave and stood there in silence for a long while. I was back in the town not too long ago and that memorial is still there.

We see my friend Alarro Shraska and his lovely wife Casipa on a regular basis, either here or at their place. He had a very successful career in the Republican army, ending up as a general before resigning and entering politics. Alarro has always been single-mindedly determined to play his part in changing the old Imperium into the democracy it has become today and he has been a prominent member of the Senate for many years, well known for his liberal views and responsible for many of the positive changes that have taken place. He has worked with Makreet on a number of occasions and they too have become good friends. He thought of running for president once but decided he could do more as a senator. I've no doubt he would have made a great president.

Casipa too has been successful. She is a well-known author and has had a number of books published, mainly novels but two non-fiction works as well – one a history of the war and the other on the changes that have occurred within the Republic since the end of the war. She and Collette are great friends and the two of them are collaborating currently on a history of the architecture of Dakota.

Caroline Ghali remained in the navy, ending up as a rear-admiral, and she, too, received a Republican decoration for her work in helping with the reconstruction. She is a family friend, also living here on Earth.

I'll end it here. The sun is setting over Kefalonia. I've just been kissed on the cheek by Collette and handed a cold bottle of beer which I shall savour while watching the sunset. As I mentioned before, I never get tired of it and this evening is no exception.